# Around the World

# AROUND
# THE
# WORLD

## Matt Phelan

CANDLEWICK PRESS

For my brother, Chris

First edition 2011

Library of Congress Cataloging-in-Publication Data

Phelan, Matt.
Around the world / Matt Phelan. — 1st ed.
p.   cm.
Summary: Challenged with circling the world at the end of the nineteenth century, three
very different adventurers — avid bicyclist Thomas Stevens, fearless reporter Nellie Bly,
and retired sea captain Joshua Slocum — embark on epic journeys.
ISBN 978-0-7636-3619-7
1. Graphic novels. [1. Graphic novels. 2. Voyages around the
world — Fiction. 3. Adventure and adventurers — Fiction. 4. Stevens,
Thomas, 1854–1935 — Fiction. 5. Bly, Nellie, 1864–1922 — Fiction.
6. Slocum, Joshua, b. 1844 — Fiction.] I. Title.
PZ7.7.P52Ar 2011
741.5'973—dc22      2010043153


11 12 13 14 15 16 SCP 10 9 8 7 6 5 4 3 2 1


Printed in Humen, Dongguan, China

This book was typeset in Erasmus Light and Windsor.
The illustrations were done in pencil, ink, gouache, and watercolor.

Candlewick Press
99 Dover Street
Somerville, Massachusetts 02144

visit us at www.candlewick.com

It all began,
as many great adventures begin,
with a story.

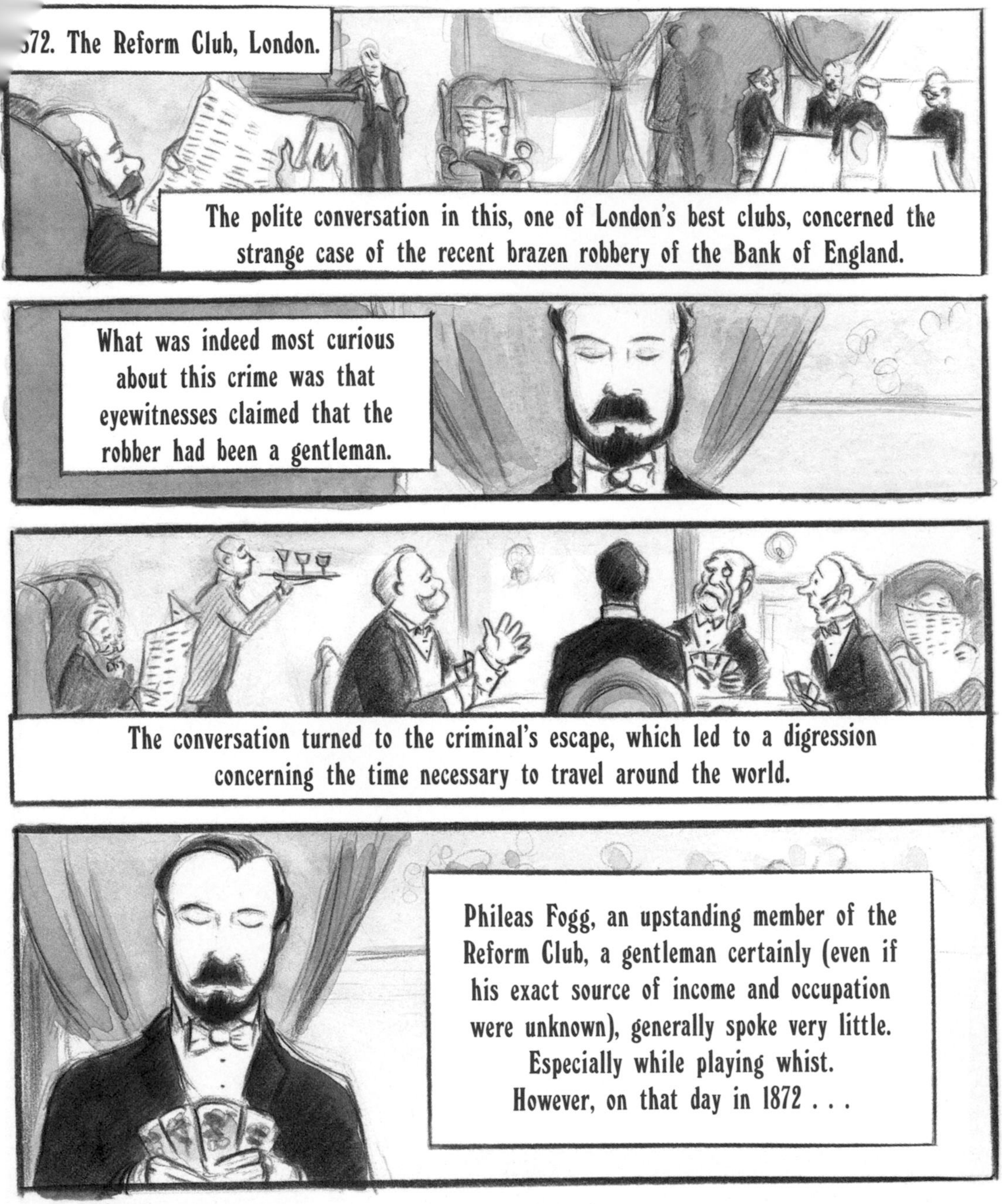

72. The Reform Club, London.
The polite conversation in this, one of London's best clubs, concerned the strange case of the recent brazen robbery of the Bank of England.
What was indeed most curious about this crime was that eyewitnesses claimed that the robber had been a gentleman.
The conversation turned to the criminal's escape, which led to a digression concerning the time necessary to travel around the world.
Phileas Fogg, an upstanding member of the Reform Club, a gentleman certainly (even if his exact source of income and occupation were unknown), generally spoke very little.
Especially while playing whist.
However, on that day in 1872 . . .

I will bet twenty thousand pounds against anyone who wishes that I will make the tour of the world in eighty days or less; in nineteen hundred and twenty hours, or one hundred and fifteen thousand two hundred minutes.

Do you accept?

Thus begins Jules Verne's rollicking adventure novel *Around the World in Eighty Days*. Verne's novel, like his previous books, was an international success. Millions read it and pondered the possibility of racing around the planet Earth. A few intrepid adventurers—for a variety of reasons both known and unknown—decided to attempt the amazing feat.

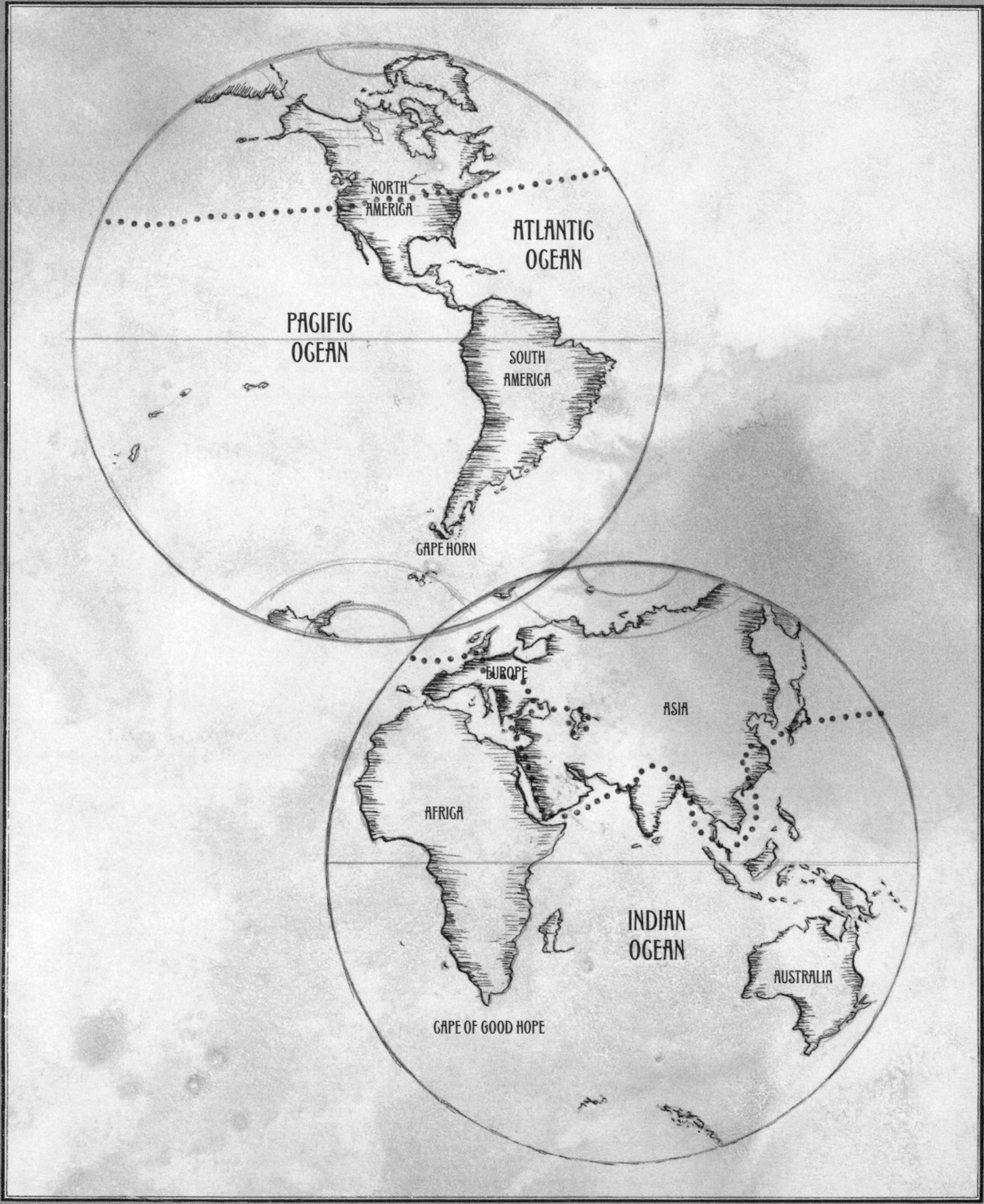
NORTH AMERICA
ATLANTIC OCEAN
PACIFIC OCEAN
SOUTH AMERICA
CAPE HORN
EUROPE
ASIA
AFRICA
INDIAN OCEAN
AUSTRALIA
CAPE OF GOOD HOPE

# The Journey of

# THOMAS STEVENS

*Wheelman*

1884

*I am making the journey partly for pleasure
and partly for other reasons.*
*— Thomas Stevens*

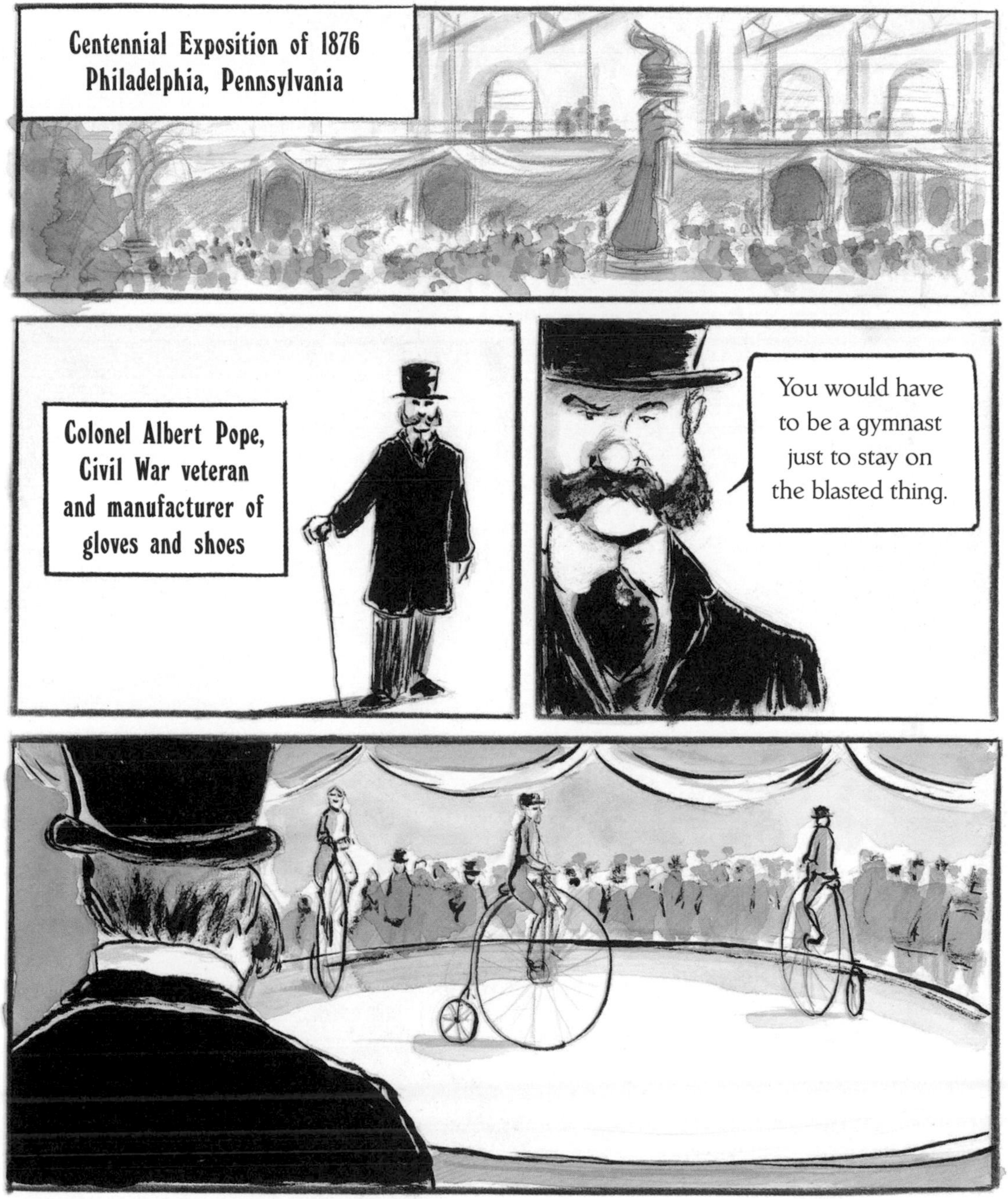

Centennial Exposition of 1876
Philadelphia, Pennsylvania
Colonel Albert Pope, Civil War veteran and manufacturer of gloves and shoes
You would have to be a gymnast just to stay on the blasted thing.

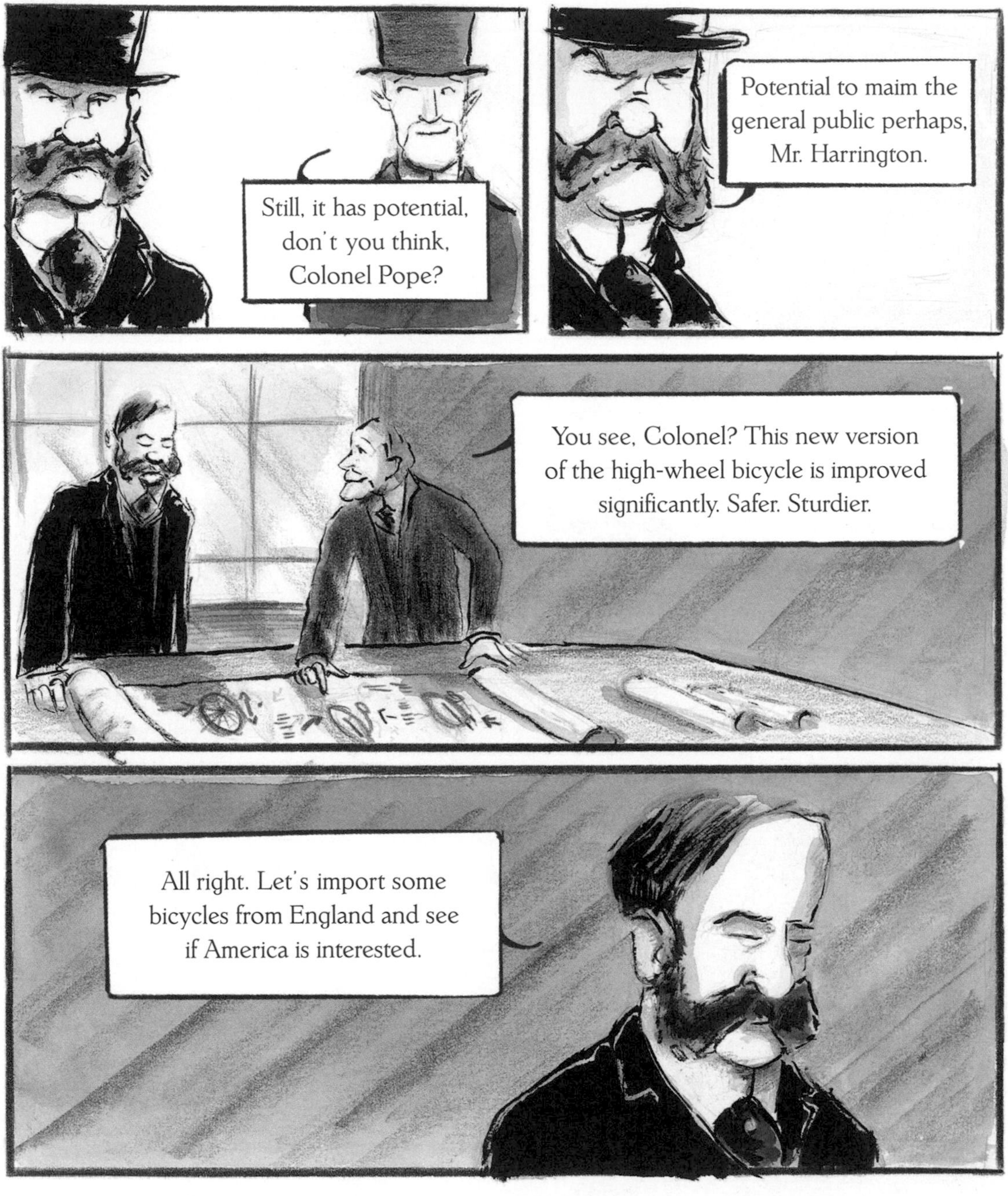
Still, it has potential, don't you think, Colonel Pope?
Potential to maim the general public perhaps, Mr. Harrington.
You see, Colonel? This new version of the high-wheel bicycle is improved significantly. Safer. Sturdier.
All right. Let's import some bicycles from England and see if America is interested.

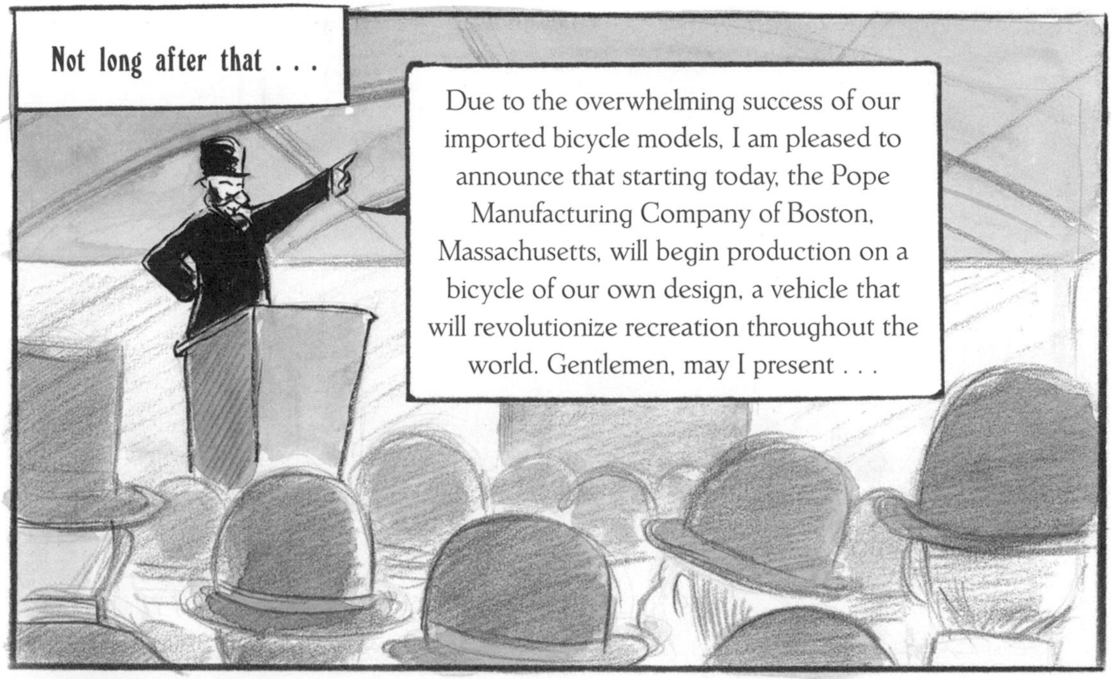
Not long after that . . .
Due to the overwhelming success of our imported bicycle models, I am pleased to announce that starting today, the Pope Manufacturing Company of Boston, Massachusetts, will begin production on a bicycle of our own design, a vehicle that will revolutionize recreation throughout the world. Gentlemen, may I present . . .

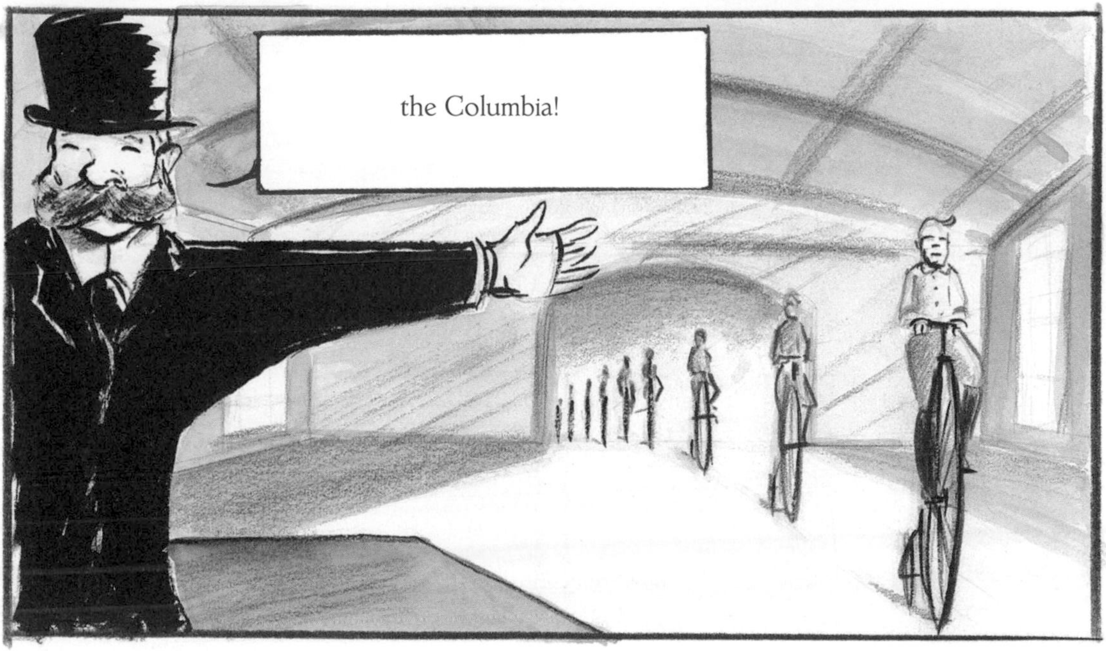
the Columbia!

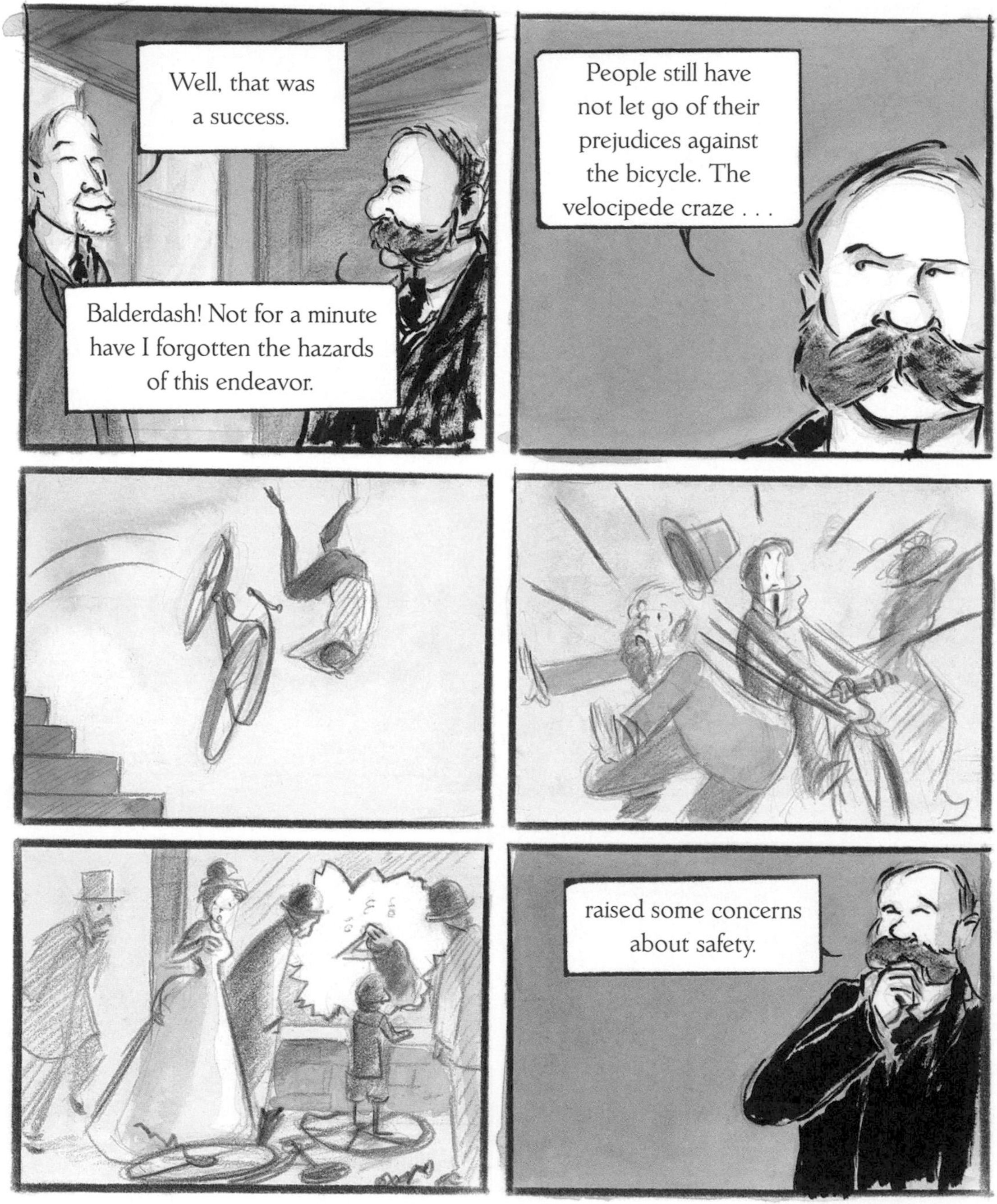
Well, that was a success.
Balderdash! Not for a minute have I forgotten the hazards of this endeavor.
People still have not let go of their prejudices against the bicycle. The velocipede craze . . .
raised some concerns about safety.

What we need to do is create the demand with one hand and the supply with the other.

We must make the bicycle popular.

Pope set out on his task with enthusiasm. First, he established the Massachusetts Bicycle Club to promote the social and health benefits of bicycling. A year later, he founded a national organization: the League of American Wheelmen (LAW).

The league's mission:
"To promote the general interests of cycling; to ascertain, defend, and protect the rights of wheelmen; and to encourage, and facilitate touring."

Touring. Pope imagined short pleasure rides, perhaps even a day trip or weekend excursion. But one man was destined to envision bicycle touring on a scale so grand that even Colonel Albert Pope would be astonished.

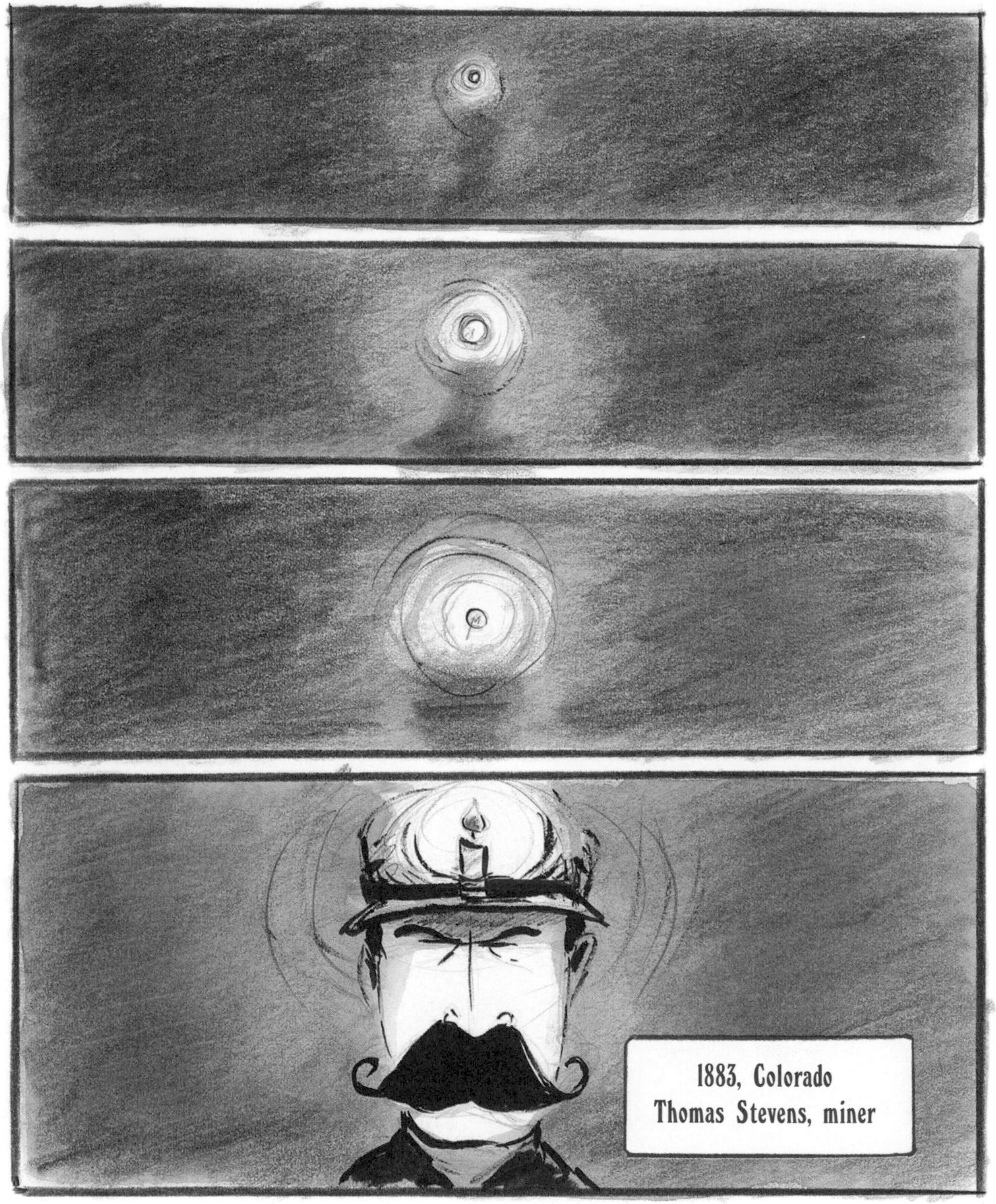
1883, Colorado
Thomas Stevens, miner

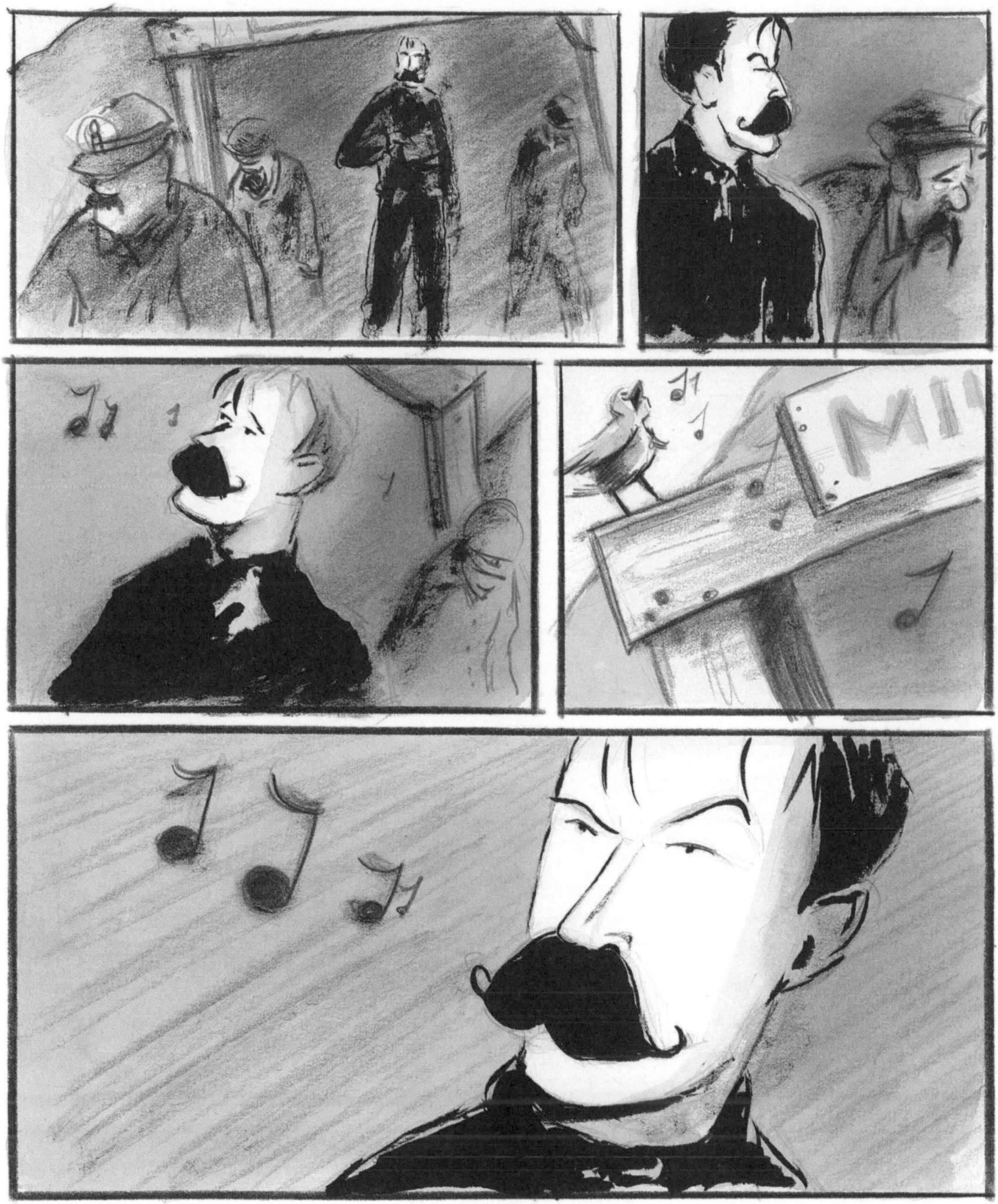

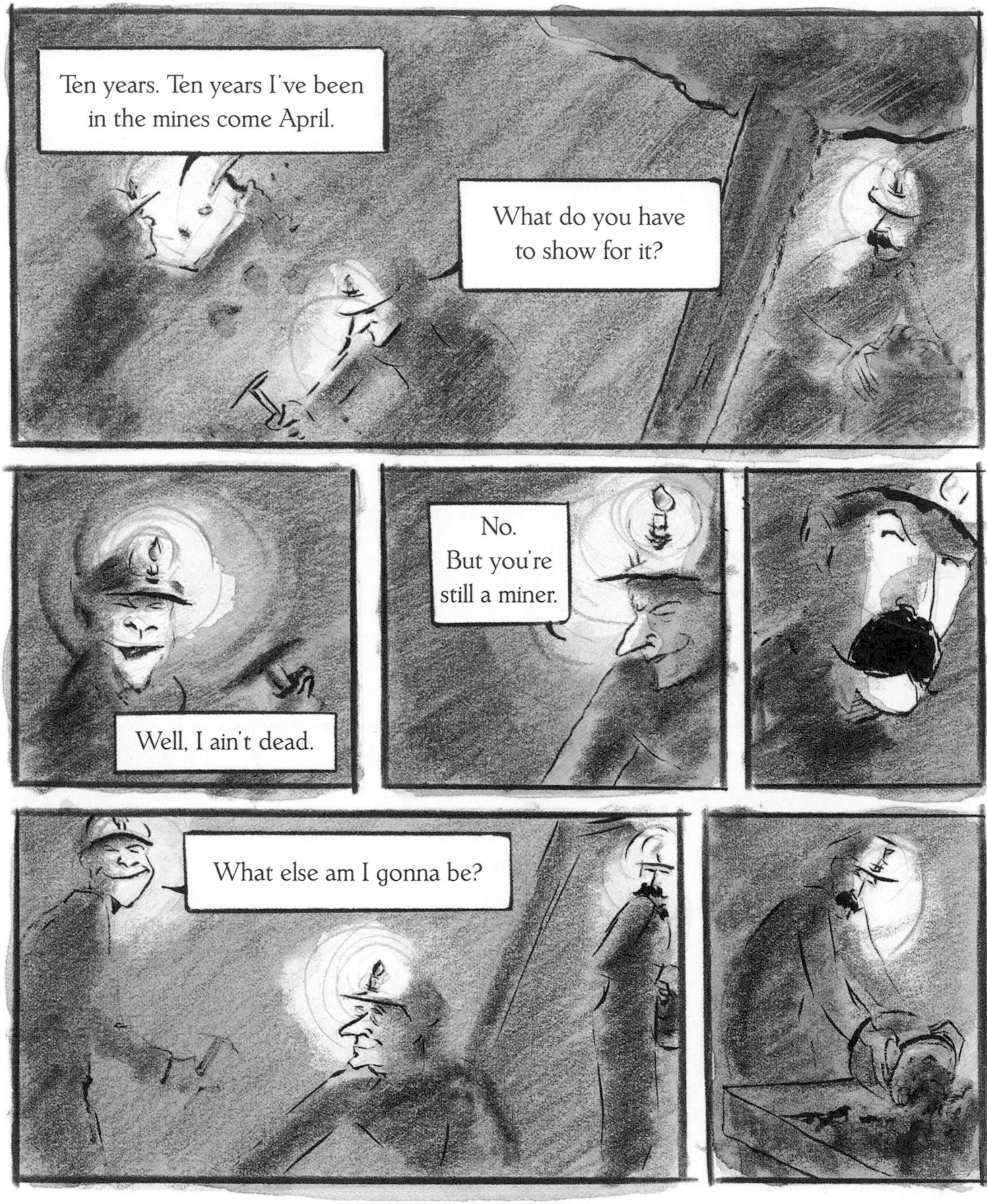
Ten years. Ten years I've been in the mines come April.
What do you have to show for it?
Well, I ain't dead.
No. But you're still a miner.
What else am I gonna be?

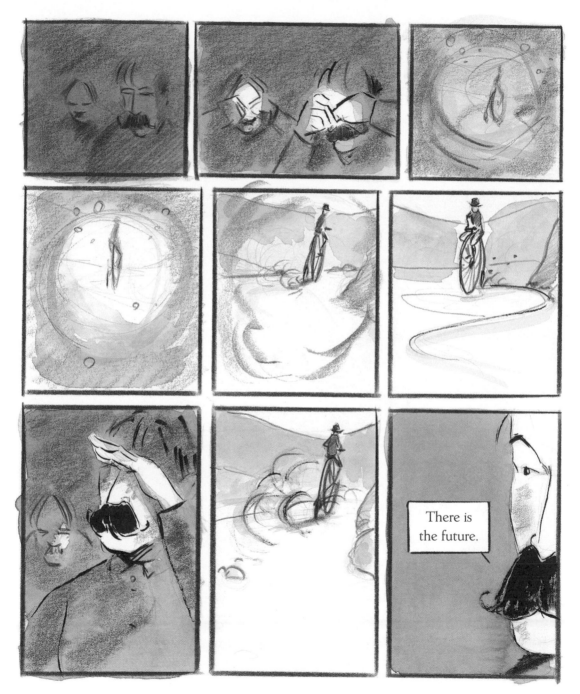

There is
the future.

Huh?

The bicycle is becoming popular. People are talking about it.

So?

I am going to do something no one has ever done. I am going to ride a bicycle across the United States.

And then people will be talking about *me*.

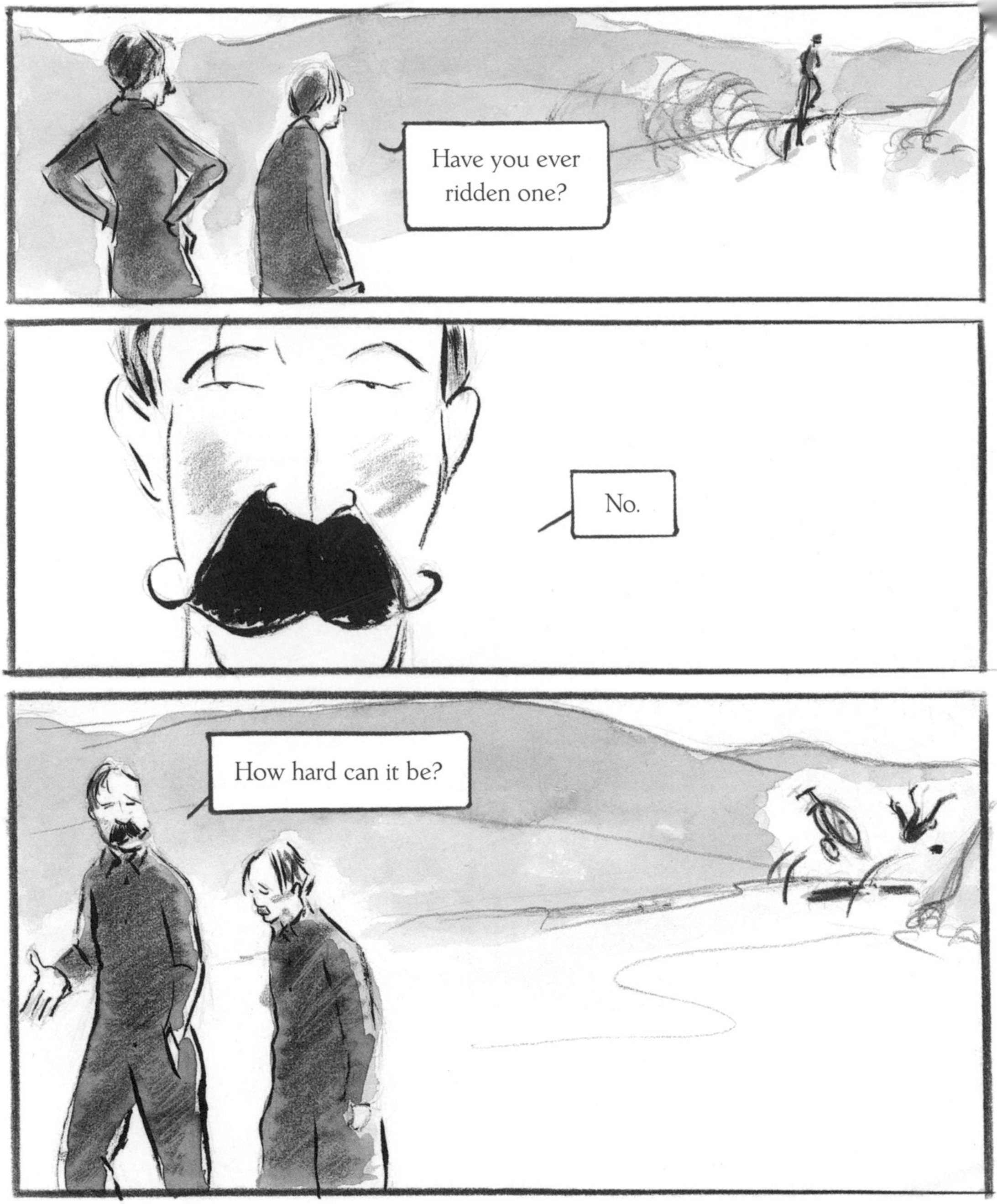
Have you ever ridden one?
No.
How hard can it be?

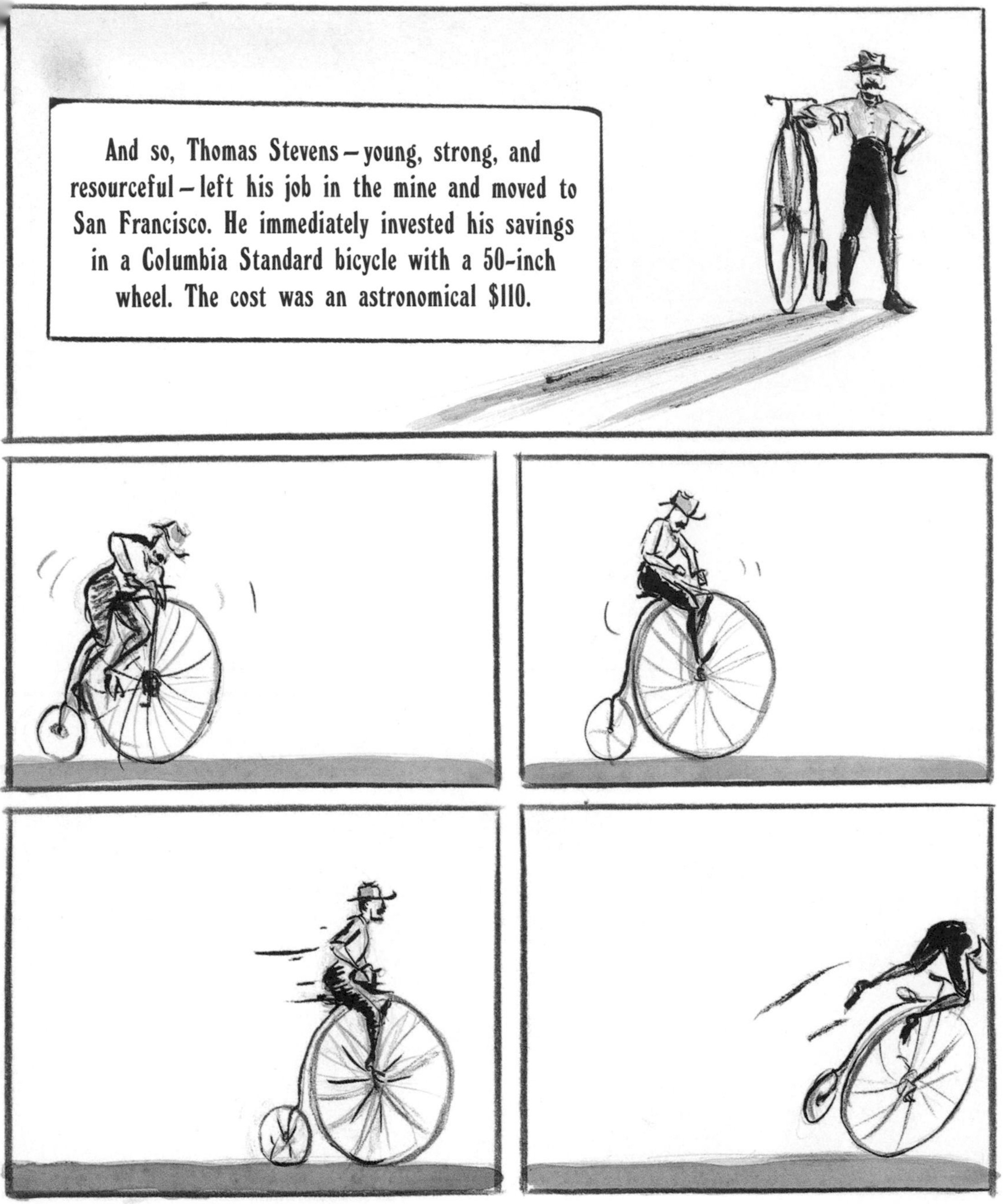
And so, Thomas Stevens – young, strong, and resourceful – left his job in the mine and moved to San Francisco. He immediately invested his savings in a Columbia Standard bicycle with a 50-inch wheel. The cost was an astronomical $110.

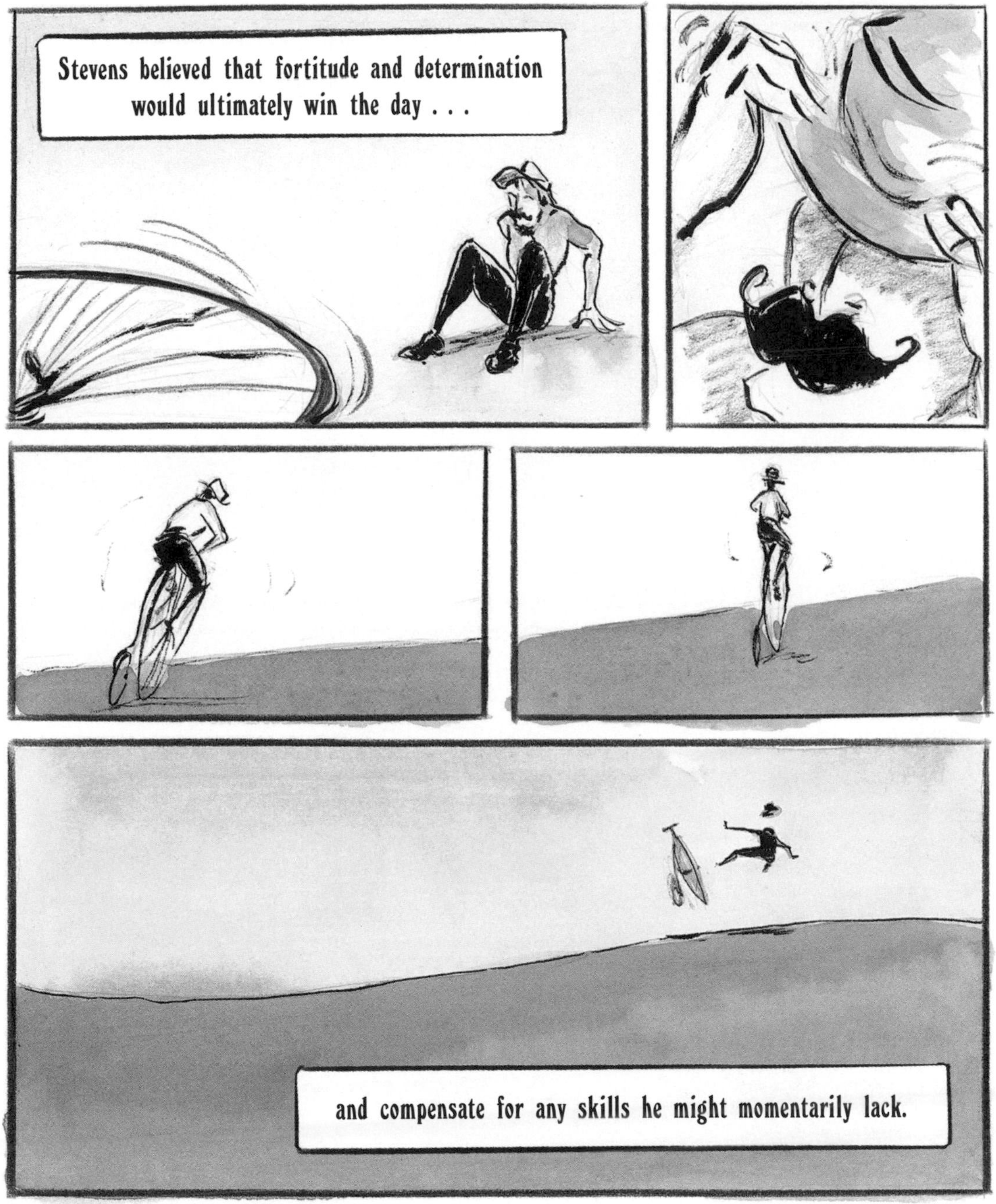
Stevens believed that fortitude and determination would ultimately win the day . . .
and compensate for any skills he might momentarily lack.

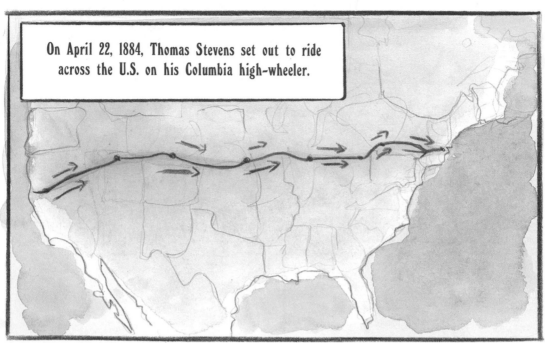

On April 22, 1884, Thomas Stevens set out to ride across the U.S. on his Columbia high-wheeler.

Attached to the back of his bicycle were his writing supplies. Thomas Stevens knew that recording his feat would be essential — and possibly lucrative.

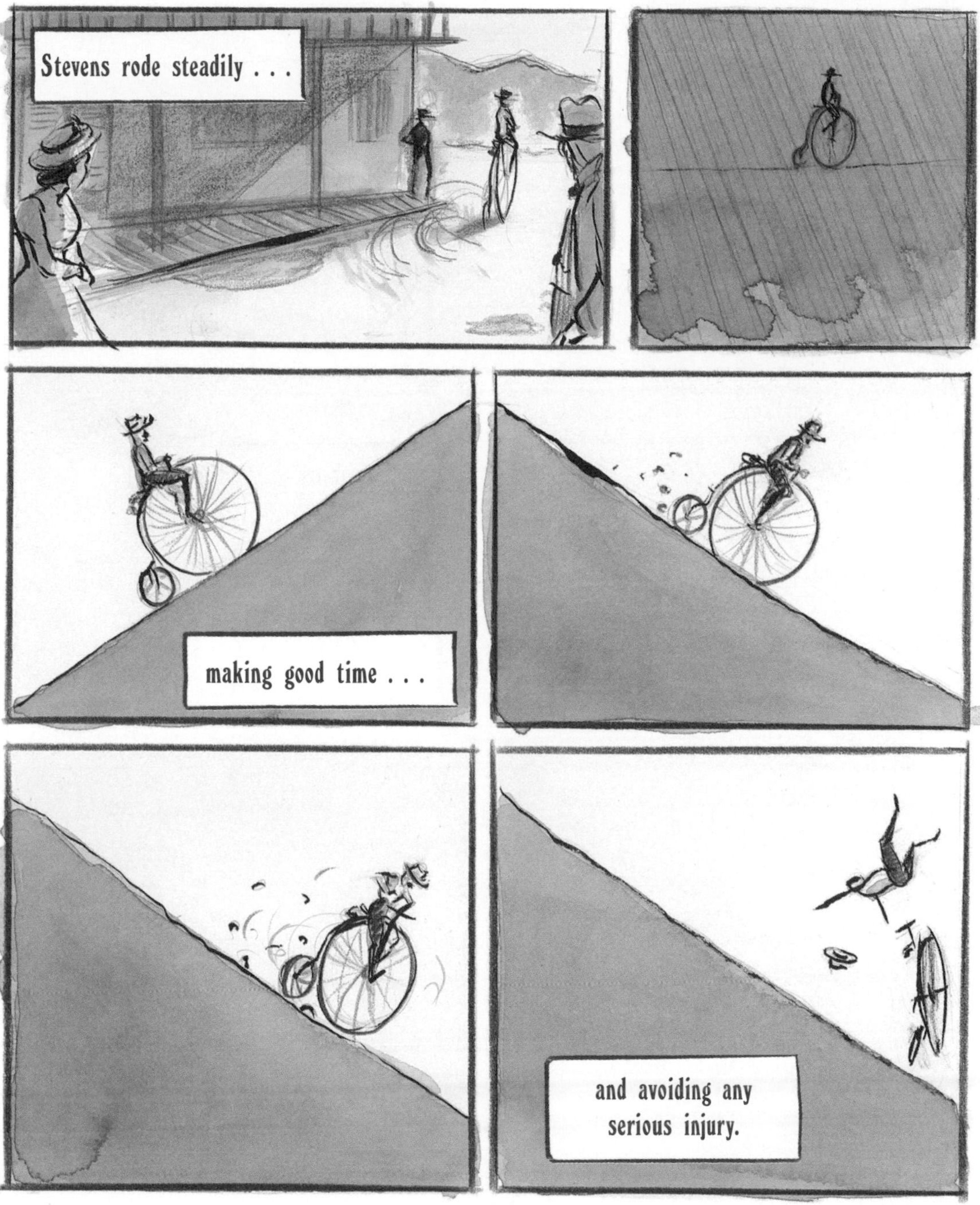
Stevens rode steadily . . .
making good time . . .
and avoiding any serious injury.

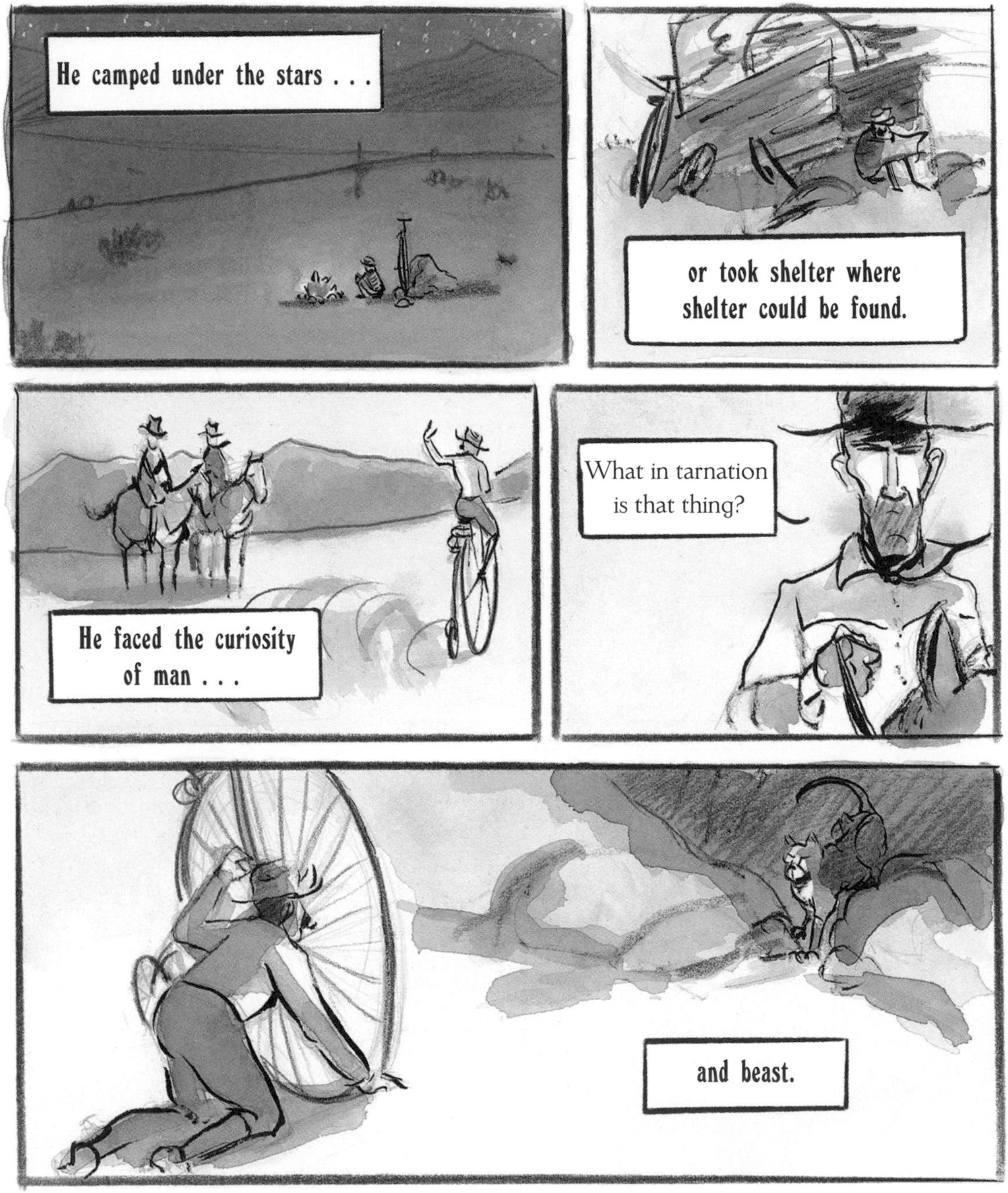
He camped under the stars . . .
or took shelter where shelter could be found.
He faced the curiosity of man . . .
What in tarnation is that thing?
and beast.

No matter what he faced, Stevens overcame it with pluck, courage, and a can-do spirit.

On August 4, 1884, Thomas Stevens rode into the city of Boston, Massachusetts, to complete his 3,700-mile journey. He arrived in fine physical condition and high spirits. He carried with him a thrilling written account of his adventure. He had something else: an idea. Thomas Stevens had decided to continue his historic ride around the world!

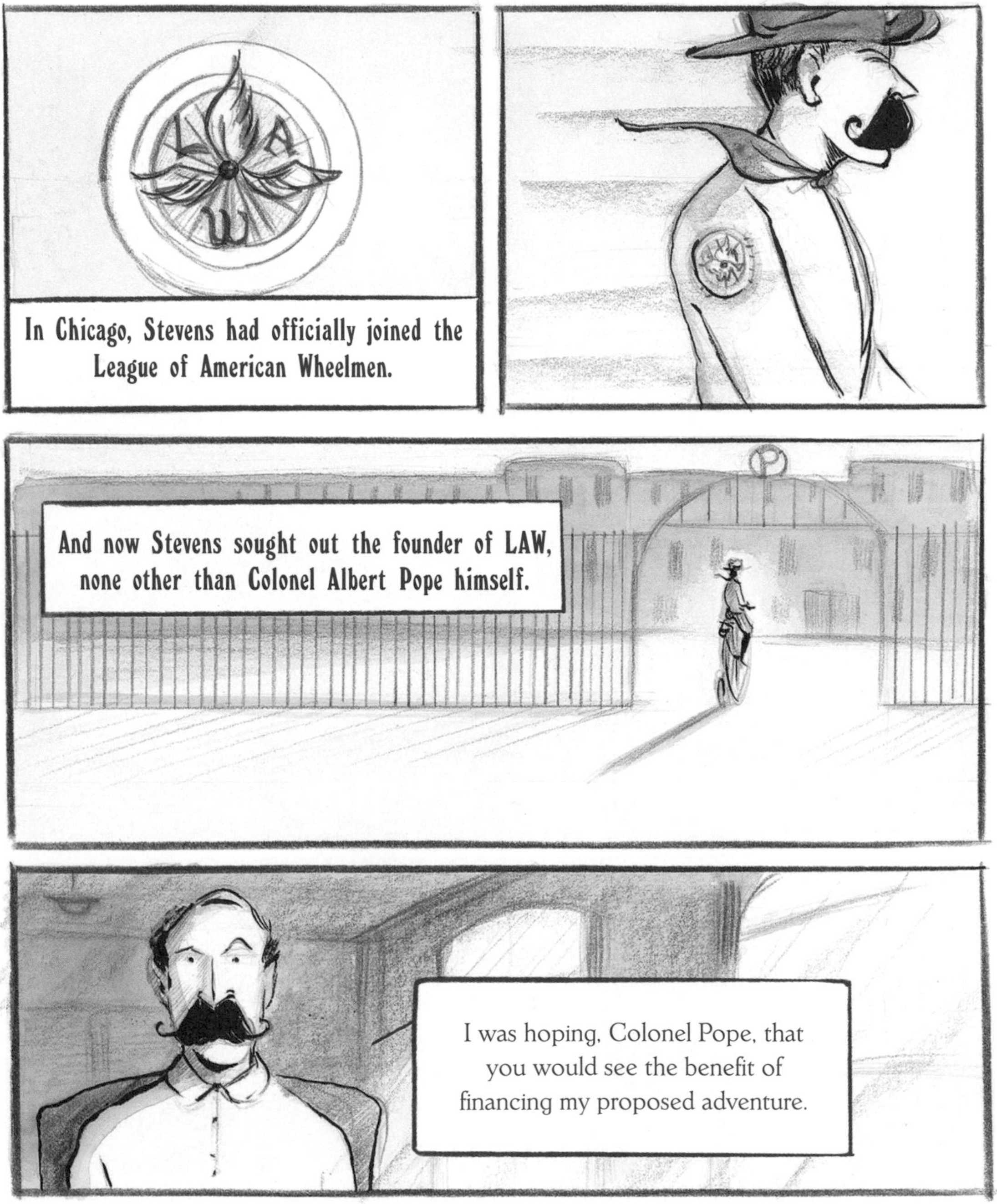
In Chicago, Stevens had officially joined the League of American Wheelmen.
And now Stevens sought out the founder of LAW, none other than Colonel Albert Pope himself.
I was hoping, Colonel Pope, that you would see the benefit of financing my proposed adventure.

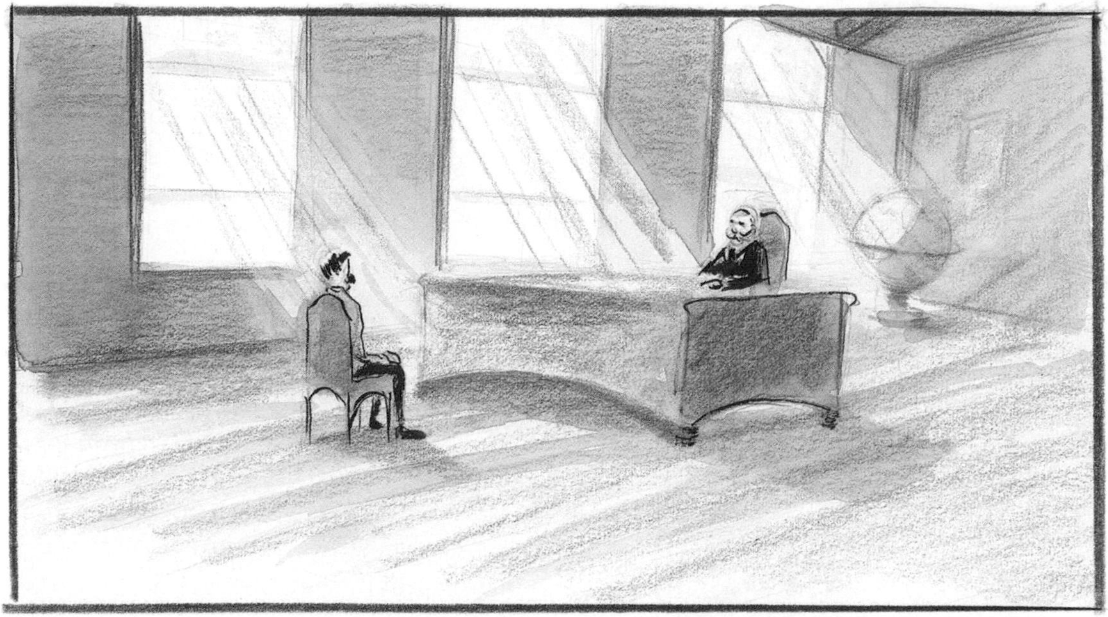

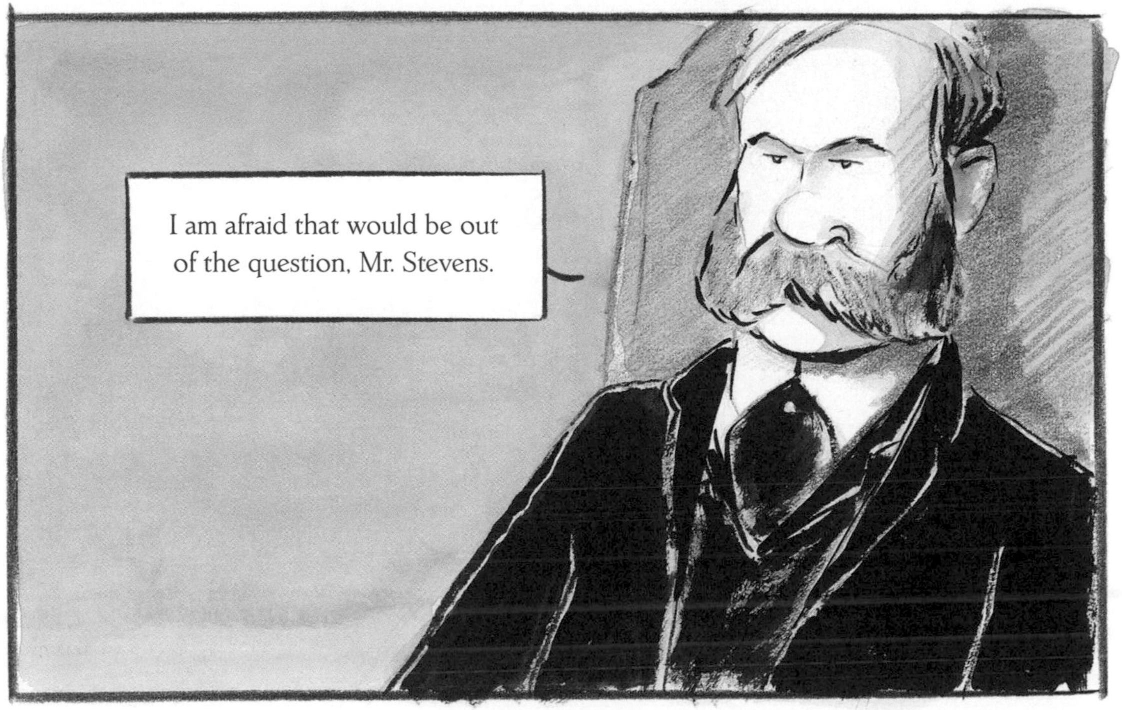
I am afraid that would be out of the question, Mr. Stevens.

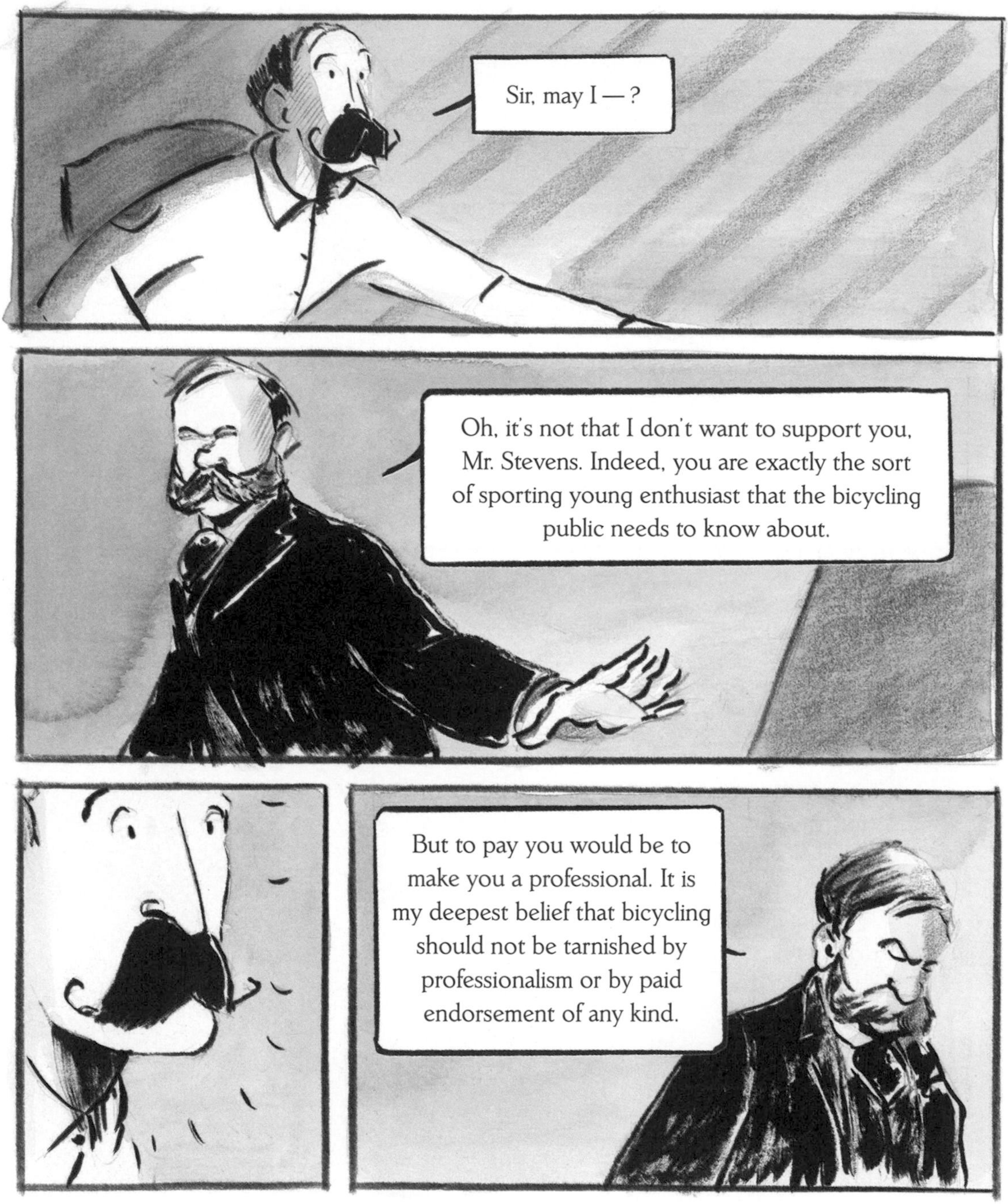
Sir, may I — ?
Oh, it's not that I don't want to support you, Mr. Stevens. Indeed, you are exactly the sort of sporting young enthusiast that the bicycling public needs to know about.
But to pay you would be to make you a professional. It is my deepest belief that bicycling should not be tarnished by professionalism or by paid endorsement of any kind.

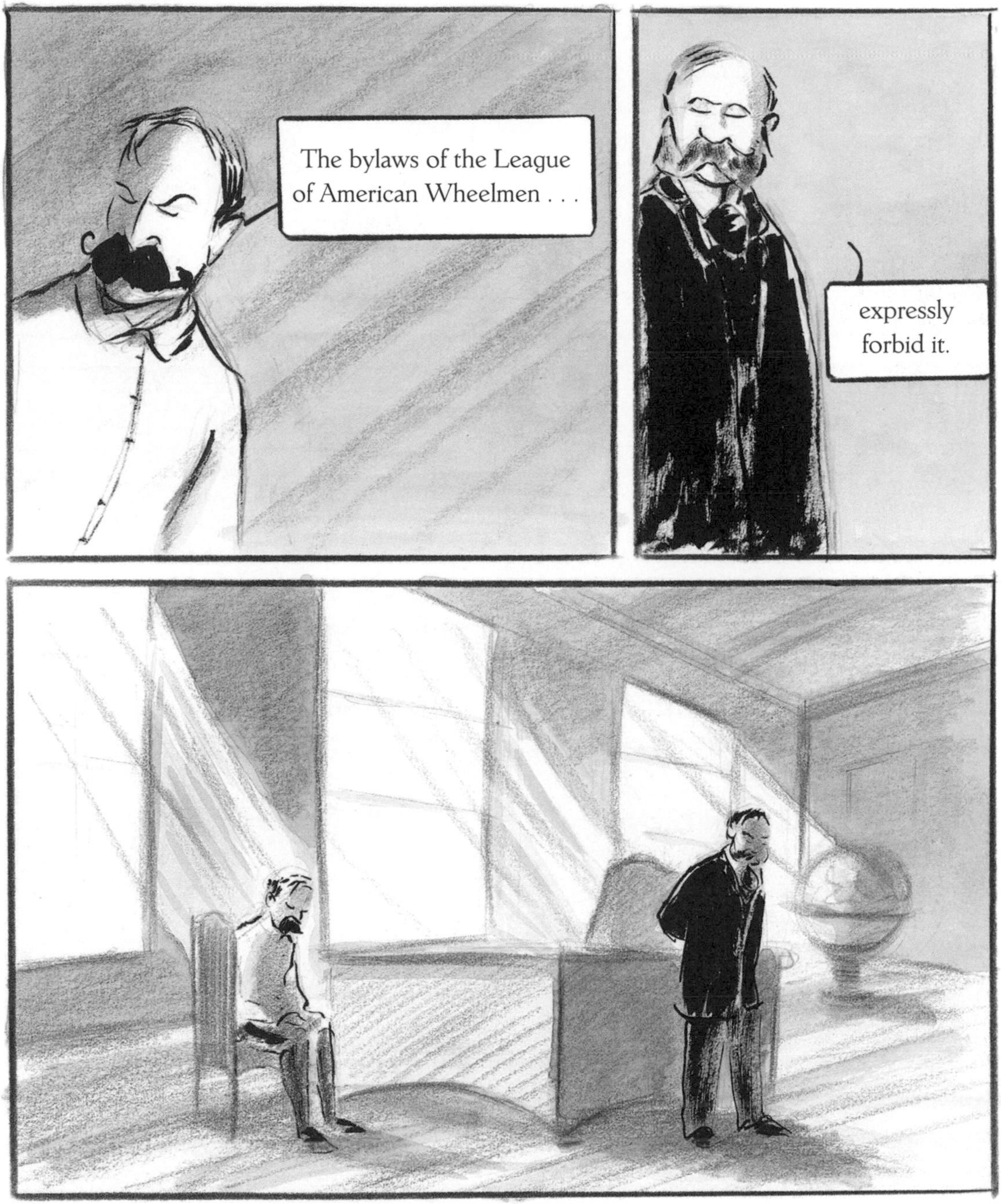

The bylaws of the League of American Wheelmen . . .
expressly forbid it.

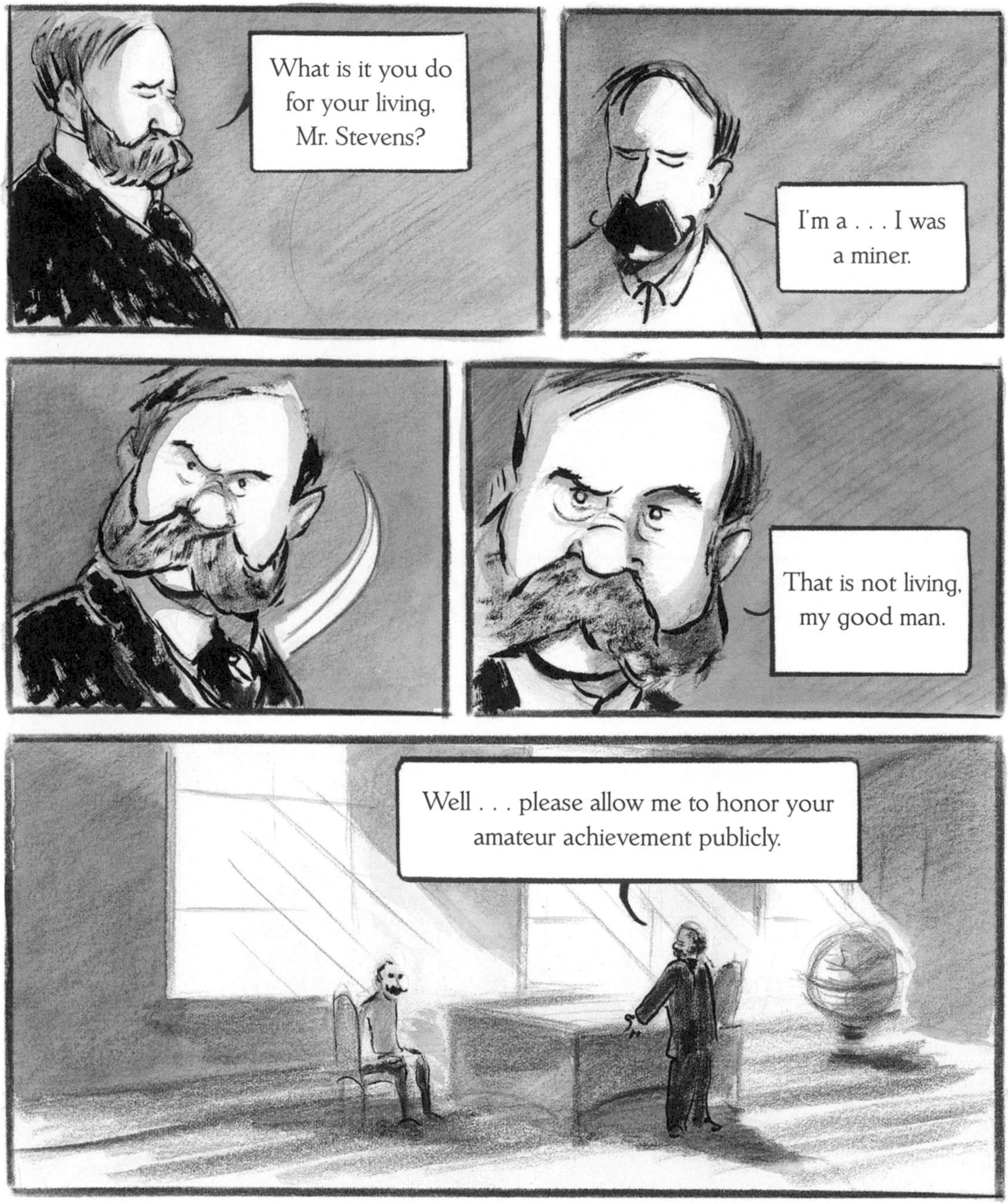
What is it you do for your living, Mr. Stevens?
I'm a . . . I was a miner.
That is not living, my good man.
Well . . . please allow me to honor your amateur achievement publicly.

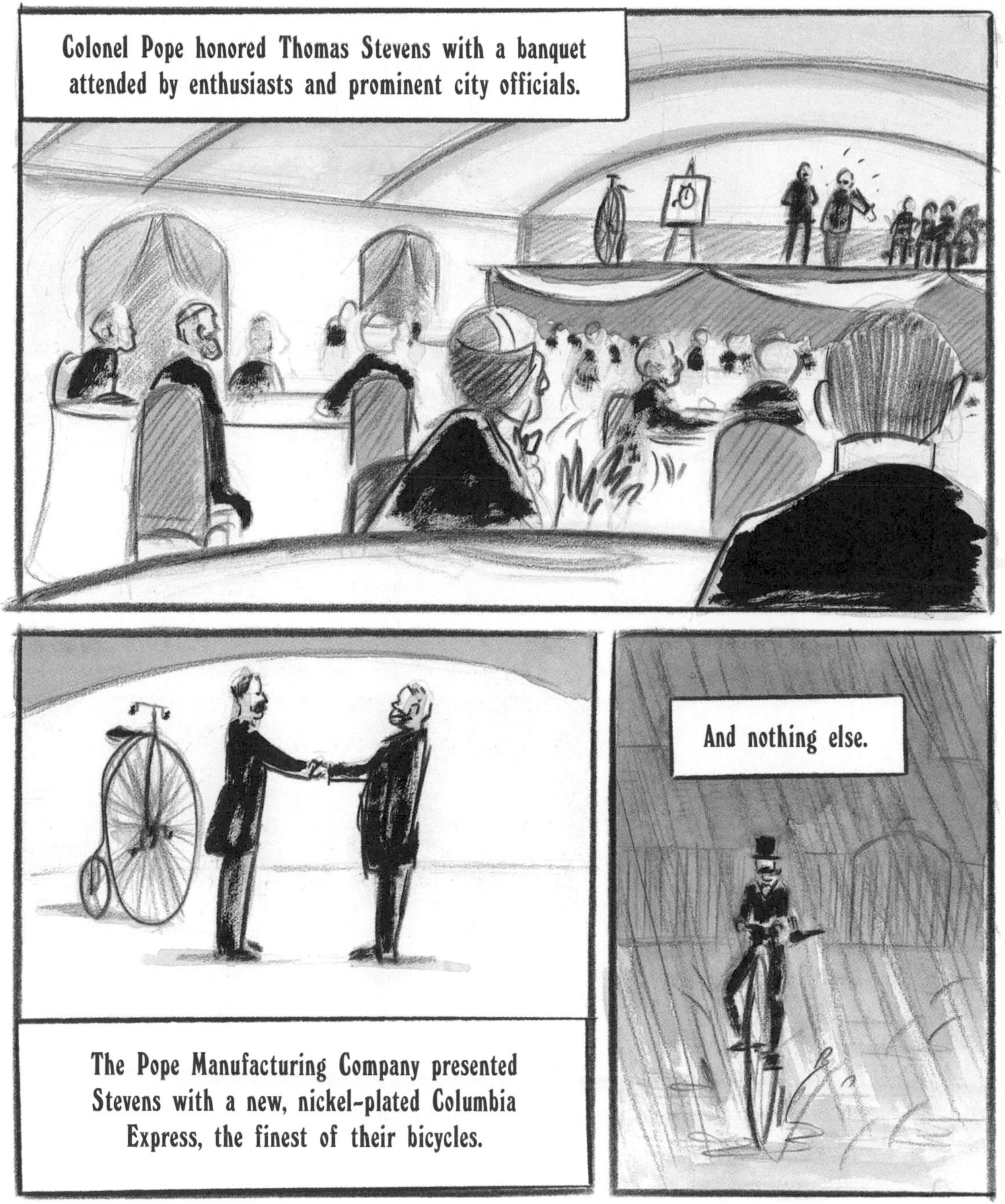
Colonel Pope honored Thomas Stevens with a banquet attended by enthusiasts and prominent city officials.
The Pope Manufacturing Company presented Stevens with a new, nickel-plated Columbia Express, the finest of their bicycles.
And nothing else.

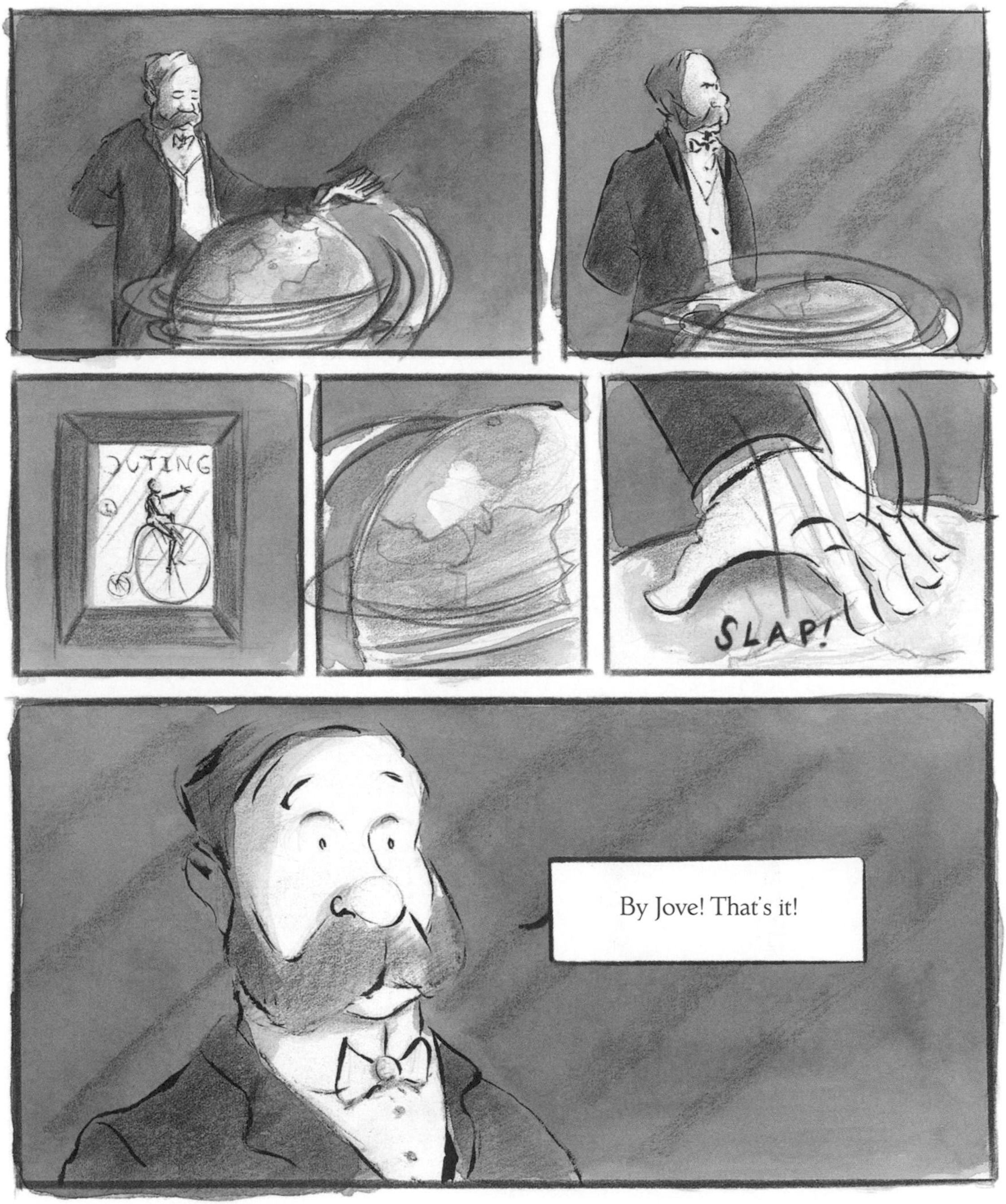
OUTING
SLAP!
By Jove! That's it!

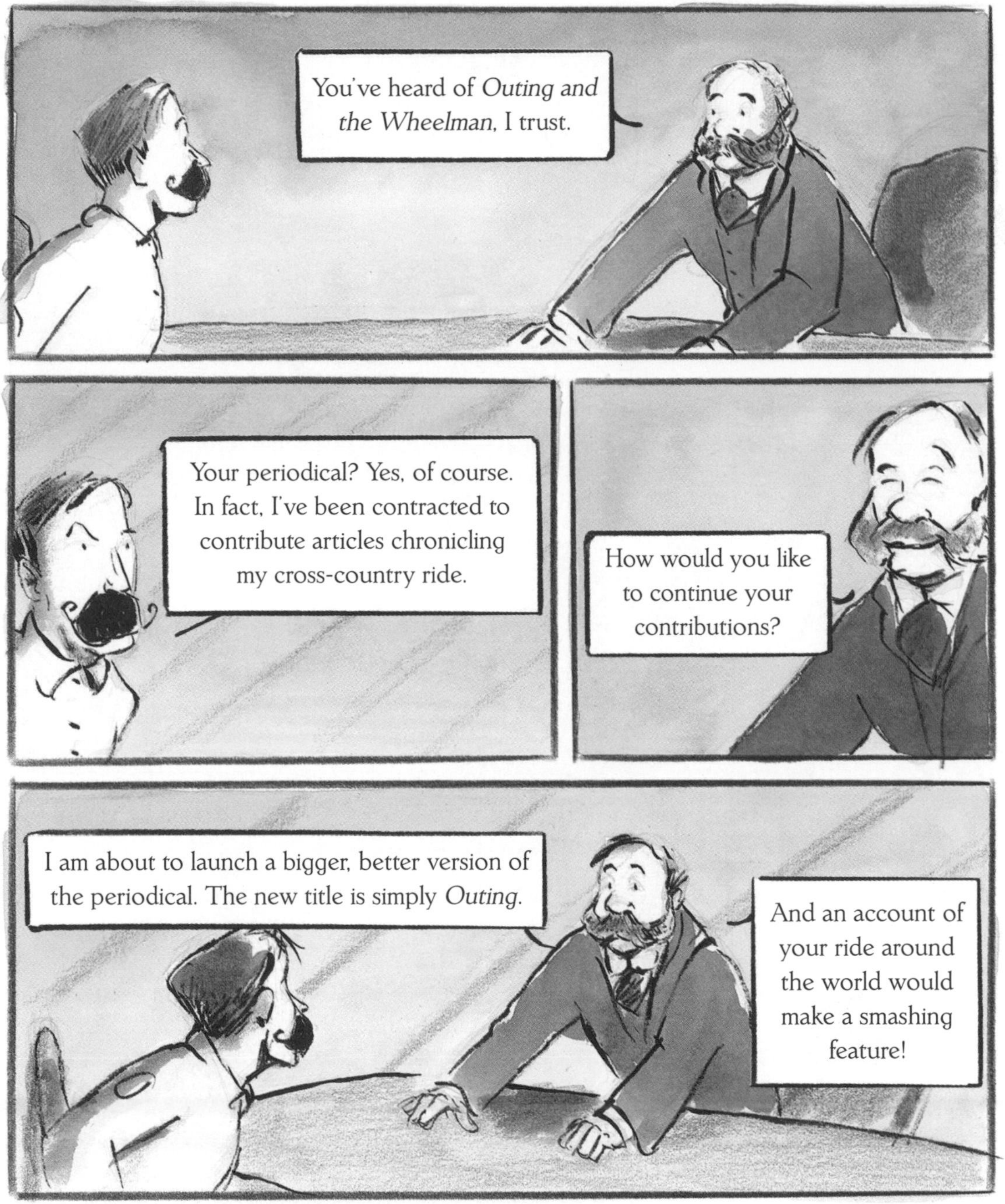
You've heard of *Outing and the Wheelman*, I trust.
Your periodical? Yes, of course. In fact, I've been contracted to contribute articles chronicling my cross-country ride.
How would you like to continue your contributions?
I am about to launch a bigger, better version of the periodical. The new title is simply *Outing*.
And an account of your ride around the world would make a smashing feature!

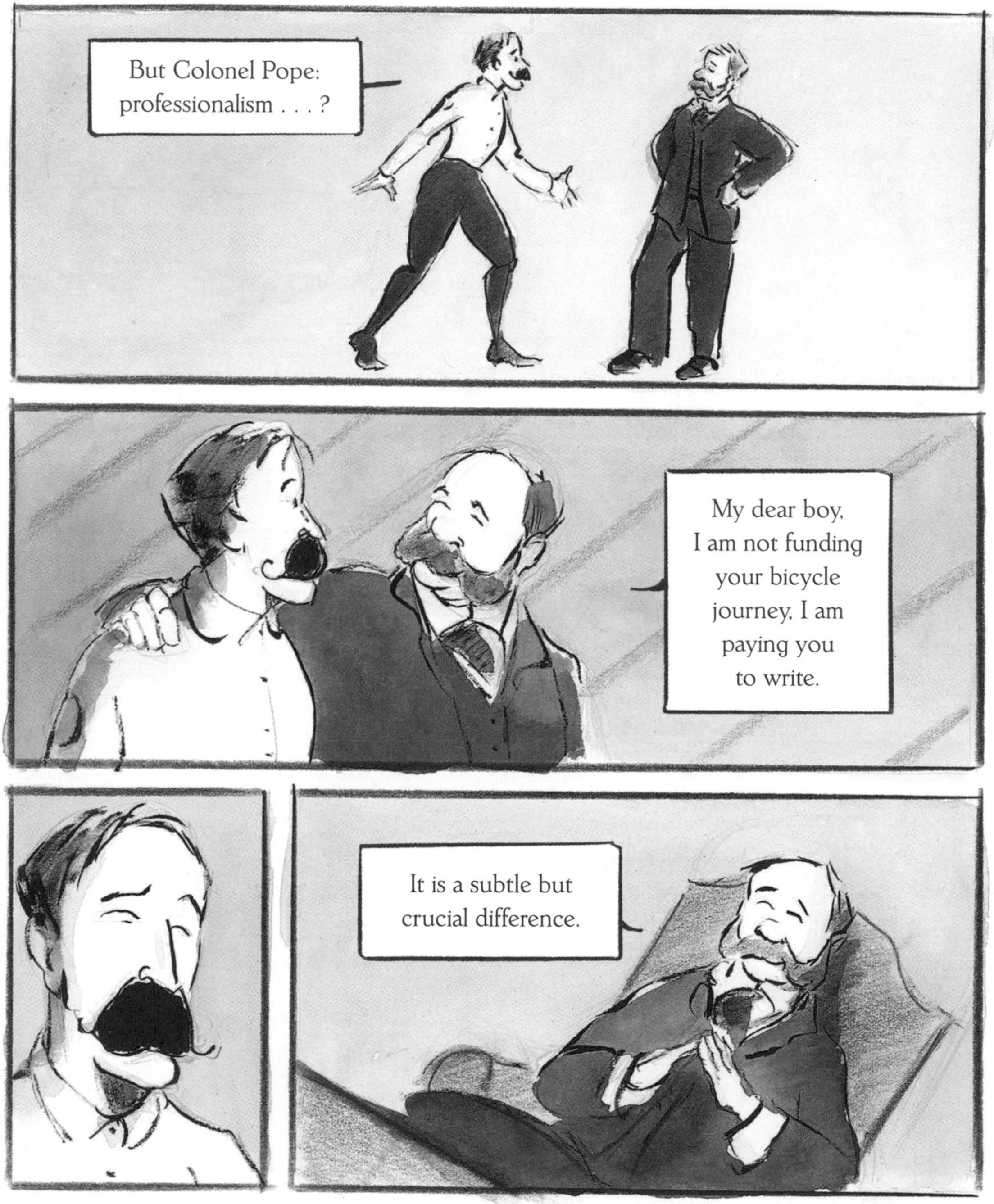
But Colonel Pope: professionalism . . . ?
My dear boy, I am not funding your bicycle journey, I am paying you to write.
It is a subtle but crucial difference.

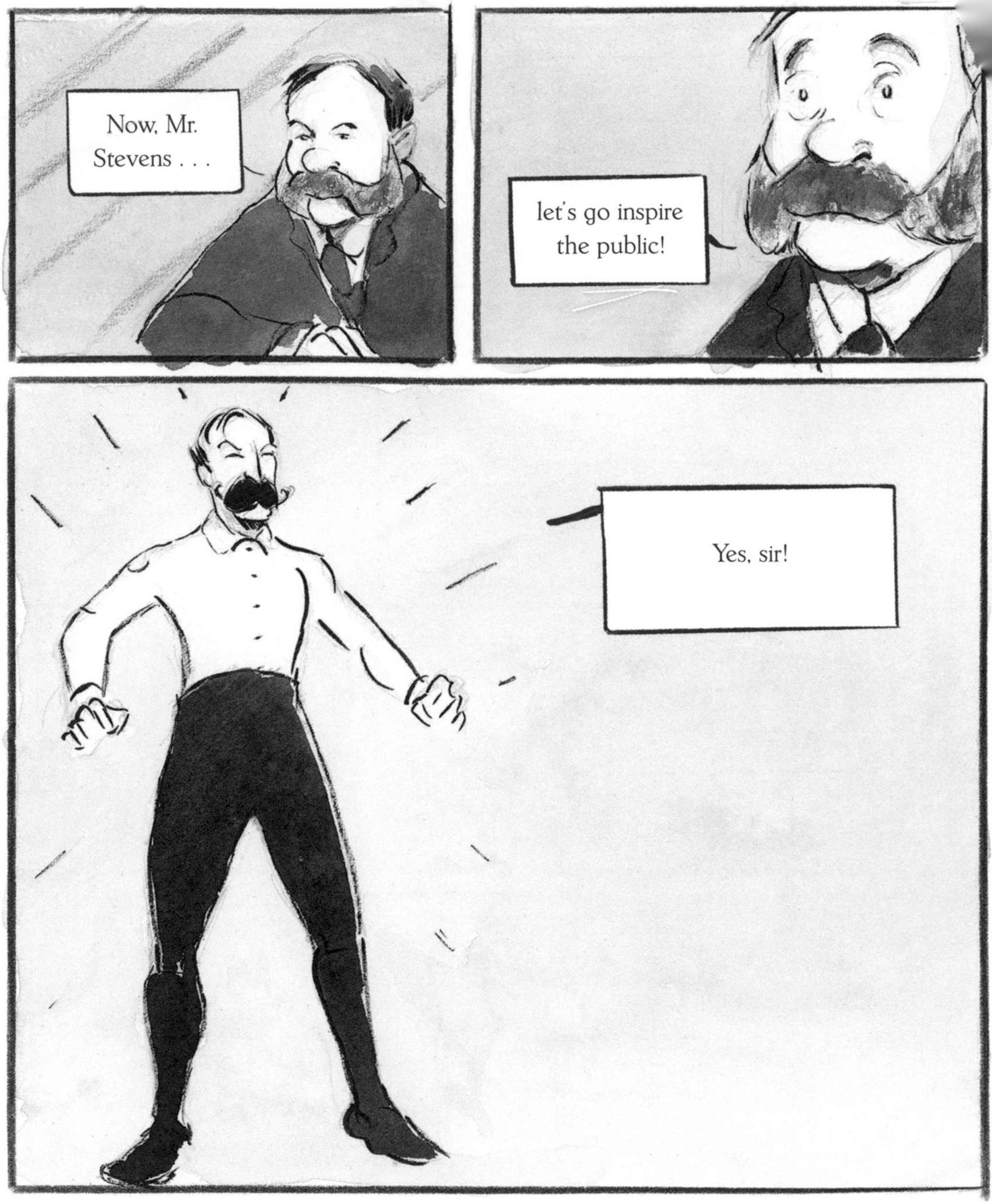
Now, Mr. Stevens . . .
let's go inspire the public!
Yes, sir!

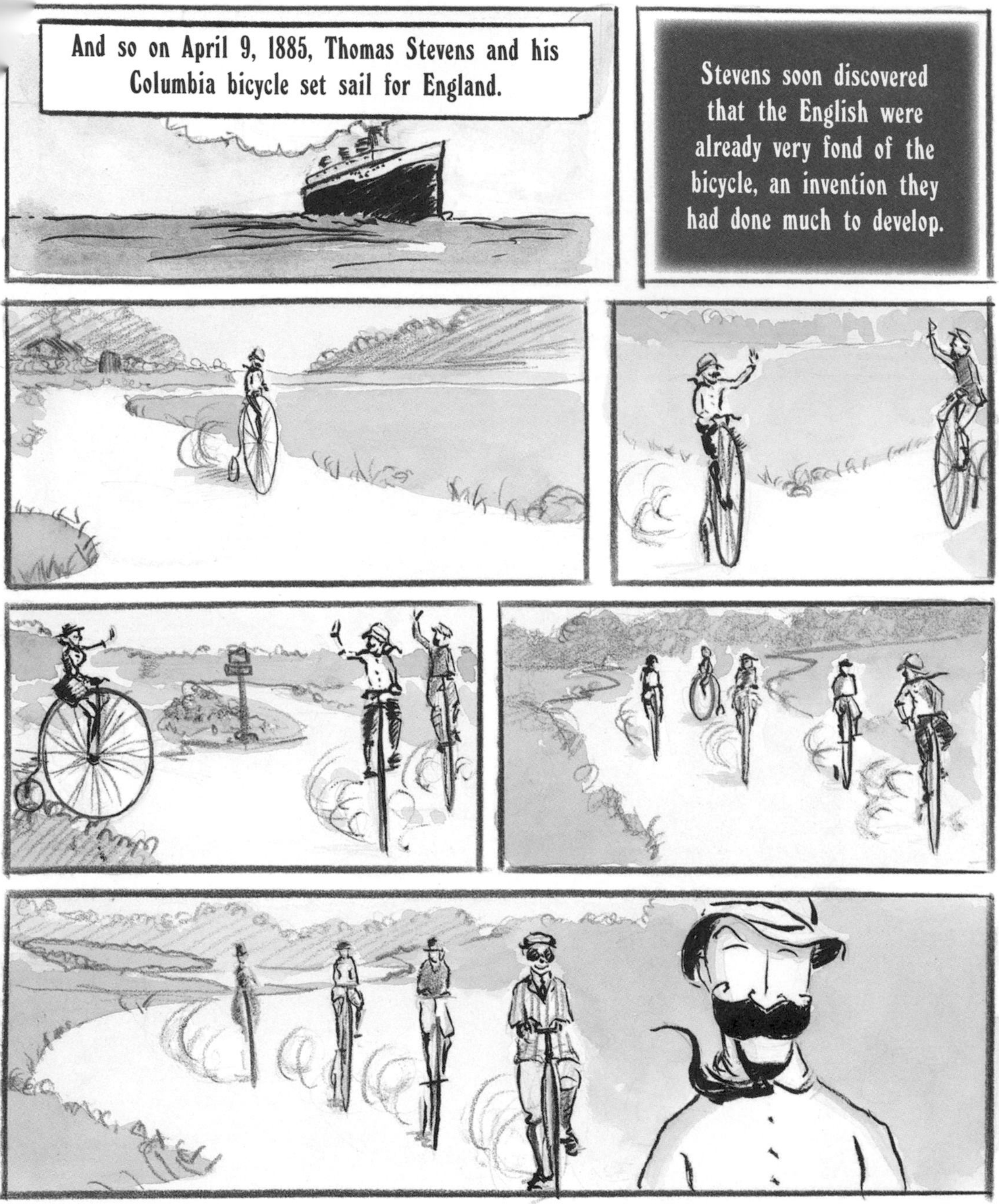
And so on April 9, 1885, Thomas Stevens and his Columbia bicycle set sail for England.
Stevens soon discovered that the English were already very fond of the bicycle, an invention they had done much to develop.

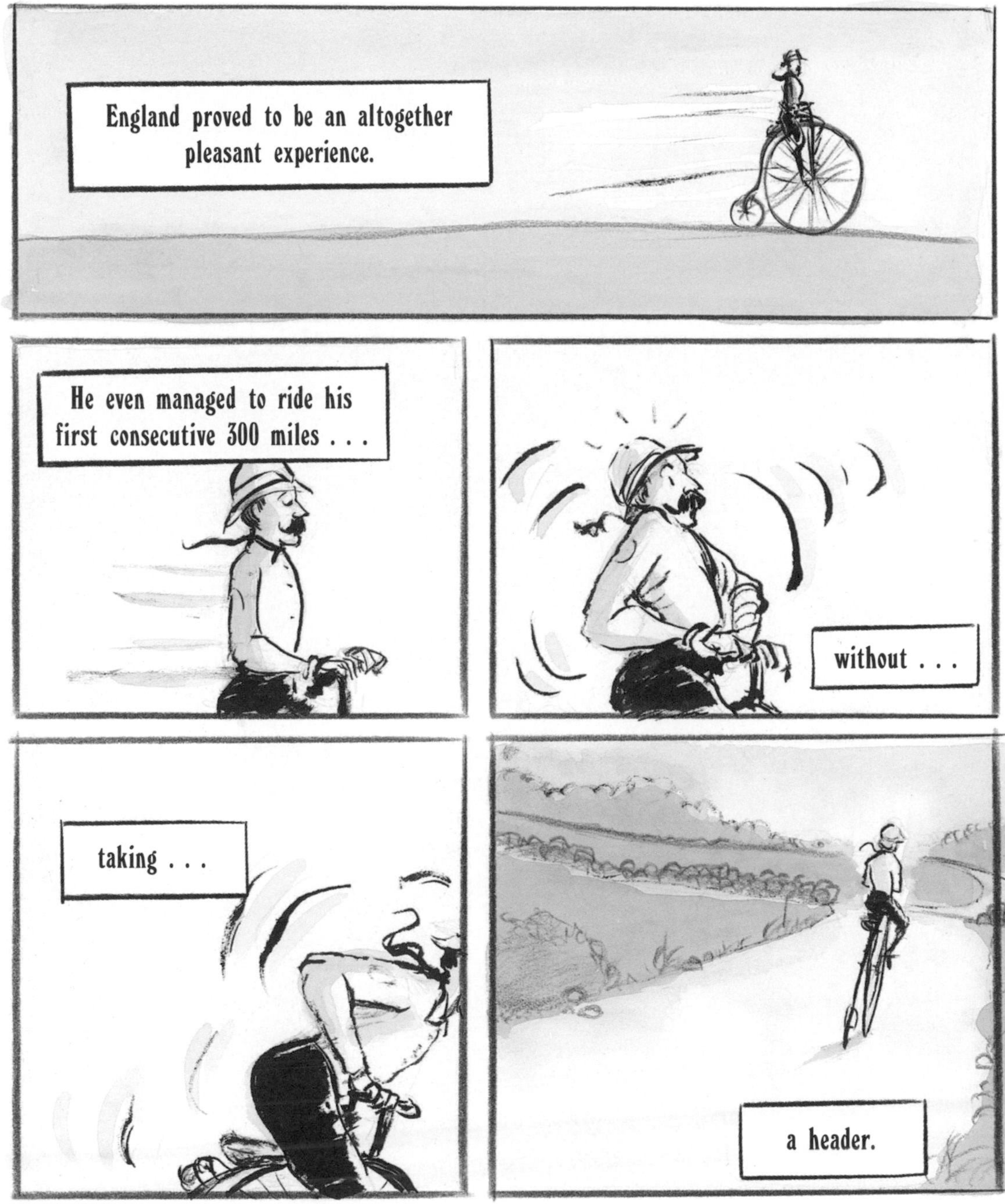
England proved to be an altogether pleasant experience.
He even managed to ride his first consecutive 300 miles . . .
without . . .
taking . . .
a header.

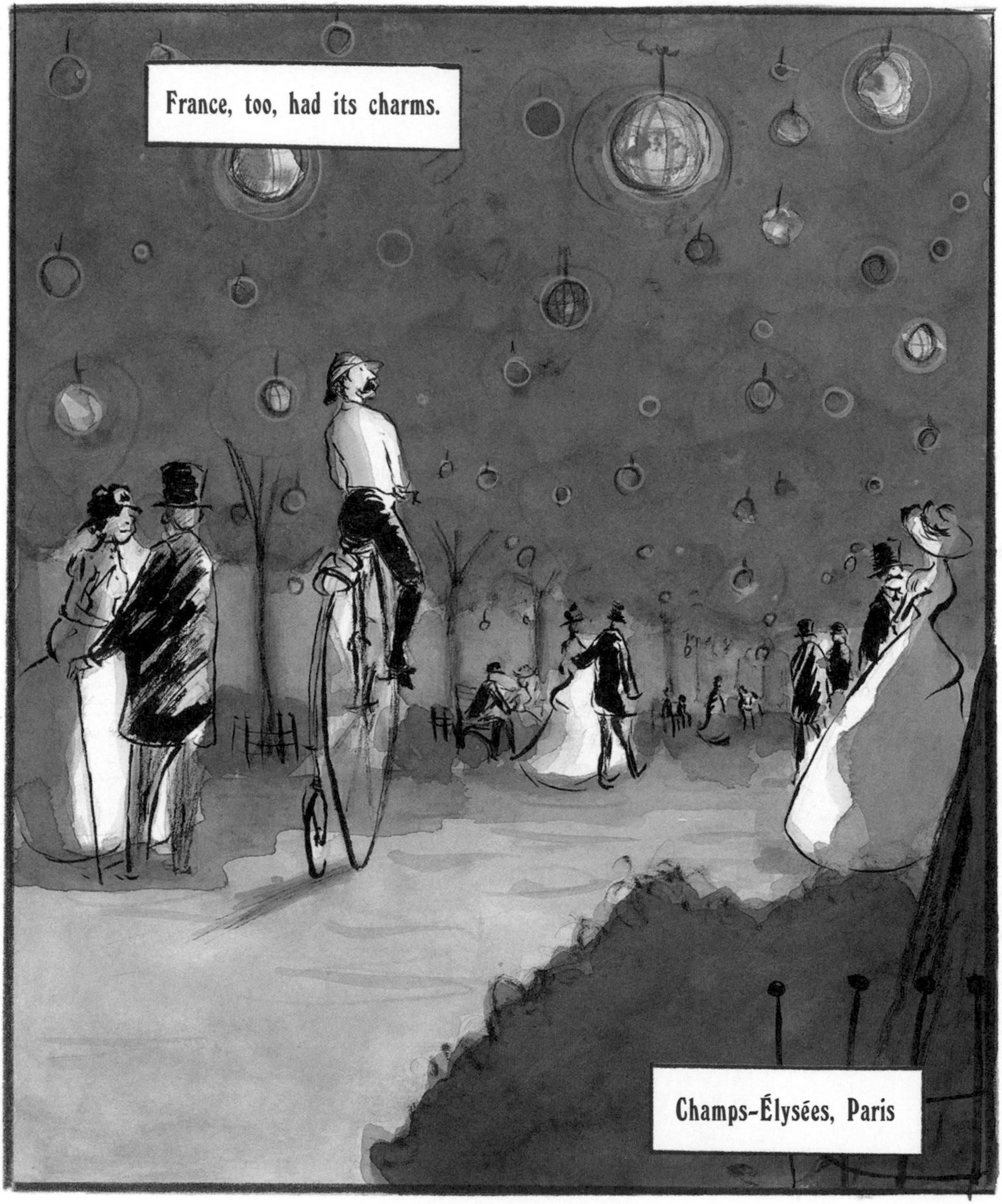
France, too, had its charms.
Champs-Élysées, Paris

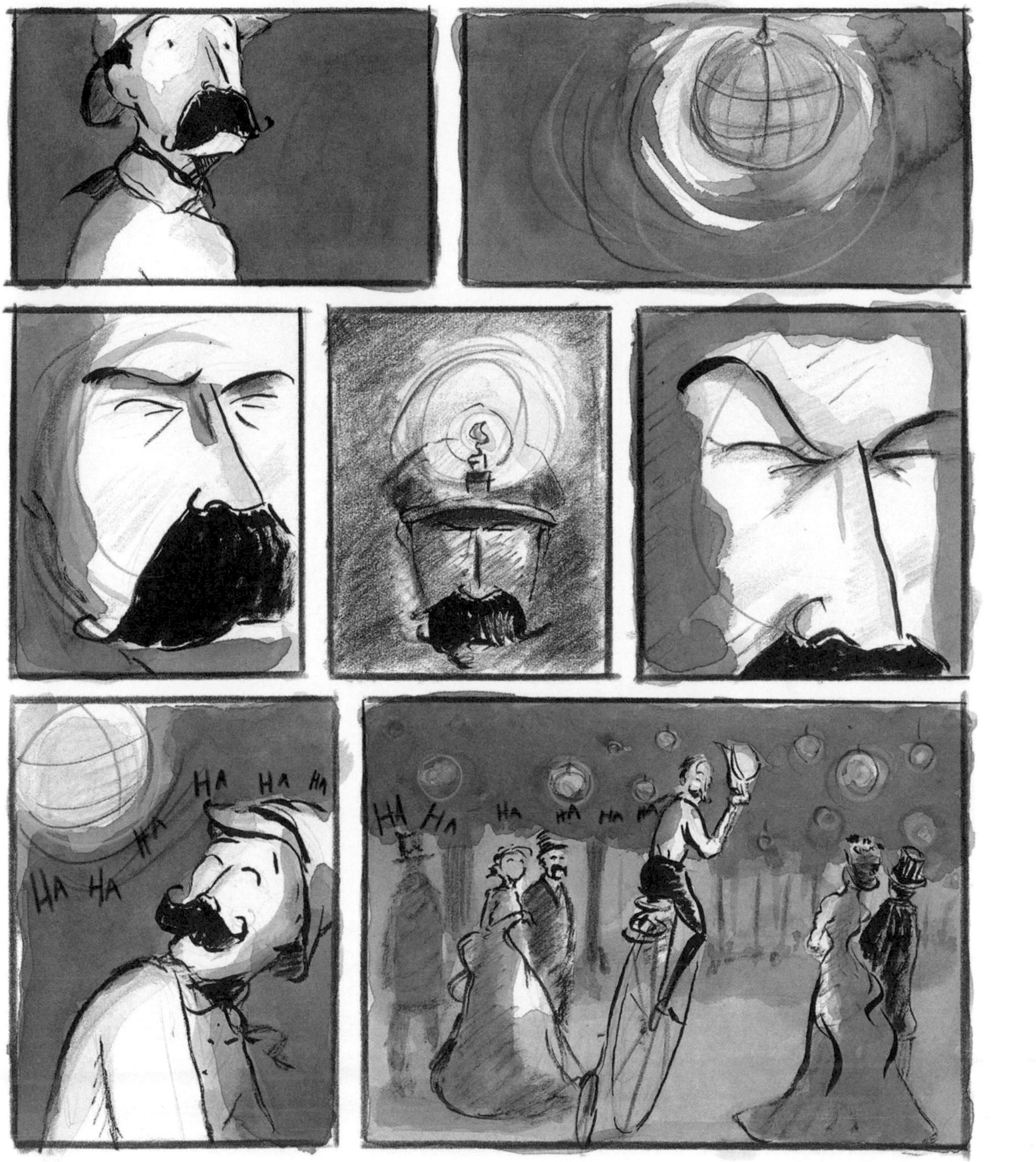
HA HA HA HA HA HA
HA HA HA HA HA HA

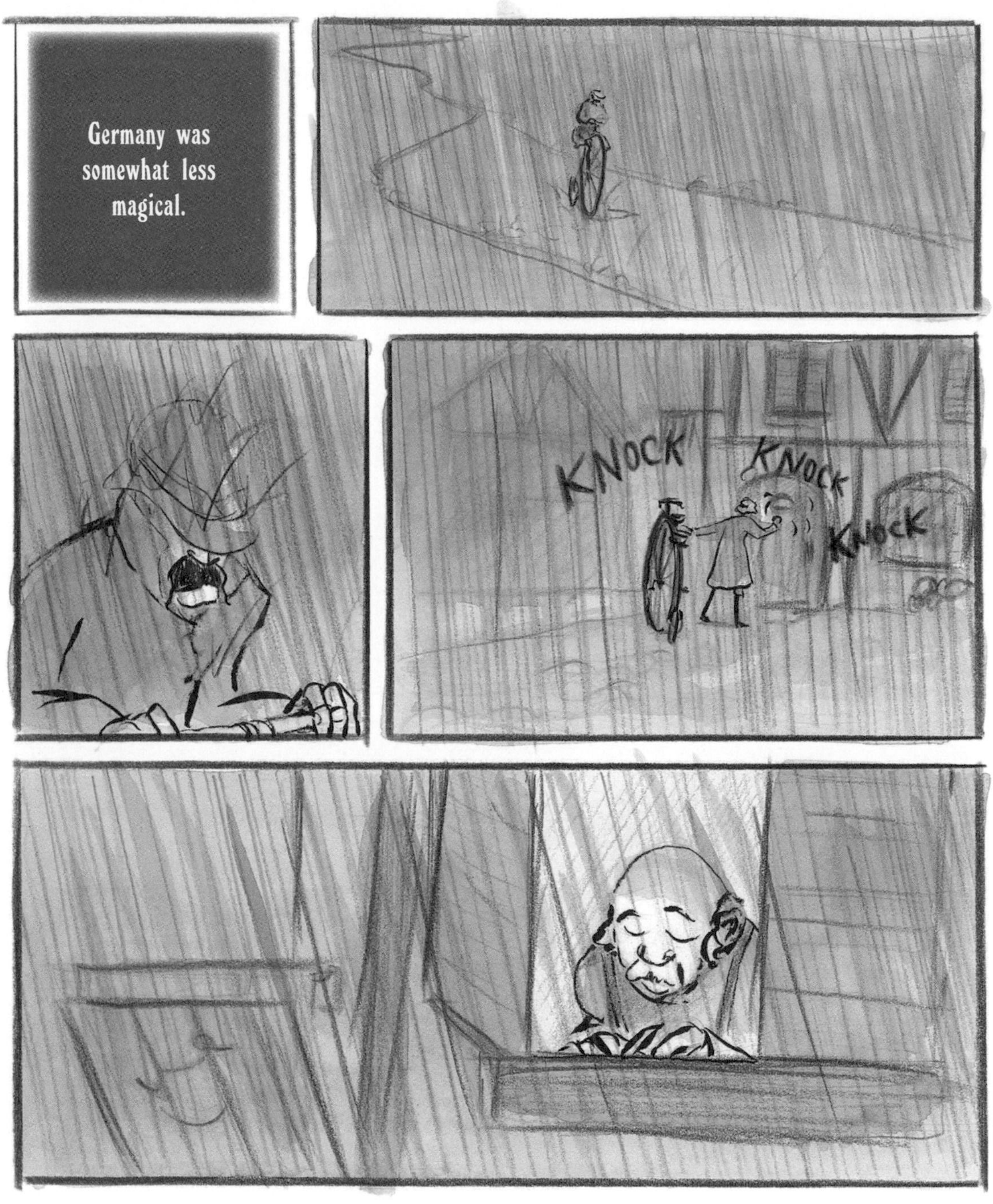
Germany was somewhat less magical.
KNOCK
KNOCK
KNOCK

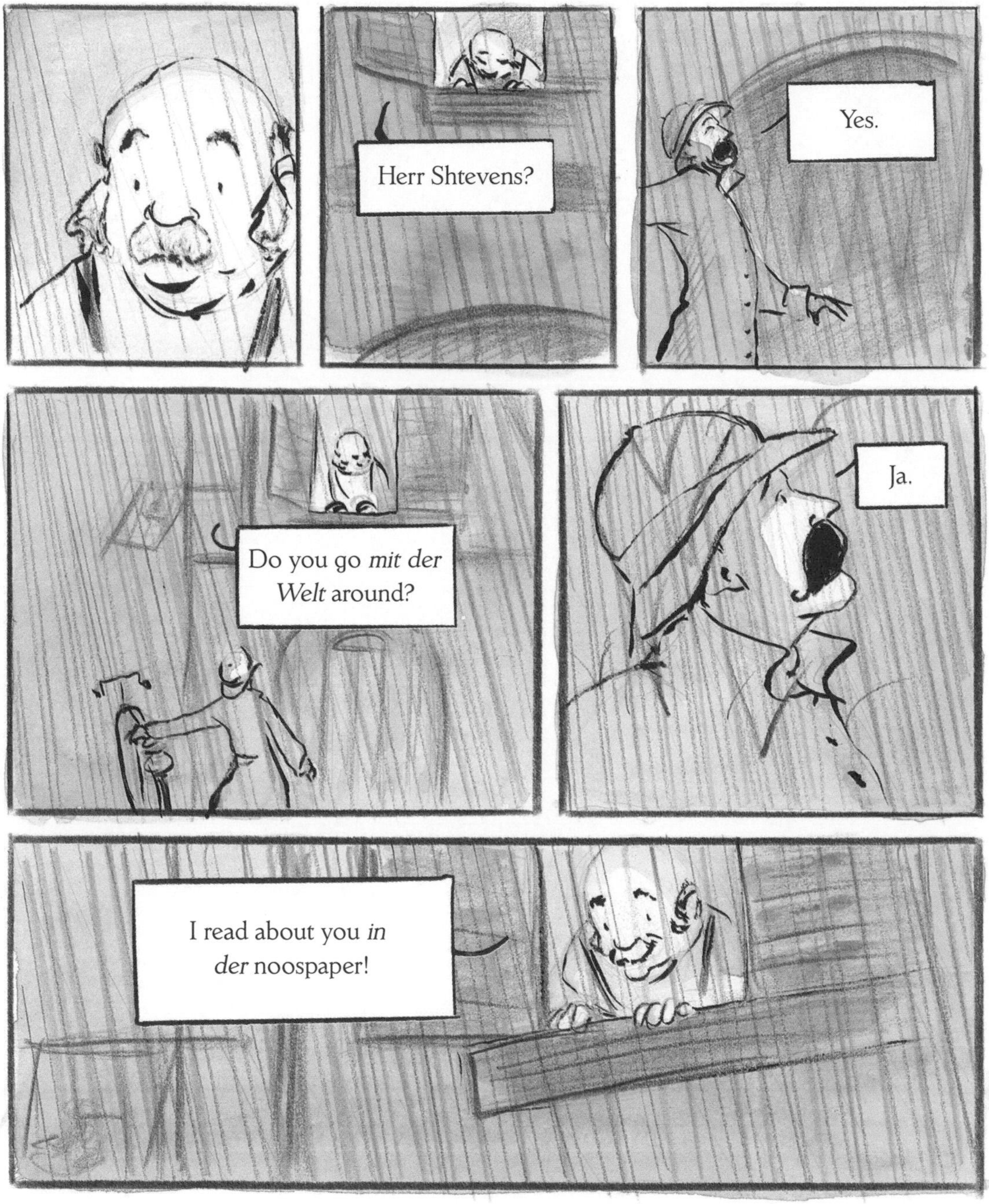

Herr Shtevens?
Yes.
Do you go *mit der Welt* around?
Ja.
I read about you *in der* noospaper!

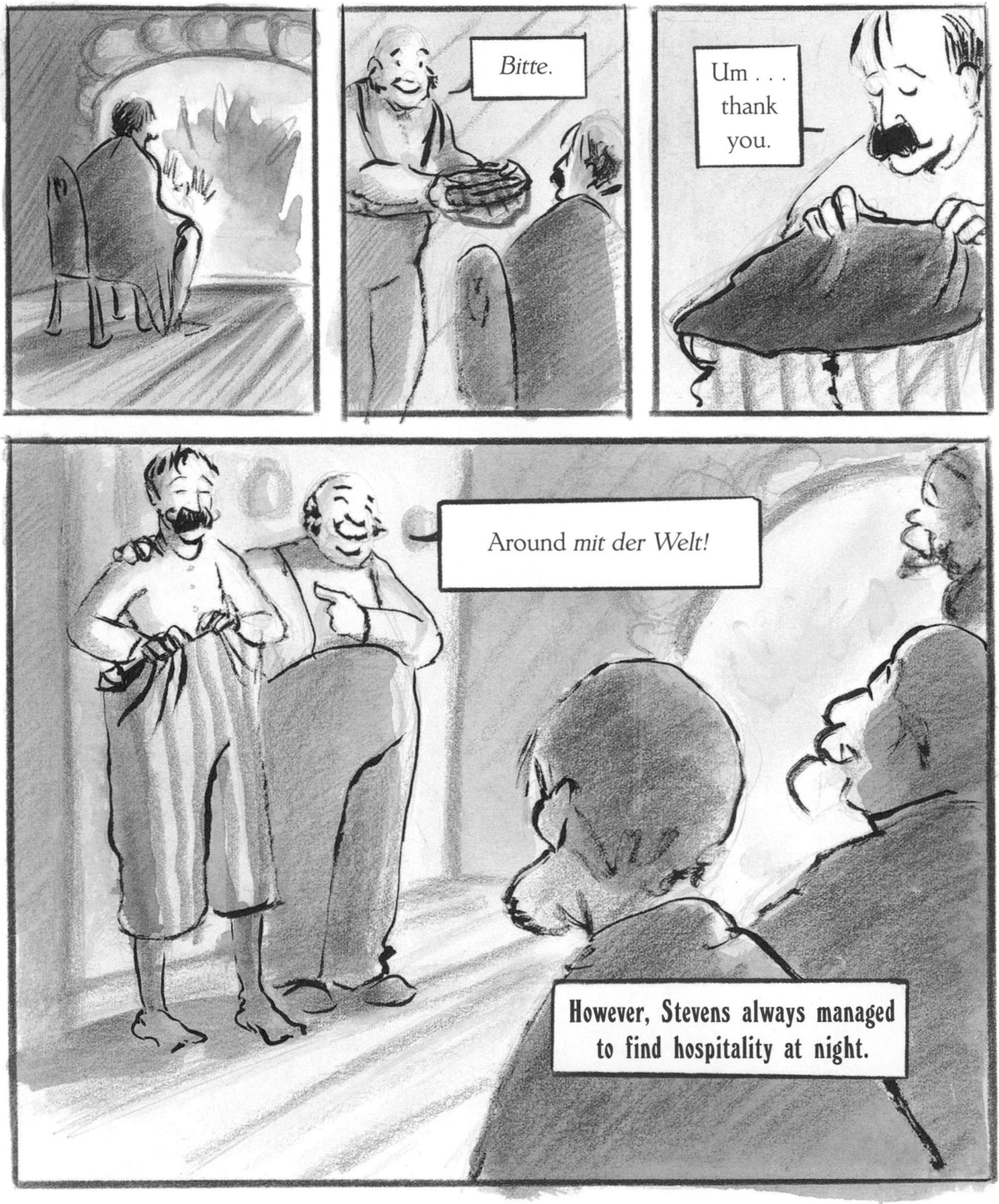

*Bitte.*
Um . . . thank you.
Around *mit der Welt!*
However, Stevens always managed to find hospitality at night.

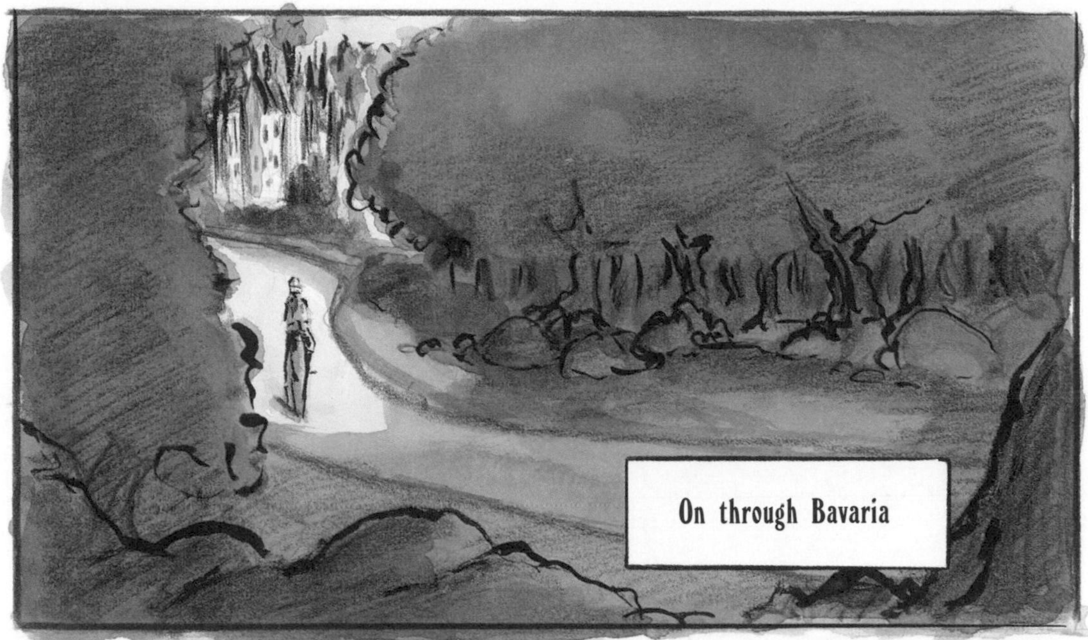
On through Bavaria

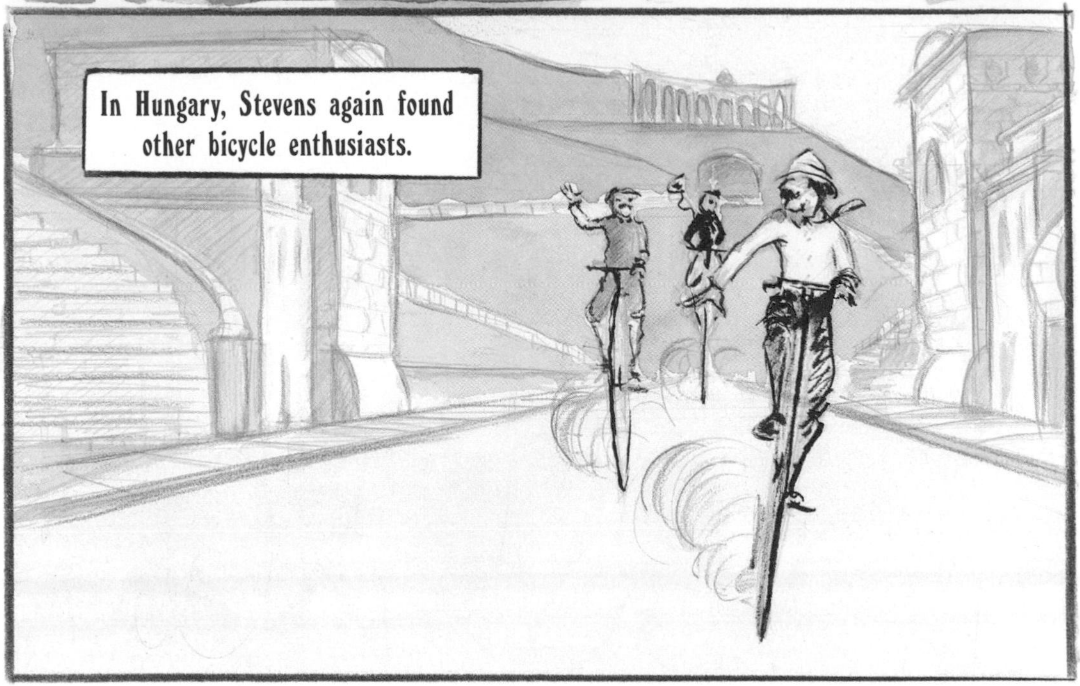
In Hungary, Stevens again found other bicycle enthusiasts.

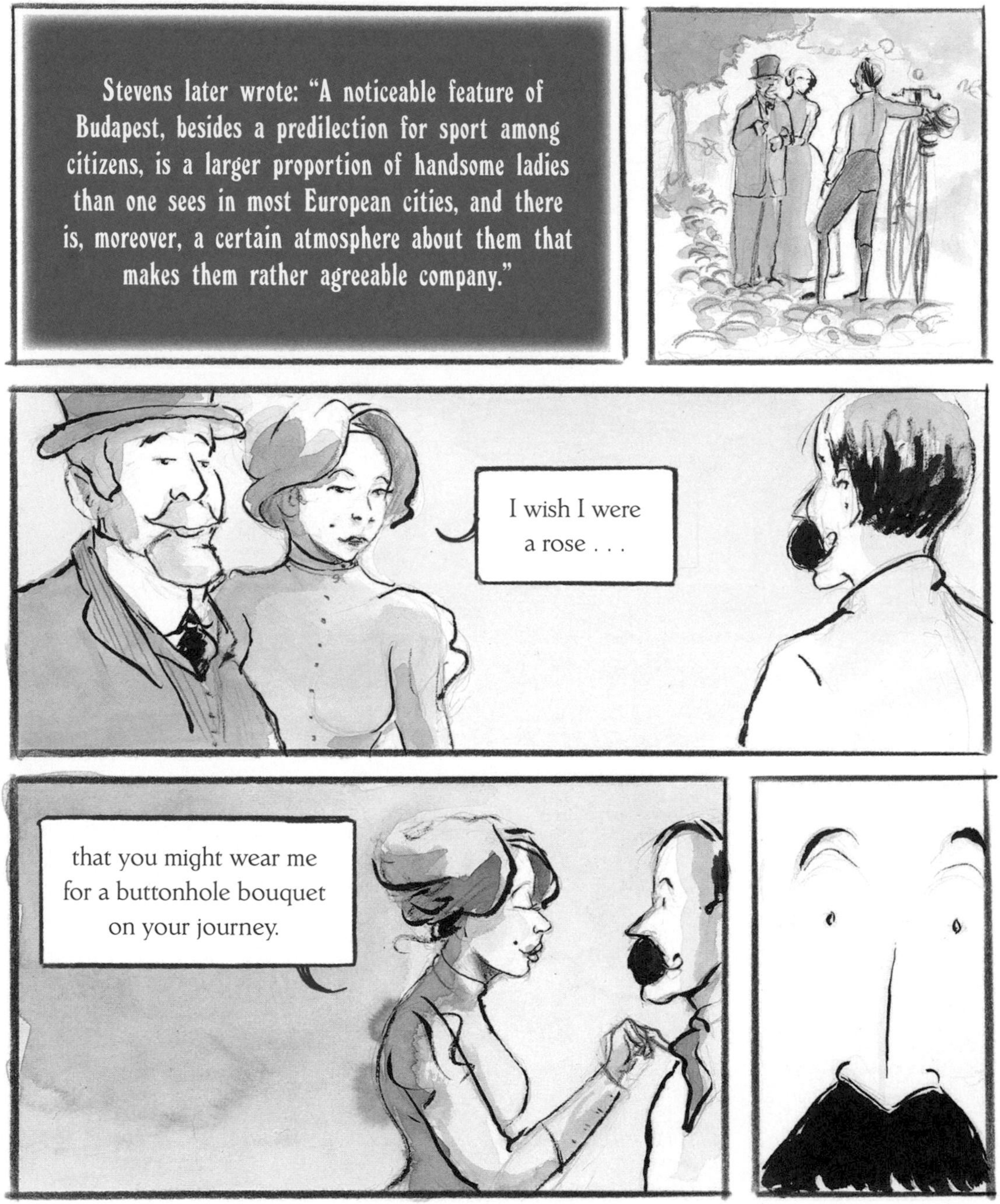
Stevens later wrote: "A noticeable feature of Budapest, besides a predilection for sport among citizens, is a larger proportion of handsome ladies than one sees in most European cities, and there is, moreover, a certain atmosphere about them that makes them rather agreeable company."
I wish I were a rose . . .
that you might wear me for a buttonhole bouquet on your journey.

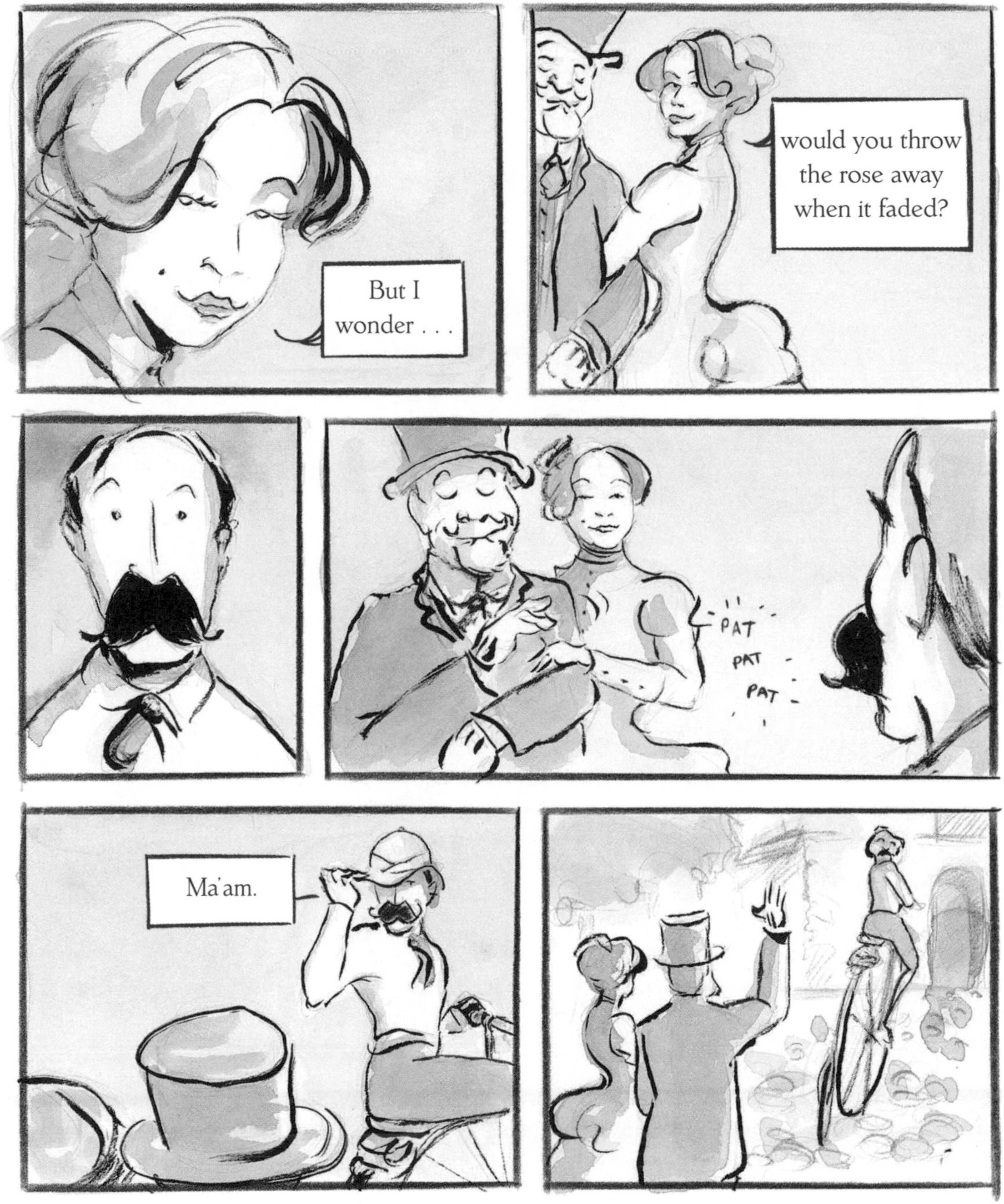
But I wonder . . .
would you throw the rose away when it faded?
PAT
PAT
PAT
Ma'am.

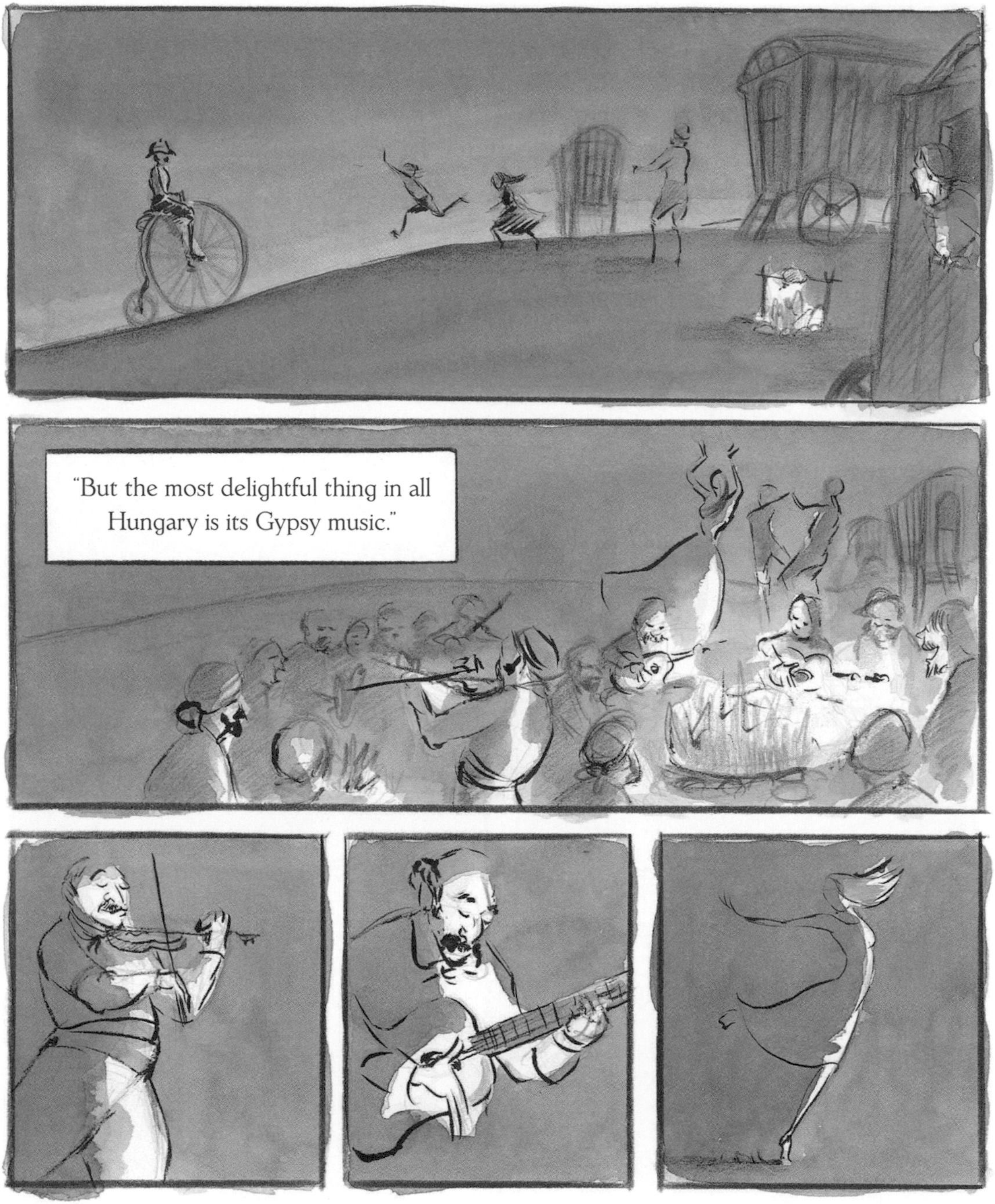
"But the most delightful thing in all Hungary is its Gypsy music."

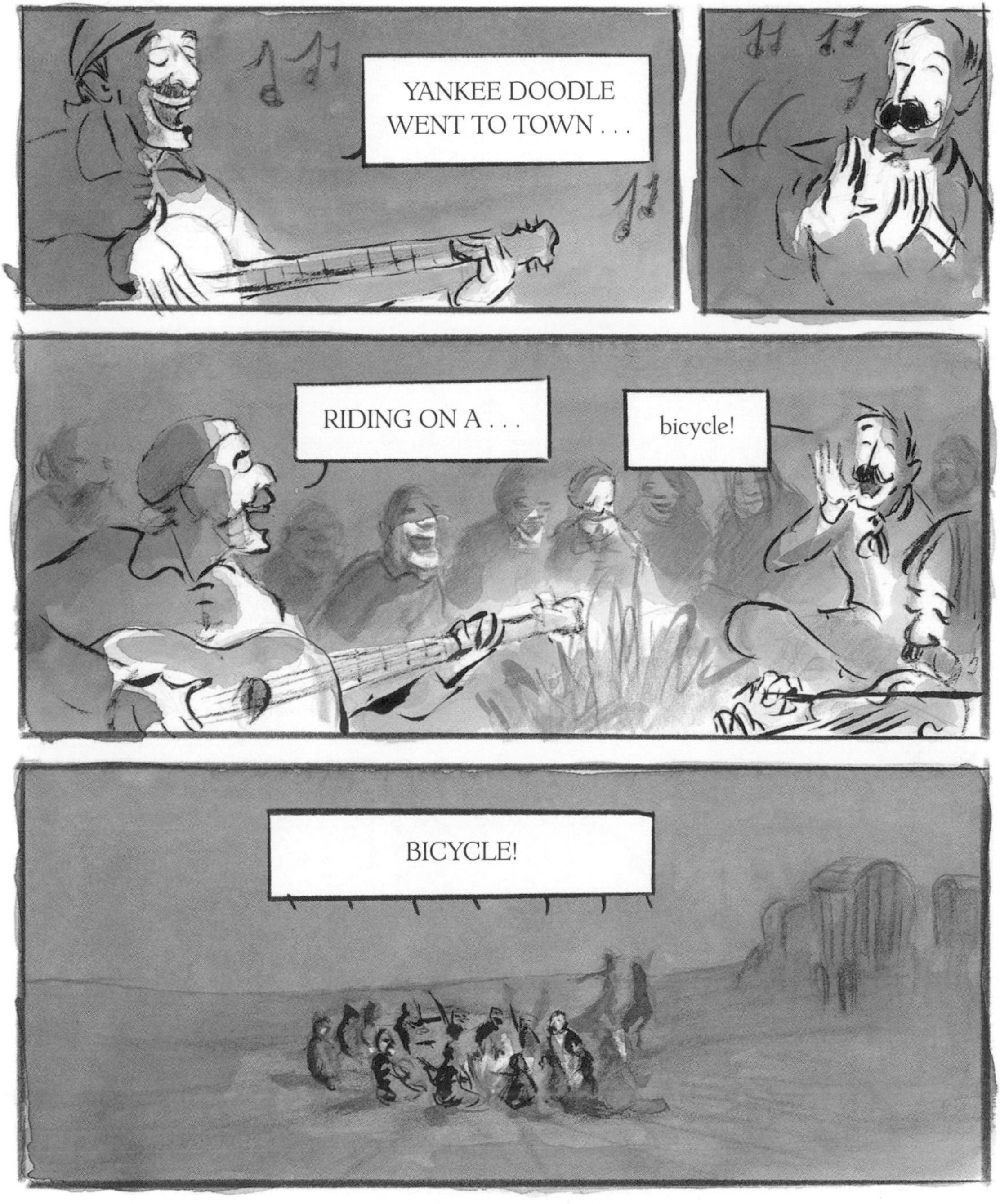
YANKEE DOODLE WENT TO TOWN . . .
RIDING ON A . . .
bicycle!
BICYCLE!

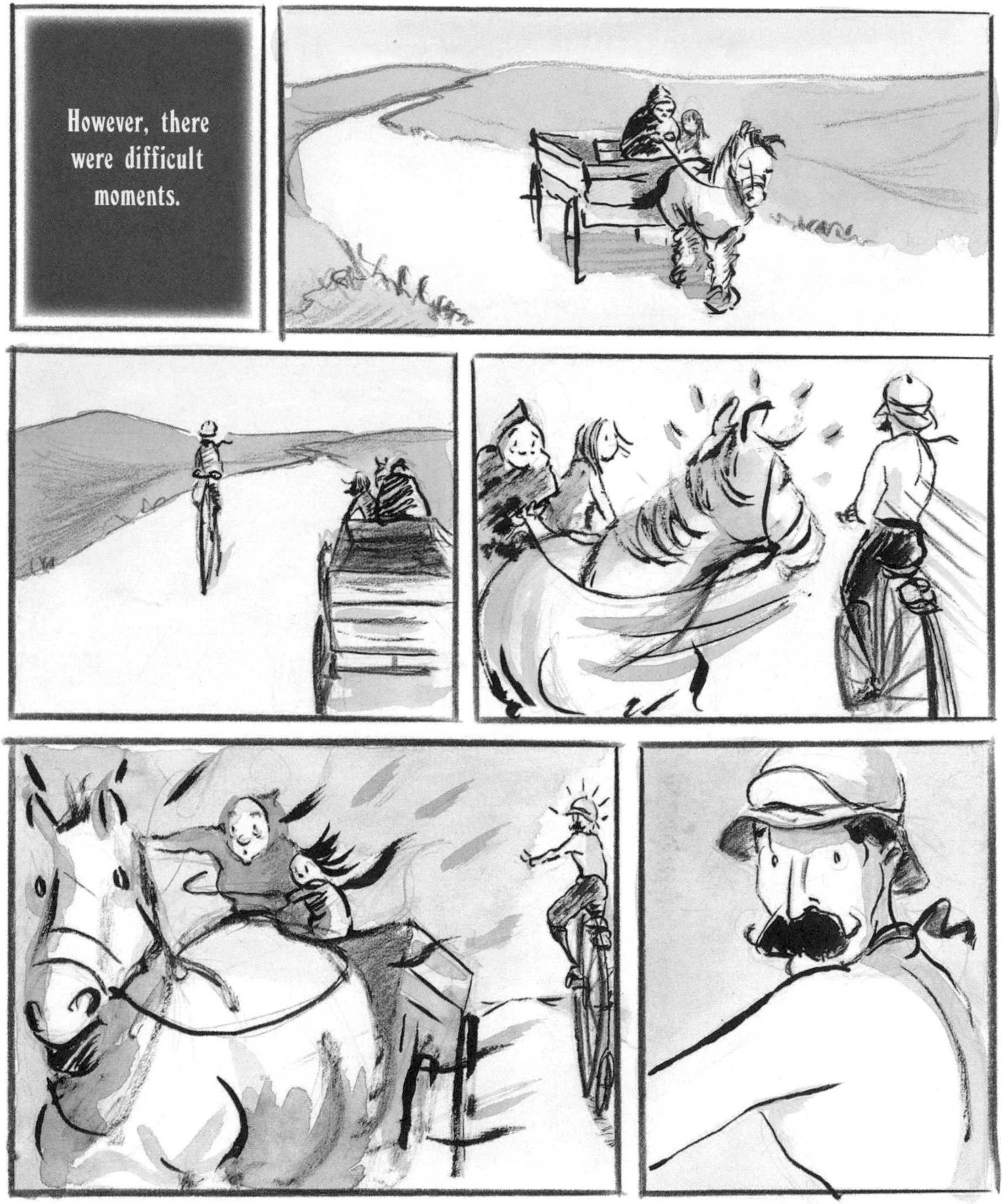
However, there were difficult moments.

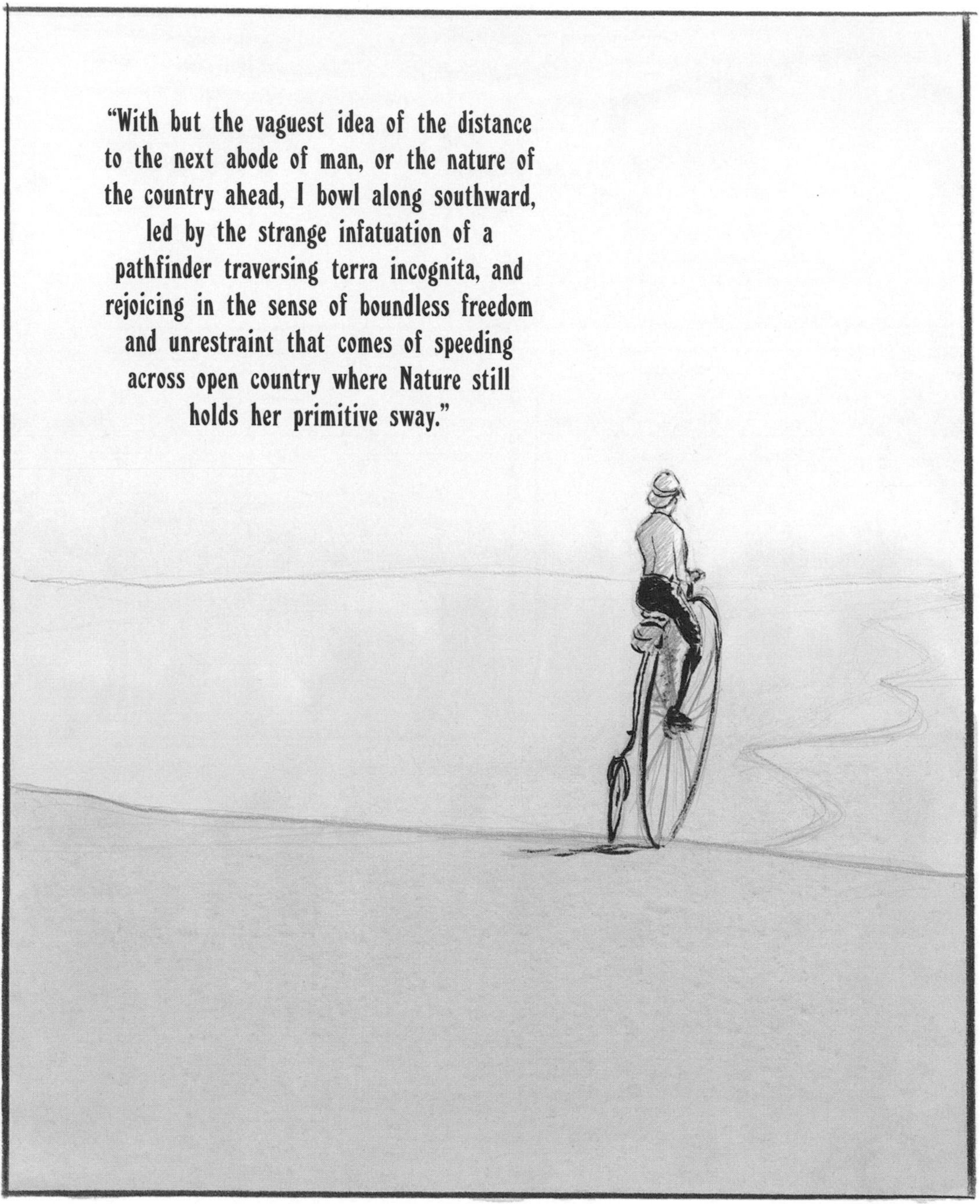
"With but the vaguest idea of the distance to the next abode of man, or the nature of the country ahead, I bowl along southward, led by the strange infatuation of a pathfinder traversing terra incognita, and rejoicing in the sense of boundless freedom and unrestraint that comes of speeding across open country where Nature still holds her primitive sway."

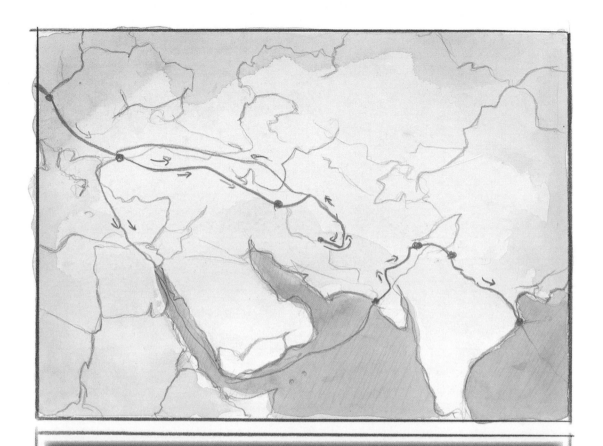

Thomas Stevens continued east on his journey around the world. He had many adventures, saw many interesting things, and met fascinating people. He also had many pleasant days of relatively easy riding (considering the lack of paved roads). This portion of his journey is thoroughly recounted in his book, *Around the World on a Bicycle*. It is so thorough, in fact, that it takes up 859 pages. In the interests of brevity, we now humbly present a condensed account of this portion of his journey.

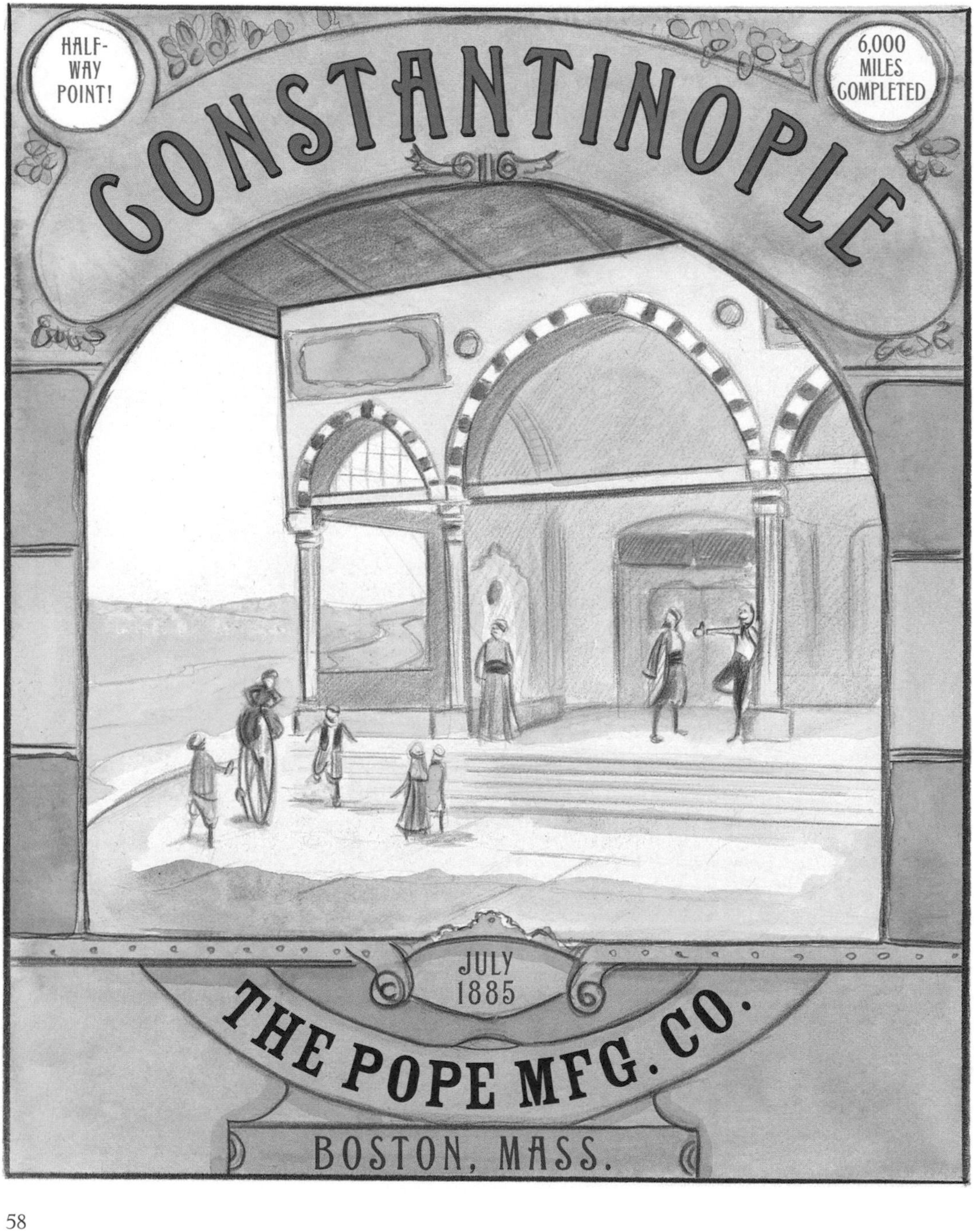
HALF-WAY POINT!
6,000 MILES COMPLETED
CONSTANTINOPLE
JULY 1885
THE POPE MFG. CO.
BOSTON, MASS.

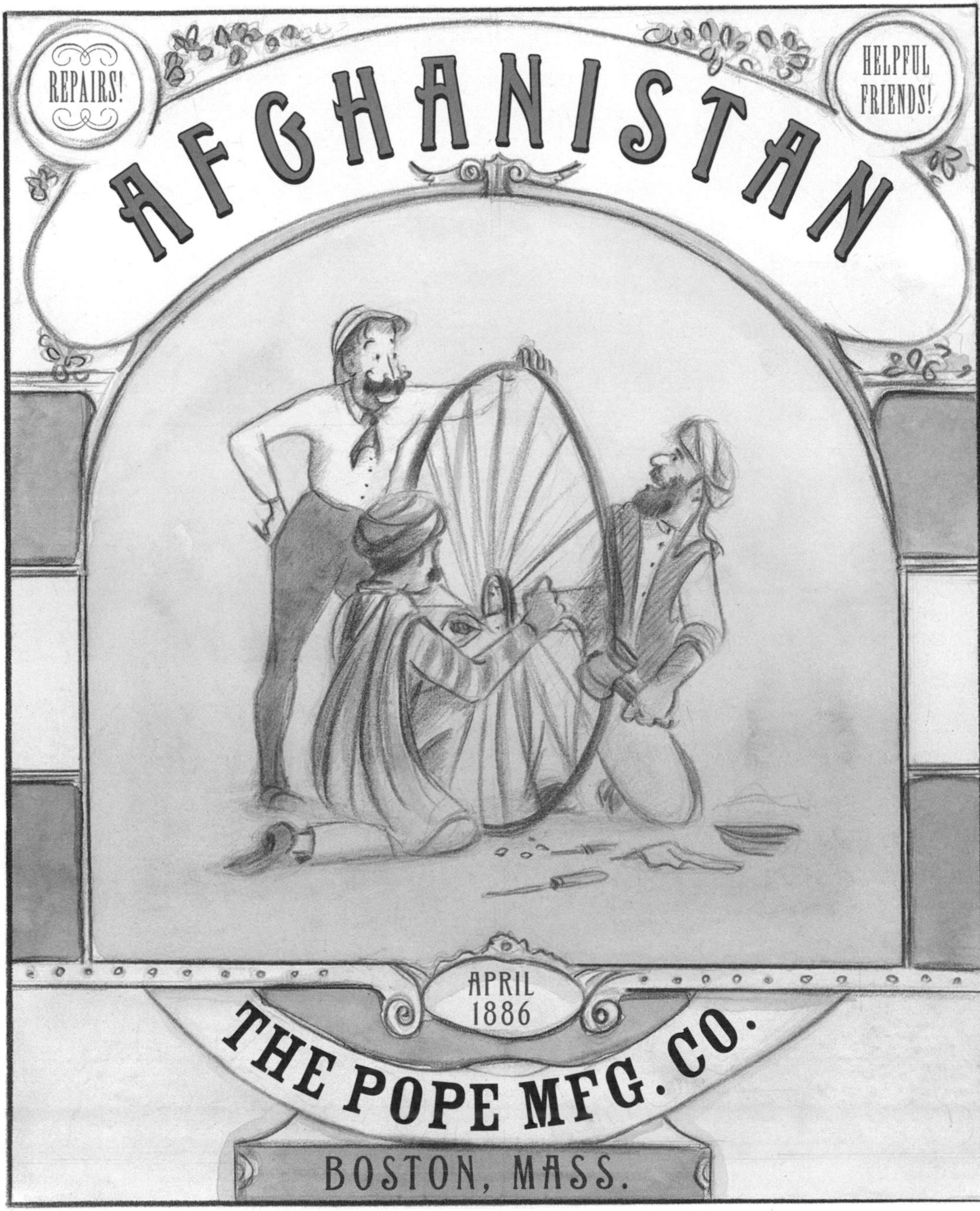
REPAIRS!
HELPFUL FRIENDS!
AFGHANISTAN
APRIL 1886
THE POPE MFG. CO.
BOSTON, MASS.

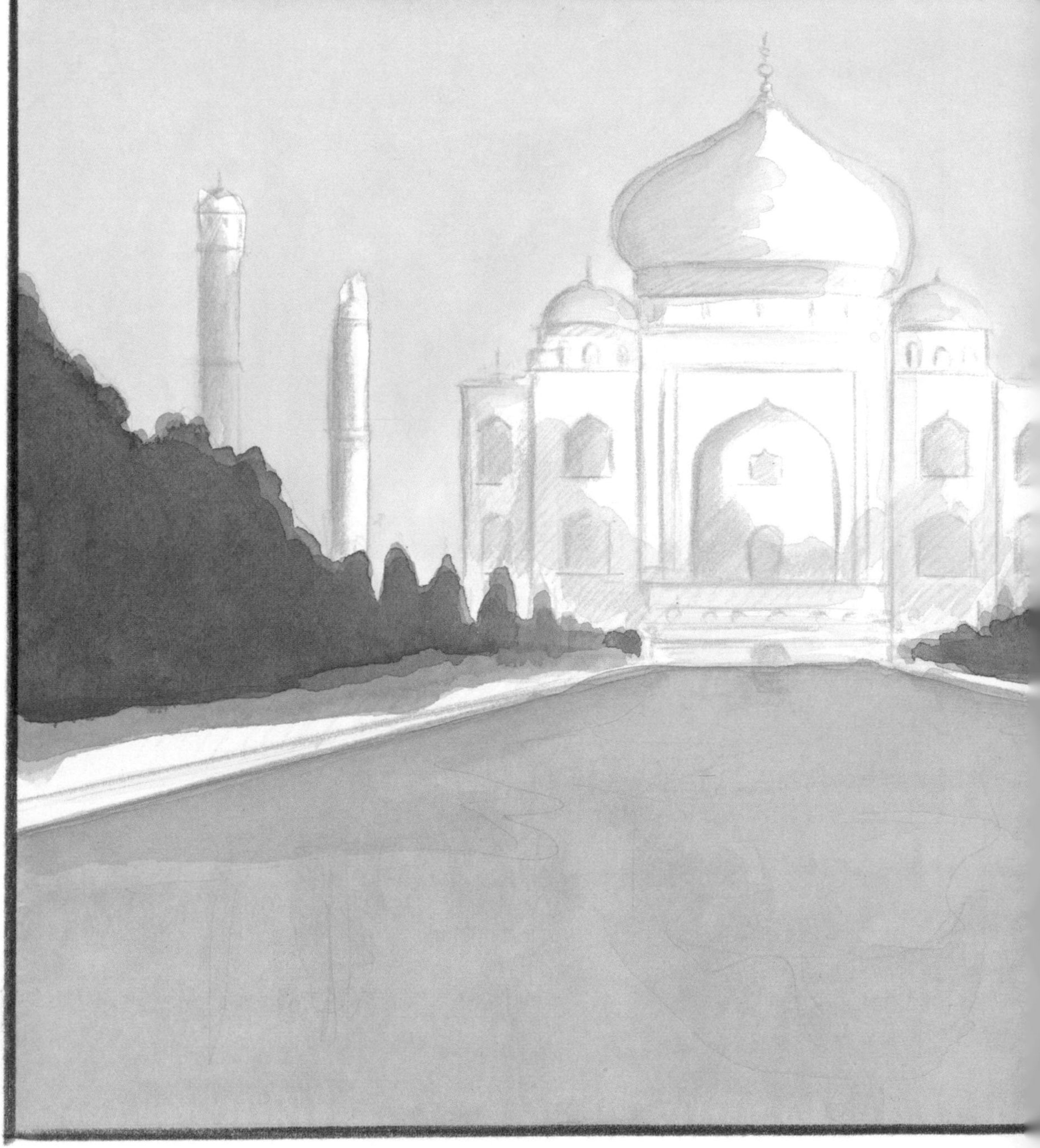

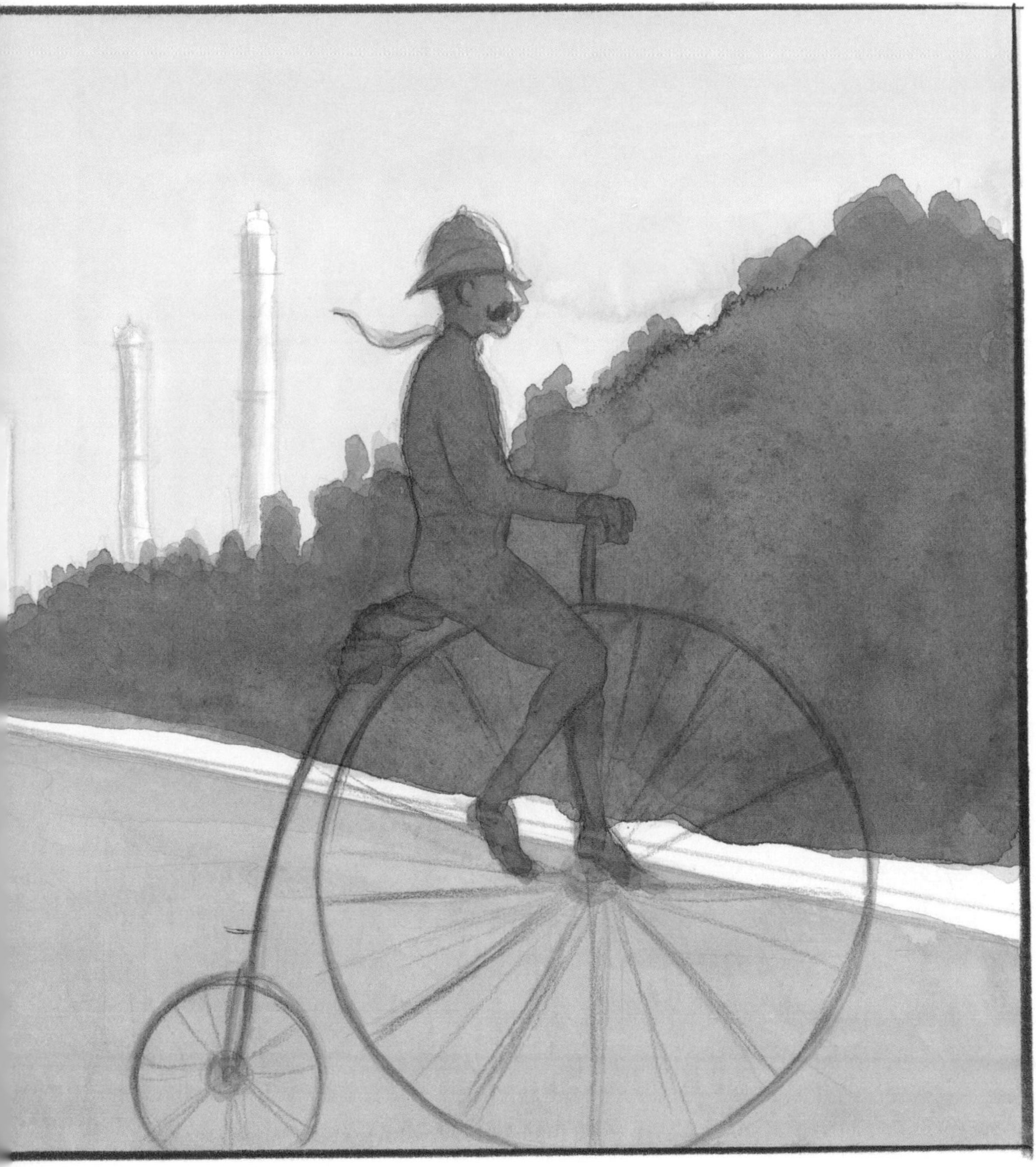

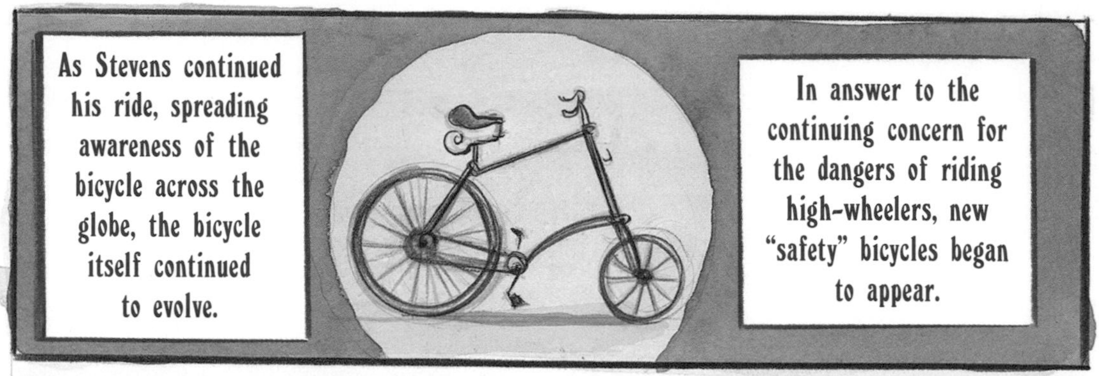
As Stevens continued his ride, spreading awareness of the bicycle across the globe, the bicycle itself continued to evolve.
In answer to the continuing concern for the dangers of riding high-wheelers, new "safety" bicycles began to appear.

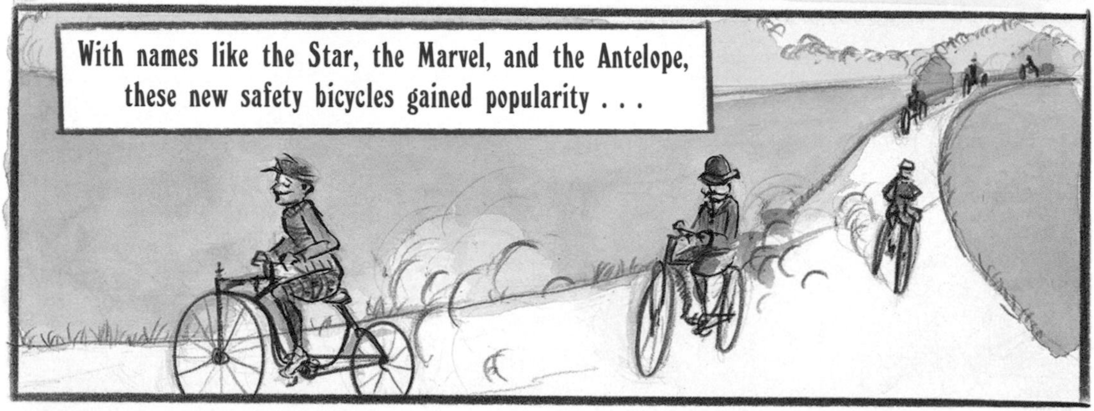
With names like the Star, the Marvel, and the Antelope, these new safety bicycles gained popularity . . .

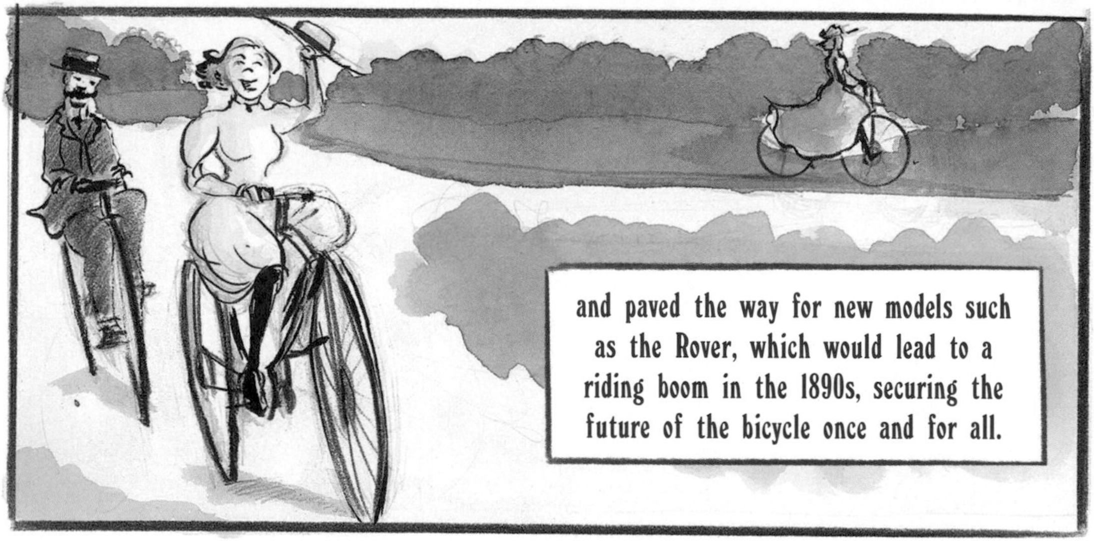
and paved the way for new models such as the Rover, which would lead to a riding boom in the 1890s, securing the future of the bicycle once and for all.

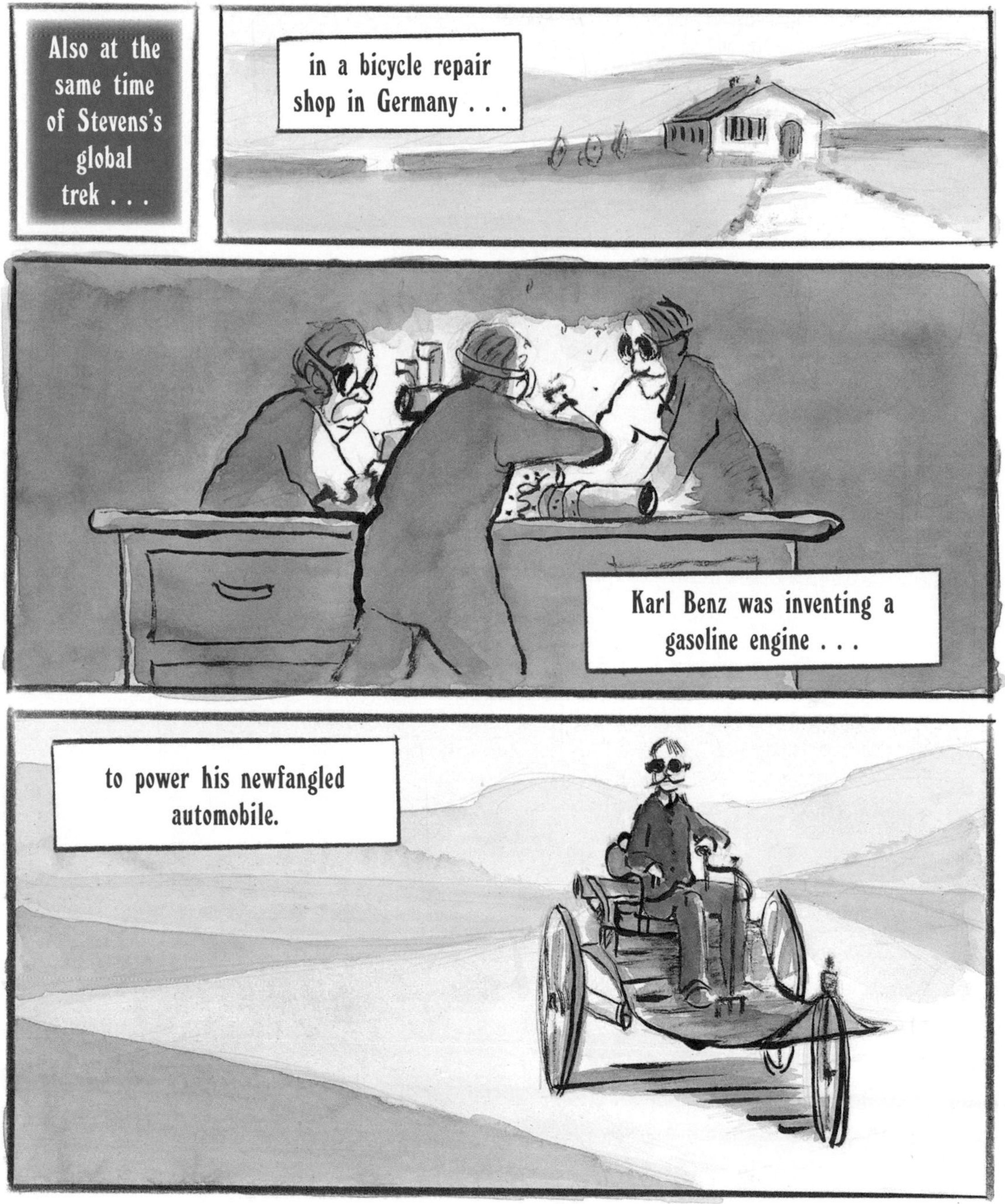
Also at the same time of Stevens's global trek . . .
in a bicycle repair shop in Germany . . .
Karl Benz was inventing a gasoline engine . . .
to power his newfangled automobile.

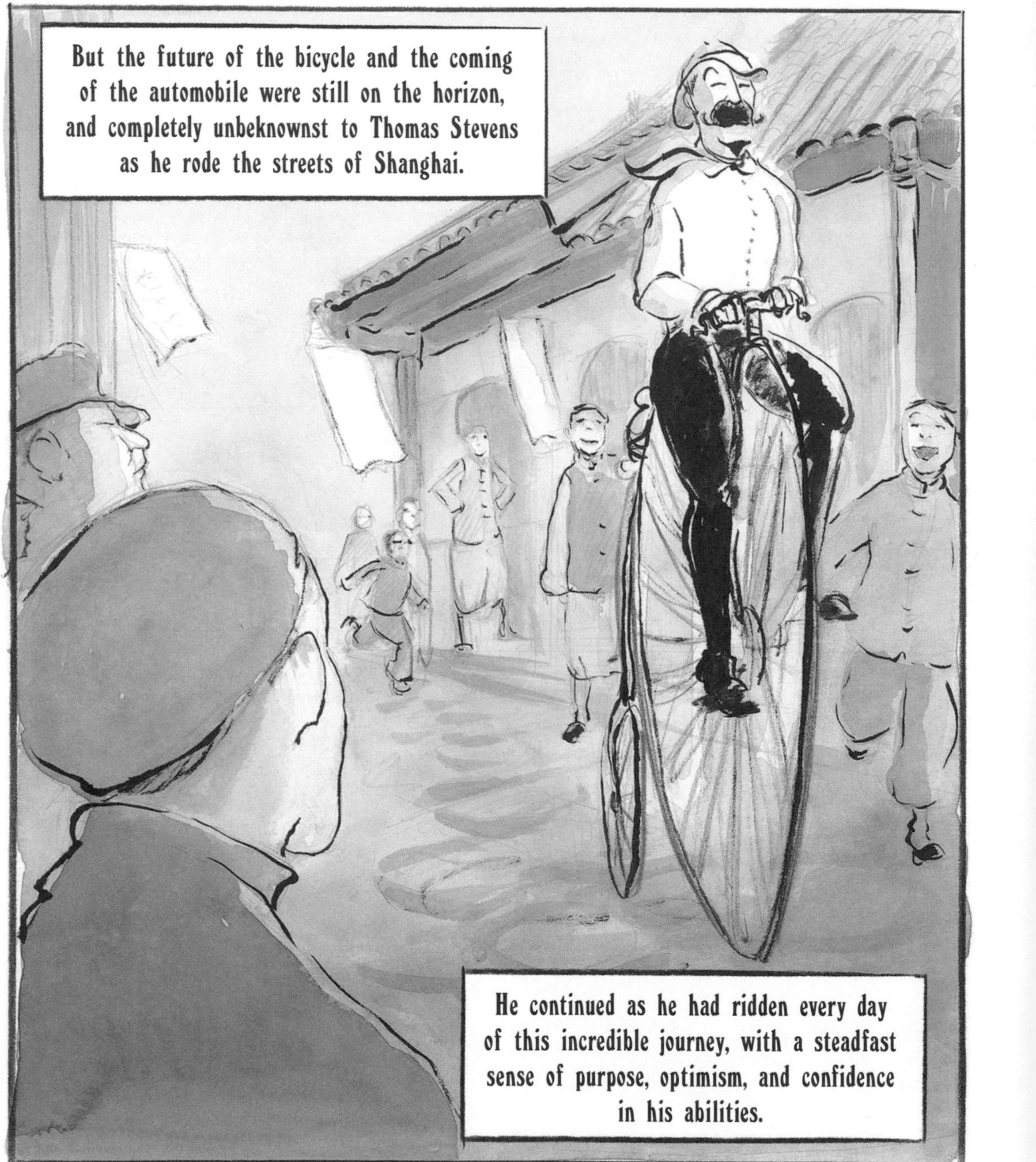
But the future of the bicycle and the coming of the automobile were still on the horizon, and completely unbeknownst to Thomas Stevens as he rode the streets of Shanghai.
He continued as he had ridden every day of this incredible journey, with a steadfast sense of purpose, optimism, and confidence in his abilities.

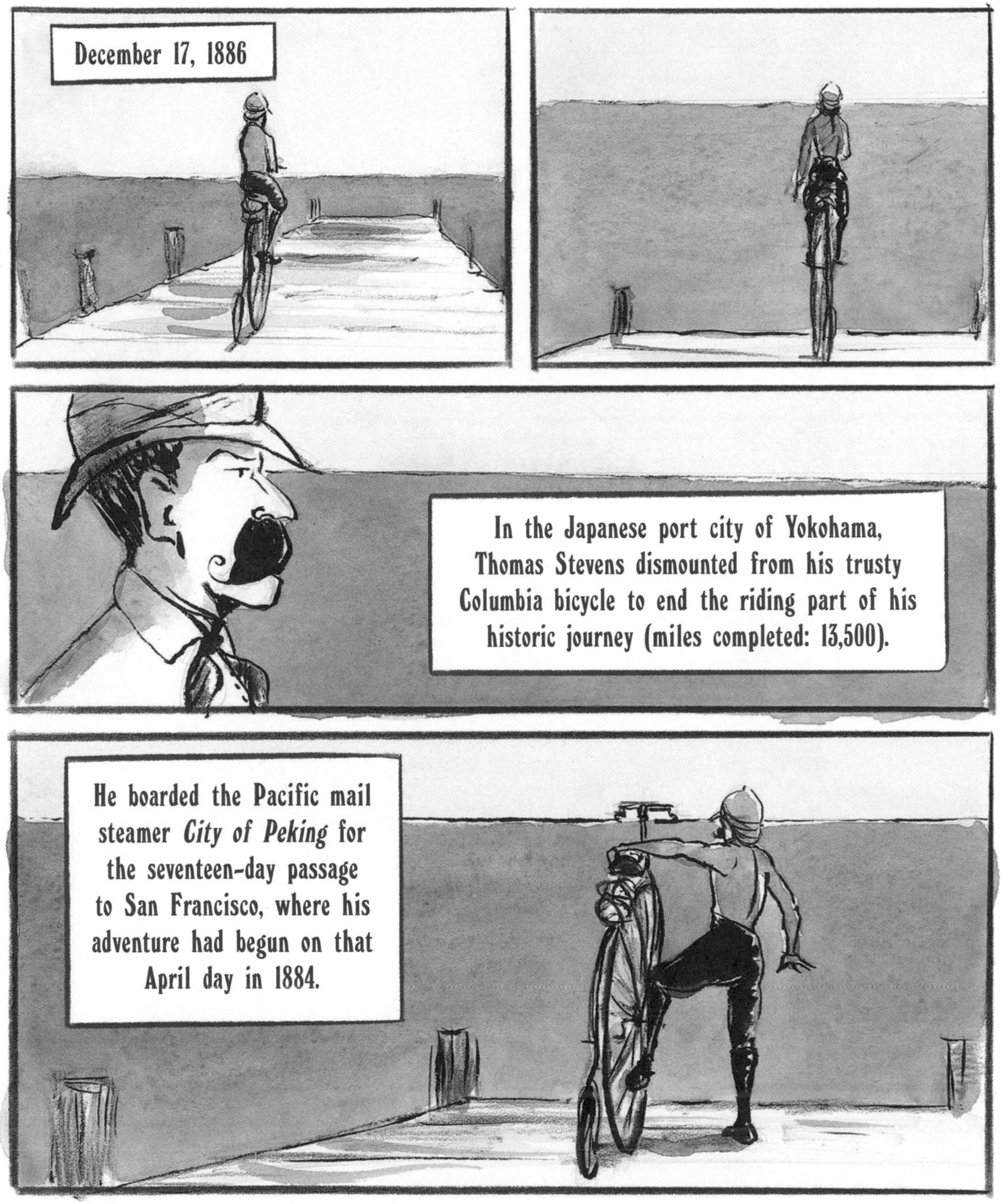
December 17, 1886
In the Japanese port city of Yokohama, Thomas Stevens dismounted from his trusty Columbia bicycle to end the riding part of his historic journey (miles completed: 13,500).
He boarded the Pacific mail steamer *City of Peking* for the seventeen-day passage to San Francisco, where his adventure had begun on that April day in 1884.

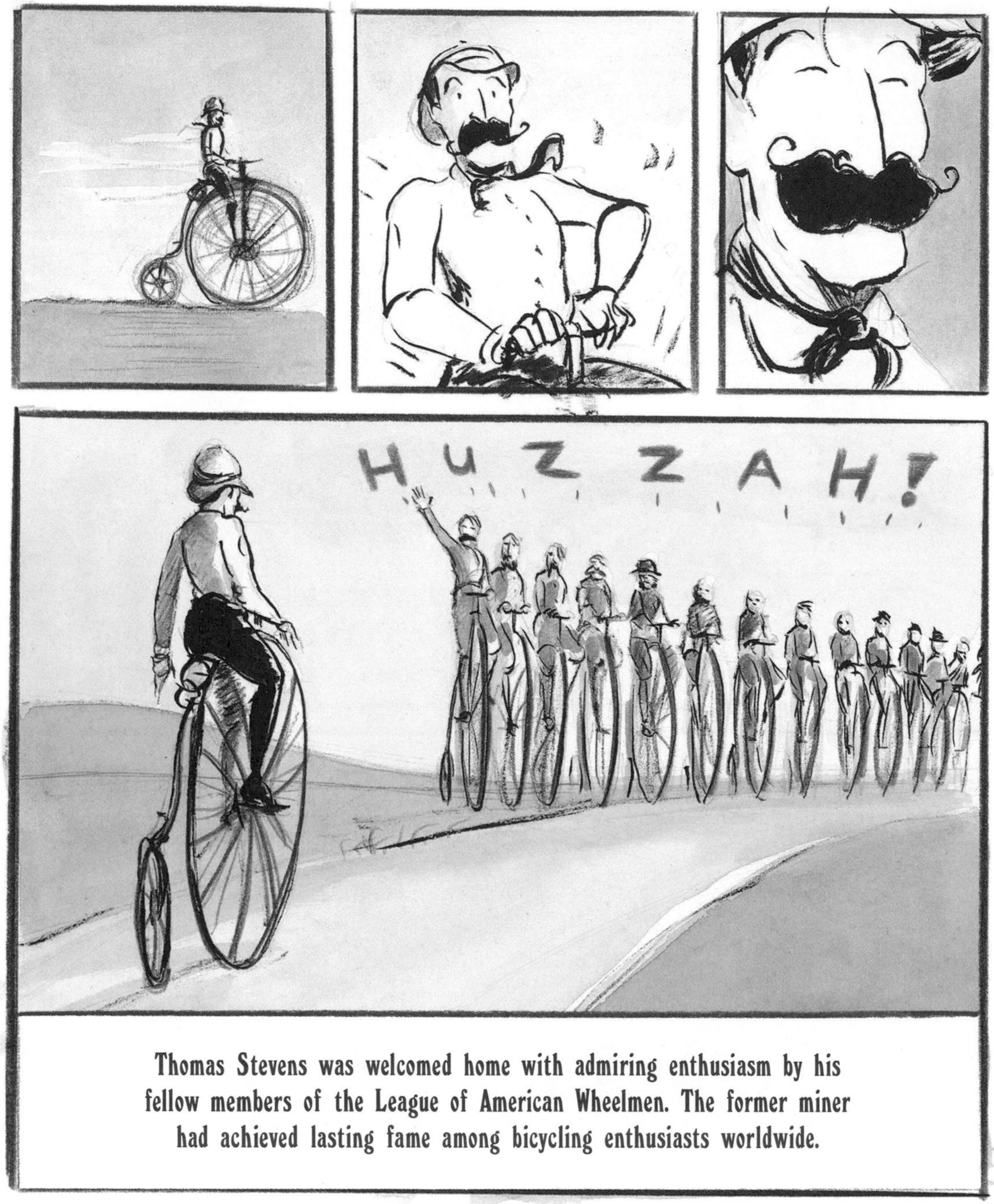
HUZZAH!
Thomas Stevens was welcomed home with admiring enthusiasm by his fellow members of the League of American Wheelmen. The former miner had achieved lasting fame among bicycling enthusiasts worldwide.

We found that modern mechanical invention, instead of disenchanting the universe, had really afforded the means of exploring its marvels the more surely. Instead of going round the world with a rifle, for the purpose of killing something . . . this bold youth simply went round the globe to see the people who were on it; and since he always had something to show them as interesting as anything that they could show him, he made his way among all nations.

—Thomas Wentworth Higginson, from the preface to *Around the World on a Bicycle* by Thomas Stevens

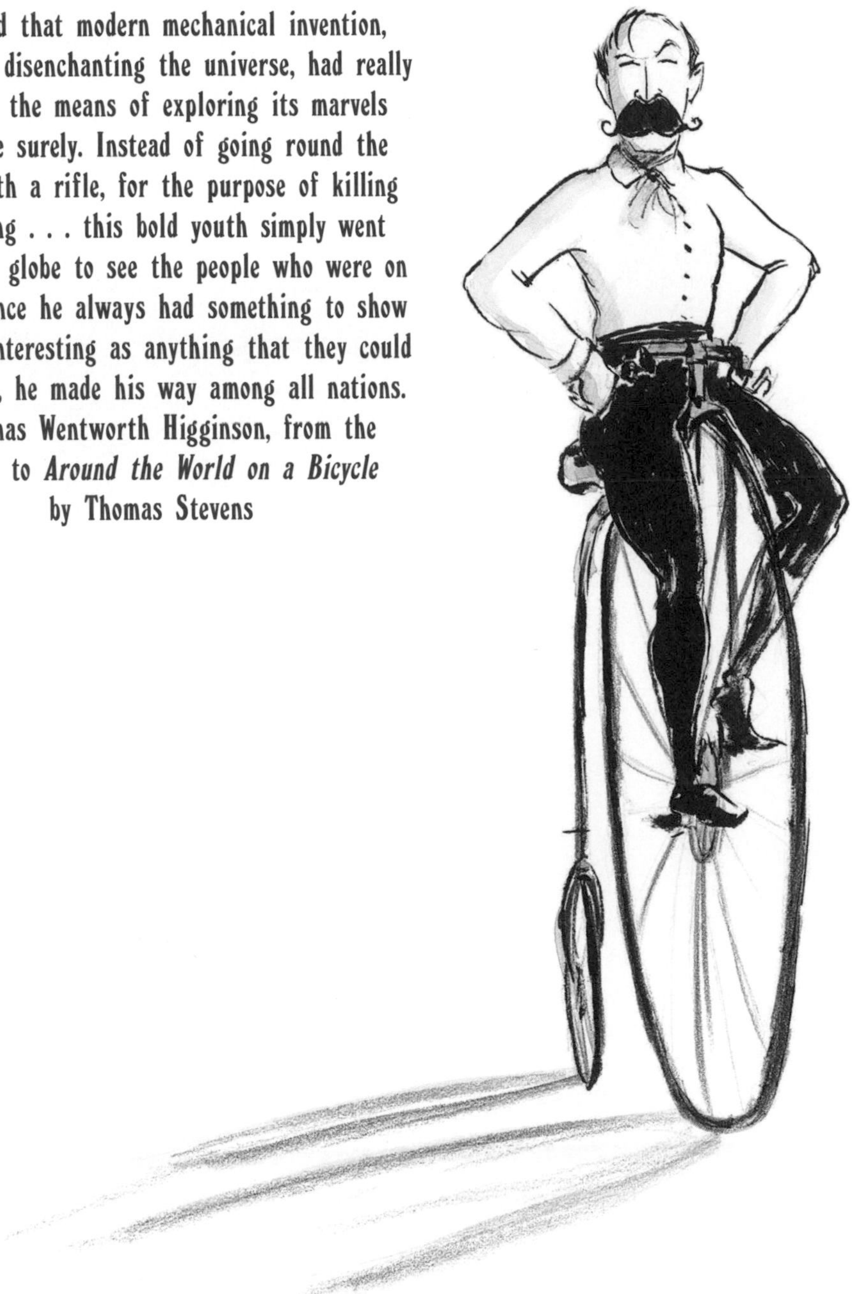

EPILOGUE

After his historic ride, Thomas Stevens arranged his notes and observations into articles for Pope's *Outing* magazine. The story of his ride was spread over several issues of *Outing* from 1885 until 1888. In 1889, he compiled the articles into his two-volume book, *Around the World on a Bicycle*.

His book was dedicated "To Colonel Albert A. Pope, of Boston, Massachusetts, whose liberal spirit of enterprise, and generous confidence in the integrity and ability of the author, made the tour around the world on a bicycle possible, by unstinted financial patronage."

The popularity of the bicycle, as you well know, continued to grow and grow over the years. The bicycle can now be seen everywhere in the world, including the regions where the first bicycle ever seen was ridden by Thomas Stevens.

Stevens continued his life of adventure. In additon to *Around the World on a Bicycle*, he is the author of *Through Russia on a Mustang*.

But that is another story.

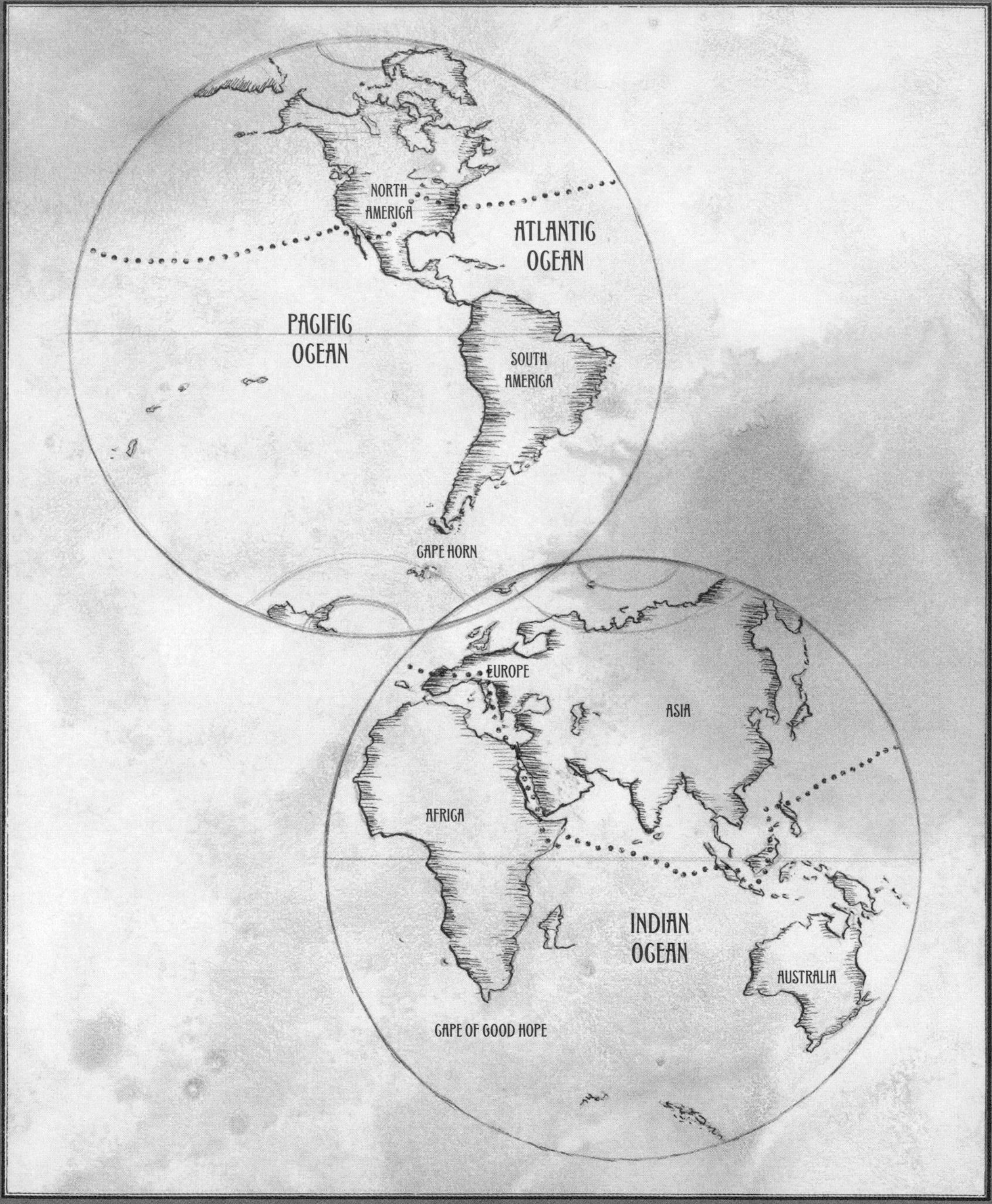
NORTH
AMERICA
ATLANTIC
OCEAN
PACIFIC
OCEAN
SOUTH
AMERICA
CAPE HORN
EUROPE
ASIA
AFRICA
INDIAN
OCEAN
AUSTRALIA
CAPE OF GOOD HOPE

THE JOURNEY OF
# NELLIE BLY
*Girl Reporter*

1889

*From you and from all those who read the chronicle of my trip I beg indulgence. These pages have been written in the spare moments snatched from the exactions of a busy life.*

*— Nellie Bly*

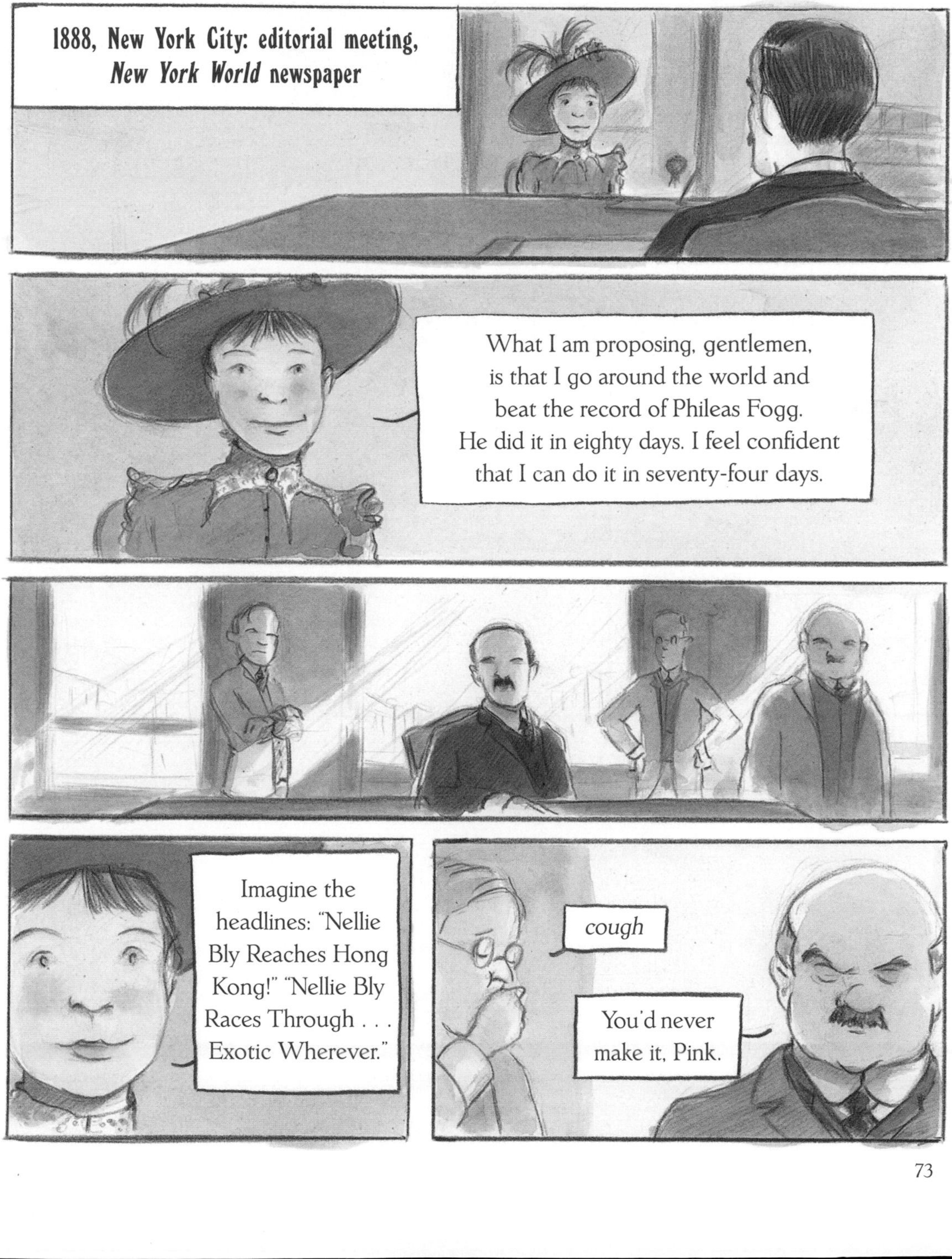
1888, New York City: editorial meeting, *New York World* newspaper
What I am proposing, gentlemen, is that I go around the world and beat the record of Phileas Fogg. He did it in eighty days. I feel confident that I can do it in seventy-four days.
Imagine the headlines: "Nellie Bly Reaches Hong Kong!" "Nellie Bly Races Through . . . Exotic Wherever."
cough
You'd never make it, Pink.

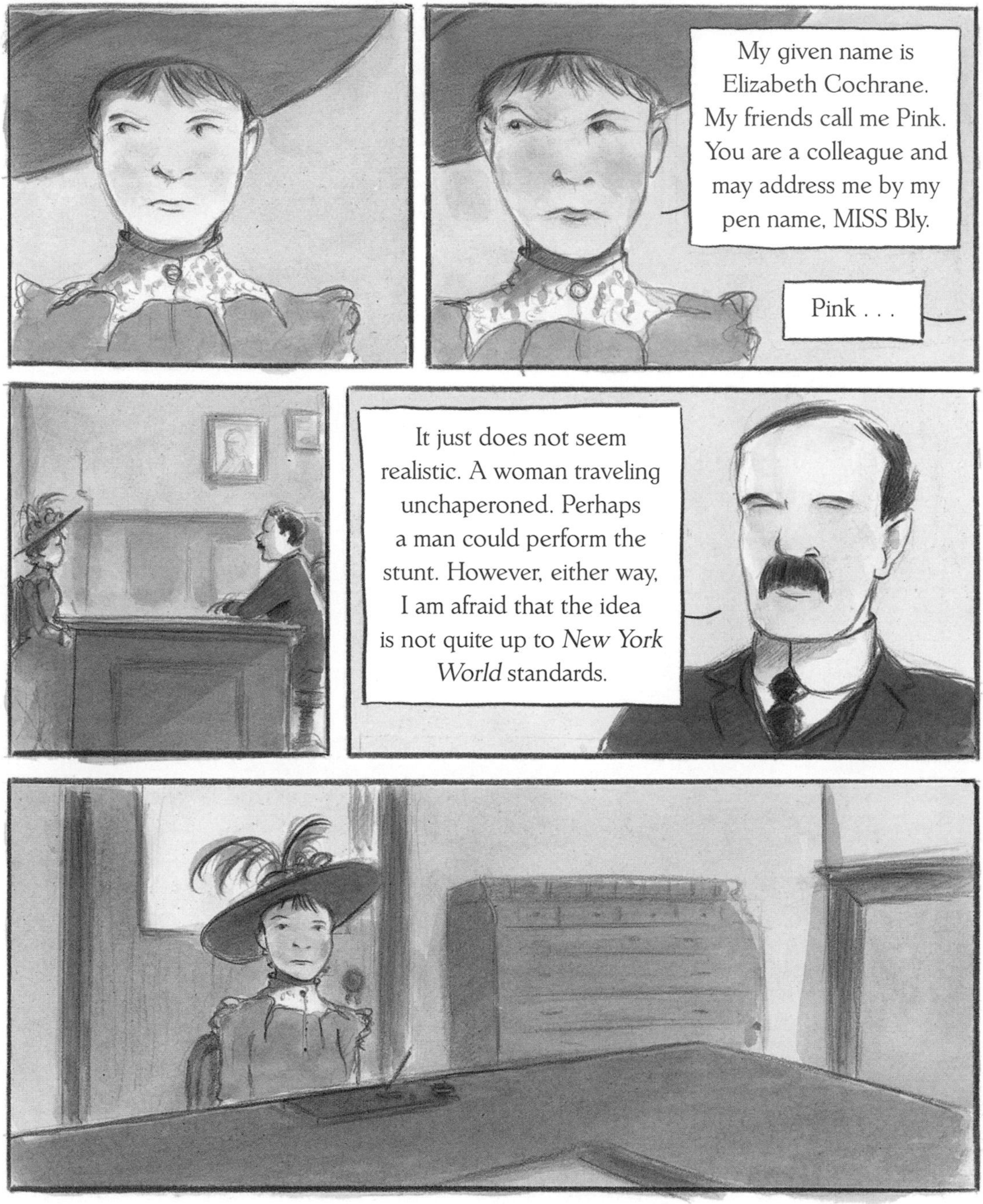
My given name is Elizabeth Cochrane. My friends call me Pink. You are a colleague and may address me by my pen name, MISS Bly.
Pink . . .
It just does not seem realistic. A woman traveling unchaperoned. Perhaps a man could perform the stunt. However, either way, I am afraid that the idea is not quite up to *New York World* standards.

One year later

We thought it might be a good idea to send you around the world in a race against time.

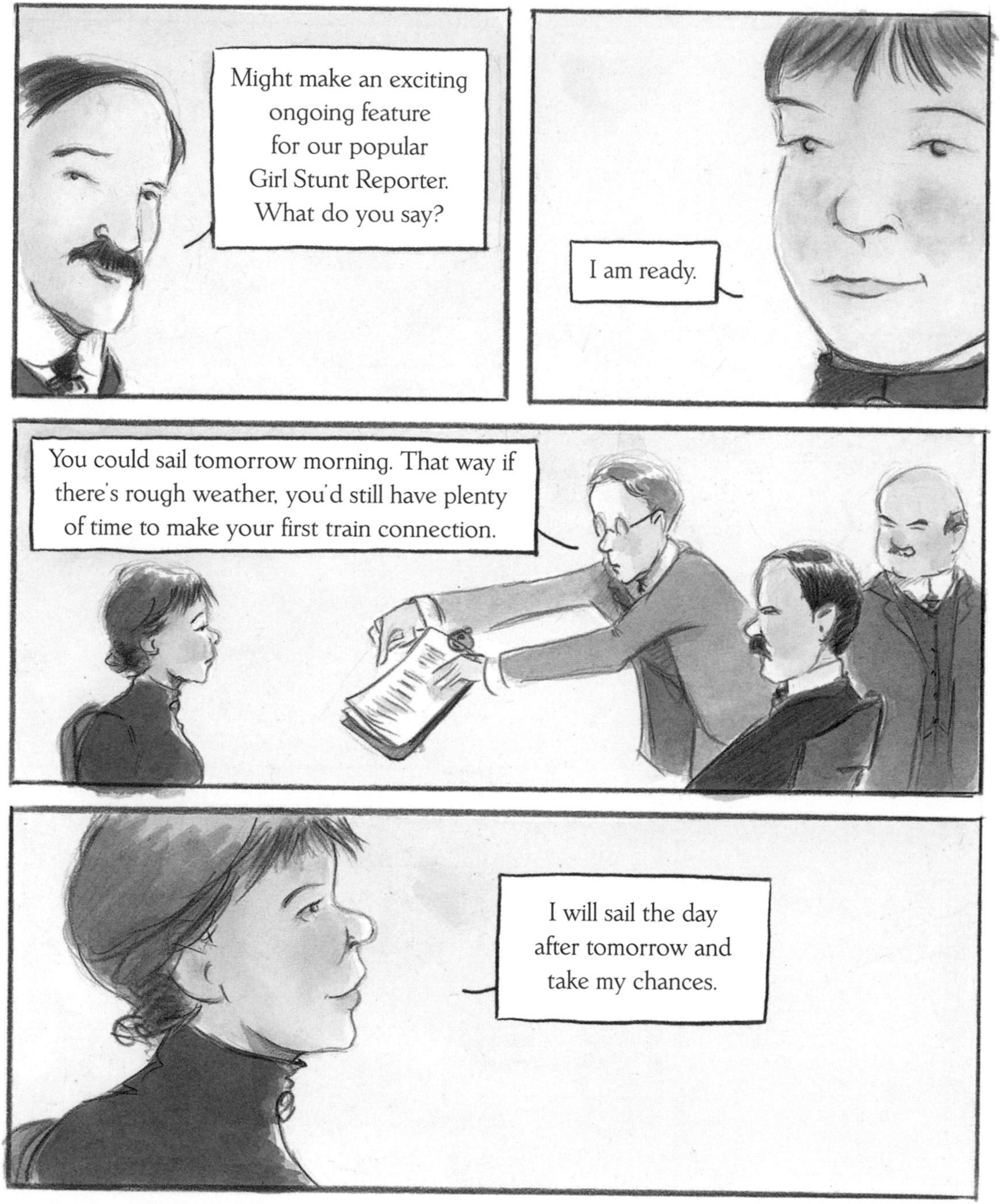
Might make an exciting ongoing feature for our popular Girl Stunt Reporter. What do you say?
I am ready.
You could sail tomorrow morning. That way if there's rough weather, you'd still have plenty of time to make your first train connection.
I will sail the day after tomorrow and take my chances.

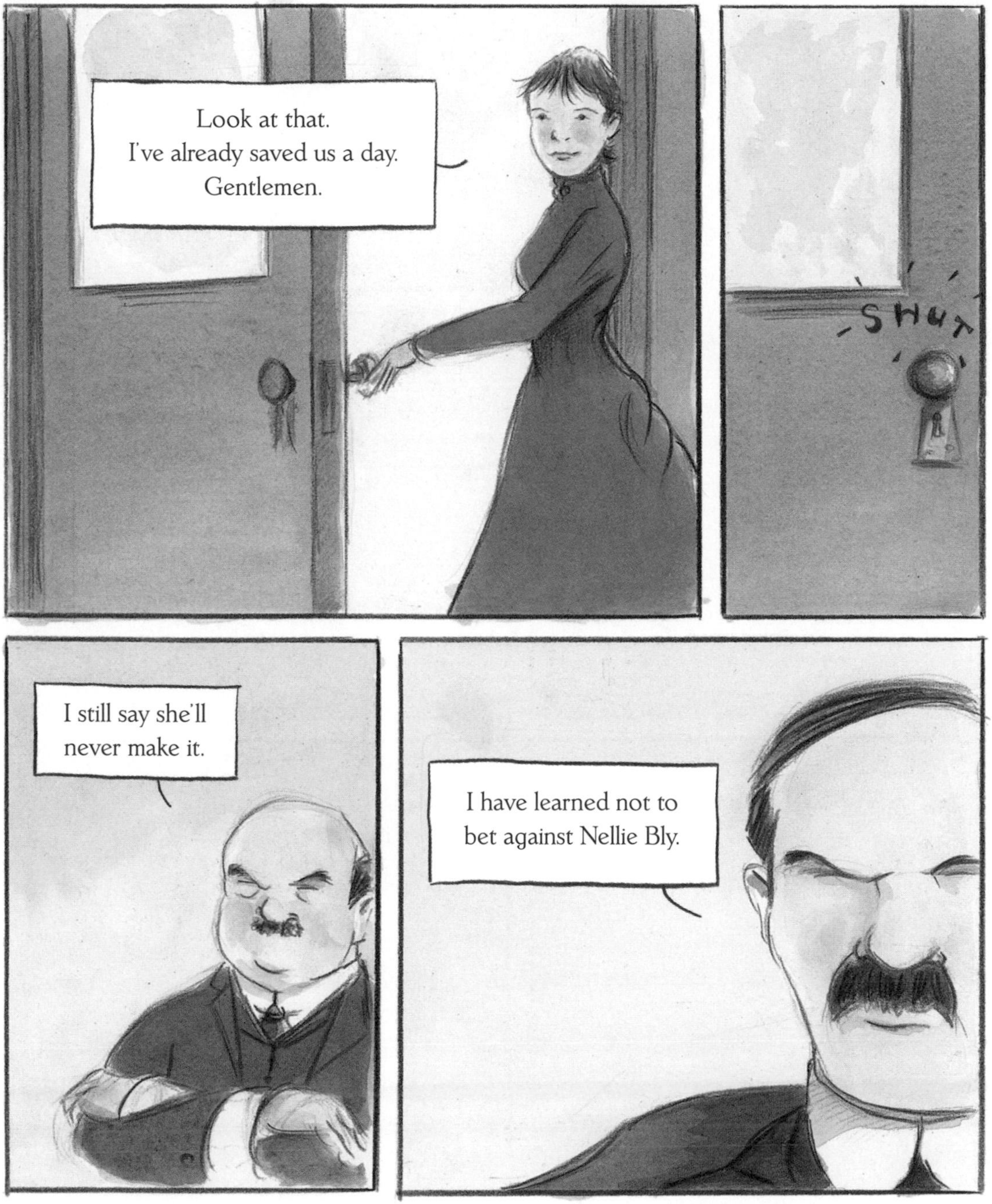
Look at that.
I've already saved us a day.
Gentlemen.
SHUT
I still say she'll never make it.
I have learned not to bet against Nellie Bly.

Miss?

I said that I want a dress that will stand constant wear for three months. And I want it by this evening.

Please.

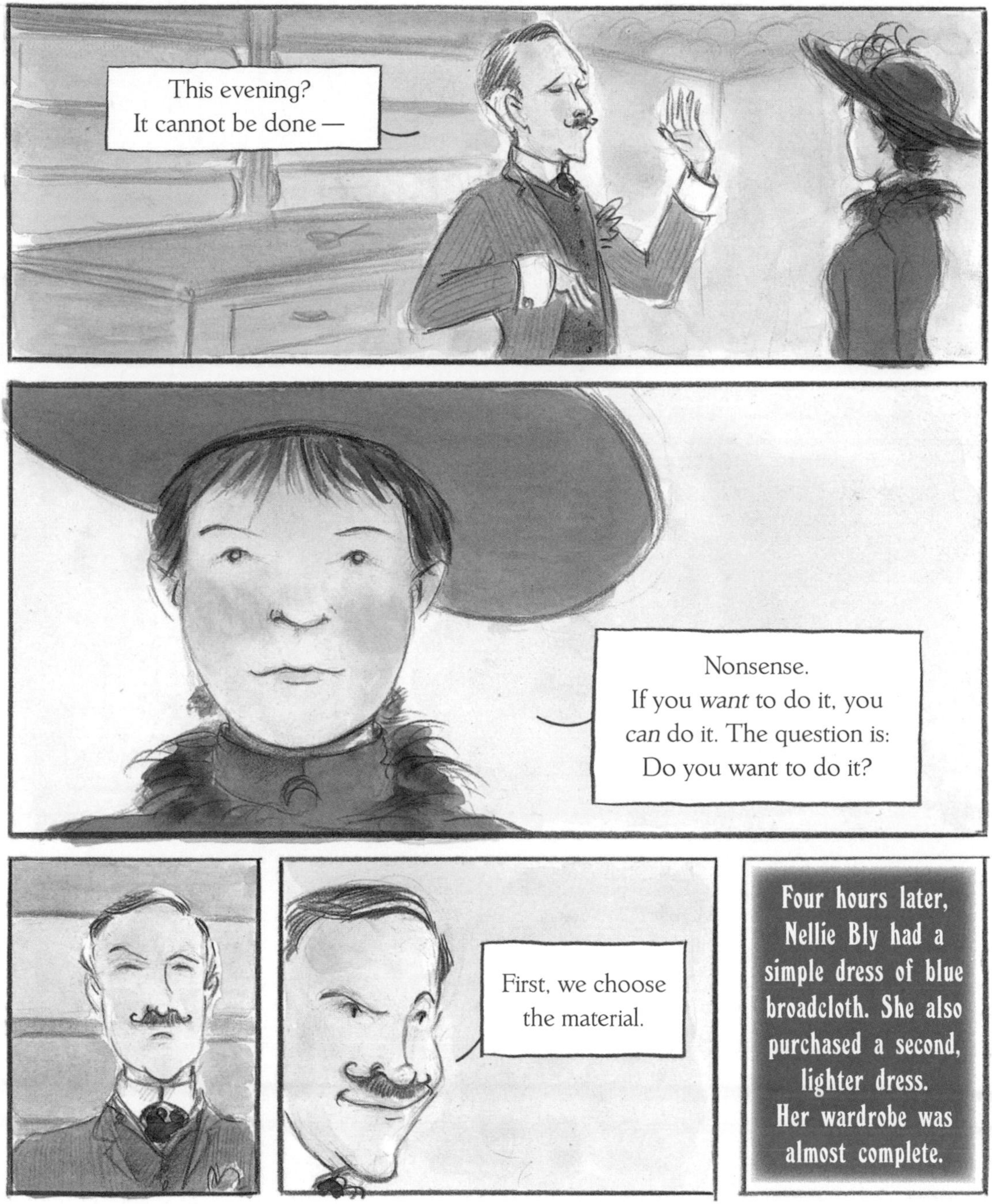
This evening?
It cannot be done —
Nonsense.
If you *want* to do it, you *can* do it. The question is: Do you want to do it?
First, we choose the material.
Four hours later, Nellie Bly had a simple dress of blue broadcloth. She also purchased a second, lighter dress. Her wardrobe was almost complete.

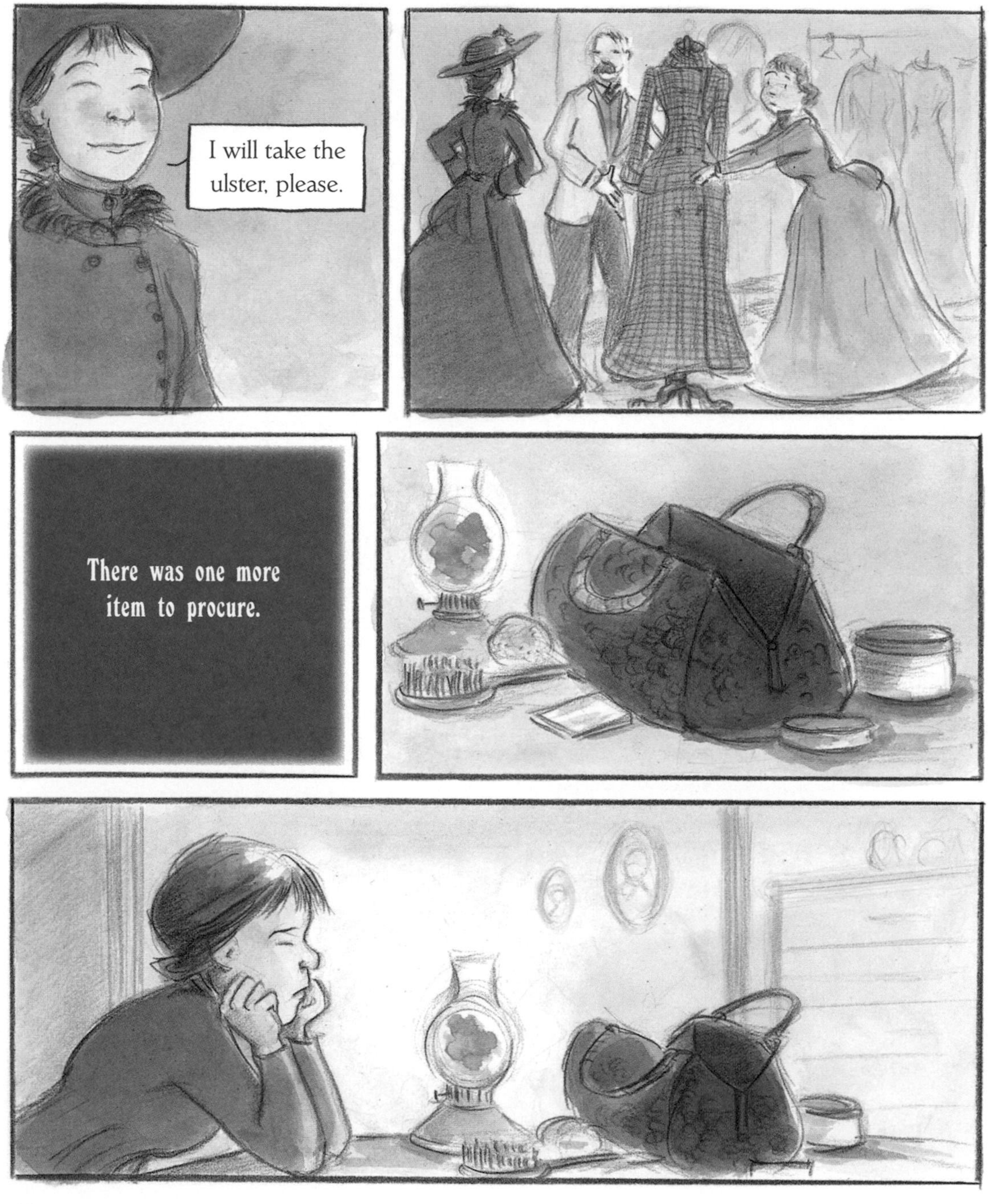
I will take the ulster, please.
There was one more item to procure.

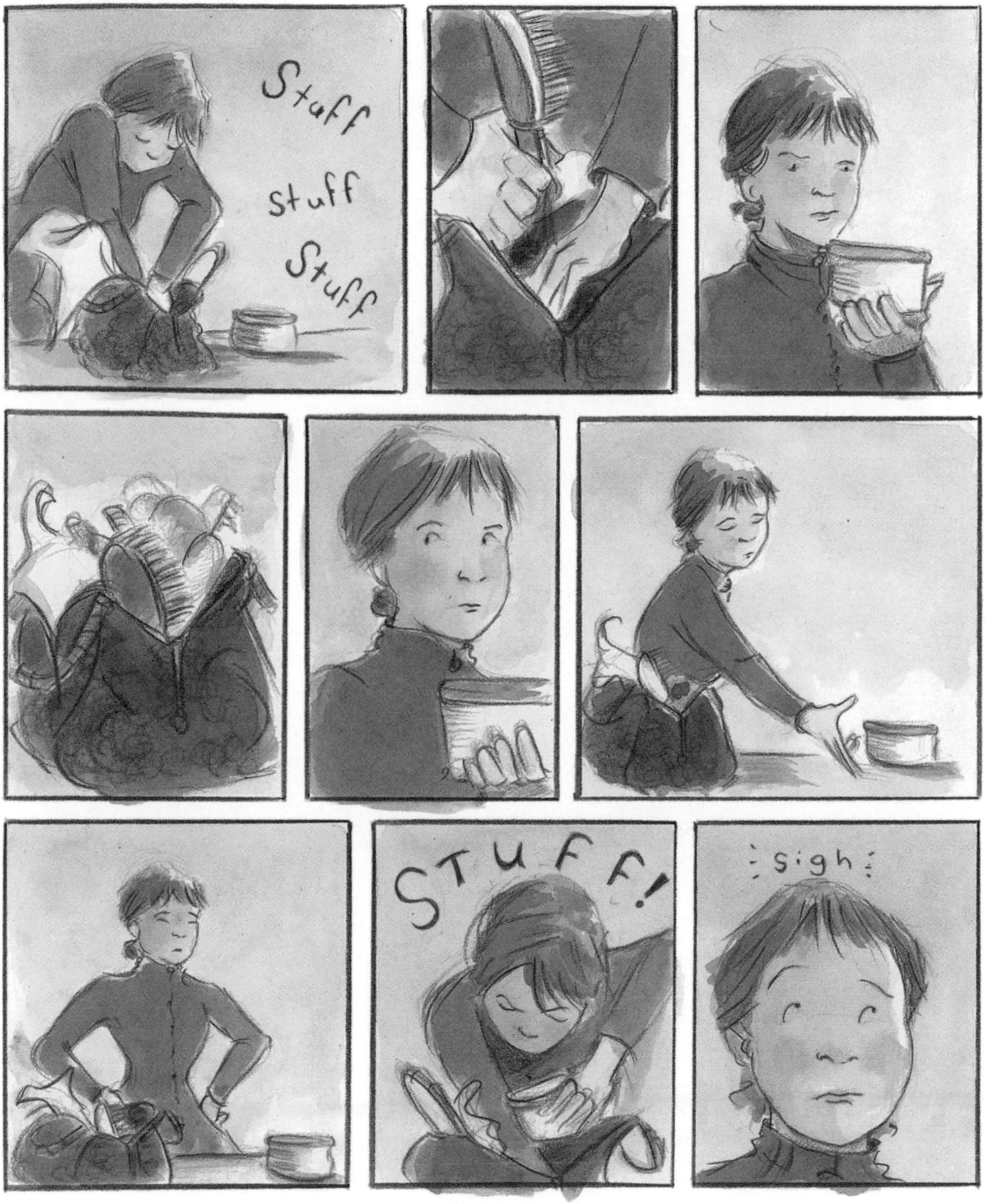
Stuff
stuff
Stuff
STUFF!
sigh

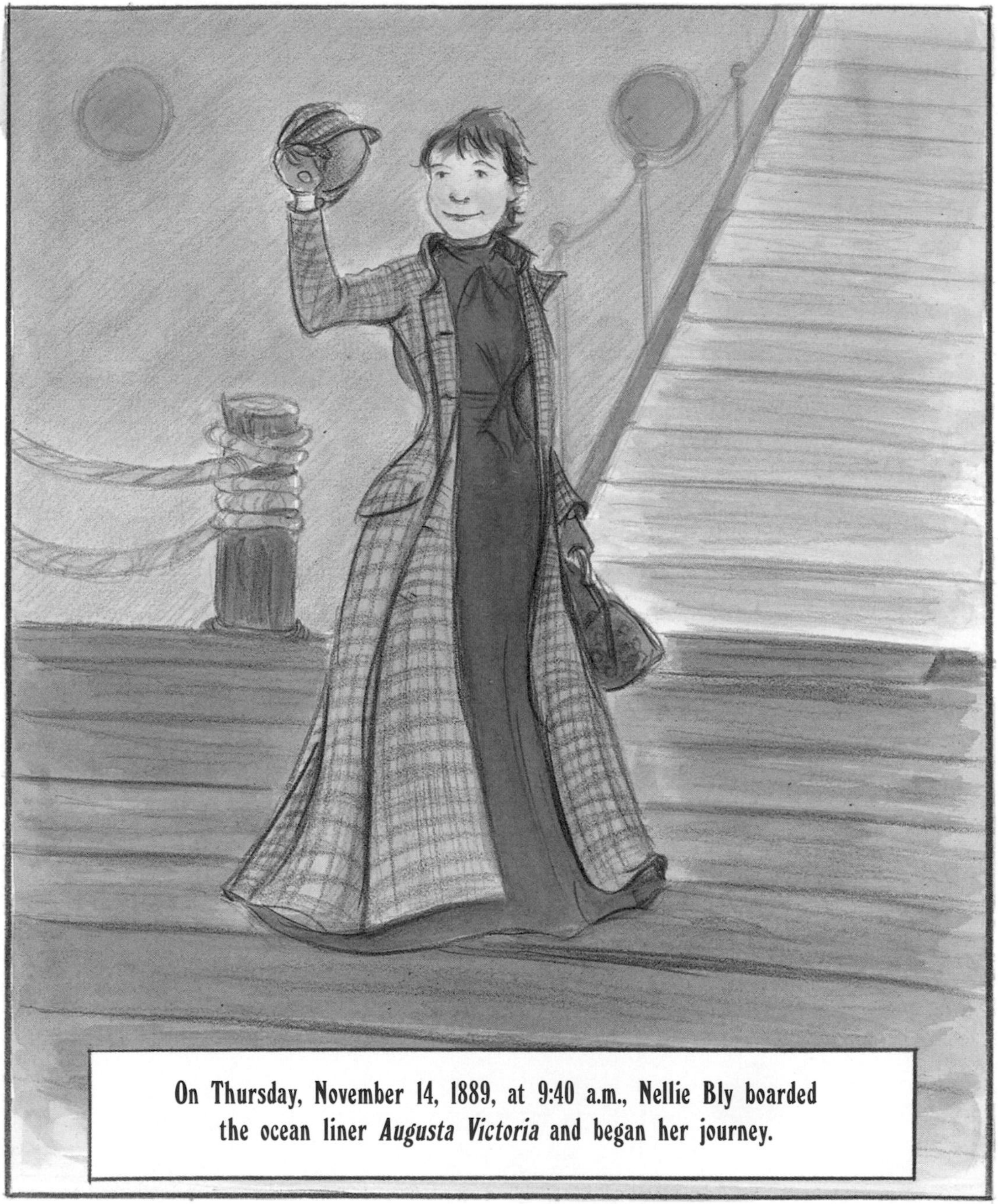
On Thursday, November 14, 1889, at 9:40 a.m., Nellie Bly boarded the ocean liner *Augusta Victoria* and began her journey.

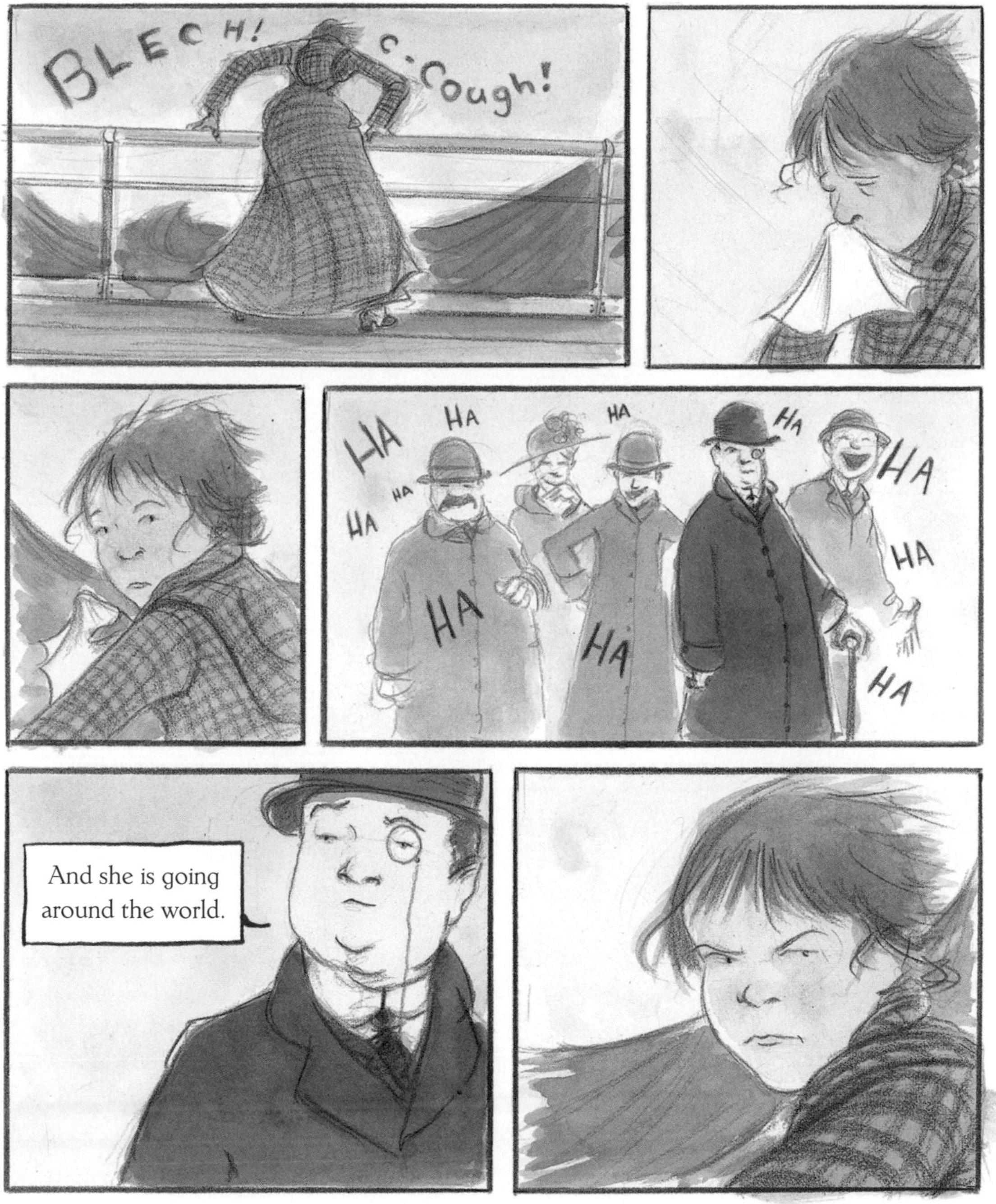
BLECH!
C-Cough!
HA HA HA HA HA HA HA HA HA HA HA HA
And she is going around the world.

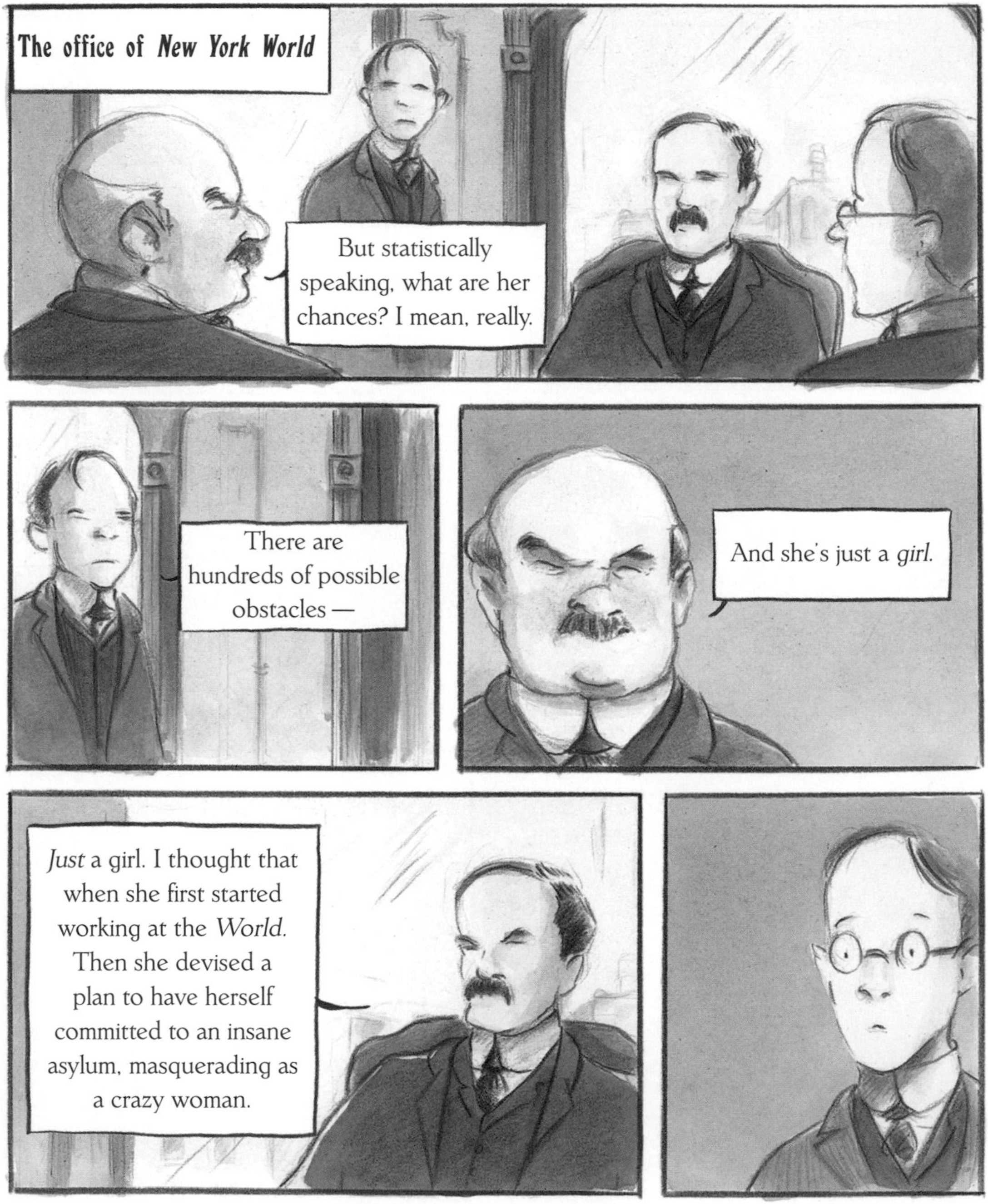
The office of *New York World*
But statistically speaking, what are her chances? I mean, really.
There are hundreds of possible obstacles —
And she's just a *girl.*
*Just* a girl. I thought that when she first started working at the *World.* Then she devised a plan to have herself committed to an insane asylum, masquerading as a crazy woman.

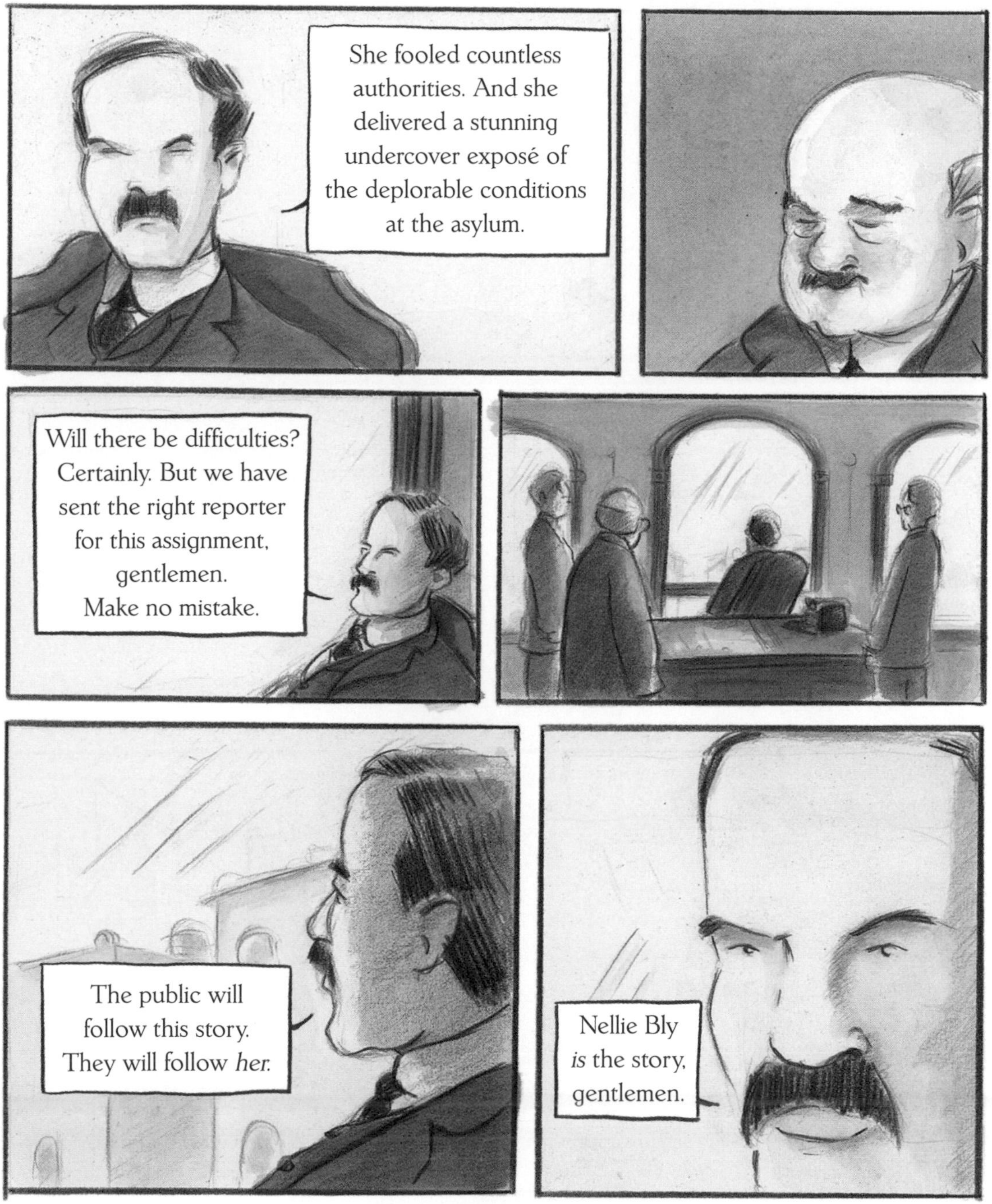
She fooled countless authorities. And she delivered a stunning undercover exposé of the deplorable conditions at the asylum.
Will there be difficulties? Certainly. But we have sent the right reporter for this assignment, gentlemen. Make no mistake.
The public will follow this story. They will follow *her.*
Nellie Bly *is* the story, gentlemen.

KNOCK
KNOCK
KNOCK!
Mmph?
Miss Bly-yyyy?
We were afraid that you were dead.

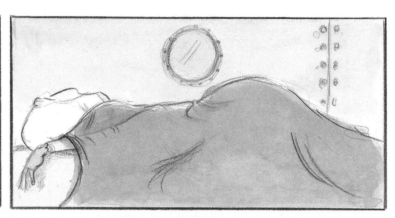

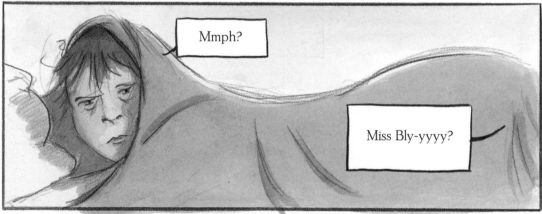

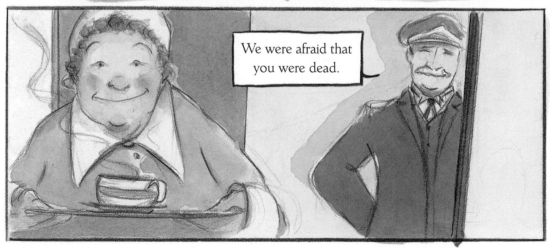

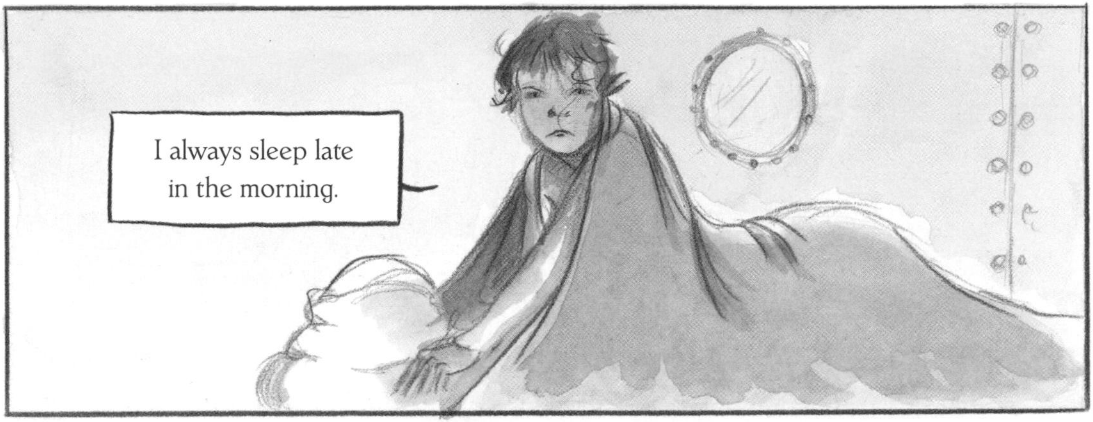
I always sleep late in the morning.

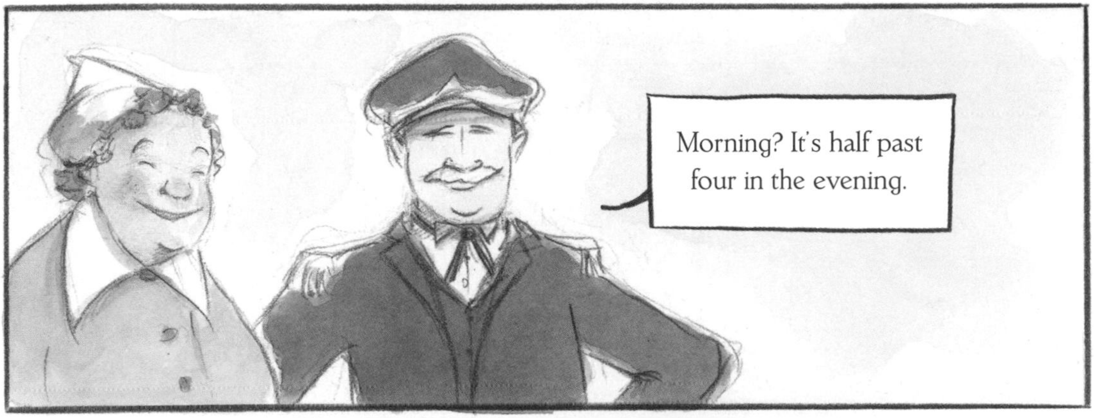
Morning? It's half past four in the evening.

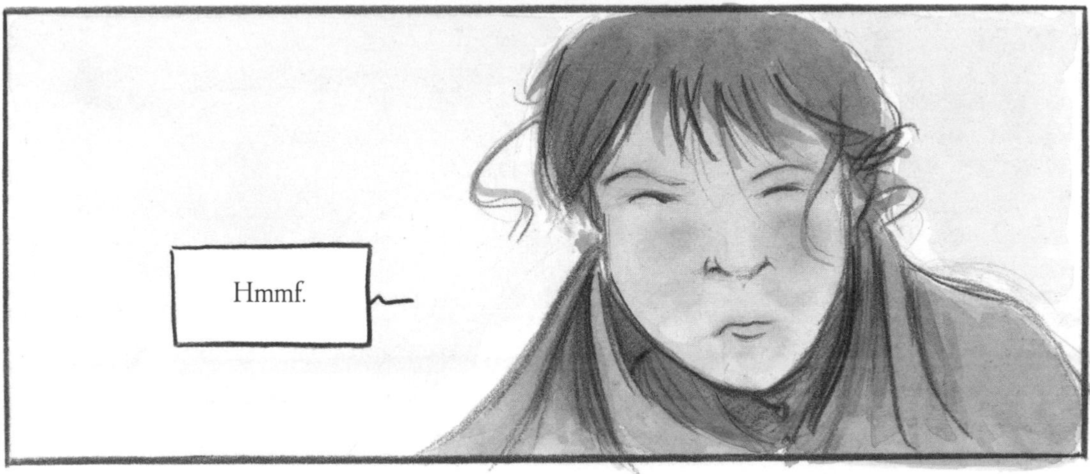
Hmmf.

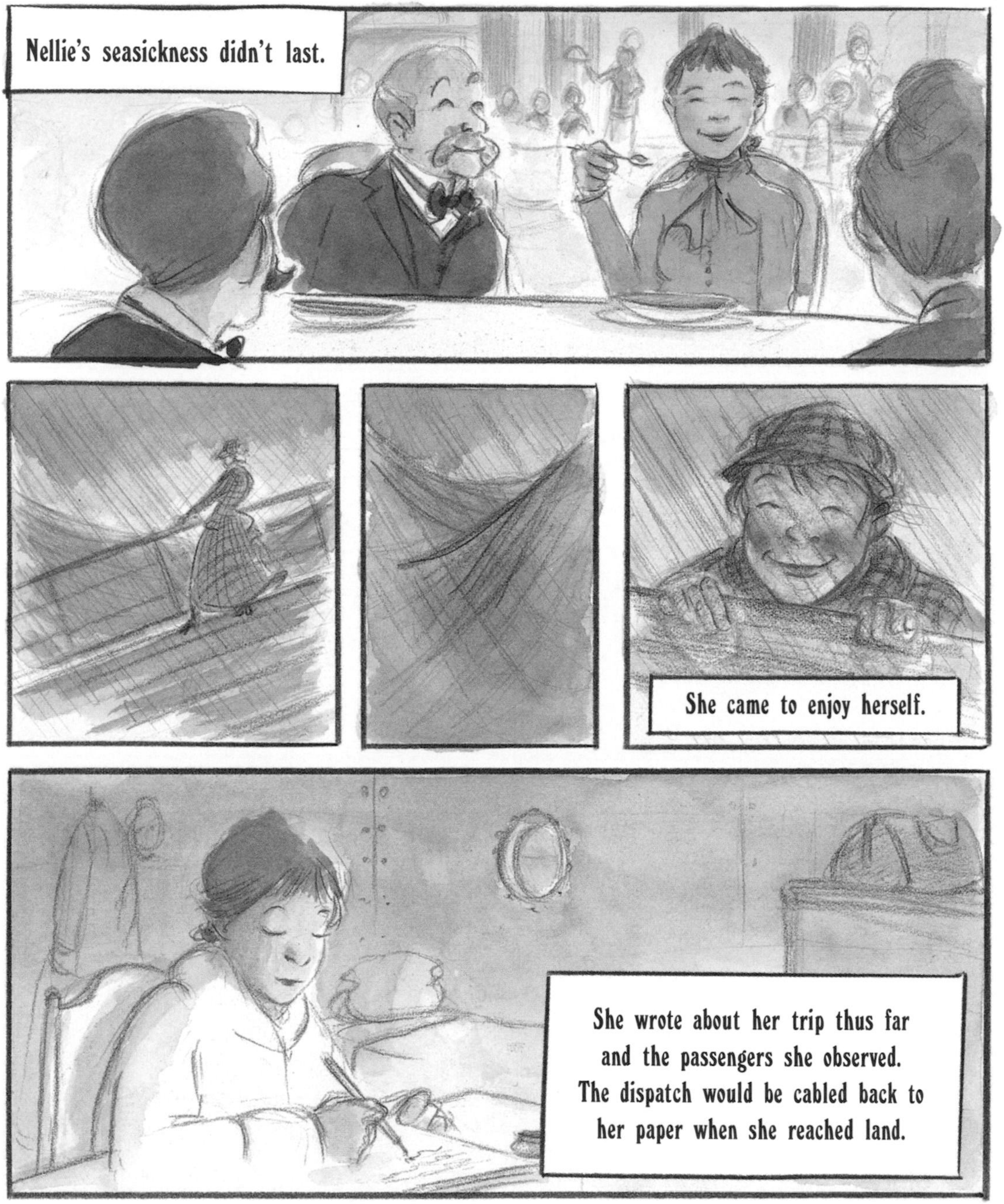
Nellie's seasickness didn't last.
She came to enjoy herself.
She wrote about her trip thus far and the passengers she observed. The dispatch would be cabled back to her paper when she reached land.

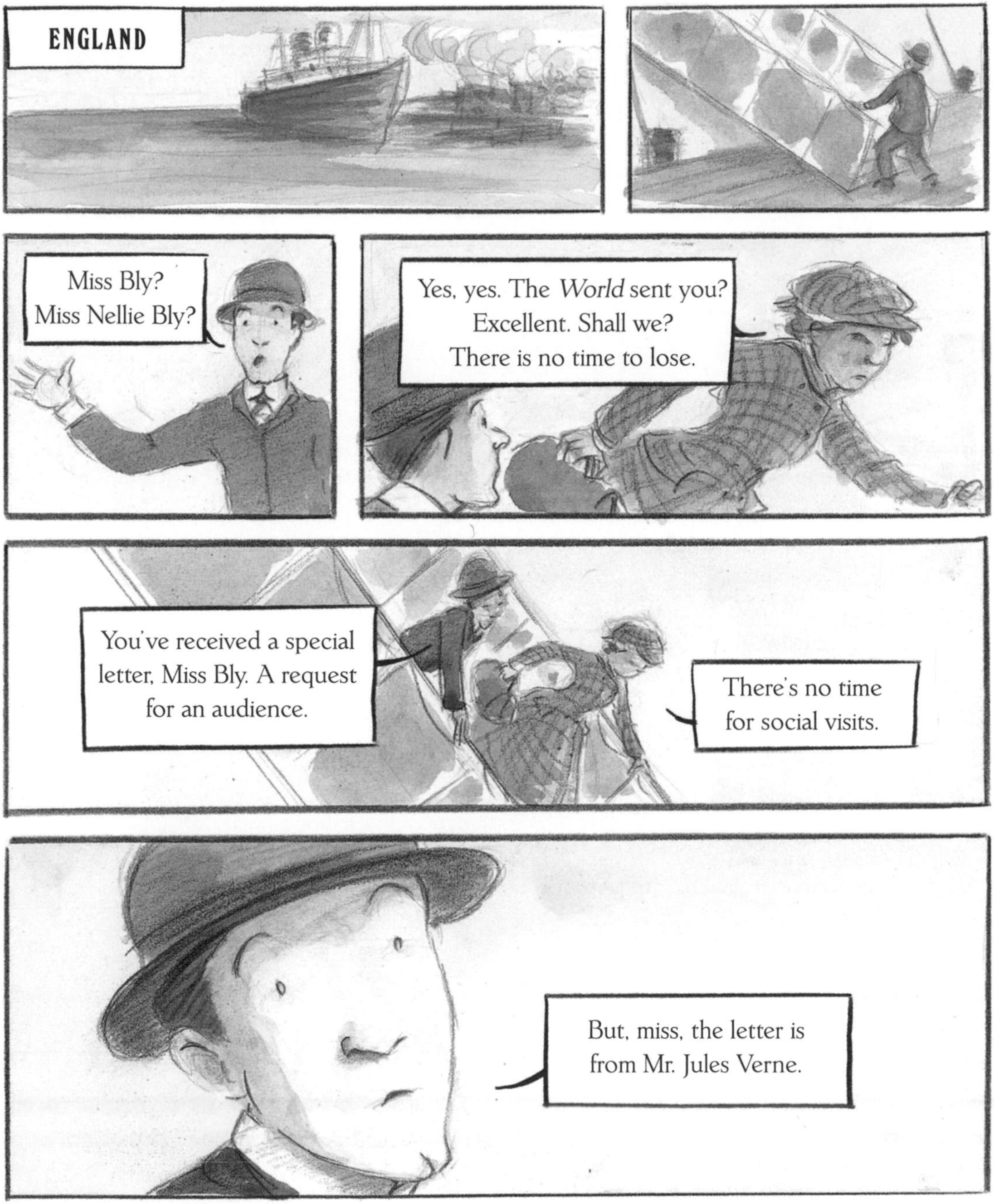
ENGLAND
Miss Bly? Miss Nellie Bly?
Yes, yes. The *World* sent you? Excellent. Shall we? There is no time to lose.
You've received a special letter, Miss Bly. A request for an audience.
There's no time for social visits.
But, miss, the letter is from Mr. Jules Verne.

Drat.

**Excerpt from** *Nellie Bly's Book,* **Chapter 3:**

"Mr. and Mrs. Jules Verne have sent a special letter asking that if possible, you will stop to see them," the London correspondent said to me, as we were on our way to the wharf.

"Oh, how I should like to see them!" I exclaimed, adding in the same breath, "Isn't it hard to be forced to decline such a treat?"

"If you are willing to go without sleep and rest for two nights, I think it can be done," he said quietly.

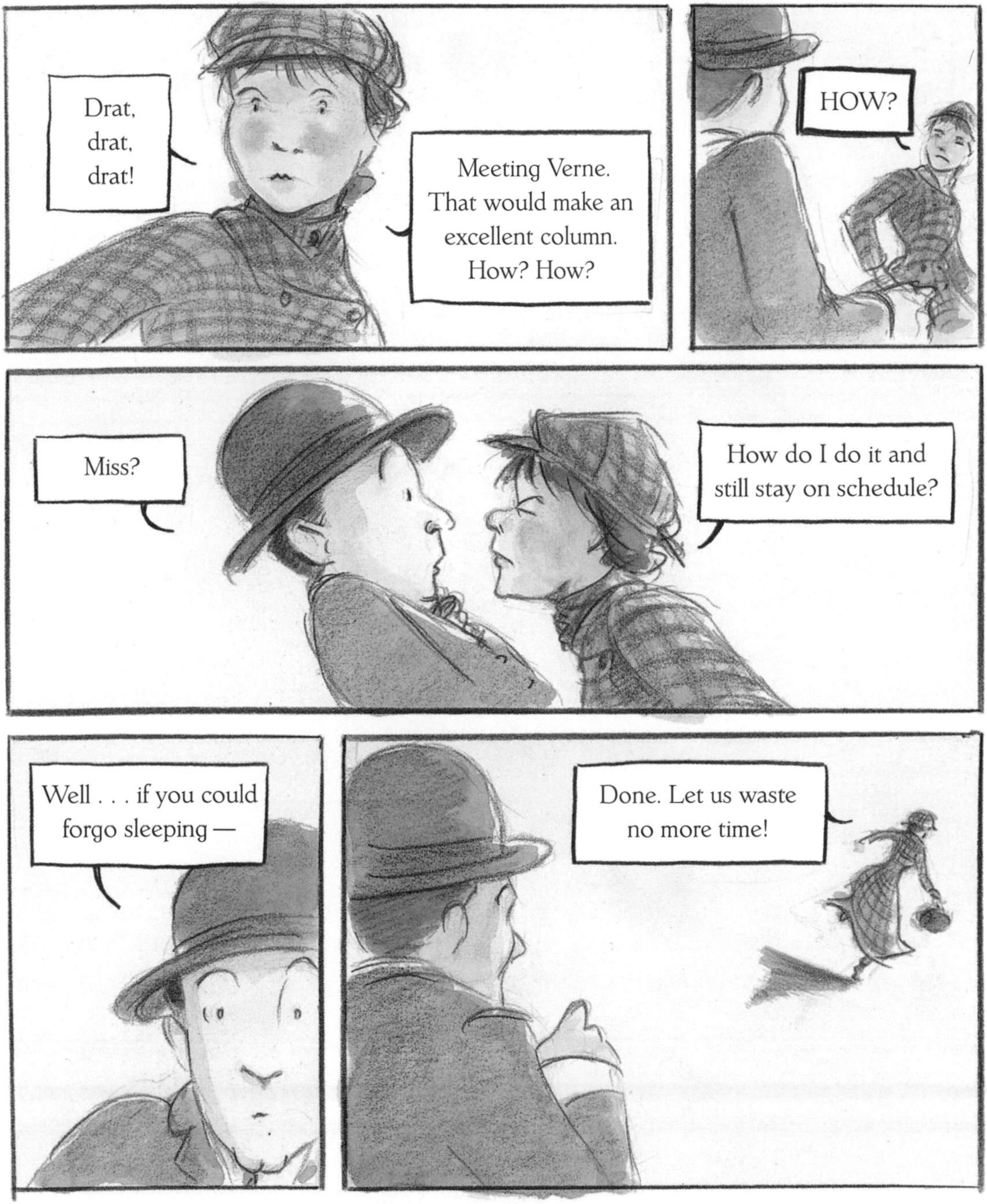

Drat,
drat,
drat!
Meeting Verne.
That would make an
excellent column.
How? How?
HOW?
Miss?
How do I do it and
still stay on schedule?
Well . . . if you could
forgo sleeping —
Done. Let us waste
no more time!

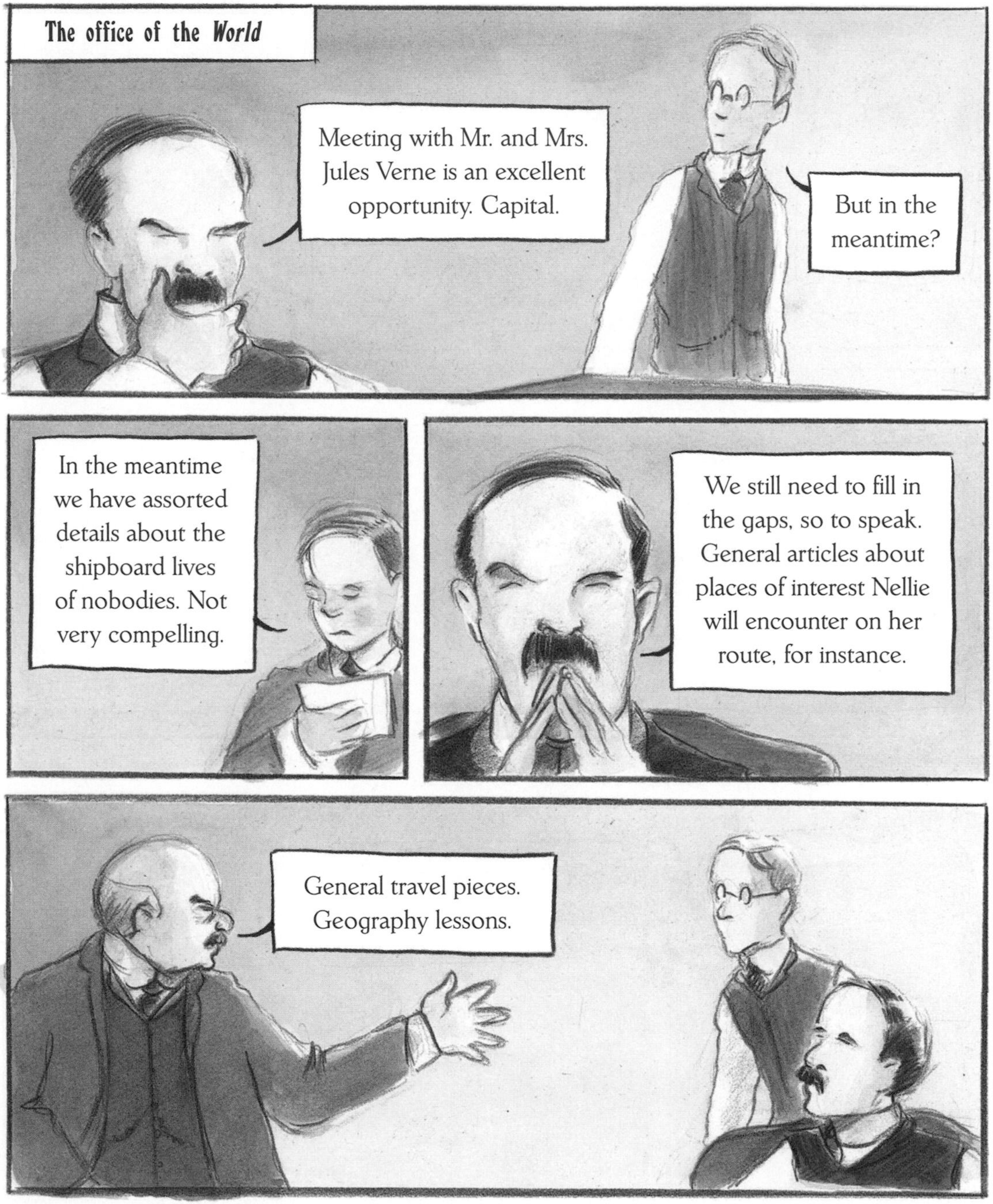
The office of the *World*
Meeting with Mr. and Mrs. Jules Verne is an excellent opportunity. Capital.
But in the meantime?
In the meantime we have assorted details about the shipboard lives of nobodies. Not very compelling.
We still need to fill in the gaps, so to speak. General articles about places of interest Nellie will encounter on her route, for instance.
General travel pieces. Geography lessons.

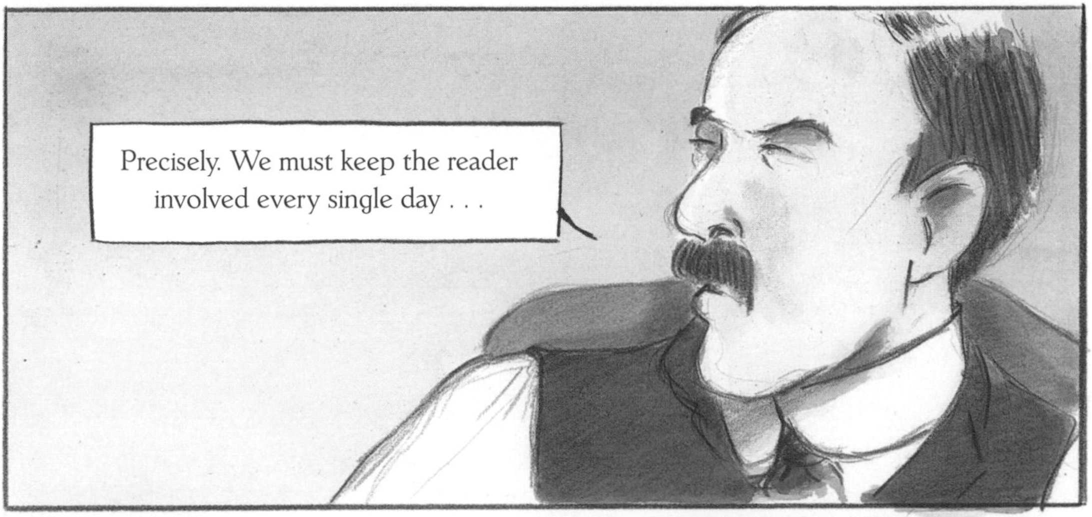
Precisely. We must keep the reader involved every single day . . .

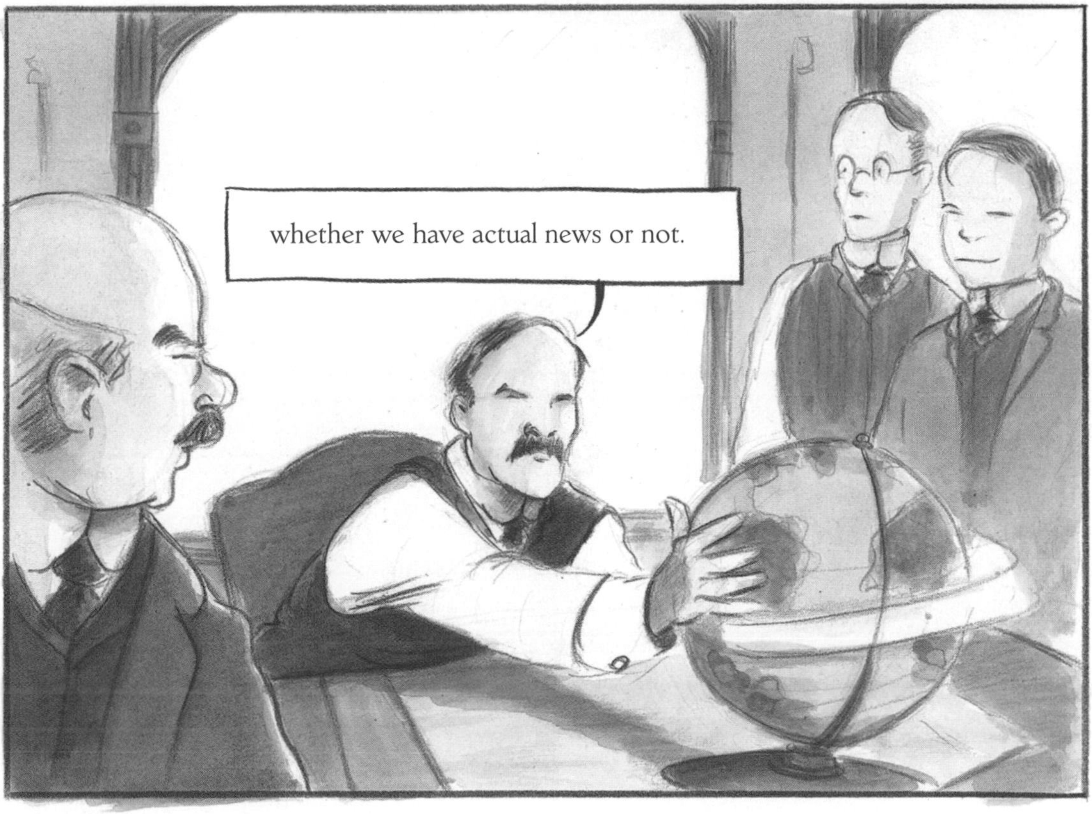
whether we have actual news or not.

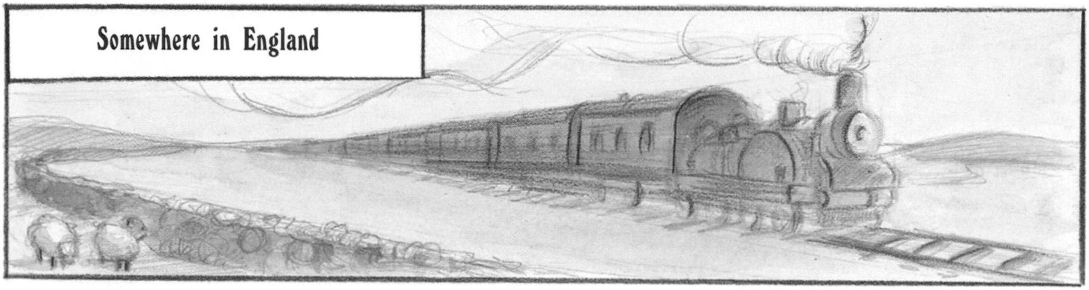
Somewhere in England

**Excerpt from** ***Nellie Bly's Book,*** **Chapter 3:**

"I want you to see the scenery along here; it is beautiful," my companion said, but I lazily thought, "What is scenery compared with sleep when one has not seen bed for over twenty-four hours?" So I said to him very crossly: "Don't you think you would better take a nap?" . . .

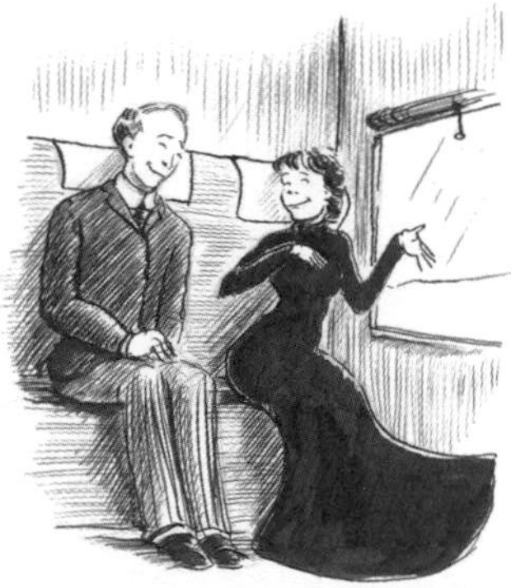

"And you?" he asked with a teasing smile. I had been up even longer. "Well, I confess, I was saying one word for you and two for myself," I replied, with a laugh that put us at ease on the subject. "Honestly, now, I care very little for scenery when I am so sleepy," I said apologetically.

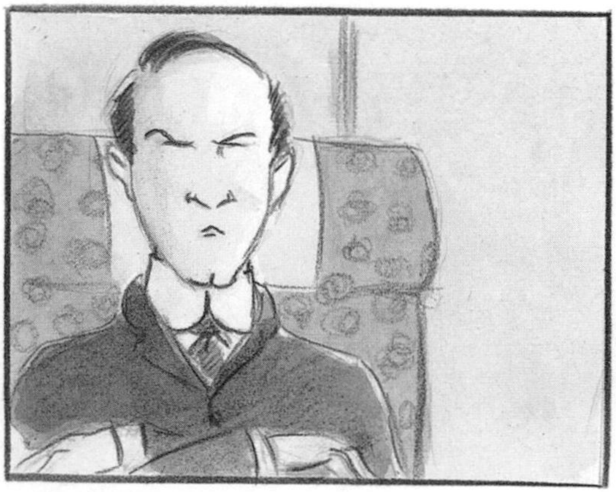

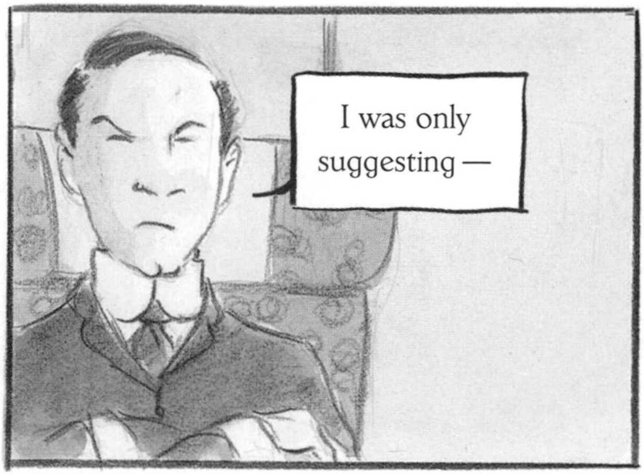
I was only suggesting —

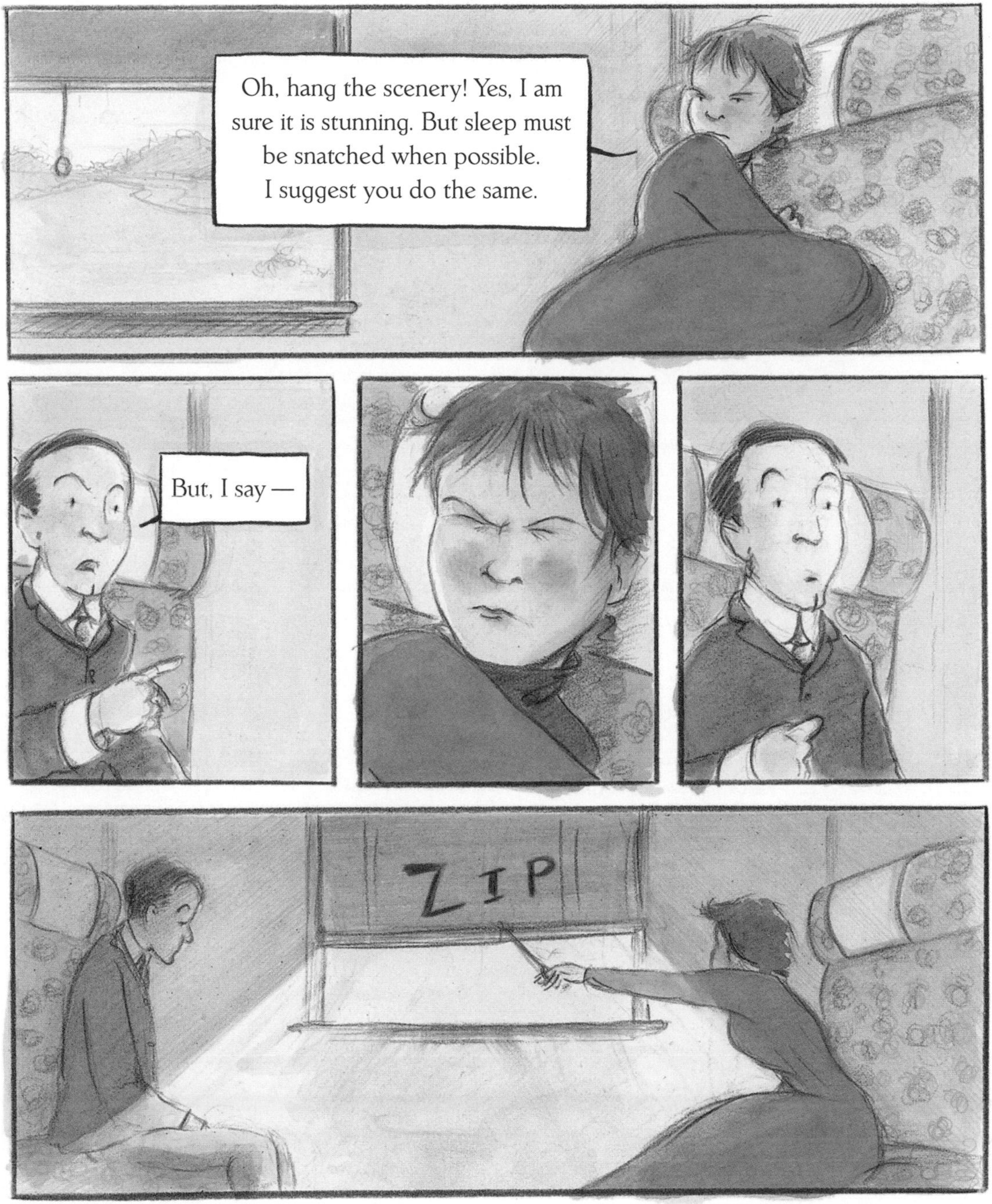
Oh, hang the scenery! Yes, I am sure it is stunning. But sleep must be snatched when possible. I suggest you do the same.
But, I say —
ZIP

The home of Jules Verne, Amiens, France

Mr. and Mrs. Verne spoke very little English.
Nellie Bly's French vocabulary consisted of the word *oui*.

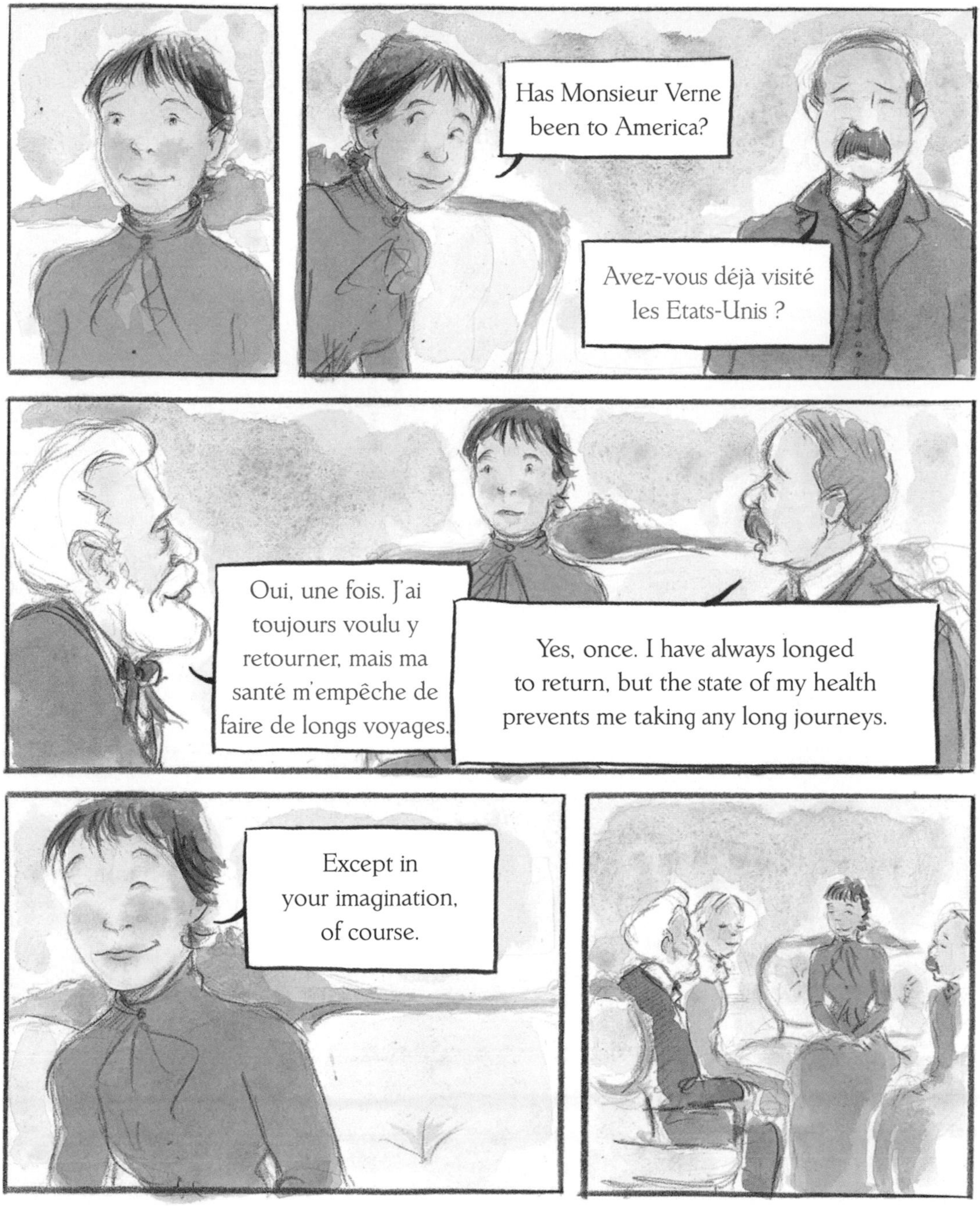
Has Monsieur Verne been to America?
Avez-vous déjà visité les Etats-Unis ?
Oui, une fois. J'ai toujours voulu y retourner, mais ma santé m'empêche de faire de longs voyages.
Yes, once. I have always longed to return, but the state of my health prevents me taking any long journeys.
Except in your imagination, of course.

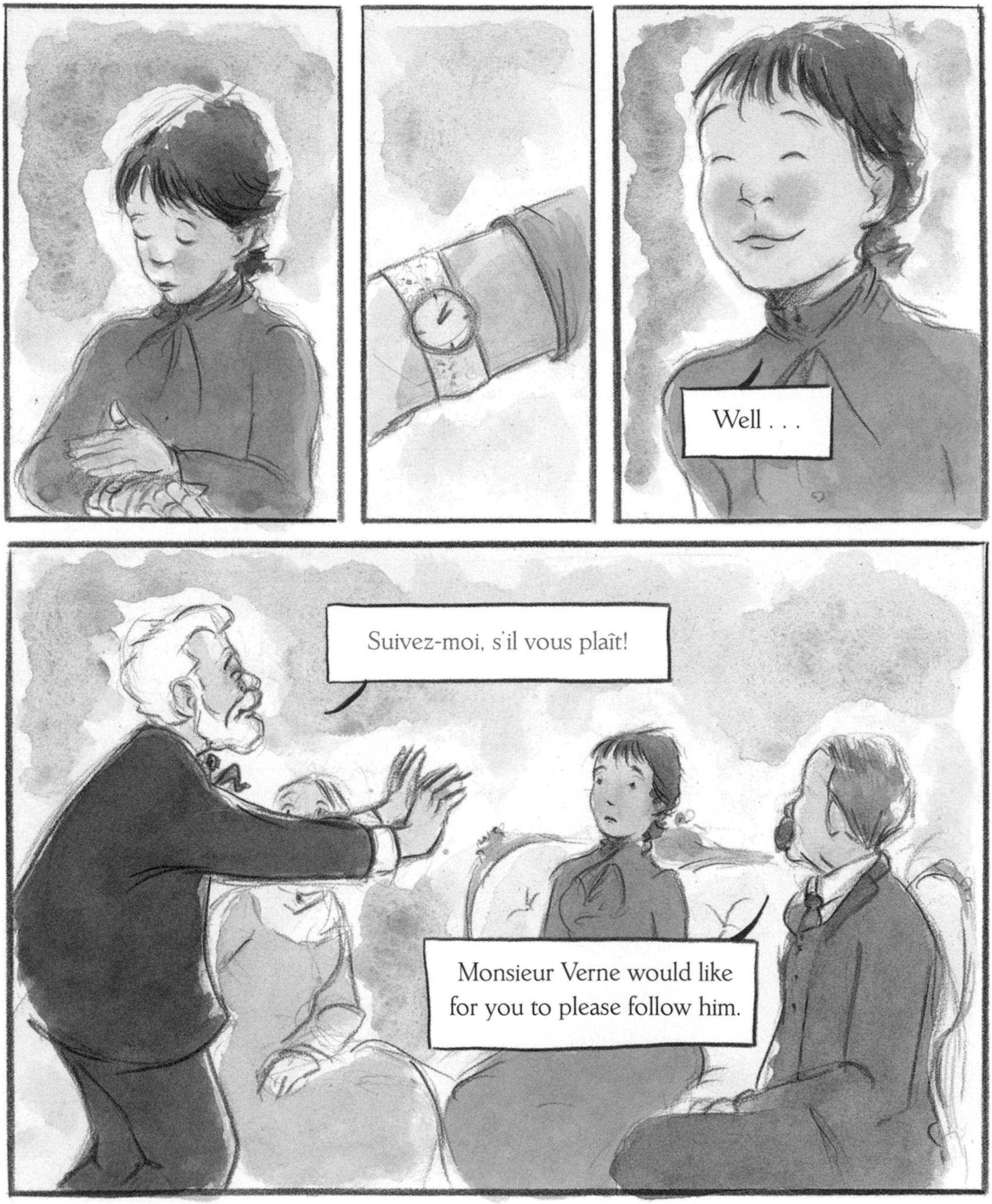
Well . . .
Suivez-moi, s'il vous plaît!
Monsieur Verne would like for you to please follow him.

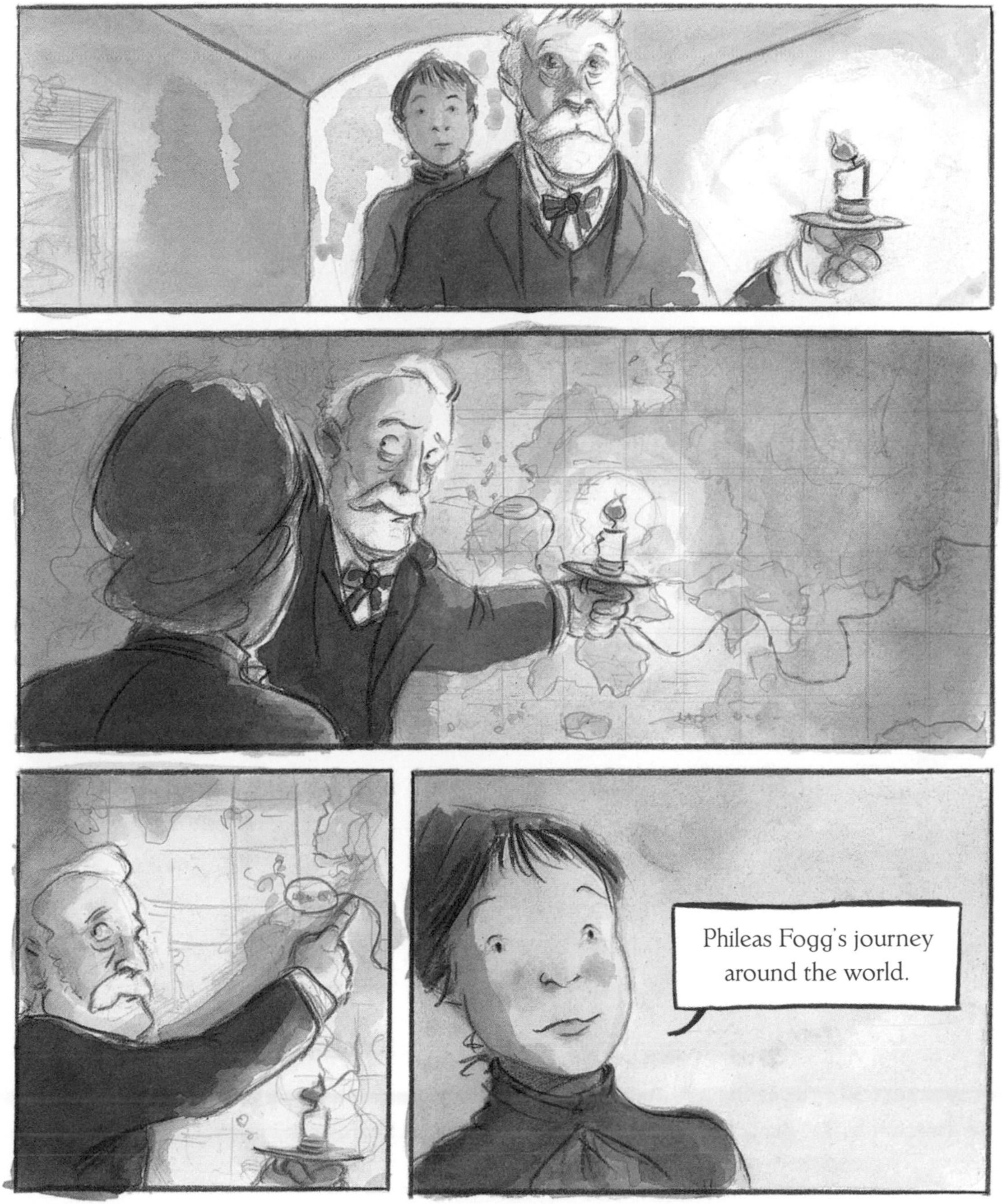
Phileas Fogg's journey around the world.

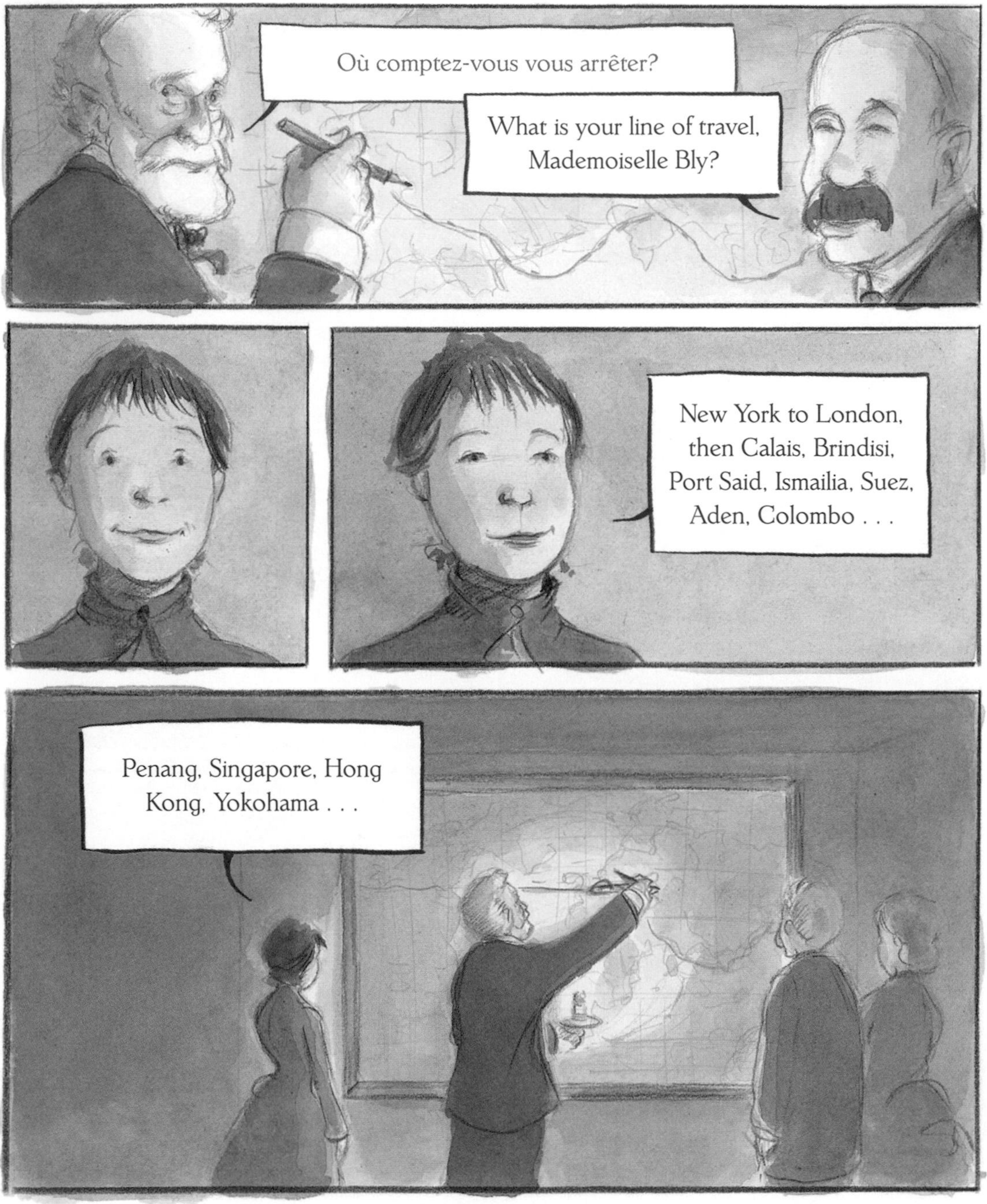
Où comptez-vous vous arrêter?
What is your line of travel, Mademoiselle Bly?
New York to London, then Calais, Brindisi, Port Said, Ismailia, Suez, Aden, Colombo . . .
Penang, Singapore, Hong Kong, Yokohama . . .

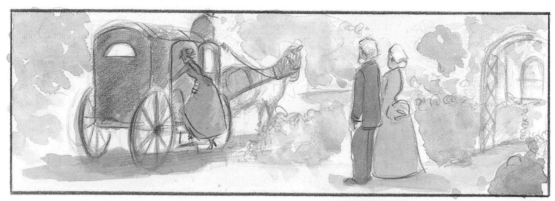

Good luck,
Nellie Bly.

Fine. Fine. That will do.

What?

The Nellie Bly Guessing Game. The public guesses and sends in a ballot. The winner receives . . .

Something.

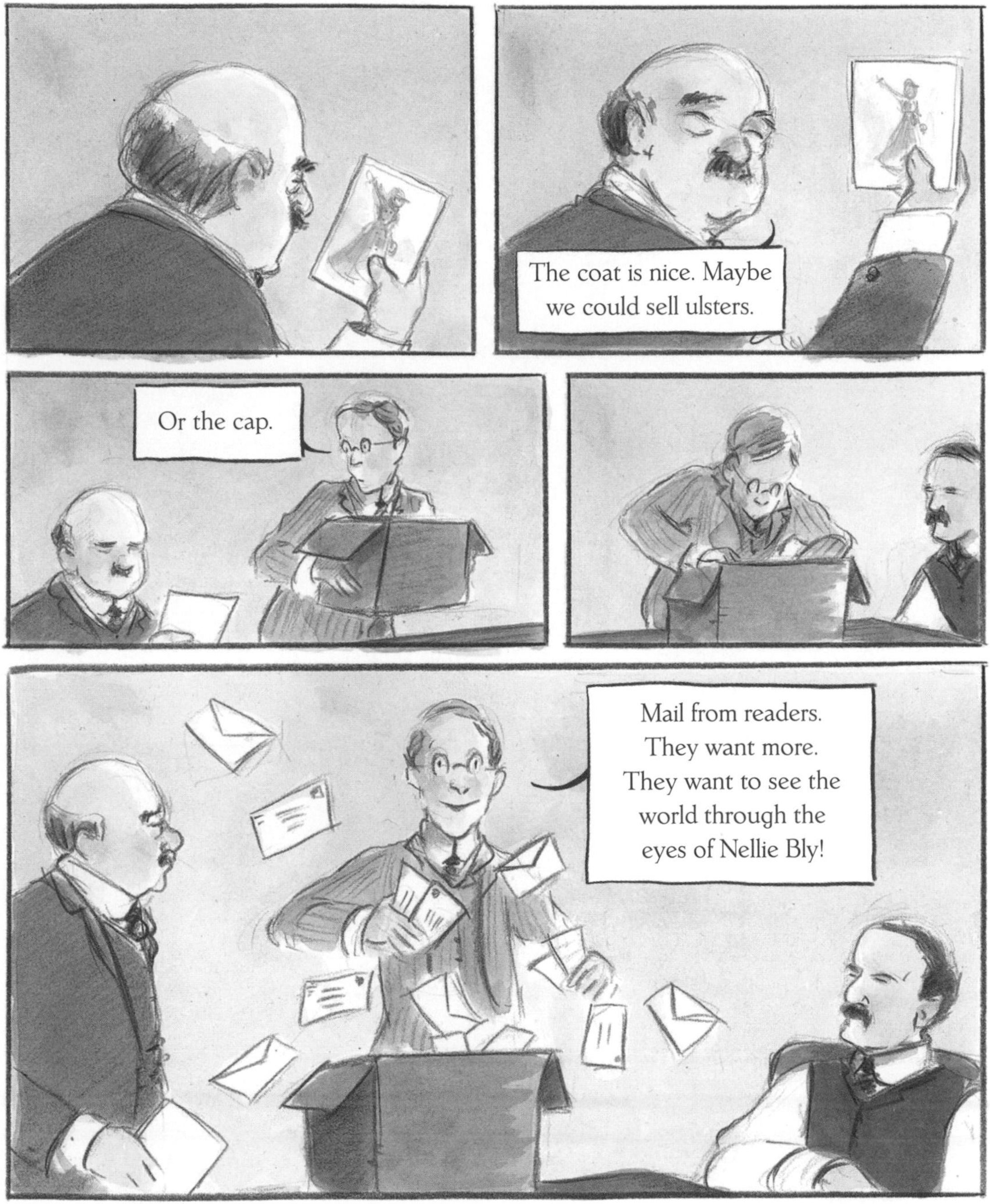
The coat is nice. Maybe we could sell ulsters.
Or the cap.
Mail from readers. They want more. They want to see the world through the eyes of Nellie Bly!

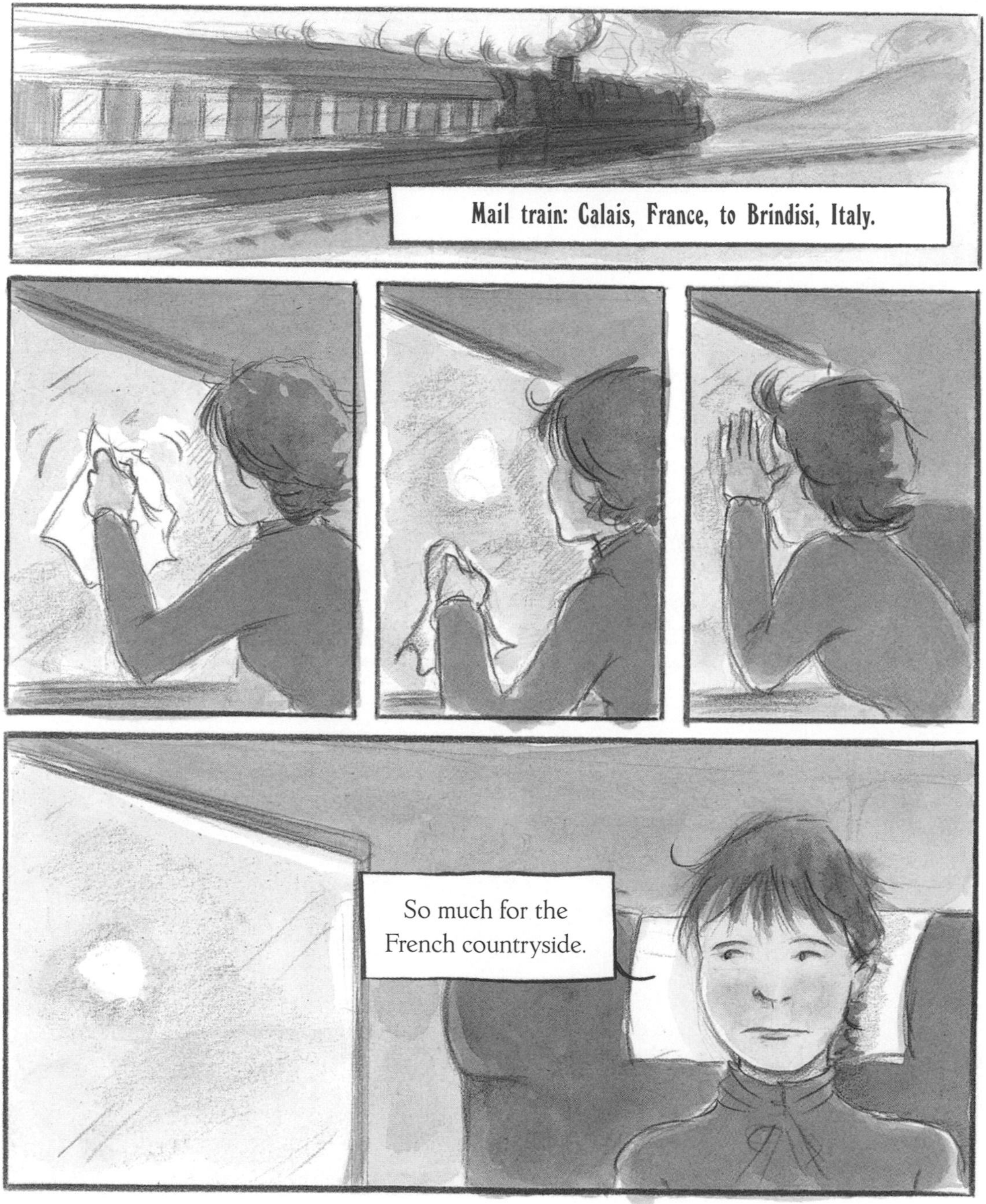
Mail train: Calais, France, to Brindisi, Italy.
So much for the French countryside.

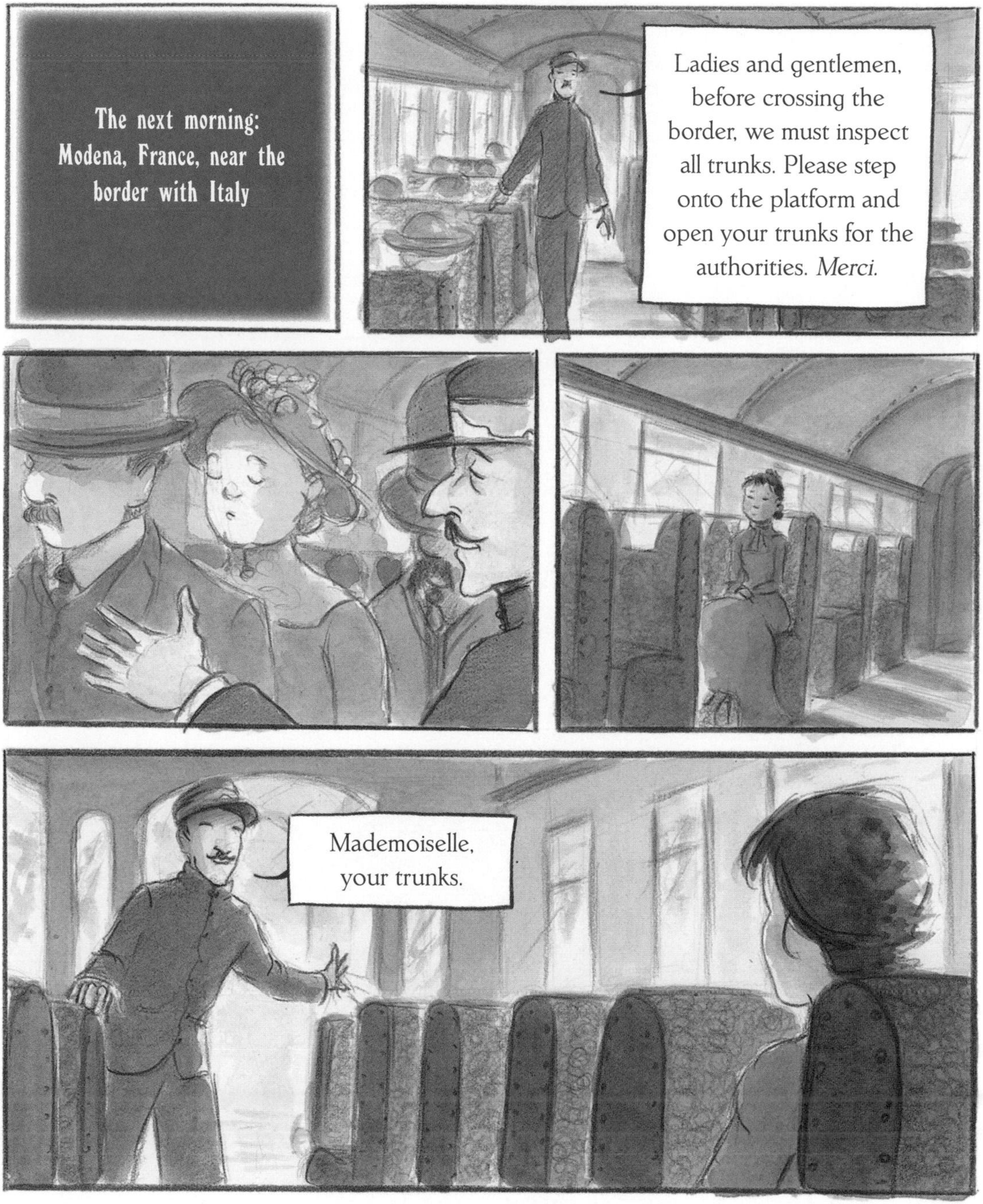

The next morning: Modena, France, near the border with Italy
Ladies and gentlemen, before crossing the border, we must inspect all trunks. Please step onto the platform and open your trunks for the authorities. *Merci.*
Mademoiselle, your trunks.

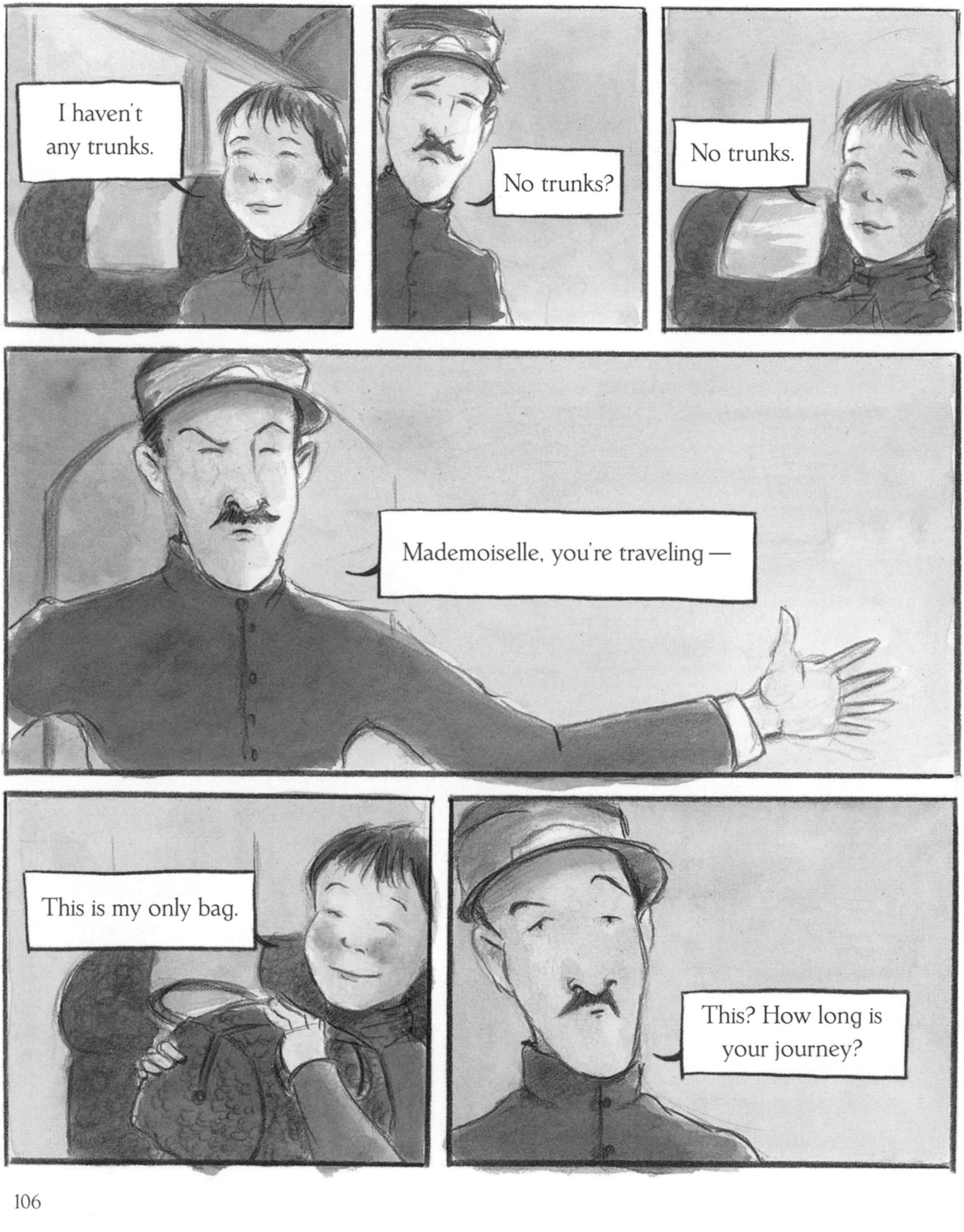
I haven't any trunks.
No trunks?
No trunks.
Mademoiselle, you're traveling —
This is my only bag.
This? How long is your journey?

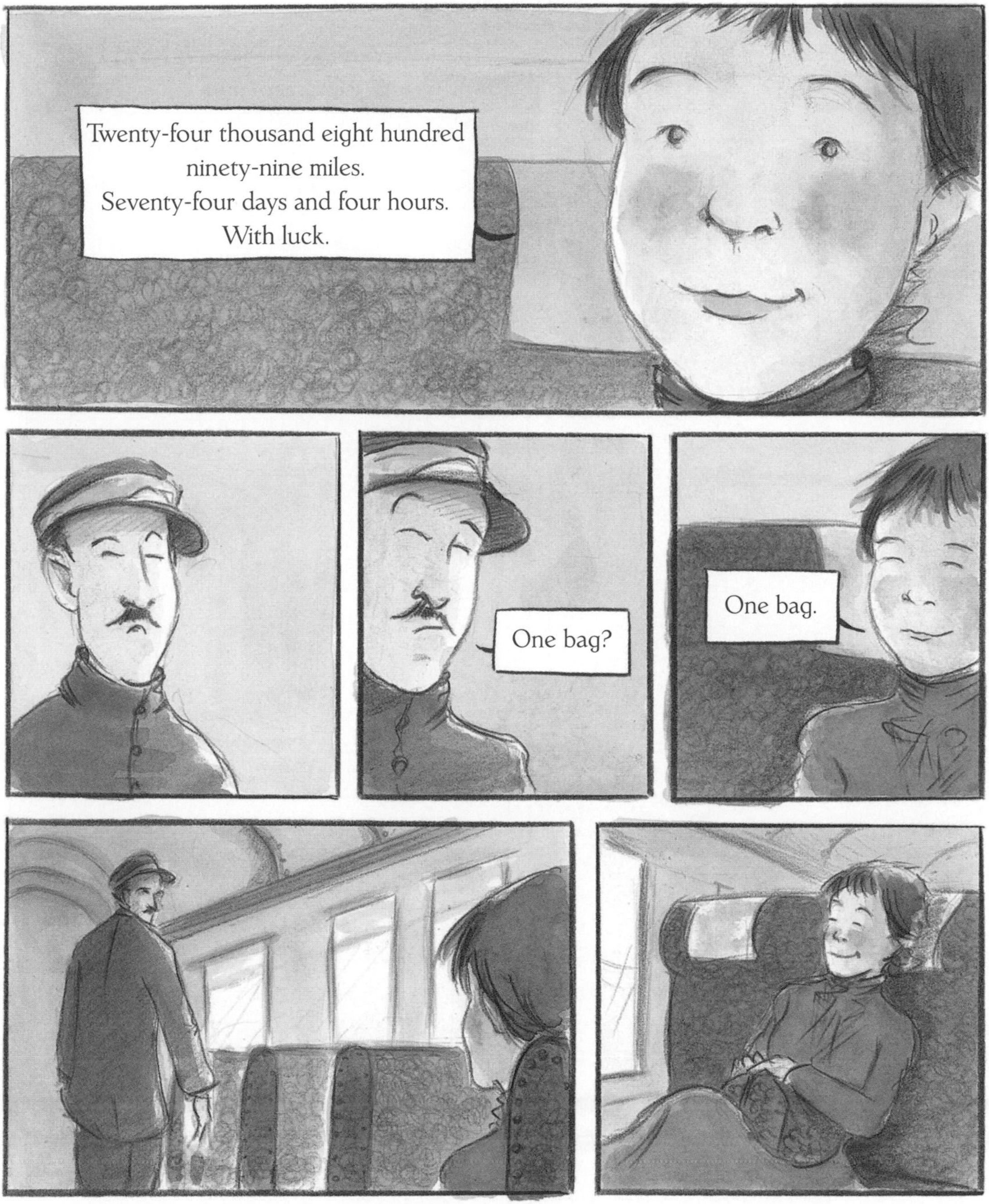
Twenty-four thousand eight hundred ninety-nine miles.
Seventy-four days and four hours.
With luck.
One bag?
One bag.

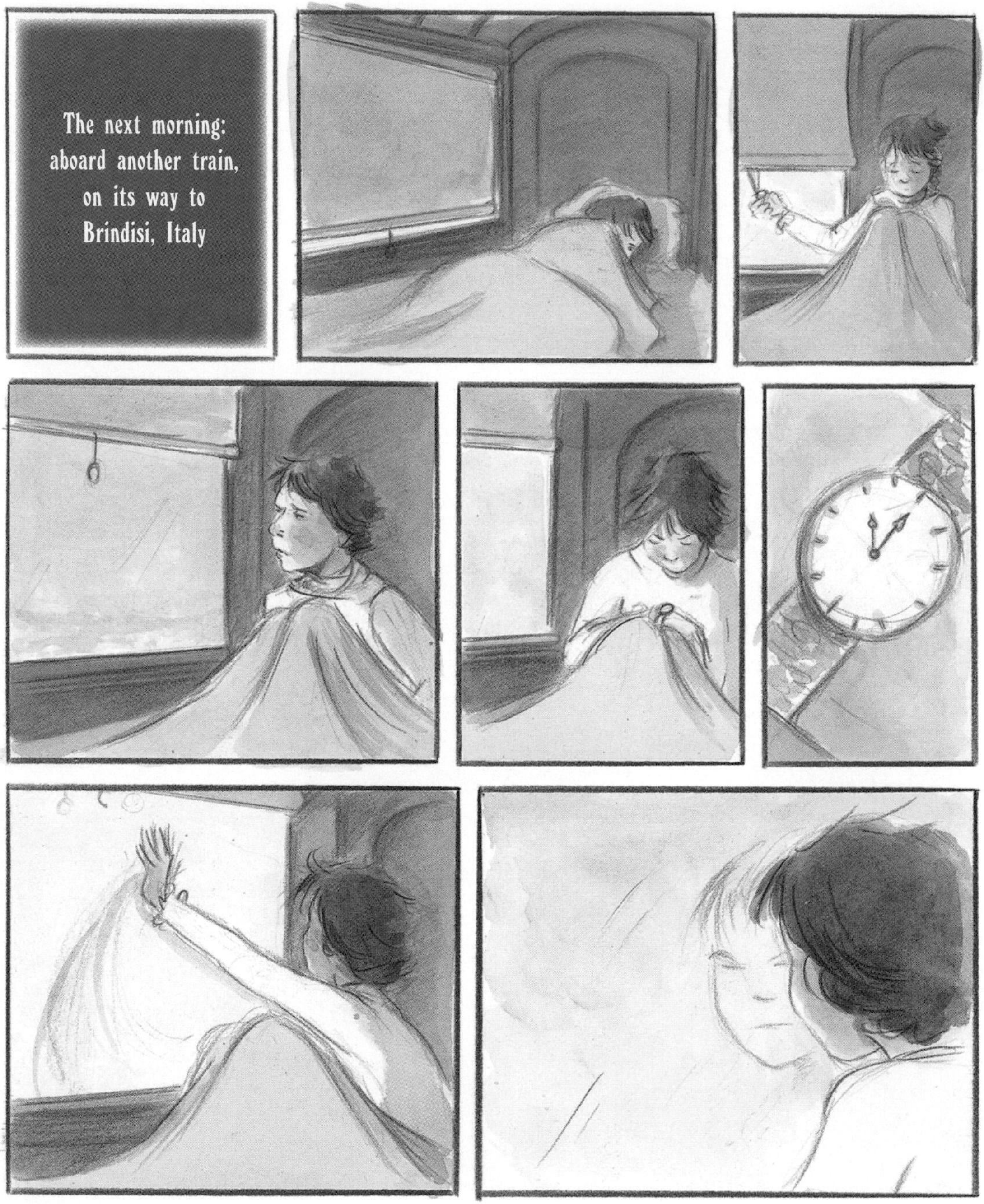
The next morning: aboard another train, on its way to Brindisi, Italy

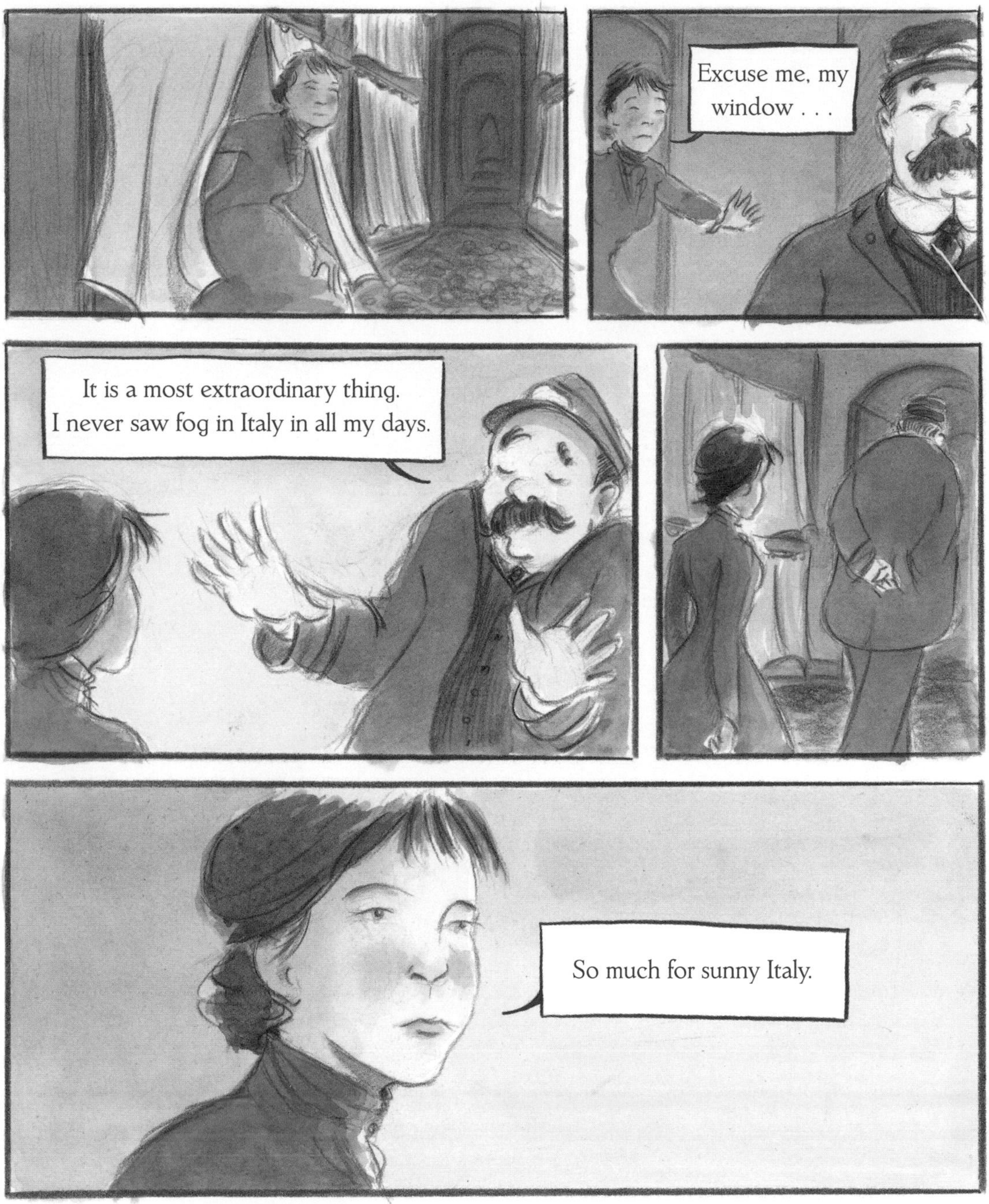

Excuse me, my window . . .
It is a most extraordinary thing. I never saw fog in Italy in all my days.
So much for sunny Italy.

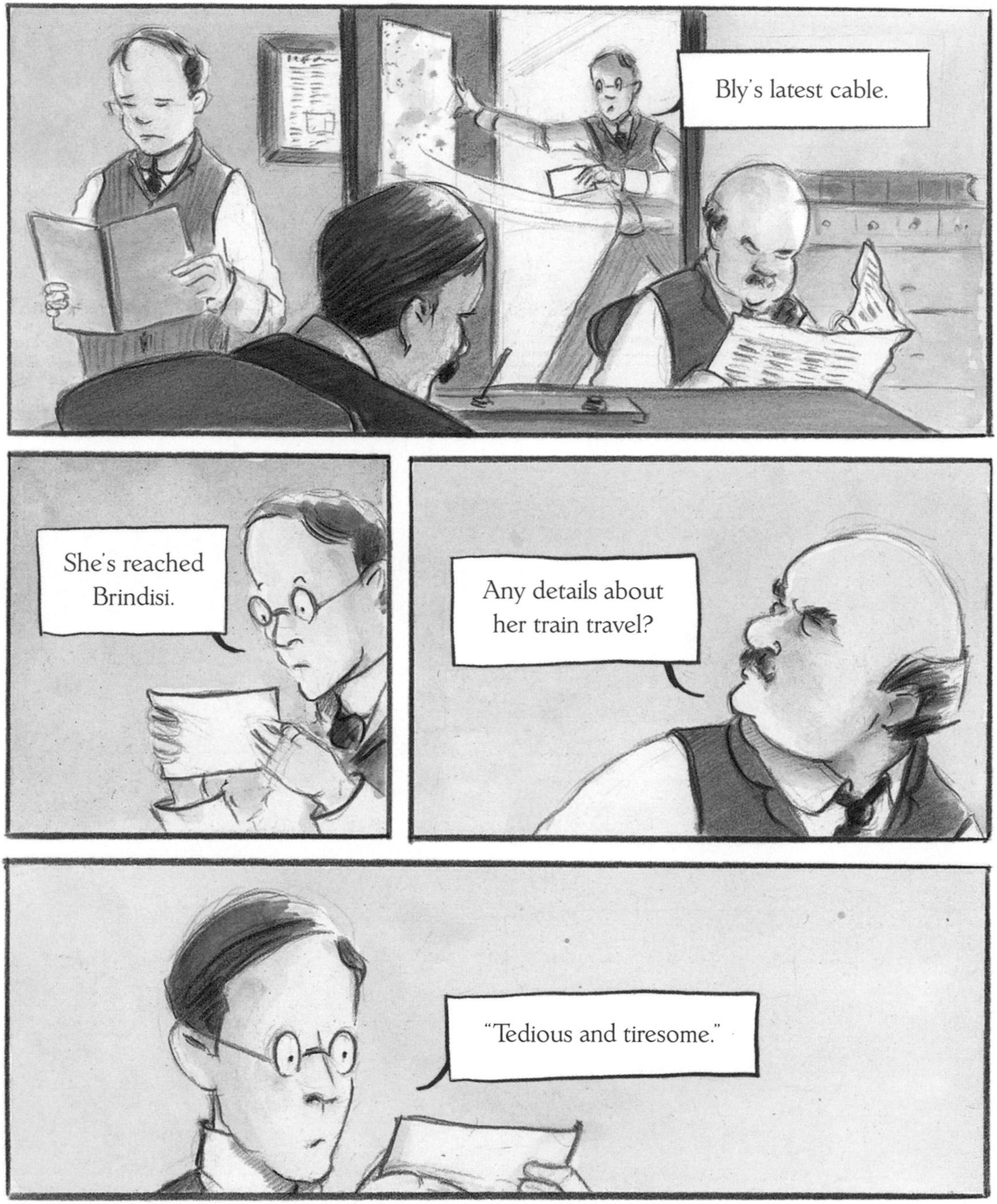
Bly's latest cable.
She's reached Brindisi.
Any details about her train travel?
"Tedious and tiresome."

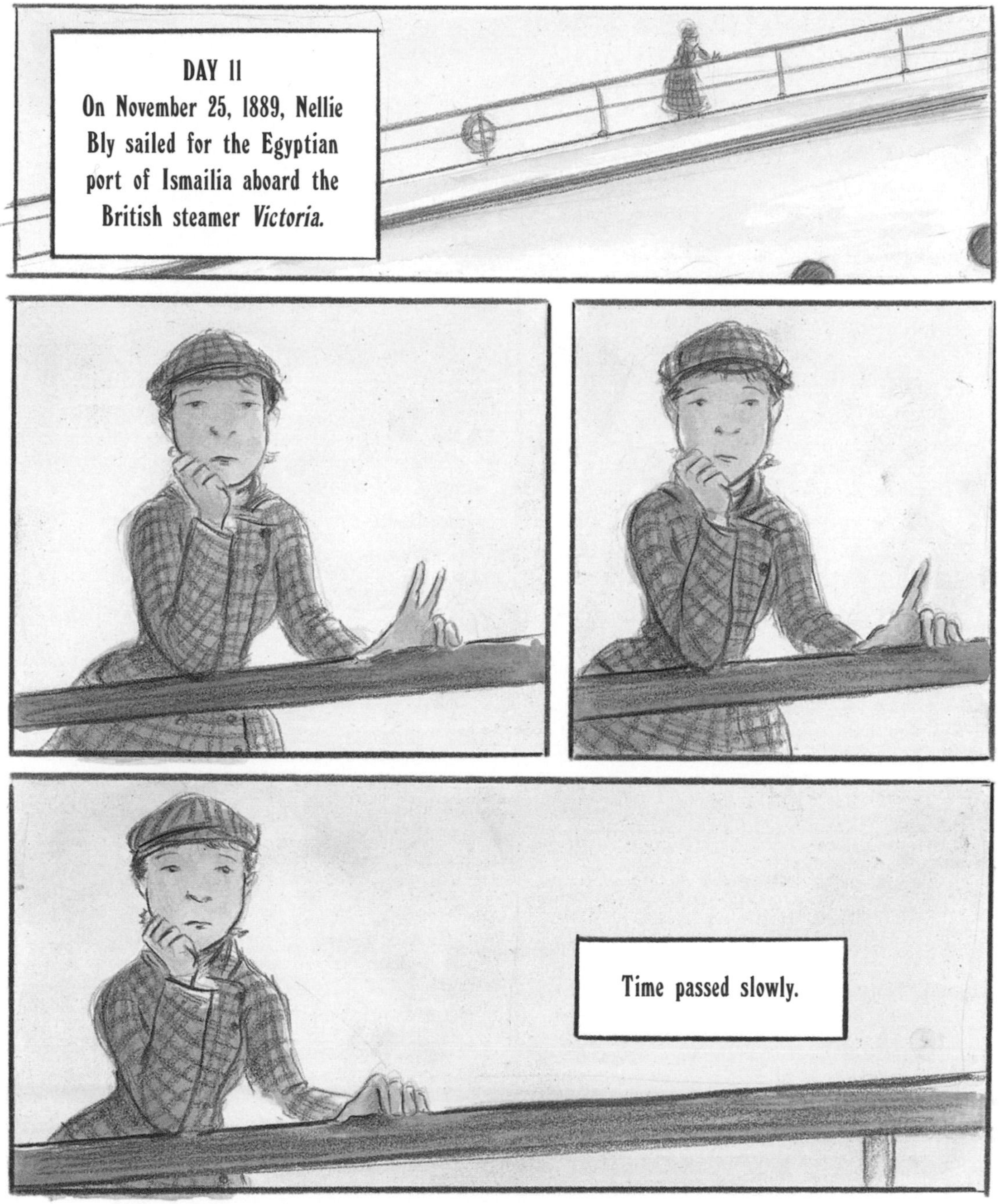
DAY 11
On November 25, 1889, Nellie Bly sailed for the Egyptian port of Ismailia aboard the British steamer *Victoria.*
Time passed slowly.

Nellie found the captain and crew intolerably rude, and she had little patience for most of the other passengers, particularly after a rumor started that she was an eccentric heiress "traveling about with a hair brush and a bank book."

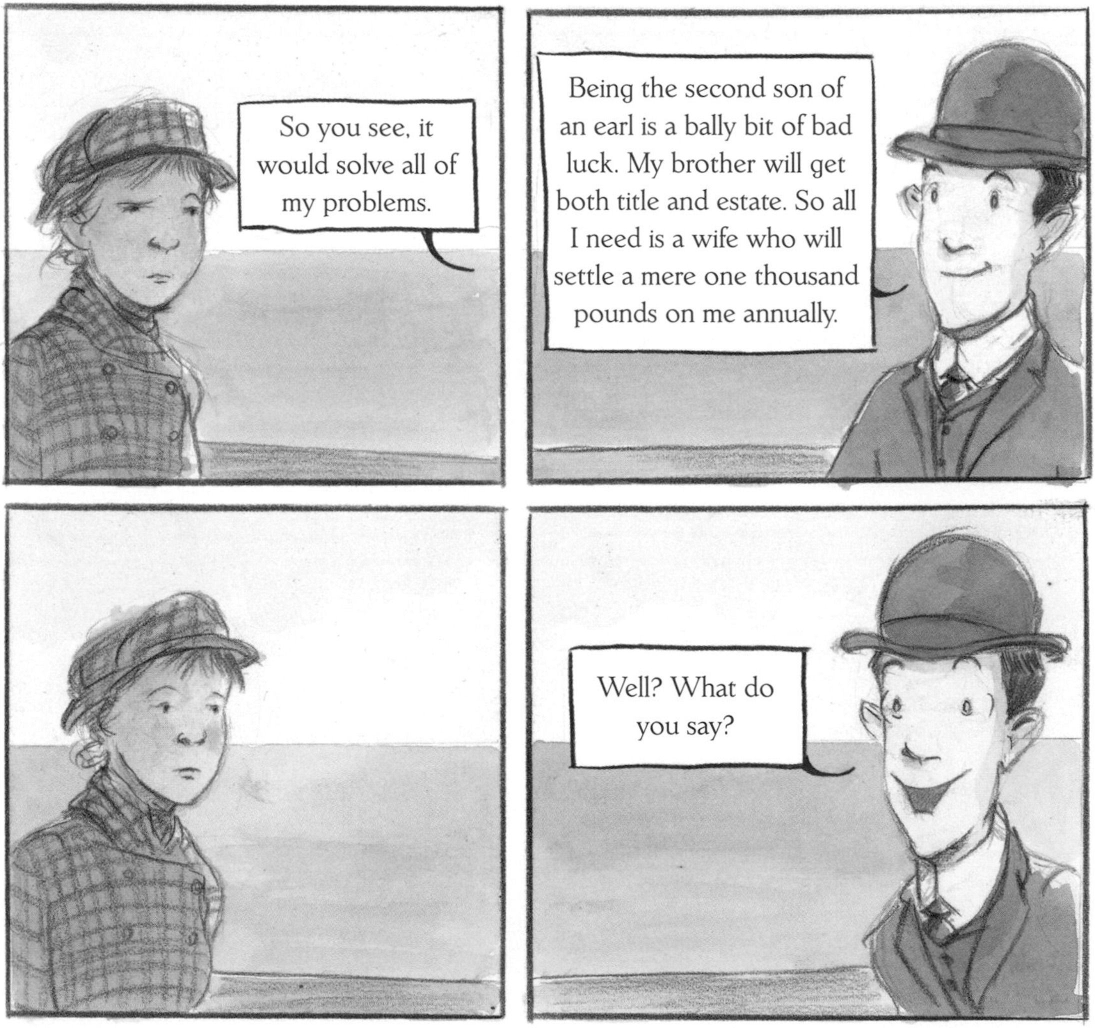

So you see, it would solve all of my problems.
Being the second son of an earl is a bally bit of bad luck. My brother will get both title and estate. So all I need is a wife who will settle a mere one thousand pounds on me annually.
Well? What do you say?

I've traveled all my life, never expecting to marry.

The truth is, I never thought I'd find a woman capable of traveling without innumerable trunks and cases.

Until now.

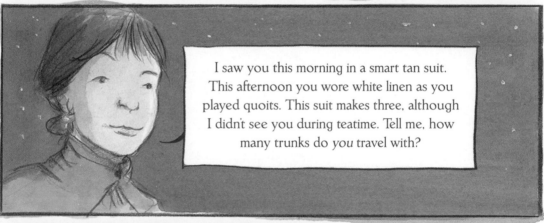

I saw you this morning in a smart tan suit. This afternoon you wore white linen as you played quoits. This suit makes three, although I didn't see you during teatime. Tell me, how many trunks do *you* travel with?

Nineteen.

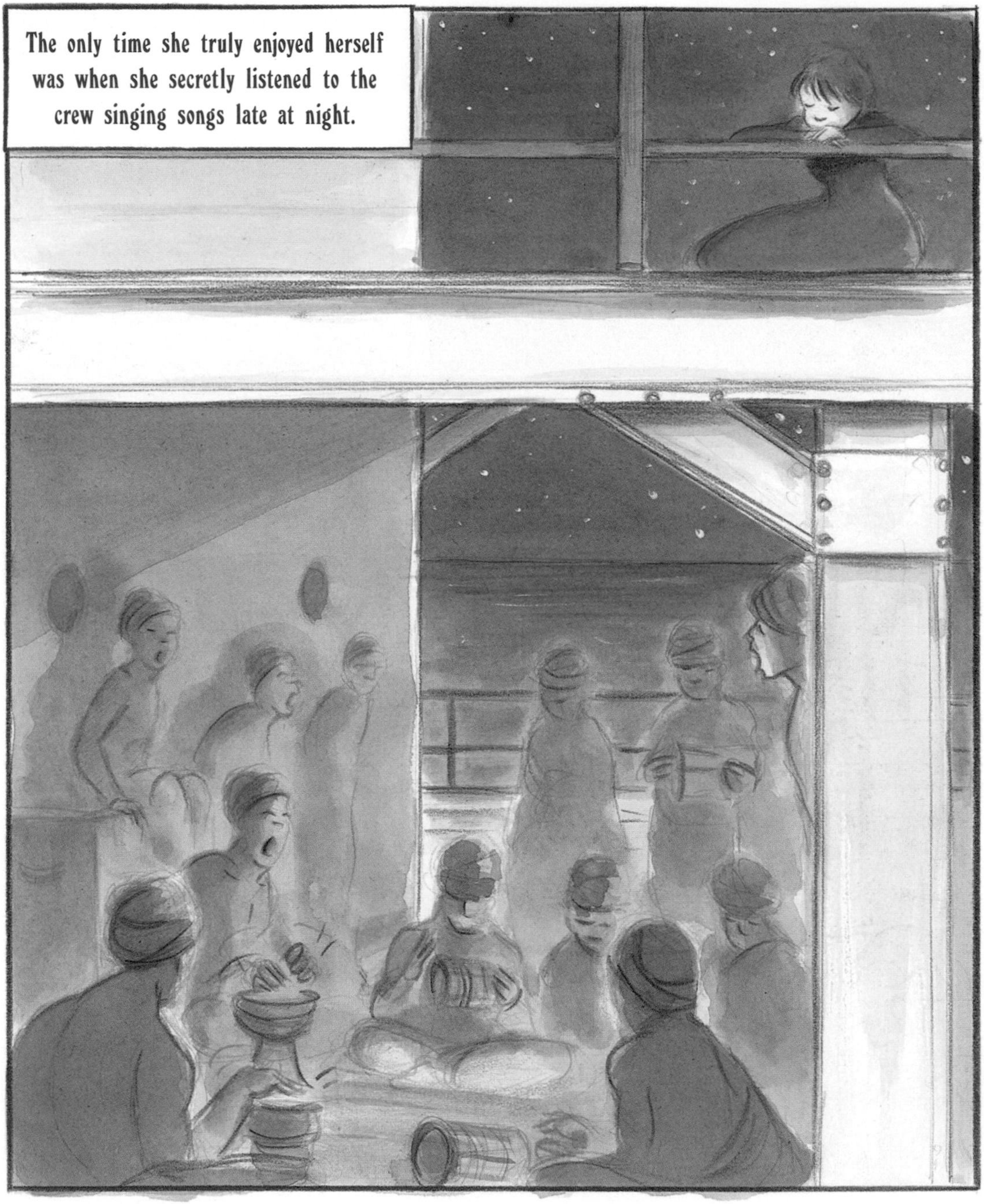
The only time she truly enjoyed herself was when she secretly listened to the crew singing songs late at night.

The *Victoria* sailed on. Occasionally they dropped anchor in an exotic port and Nellie went ashore to observe the locals firsthand.

In Port Said, Nellie purchased a hat and avoided beggars, whom she called "repulsive forms of misery."

The famous Suez Canal motivated Bly to rise several hours early for the morning passage.

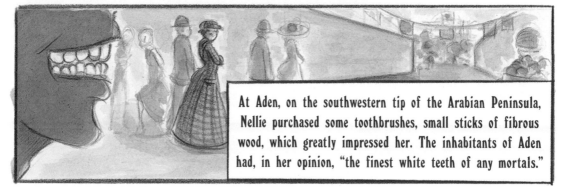

At Aden, on the southwestern tip of the Arabian Peninsula, Nellie purchased some toothbrushes, small sticks of fibrous wood, which greatly impressed her. The inhabitants of Aden had, in her opinion, "the finest white teeth of any mortals."

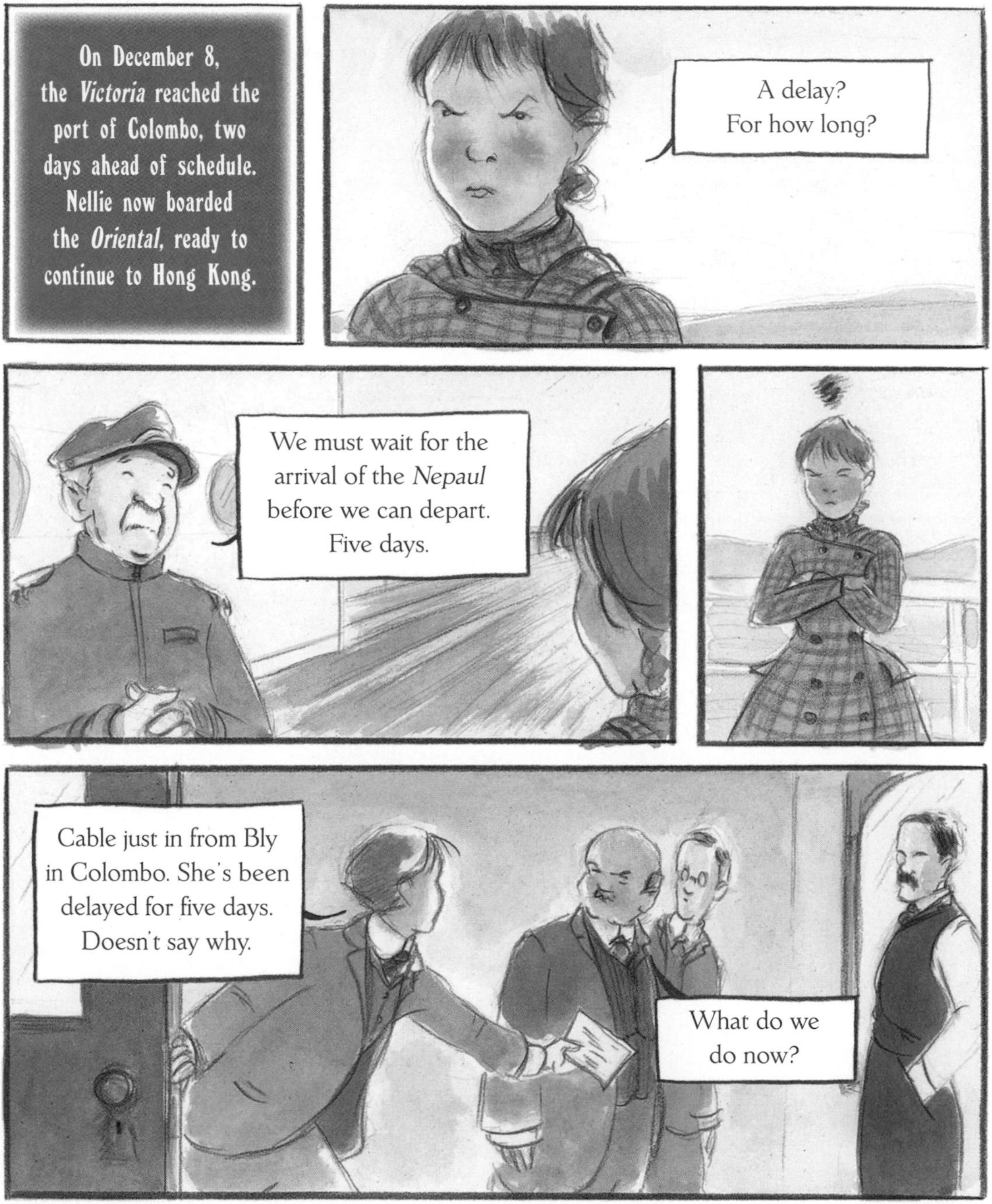
On December 8, the *Victoria* reached the port of Colombo, two days ahead of schedule. Nellie now boarded the *Oriental,* ready to continue to Hong Kong.
A delay? For how long?
We must wait for the arrival of the *Nepaul* before we can depart. Five days.
Cable just in from Bly in Colombo. She's been delayed for five days. Doesn't say why.
What do we do now?

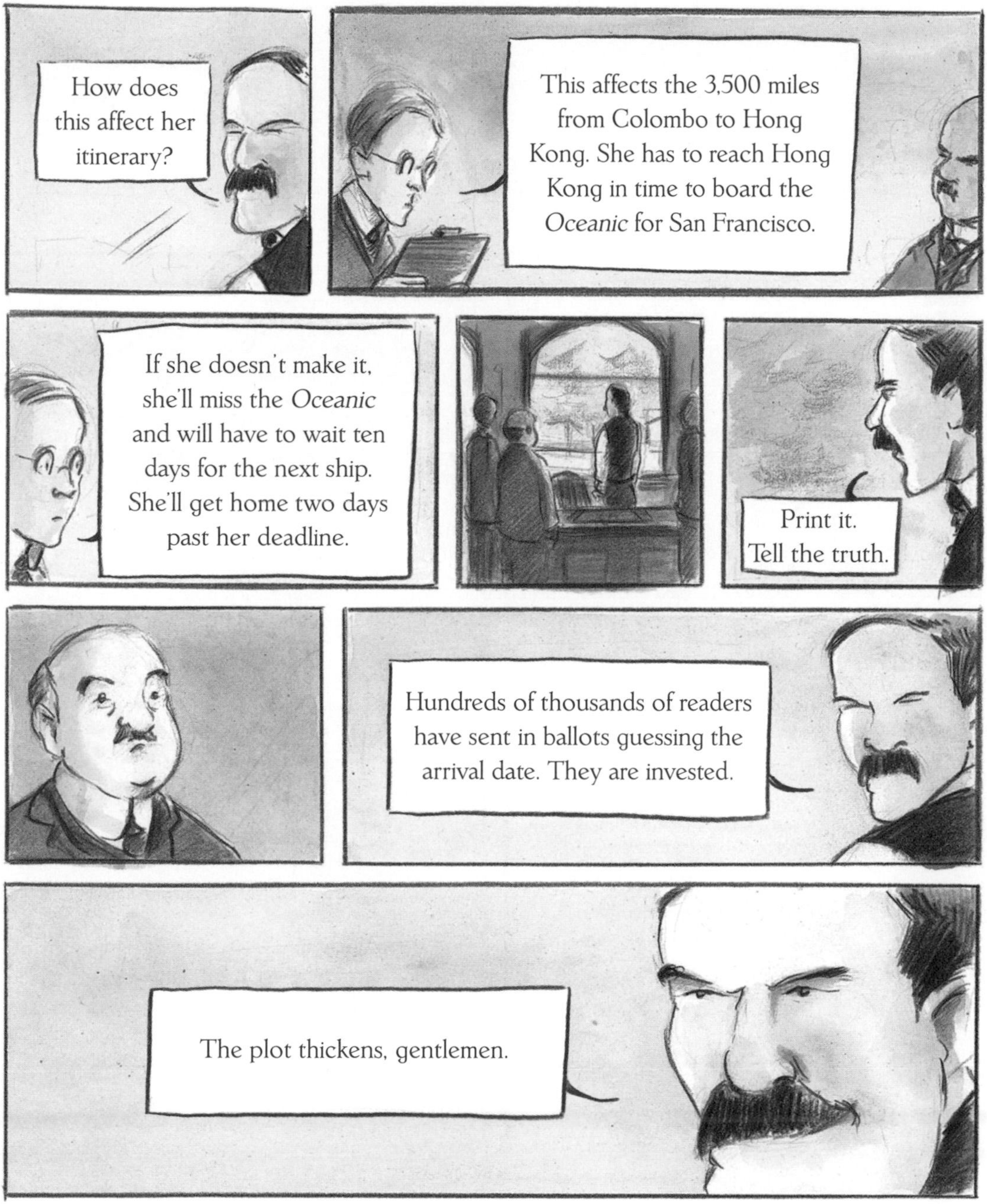
How does this affect her itinerary?
This affects the 3,500 miles from Colombo to Hong Kong. She has to reach Hong Kong in time to board the *Oceanic* for San Francisco.
If she doesn't make it, she'll miss the *Oceanic* and will have to wait ten days for the next ship. She'll get home two days past her deadline.
Print it. Tell the truth.
Hundreds of thousands of readers have sent in ballots guessing the arrival date. They are invested.
The plot thickens, gentlemen.

Nellie's delay, as the editors of the *World* suspected, did nothing to slow the flood of excitement that was spreading across the country.
Latest Novelty
IN CAPS FOR YOUNG LADIES
The "Nellie Bly."
In Plaids and Plain Colors, to retail from 50 Cents to $1.00
SEND FOR SAMPLES

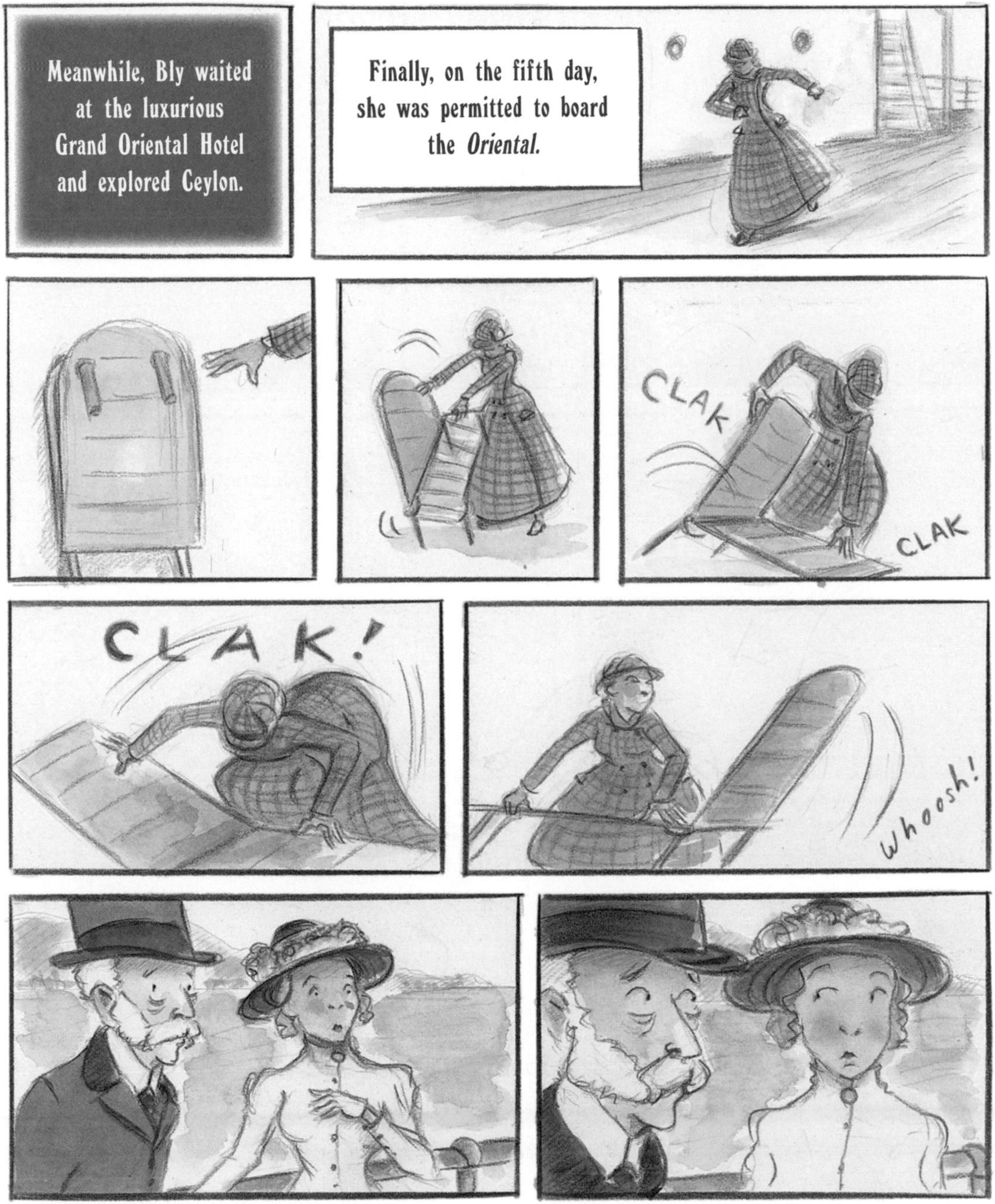
Meanwhile, Bly waited at the luxurious Grand Oriental Hotel and explored Ceylon.
Finally, on the fifth day, she was permitted to board the *Oriental.*
CLAK
CLAK
CLAK!
Whoosh!

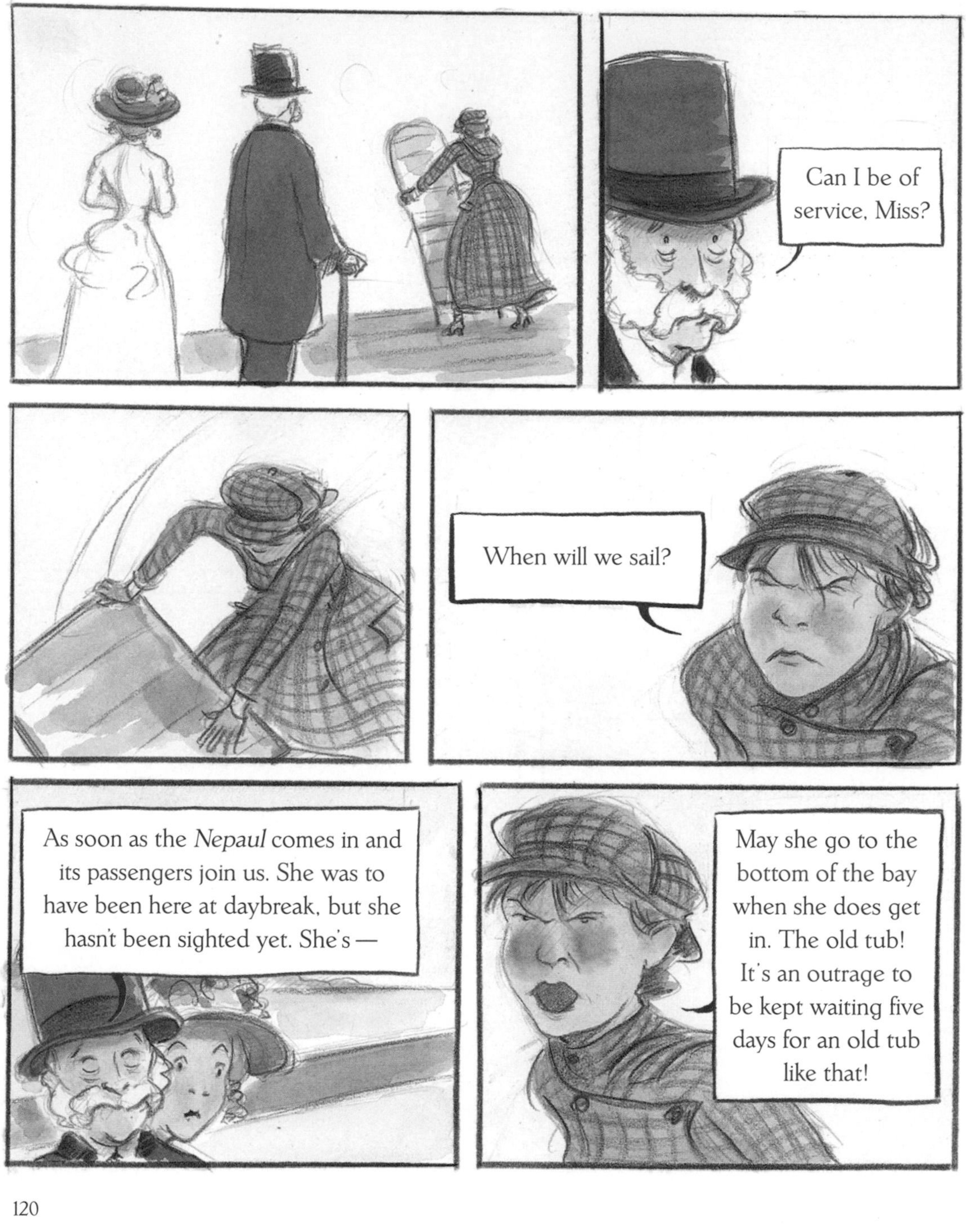
Can I be of service, Miss?
When will we sail?
As soon as the *Nepaul* comes in and its passengers join us. She was to have been here at daybreak, but she hasn't been sighted yet. She's —
May she go to the bottom of the bay when she does get in. The old tub! It's an outrage to be kept waiting five days for an old tub like that!

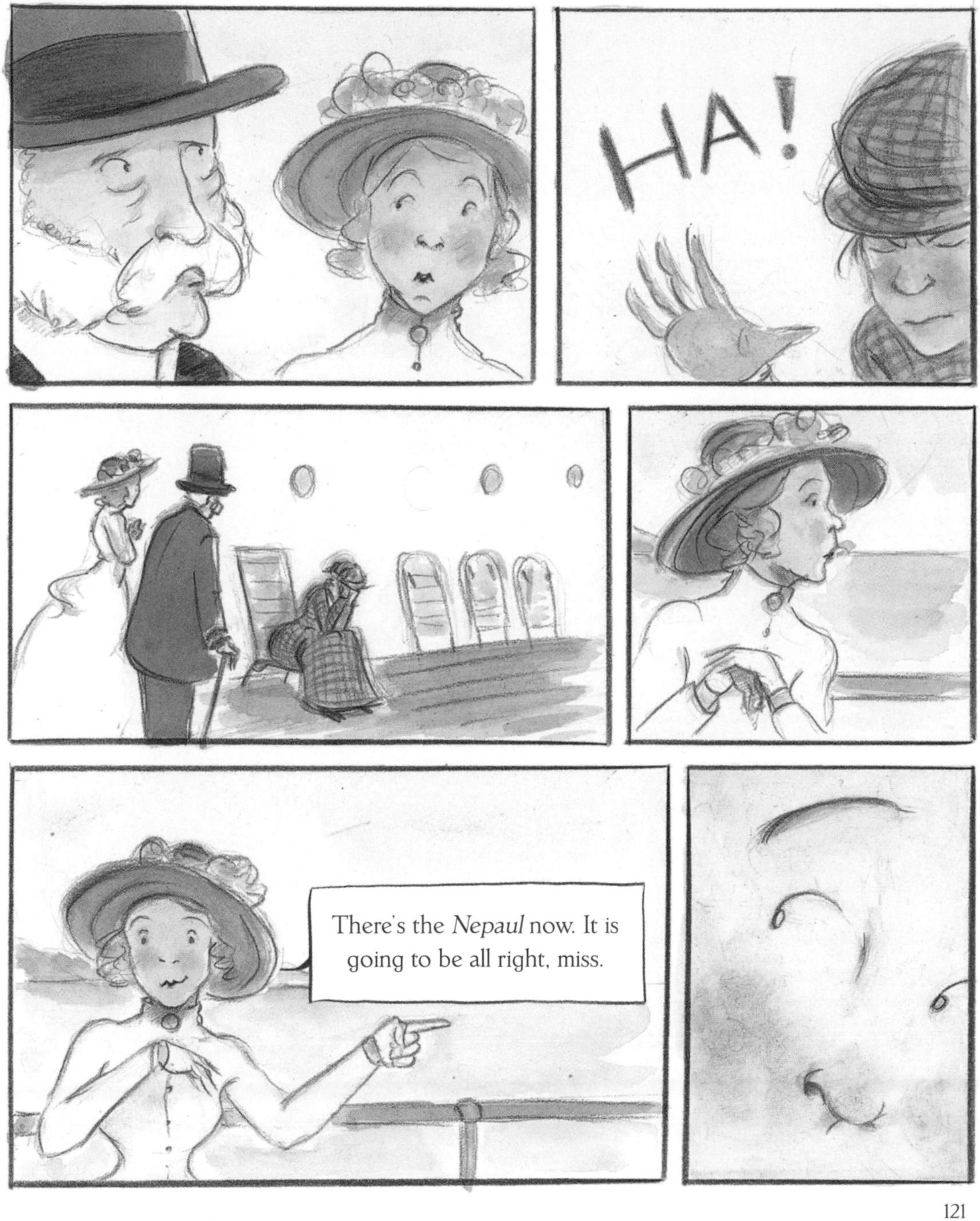
HA!
There's the *Nepaul* now. It is going to be all right, miss.

The *Oriental* sailed on, stopping briefly in Penang . . .

and Singapore.

Here Nellie was denied entrance to a Hindu temple.

No. No mudder.

I assure you I am not a mother!

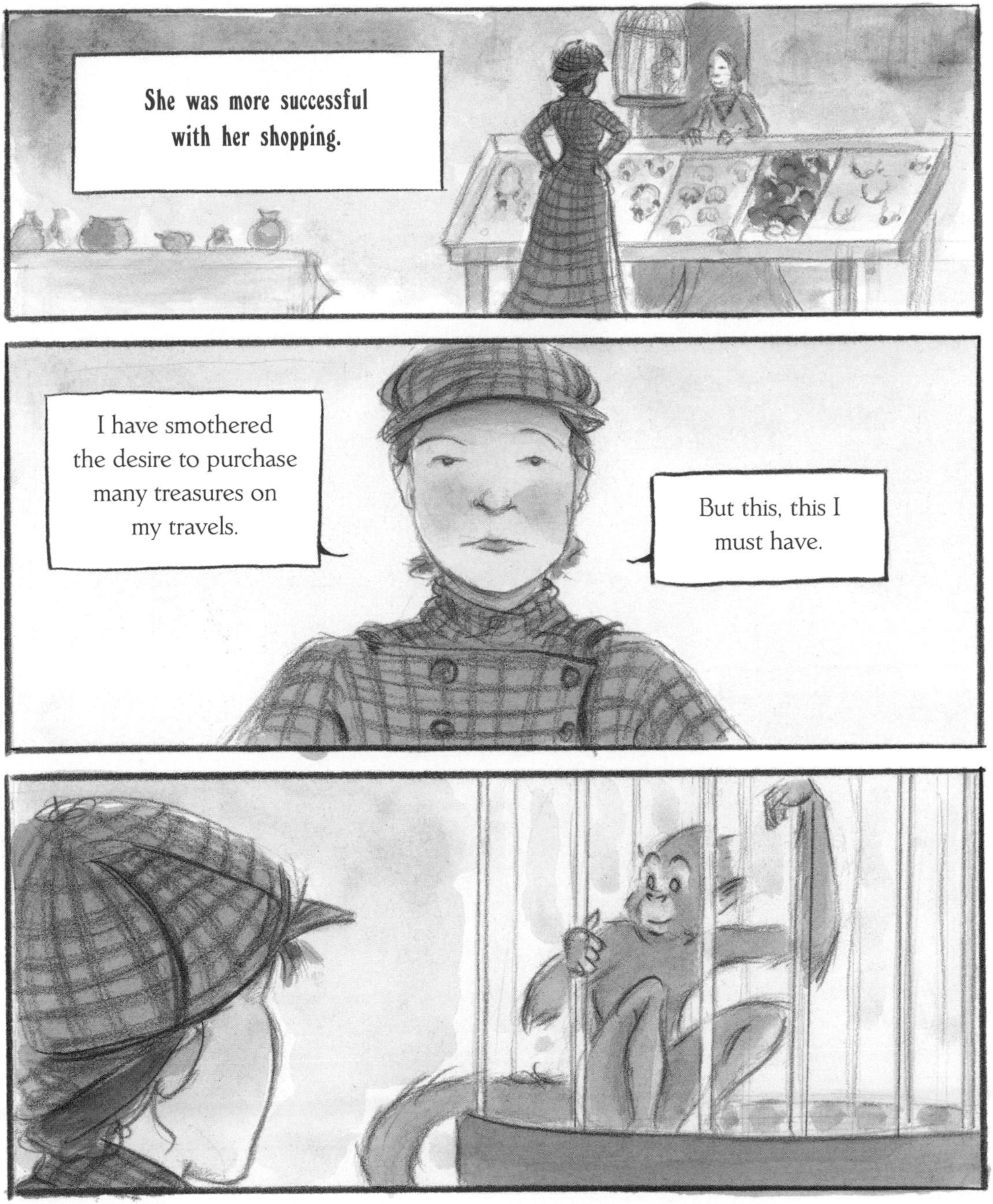
She was more successful with her shopping.
I have smothered the desire to purchase many treasures on my travels.
But this, this I must have.

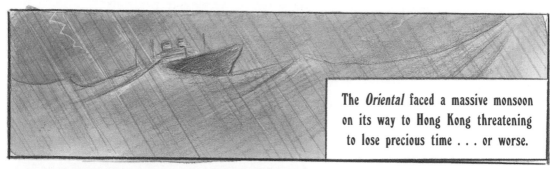

The *Oriental* faced a massive monsoon on its way to Hong Kong threatening to lose precious time . . . or worse.

Well, McGinty, my friend, if the ship does go down, at least no one will be able to tell if I could have gone around the world in seventy-four days or not.

At this rate, I'll be lucky to make it in a hundred days.

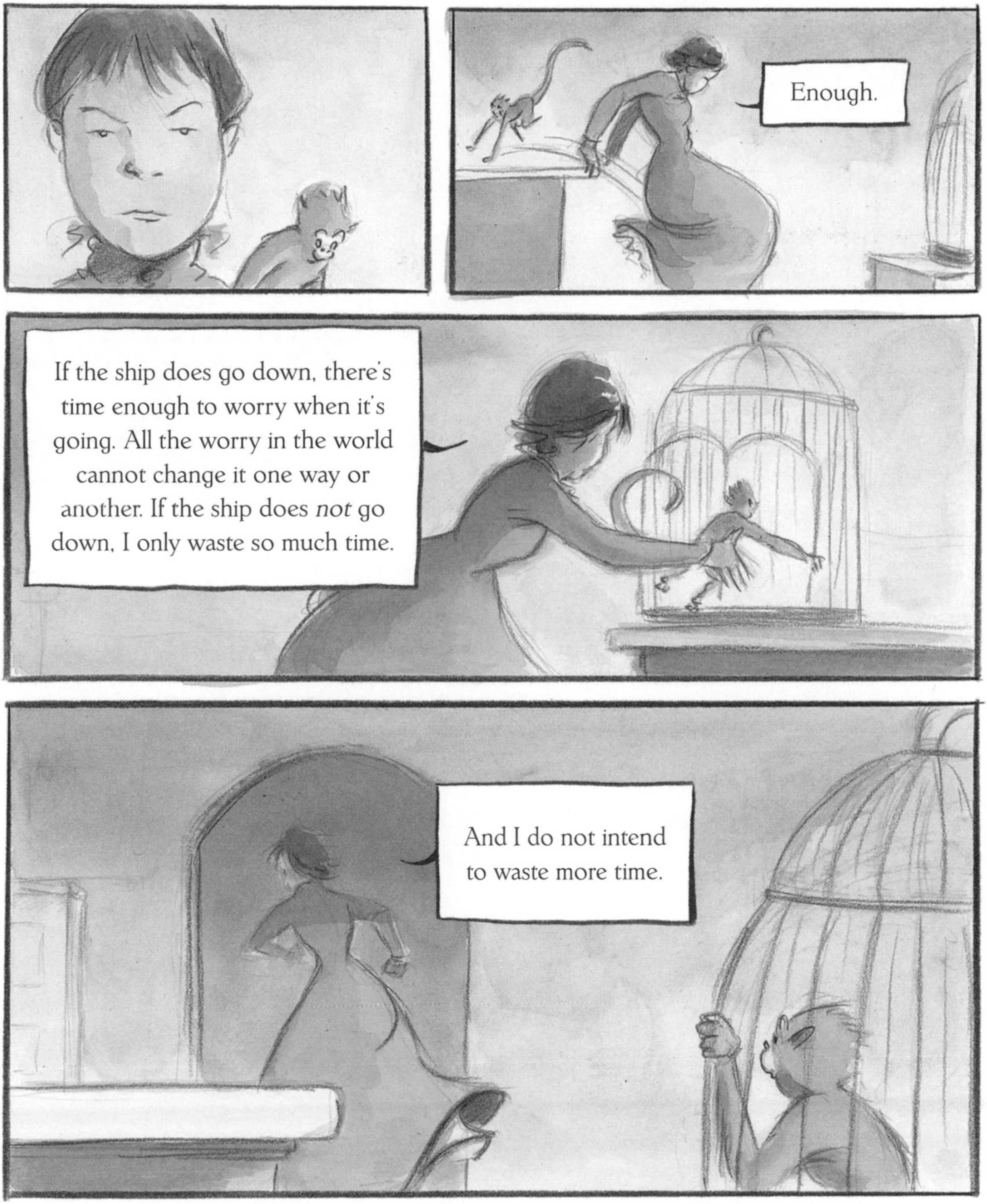
Enough.
If the ship does go down, there's time enough to worry when it's going. All the worry in the world cannot change it one way or another. If the ship does *not* go down, I only waste so much time.
And I do not intend to waste more time.

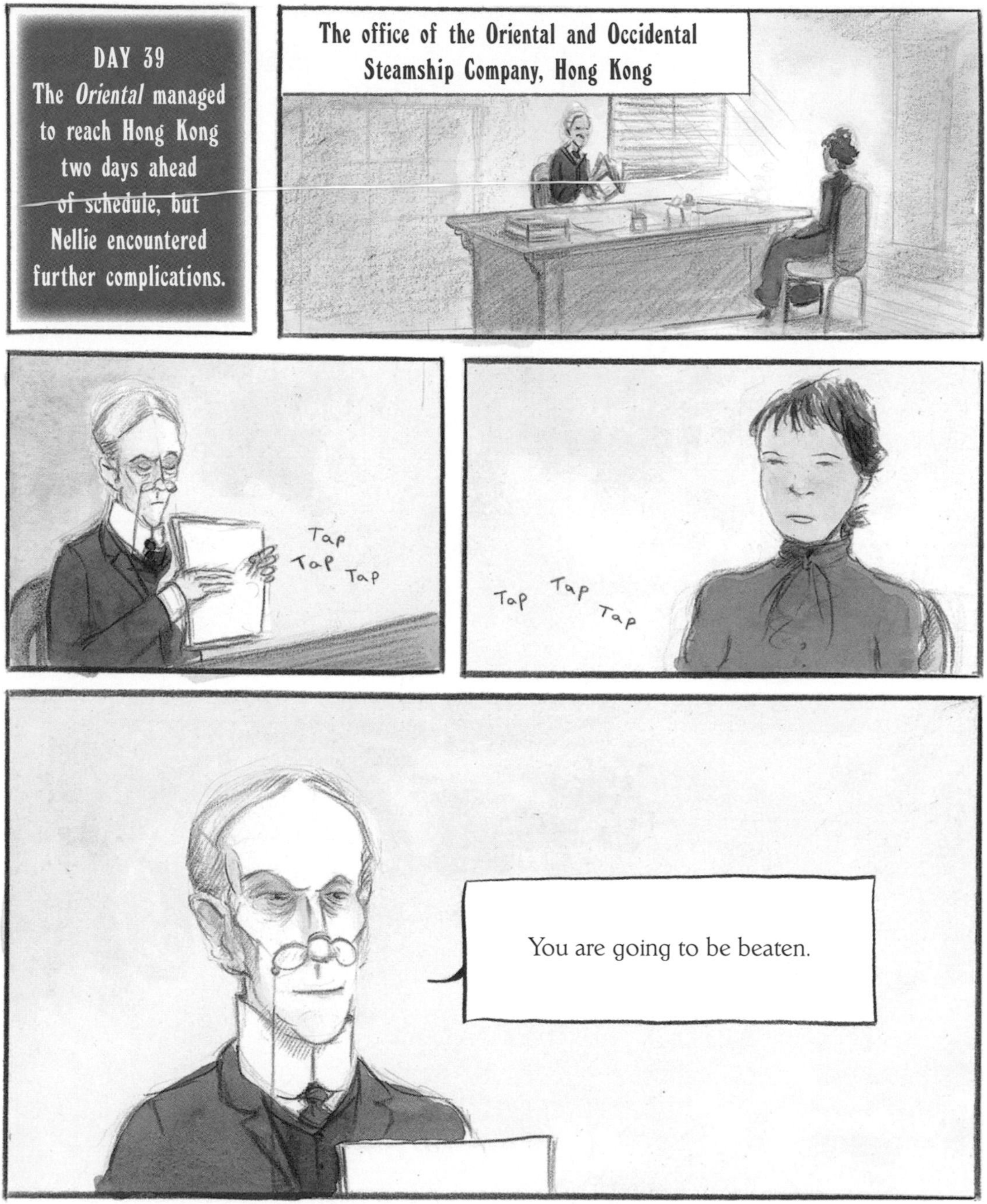
DAY 39
The *Oriental* managed to reach Hong Kong two days ahead of schedule, but Nellie encountered further complications.
The office of the Oriental and Occidental Steamship Company, Hong Kong
Tap Tap Tap
Tap Tap Tap
You are going to be beaten.

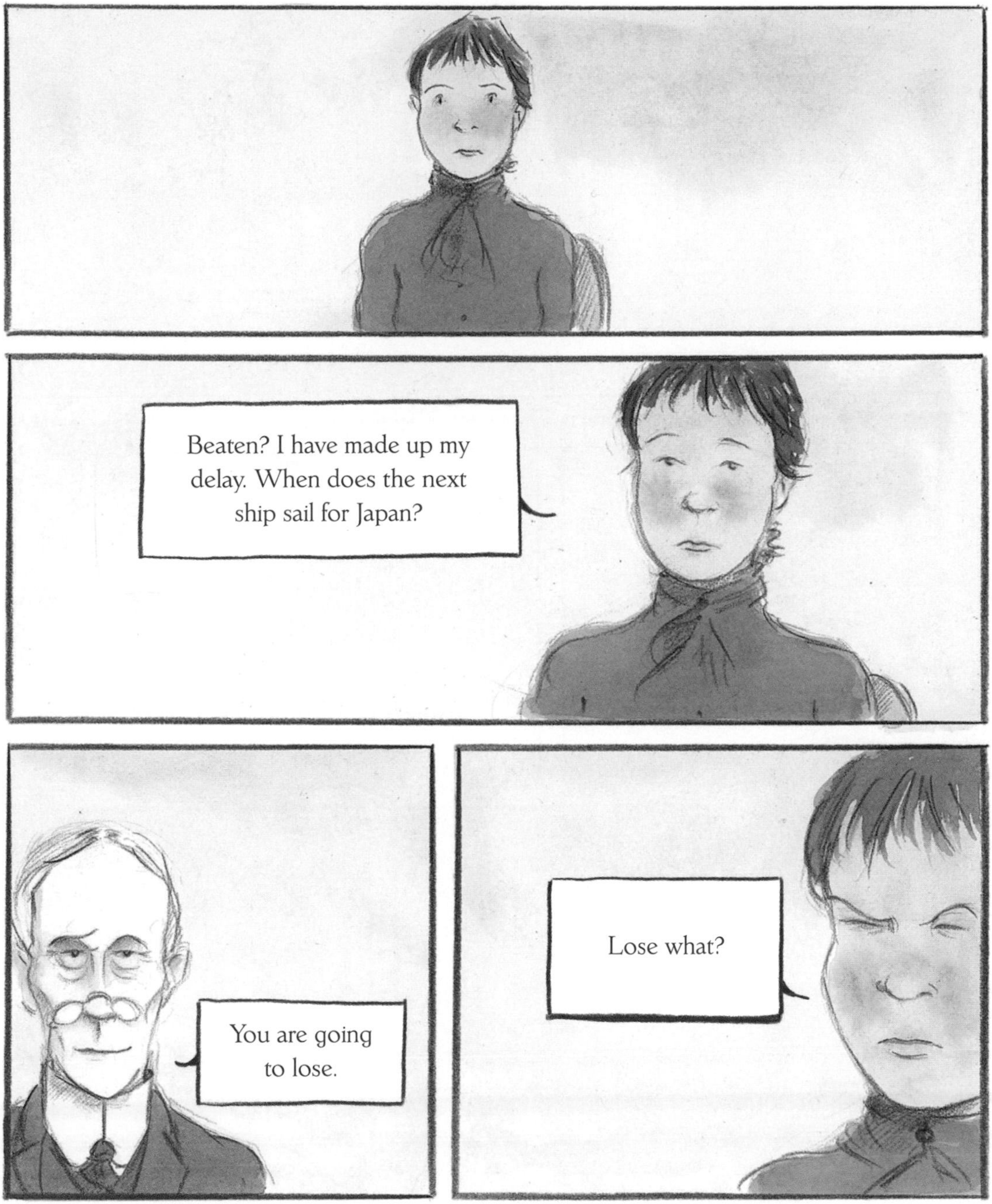
Beaten? I have made up my delay. When does the next ship sail for Japan?
You are going to lose.
Lose what?

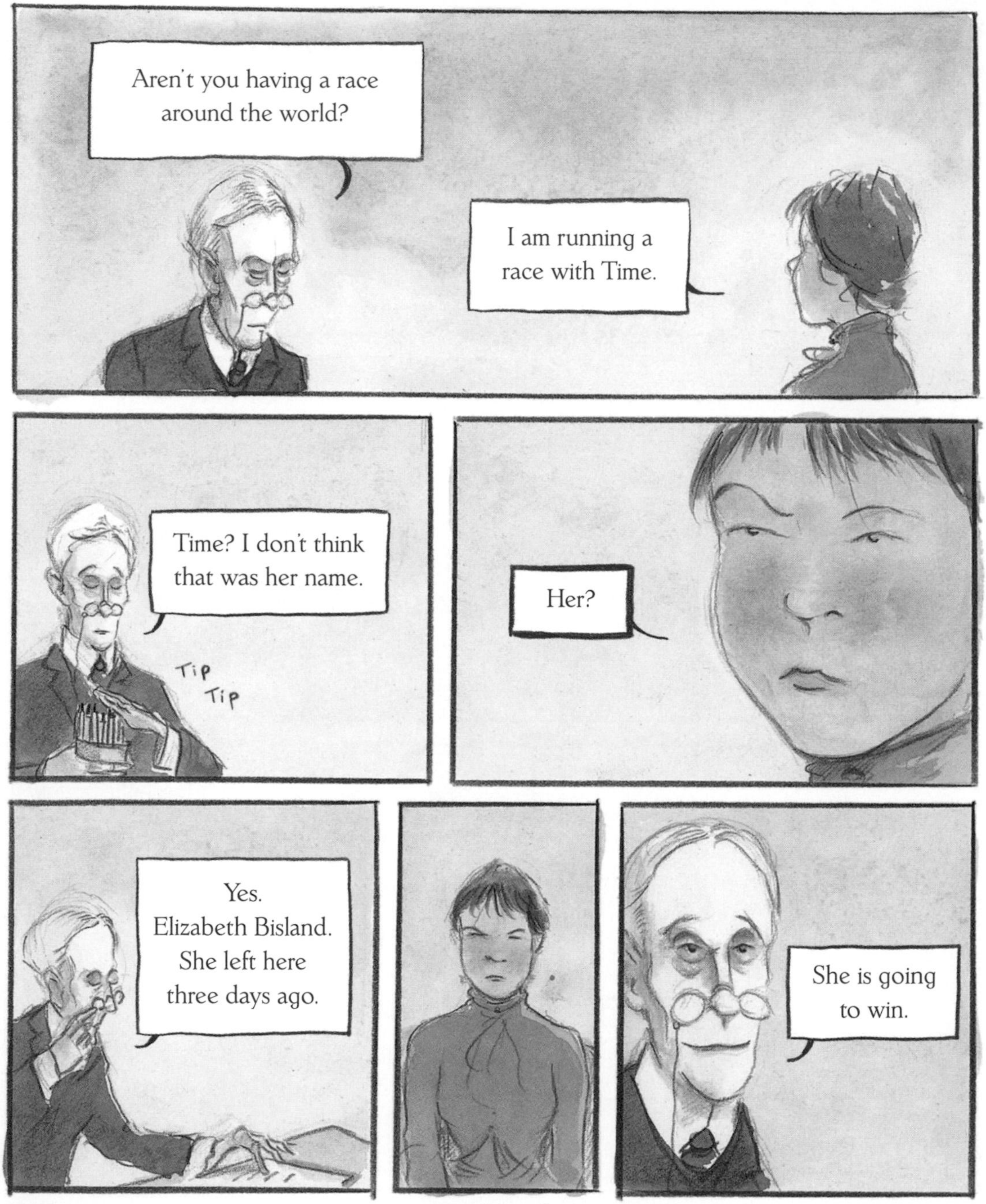
Aren't you having a race around the world?
I am running a race with Time.
Time? I don't think that was her name.
Tip Tip
Her?
Yes. Elizabeth Bisland. She left here three days ago.
She is going to win.

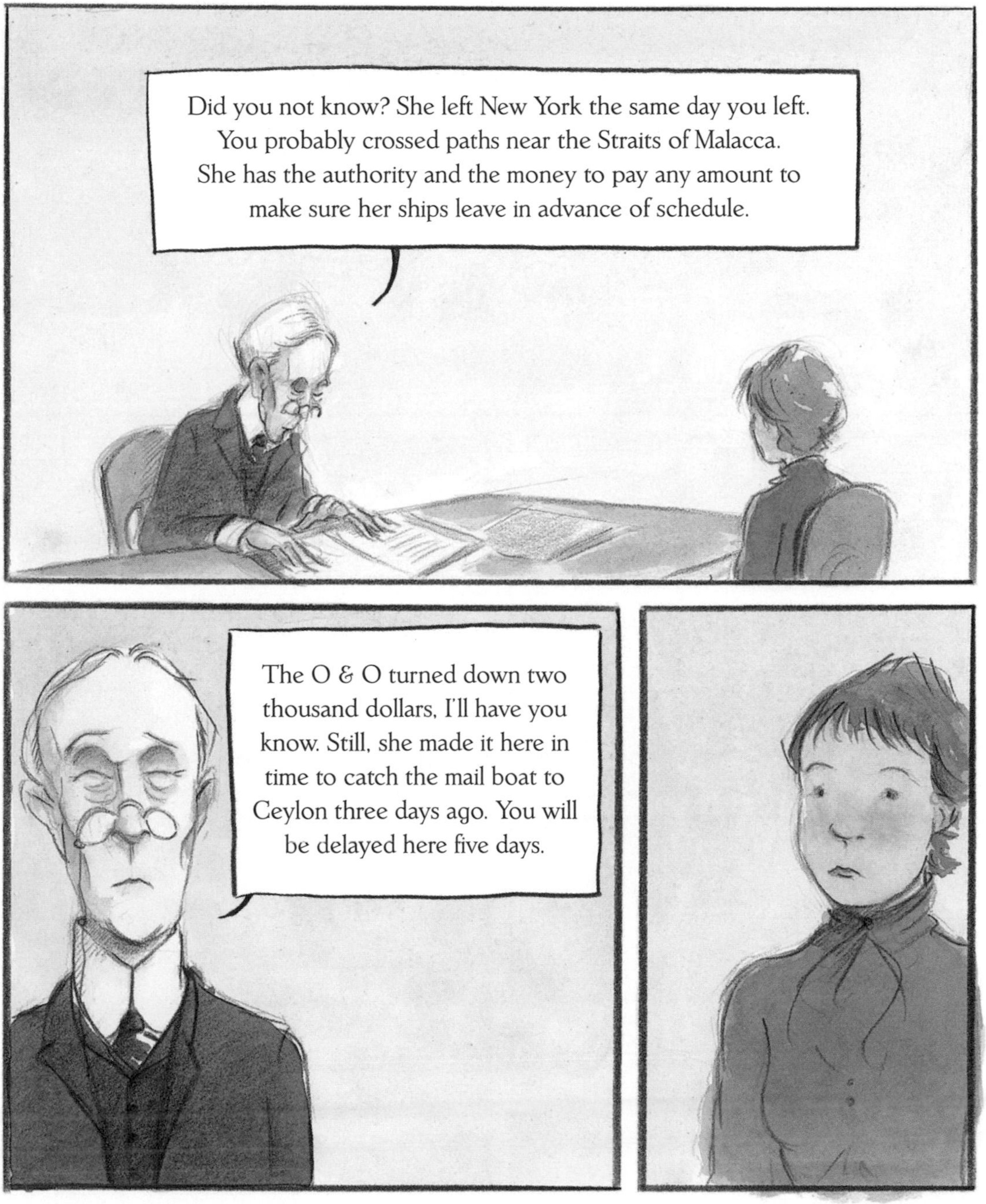
Did you not know? She left New York the same day you left. You probably crossed paths near the Straits of Malacca. She has the authority and the money to pay any amount to make sure her ships leave in advance of schedule.
The O & O turned down two thousand dollars, I'll have you know. Still, she made it here in time to catch the mail boat to Ceylon three days ago. You will be delayed here five days.

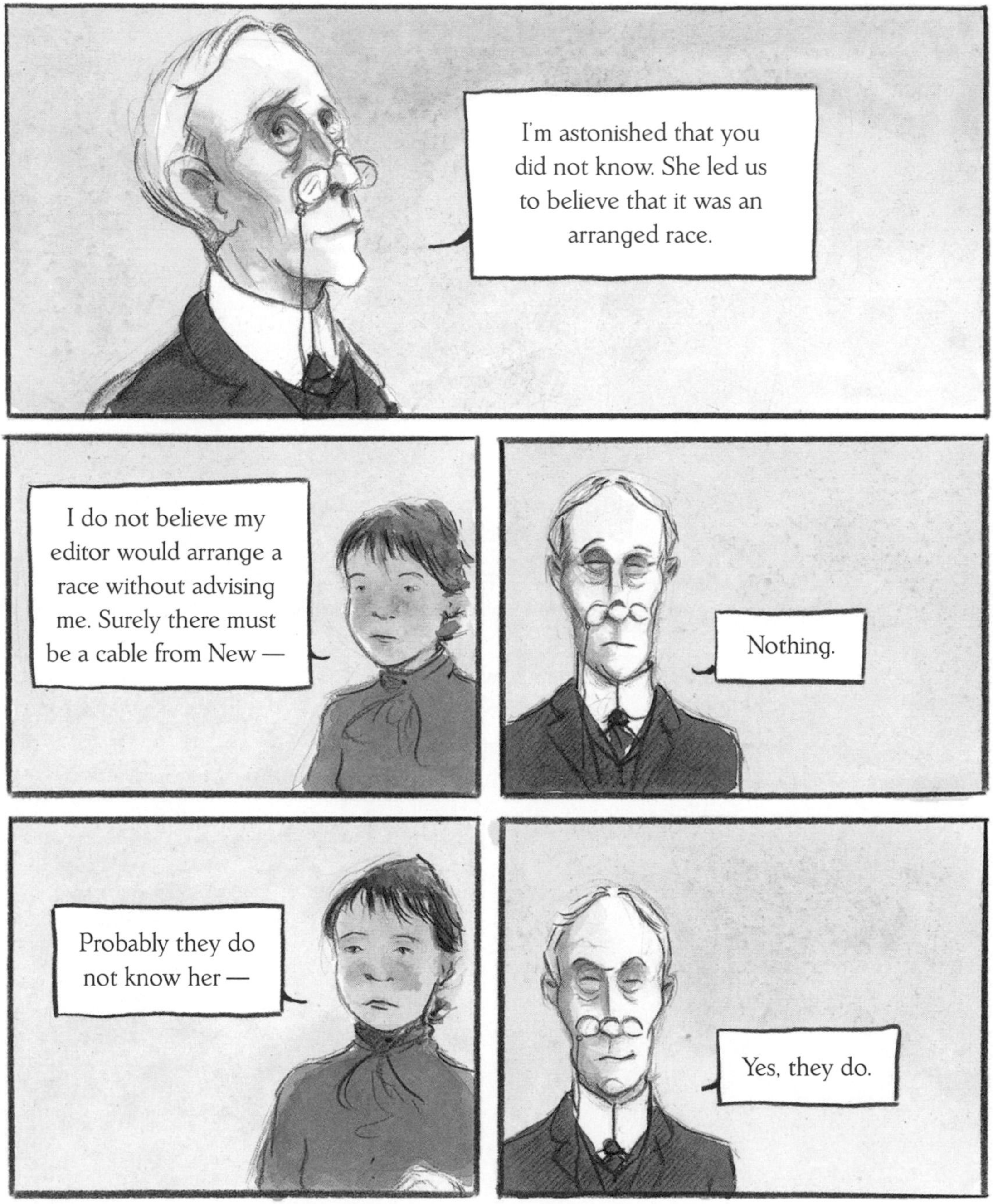
I'm astonished that you did not know. She led us to believe that it was an arranged race.
I do not believe my editor would arrange a race without advising me. Surely there must be a cable from New —
Nothing.
Probably they do not know her —
Yes, they do.

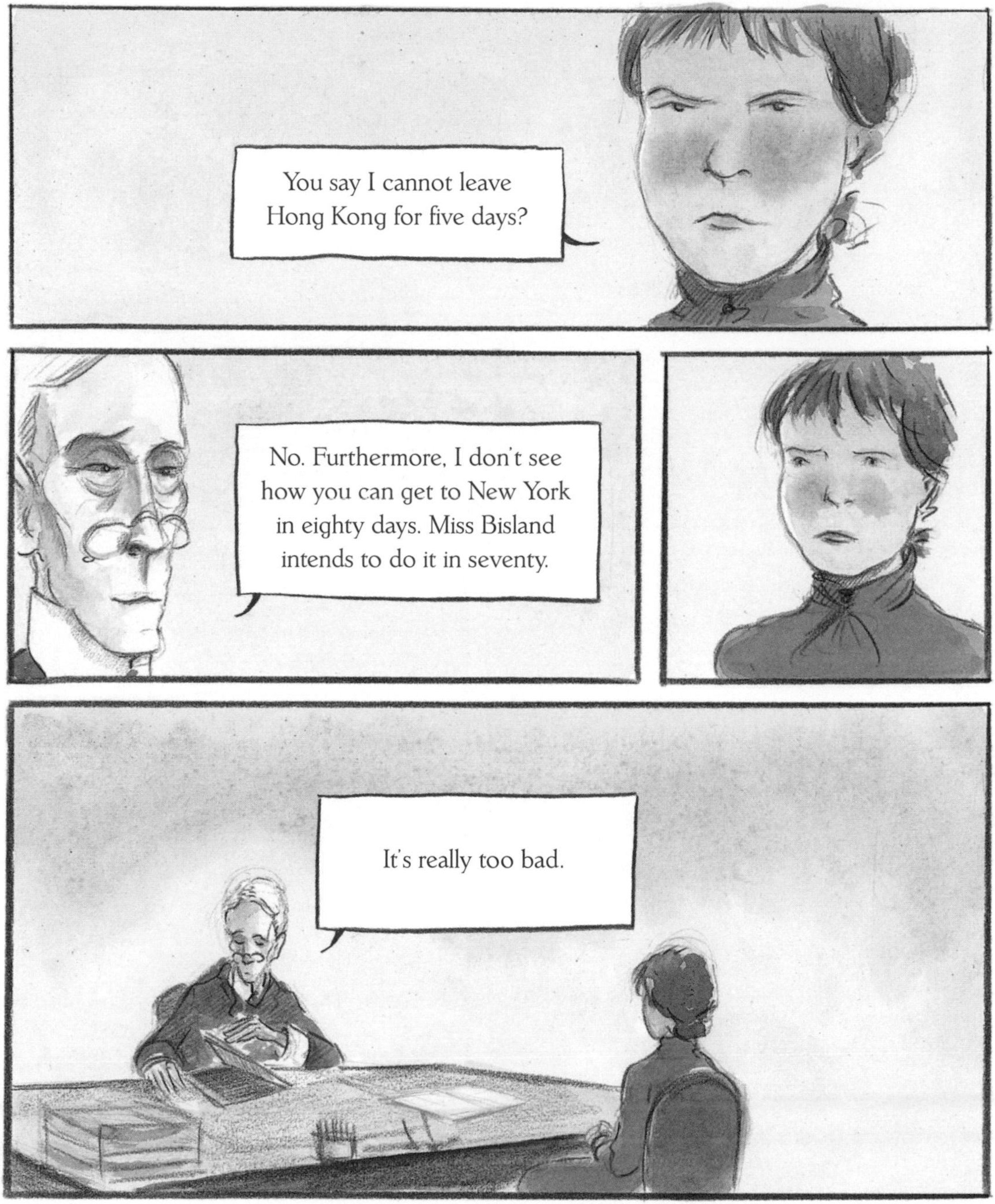
You say I cannot leave Hong Kong for five days?
No. Furthermore, I don't see how you can get to New York in eighty days. Miss Bisland intends to do it in seventy.
It's really too bad.

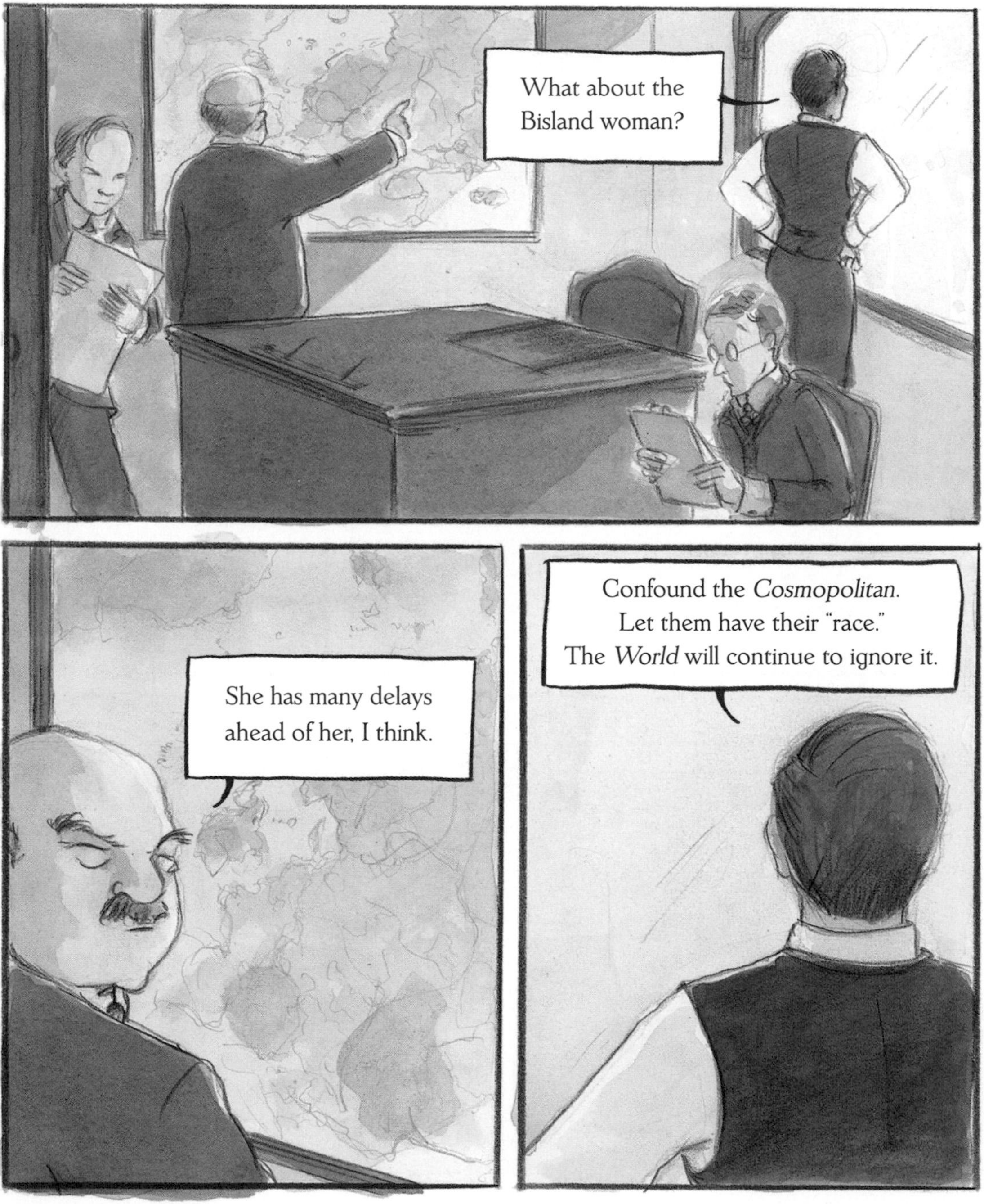
What about the Bisland woman?
She has many delays ahead of her, I think.
Confound the *Cosmopolitan*. Let them have their "race." The *World* will continue to ignore it.

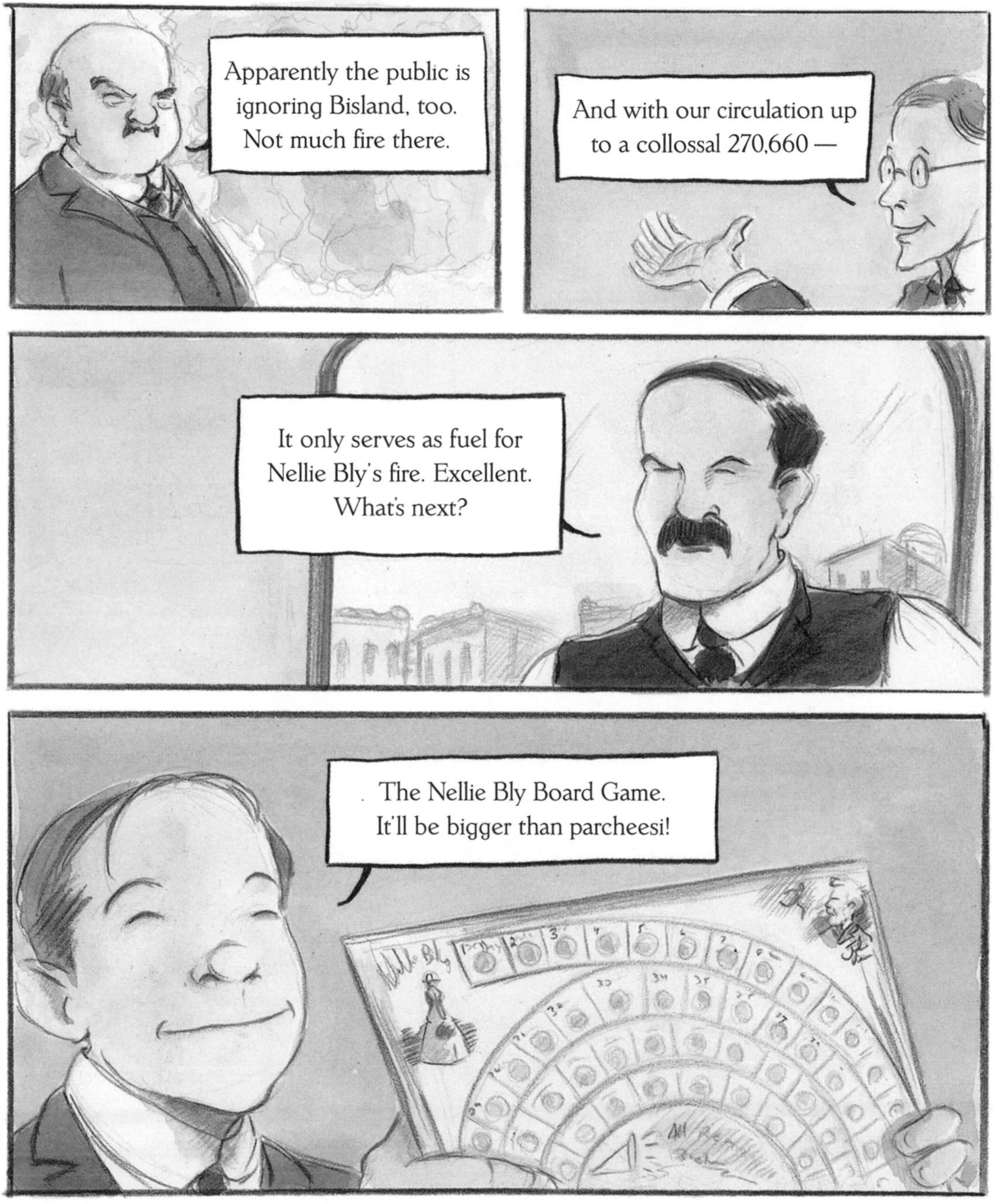
Apparently the public is ignoring Bisland, too. Not much fire there.
And with our circulation up to a collossal 270,660 —
It only serves as fuel for Nellie Bly's fire. Excellent. What's next?
The Nellie Bly Board Game. It'll be bigger than parcheesi!

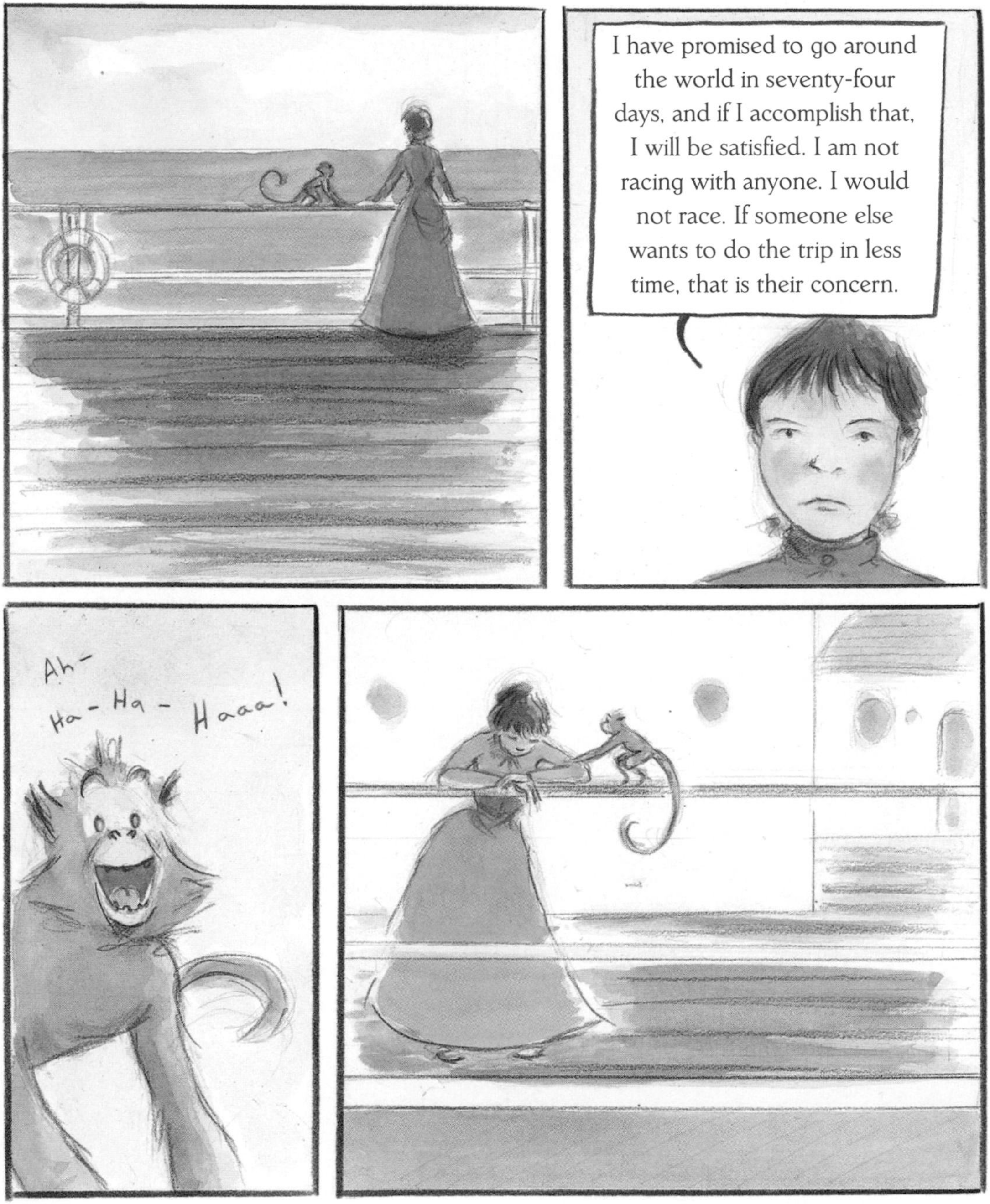
I have promised to go around the world in seventy-four days, and if I accomplish that, I will be satisfied. I am not racing with anyone. I would not race. If someone else wants to do the trip in less time, that is their concern.
Ah-Ha-Ha-Haaa!

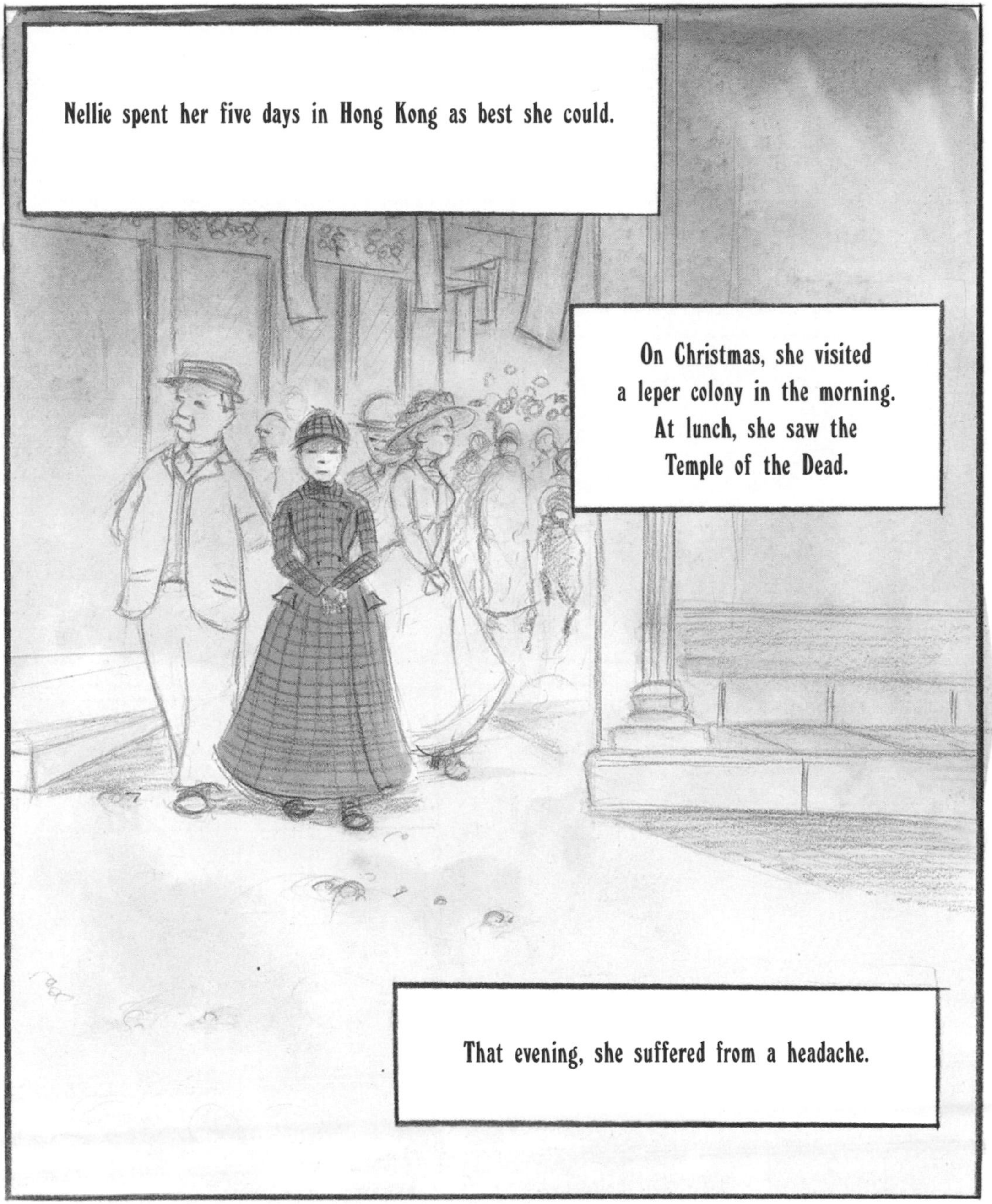
Nellie spent her five days in Hong Kong as best she could.
On Christmas, she visited a leper colony in the morning. At lunch, she saw the Temple of the Dead.
That evening, she suffered from a headache.

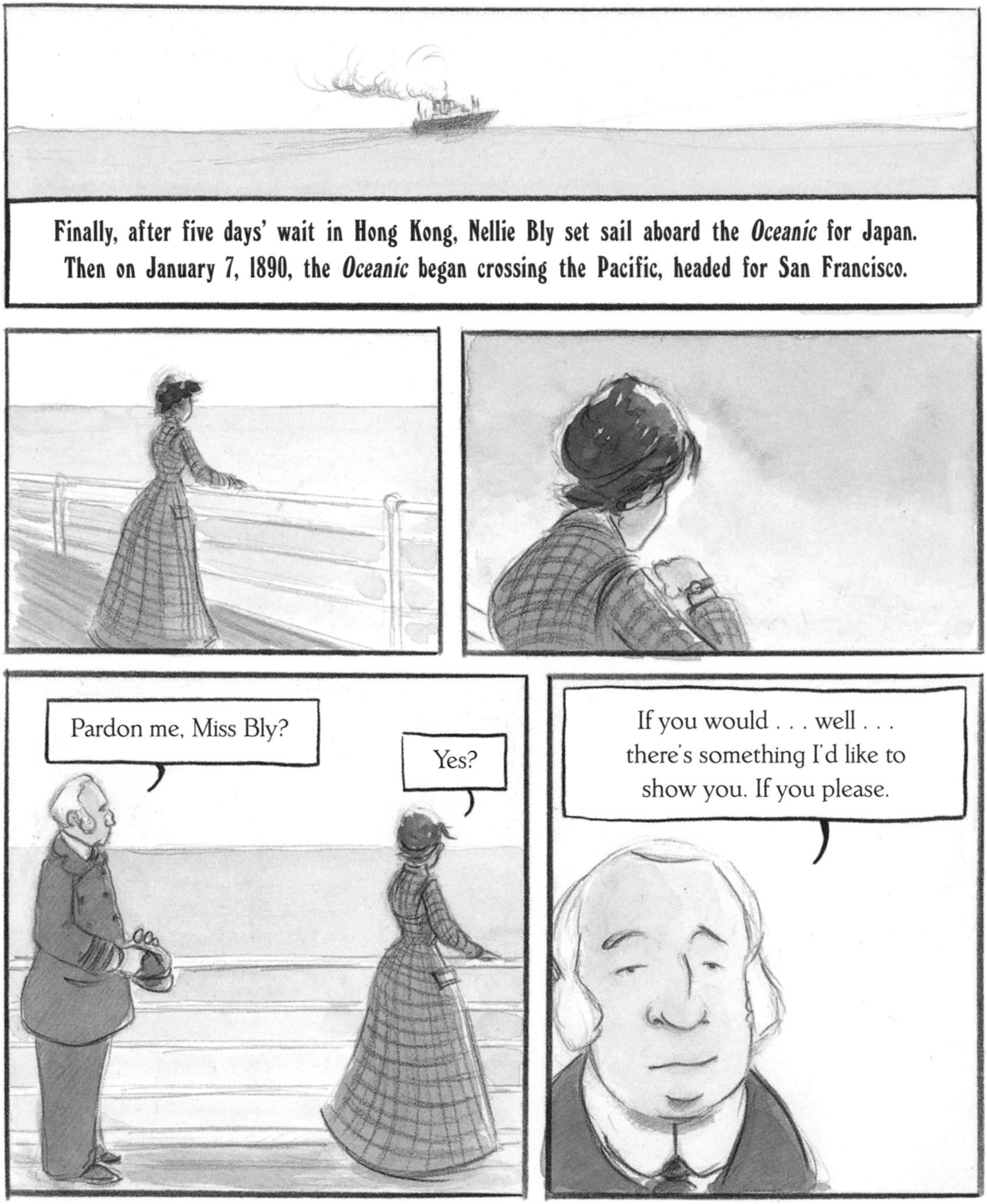
Finally, after five days' wait in Hong Kong, Nellie Bly set sail aboard the *Oceanic* for Japan. Then on January 7, 1890, the *Oceanic* began crossing the Pacific, headed for San Francisco.
Pardon me, Miss Bly?
Yes?
If you would . . . well . . . there's something I'd like to show you. If you please.

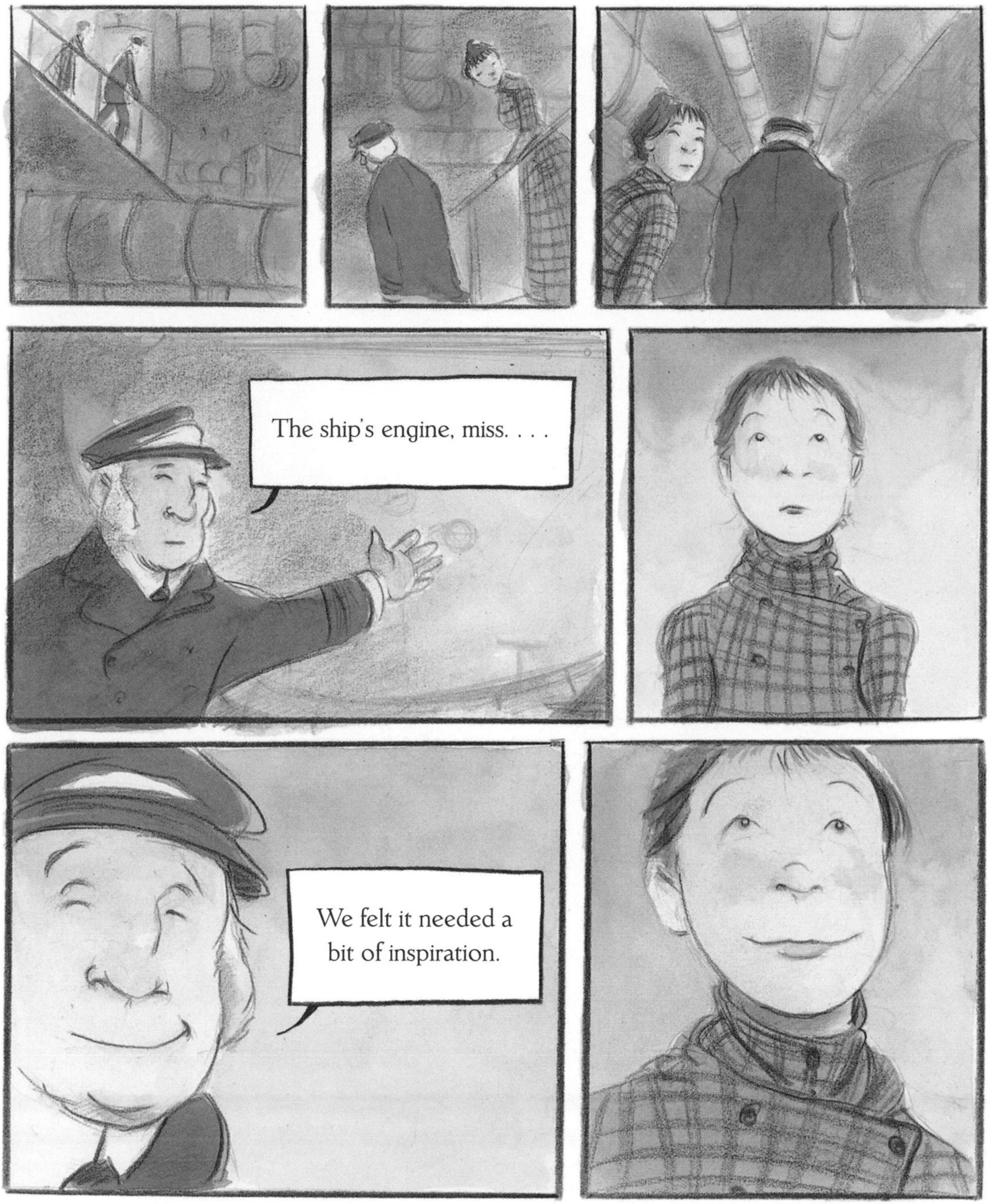
The ship's engine, miss. . . .
We felt it needed a bit of inspiration.

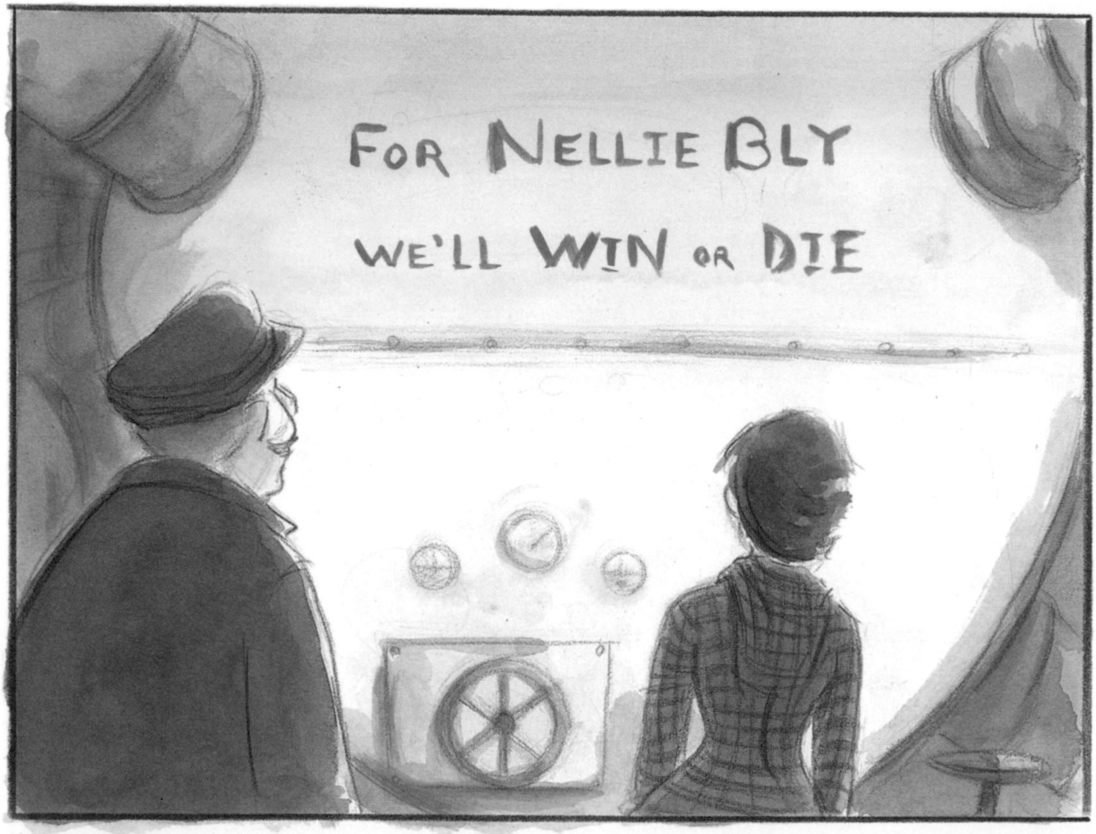
FOR NELLIE BLY
WE'LL WIN OR DIE

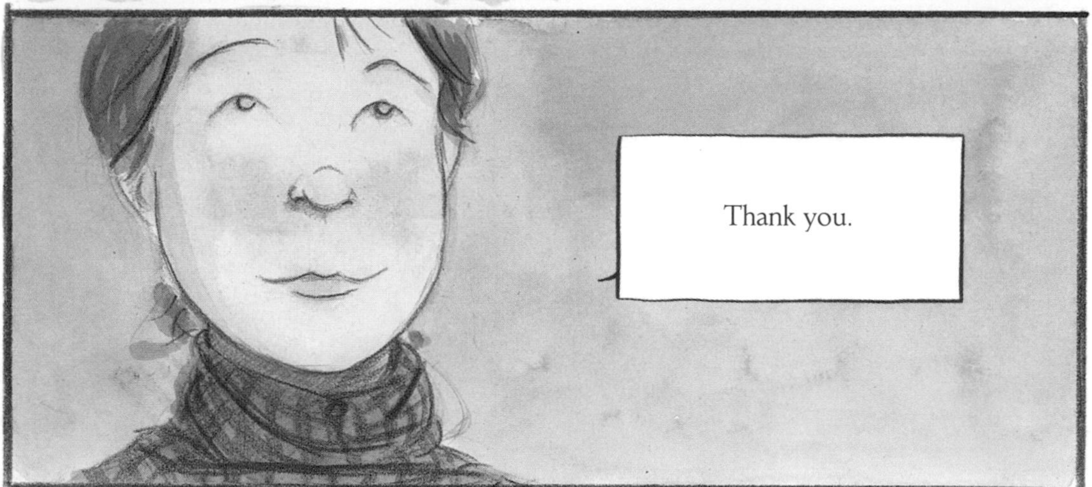
Thank you.

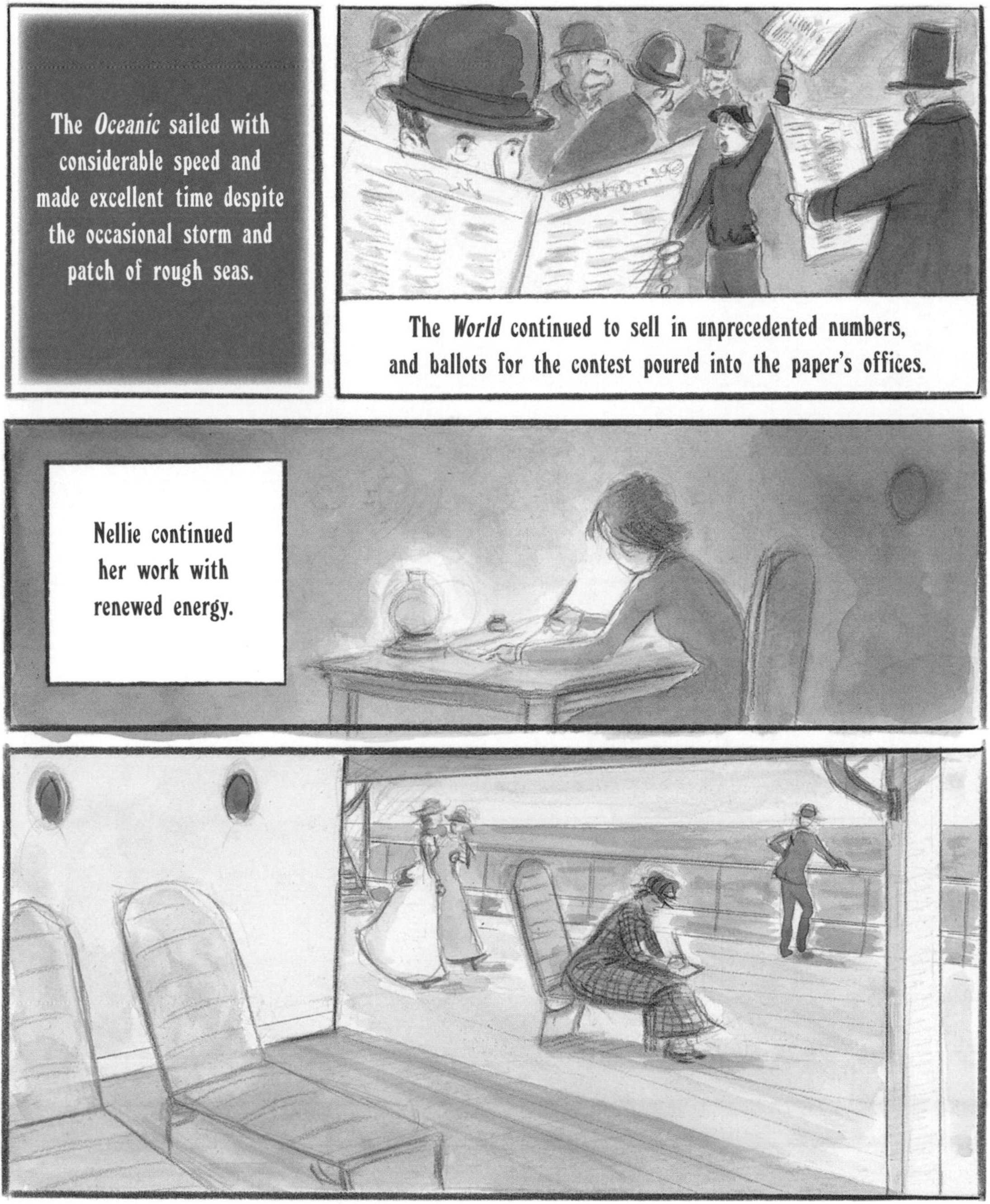
The *Oceanic* sailed with considerable speed and made excellent time despite the occasional storm and patch of rough seas.
The *World* continued to sell in unprecedented numbers, and ballots for the contest poured into the paper's offices.
Nellie continued her work with renewed energy.

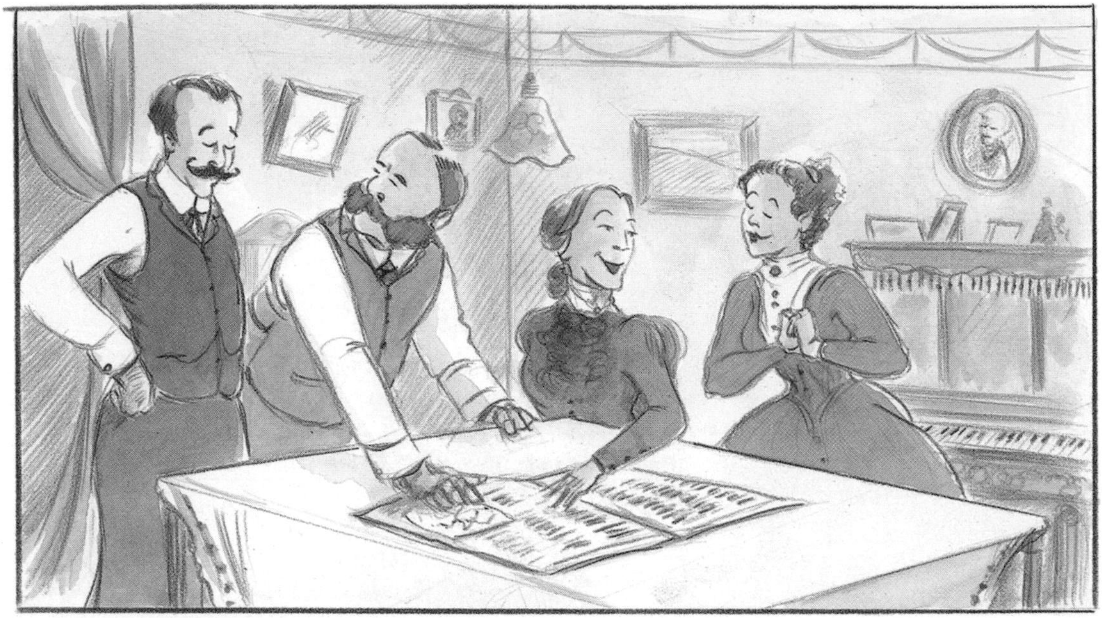

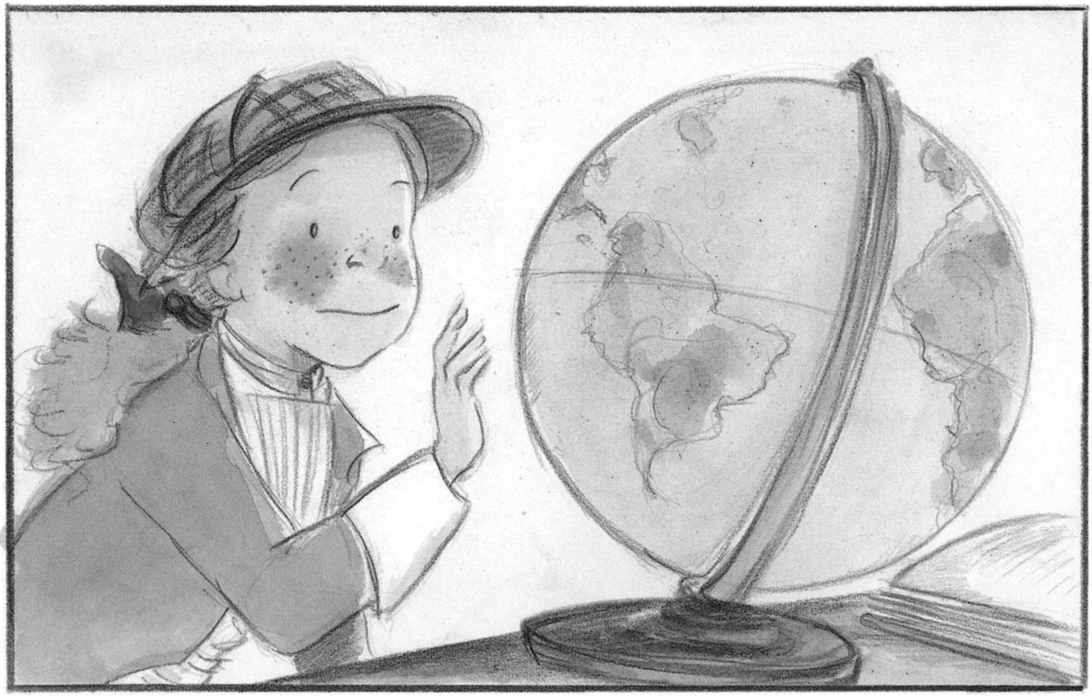

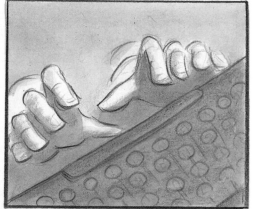

Her grit has been more than masculine. Her perseverance has been more than rare Ben Jonson ever counselled or Philosopher Ben Franklin ever practiced. She is coming home to dear old America with the scalps of the carpers and critics strung on her slender girdle, and about her head a monster wreath of laurel and forget-me-nots, as a tribute to American pluck, American womanhood and American perseverance.

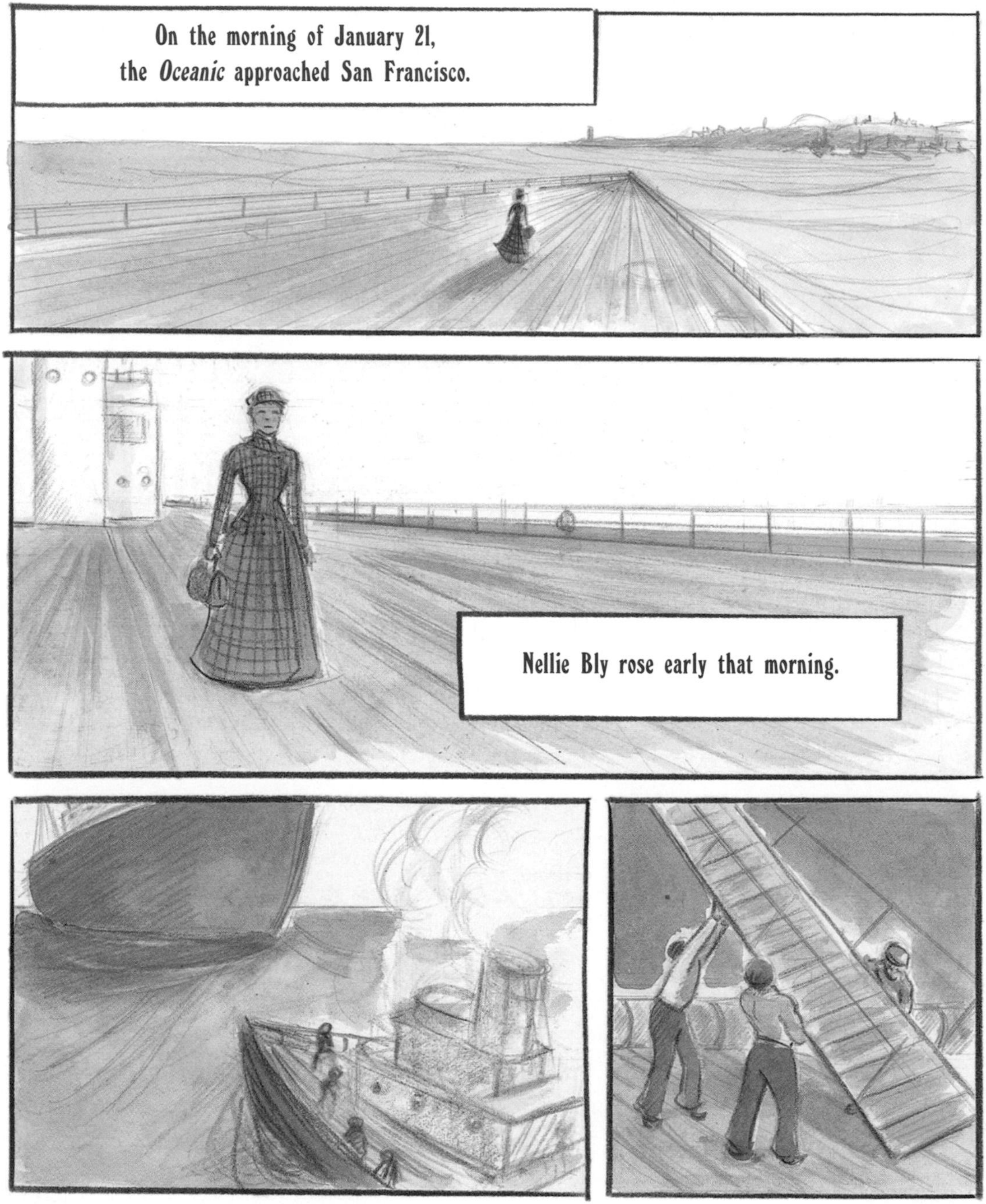
On the morning of January 21,
the *Oceanic* approached San Francisco.
Nellie Bly rose early that morning.

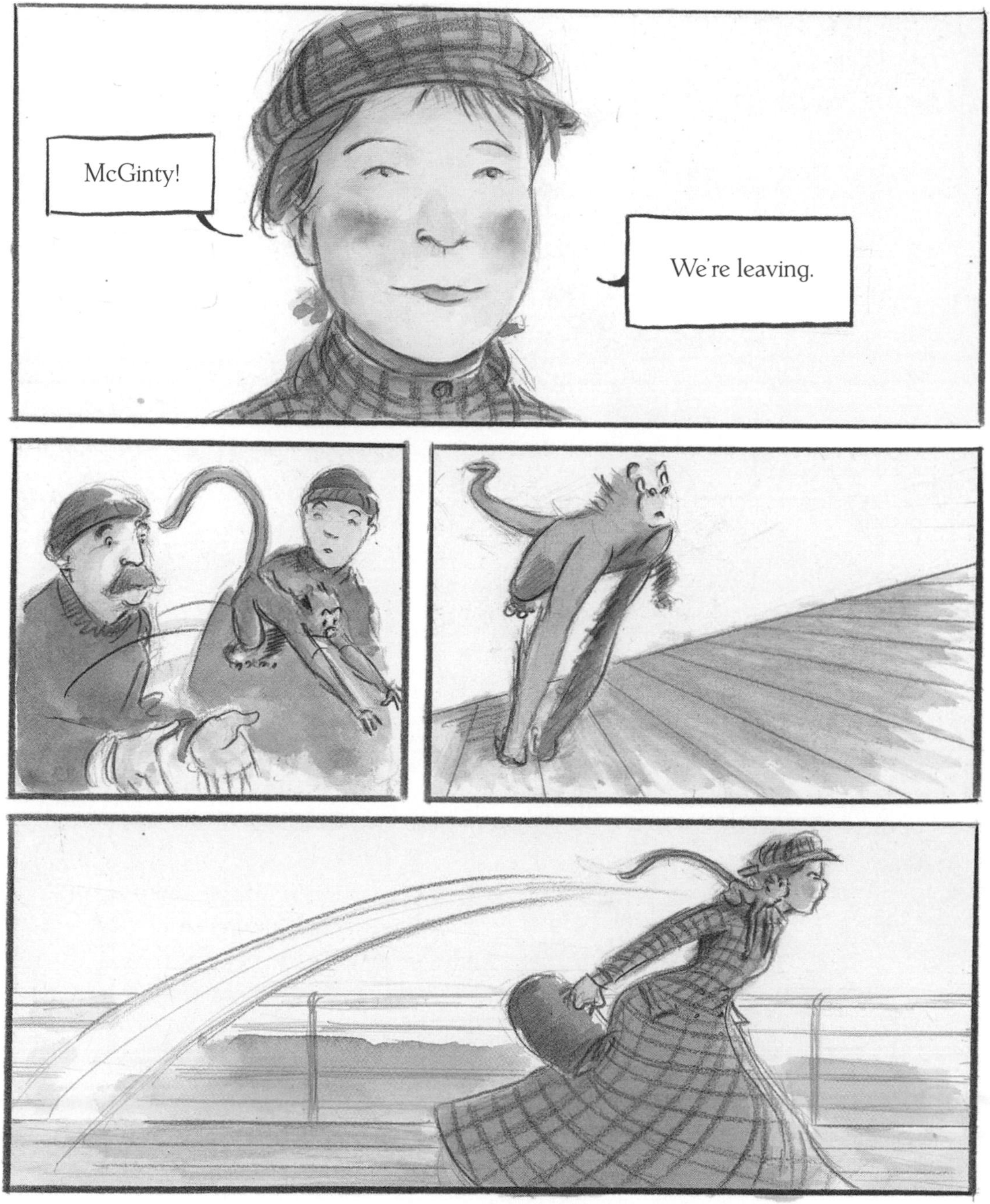
McGinty!
We're leaving.

Miss Bly, I'm from the *San Francisco Chronicle*.

A fine paper.

Yes. Thank you.

It's quite extraordinary what you've done.

Oh, I don't know. It's not so very much for a woman to do who has the pluck, energy, and independence which characterizes many women in this day of push and get-there.

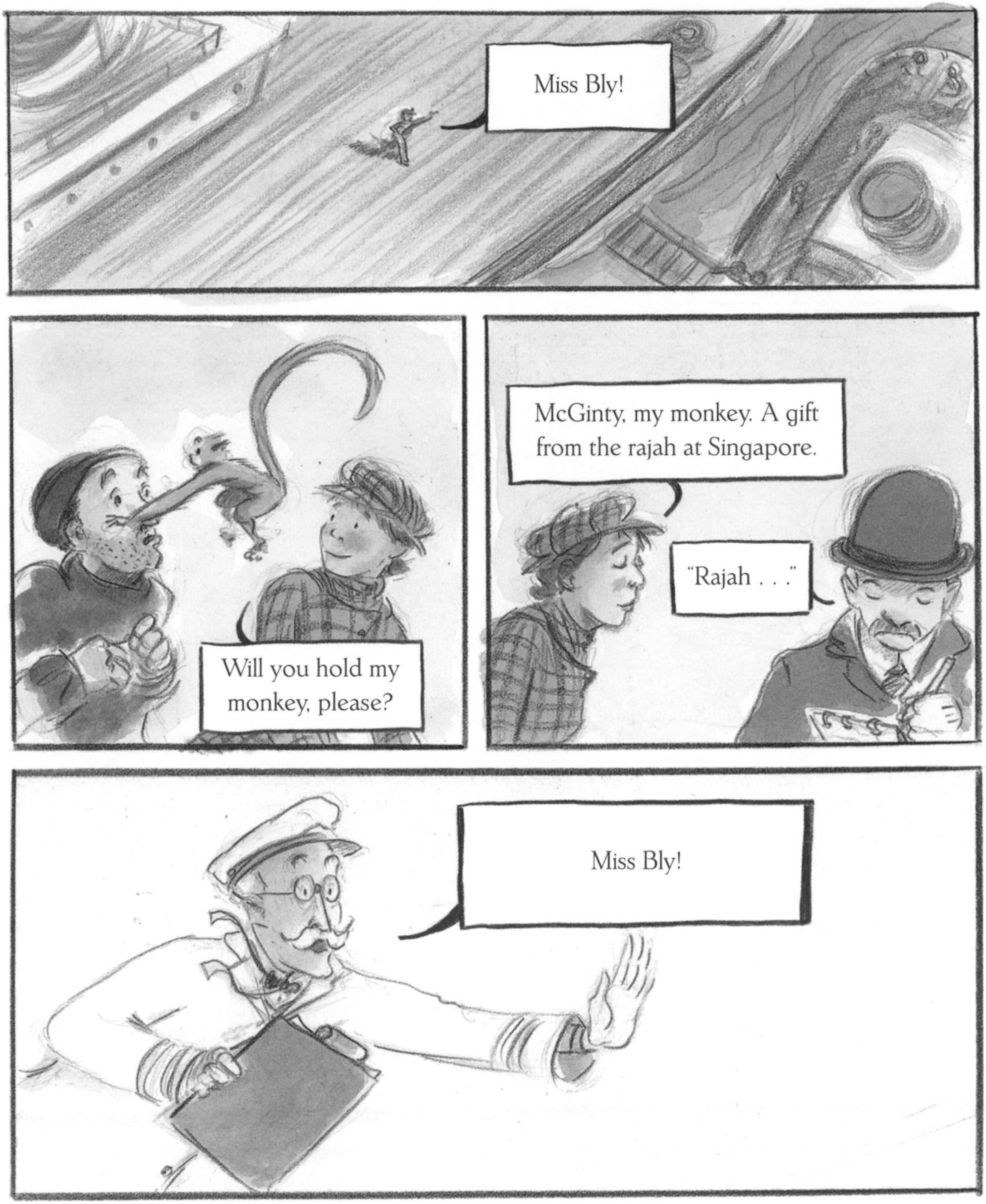
Miss Bly!
Will you hold my monkey, please?
McGinty, my monkey. A gift from the rajah at Singapore.
"Rajah . . ."
Miss Bly!

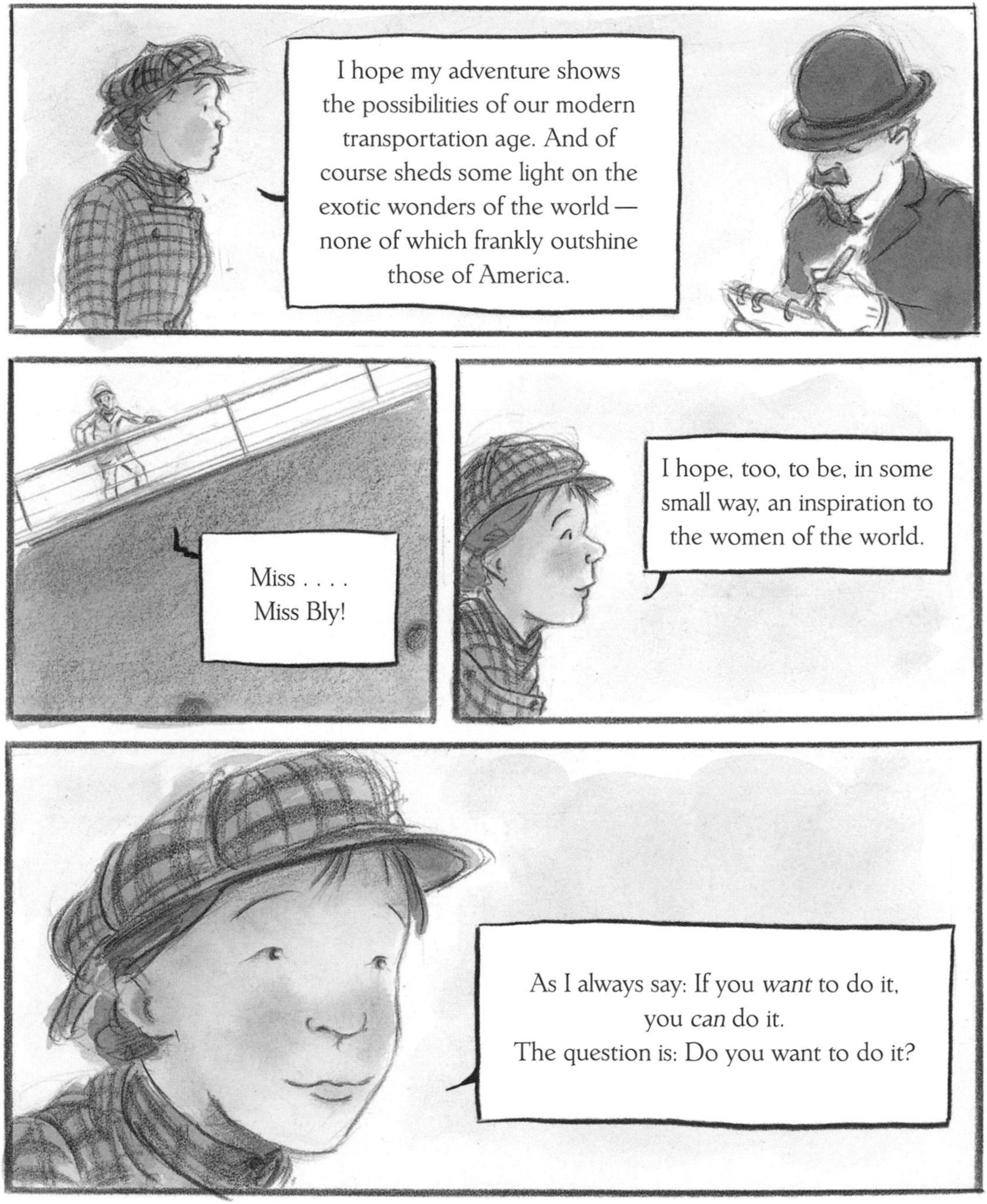
I hope my adventure shows the possibilities of our modern transportation age. And of course sheds some light on the exotic wonders of the world — none of which frankly outshine those of America.
Miss . . . .
Miss Bly!
I hope, too, to be, in some small way, an inspiration to the women of the world.
As I always say: If you *want* to do it, you *can* do it.
The question is: Do you want to do it?

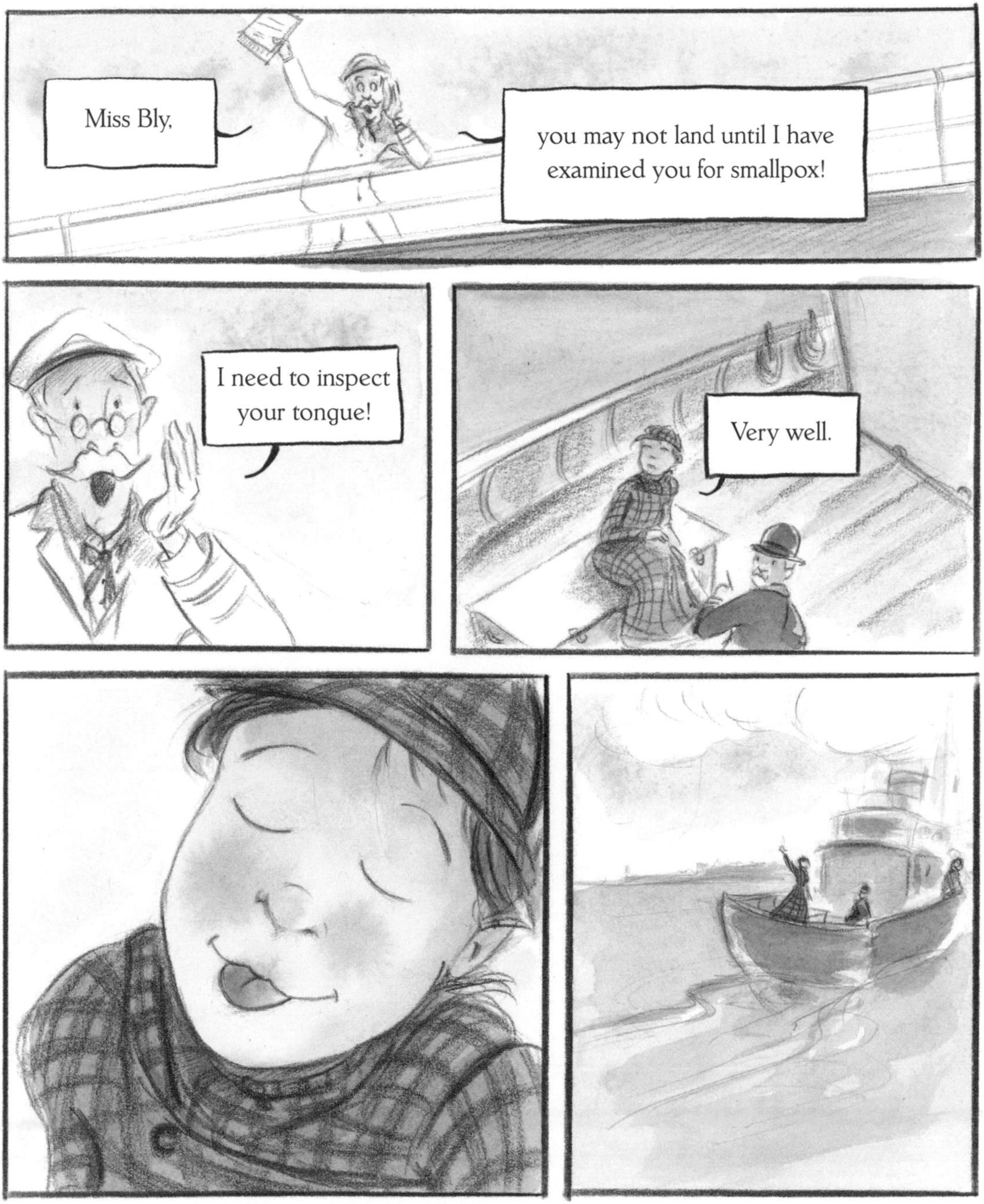
Miss Bly,
you may not land until I have examined you for smallpox!
I need to inspect your tongue!
Very well.

The *World* had arranged for a special train car to whisk
Nellie Bly from California to New York.
Her passage was swift and uneventful, and she was met by
cheering crowds in every town she passed through.

Elizabeth Bisland, rival reporter from *Cosmopolitan,* encountered
several setbacks and delays between Hong Kong and Aden.
A particularly slow boat ended her chances of swiftly crossing the Atlantic.

Nellie Bly reached her destination at 3:51 p.m. on January 25, 1890.
She was met by a roaring crowd of well-wishers.
Her journey lasted seventy-two days, six hours, eleven minutes, and fourteen seconds.

She was two days ahead of schedule.

EPILOGUE

Although her famous journey sold more papers than the *World* had ever sold, Nellie Bly received very little in return. Joseph Pulitzer, owner of the paper, offered a simple "Congratulations." Her editors said even less. She had expected, and rightly so, a raise or even a bonus for her feat, but neither was given.

Nellie Bly resigned from the *New York World* and vowed never to return. In August 1890, she published *Nellie Bly's Book: Around the World in Seventy-two Days.* It was an instant bestseller and brought the intrepid Nellie Bly fortune as well as increased fame.

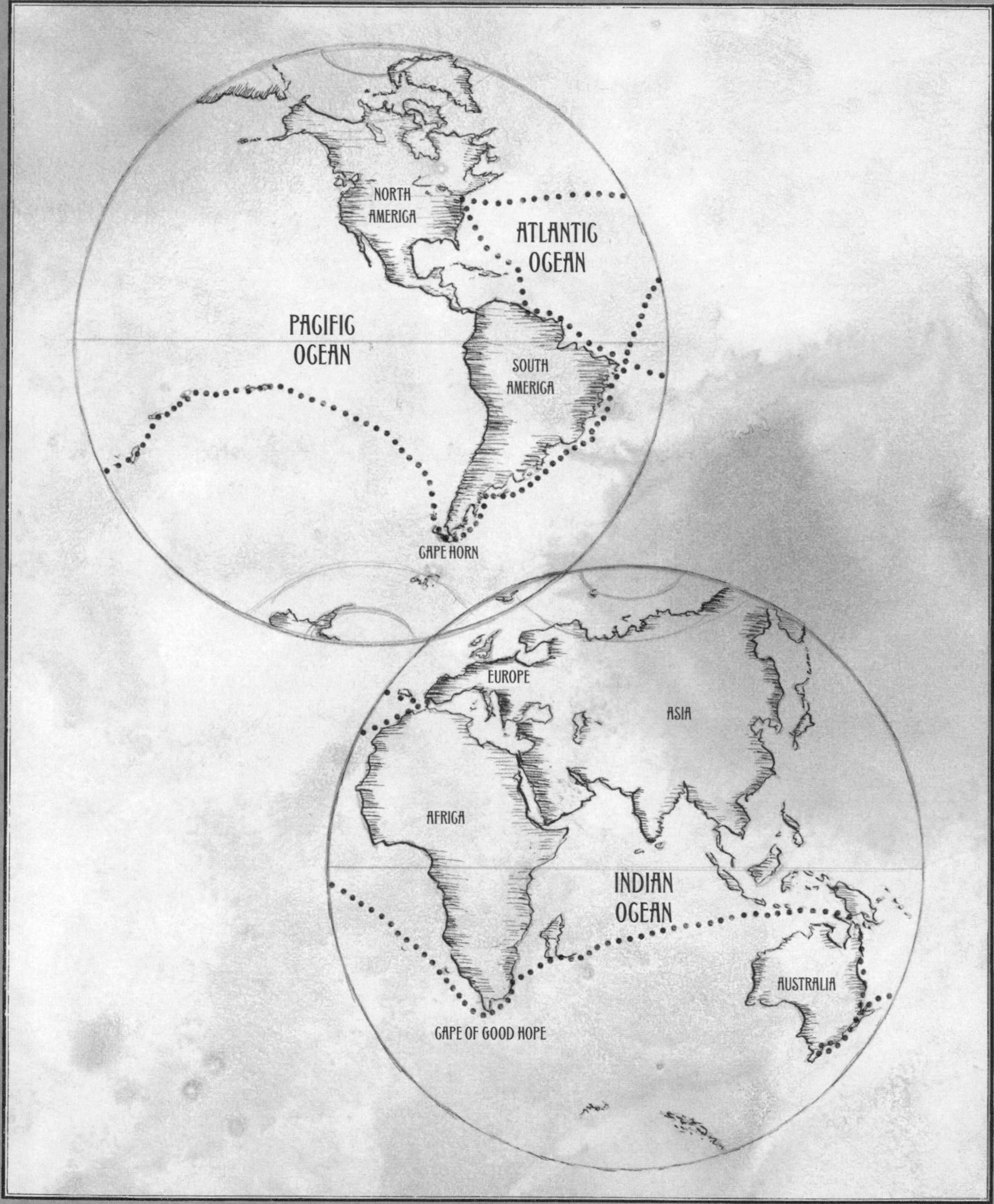
NORTH AMERICA
ATLANTIC OCEAN
PACIFIC OCEAN
SOUTH AMERICA
CAPE HORN
EUROPE
ASIA
AFRICA
INDIAN OCEAN
AUSTRALIA
CAPE OF GOOD HOPE

THE JOURNEY OF

# JOSHUA SLOCUM

*Mariner*

1895

*I will only say that I have endeavored to tell
just the story of the adventure itself.*
— *Joshua Slocum*

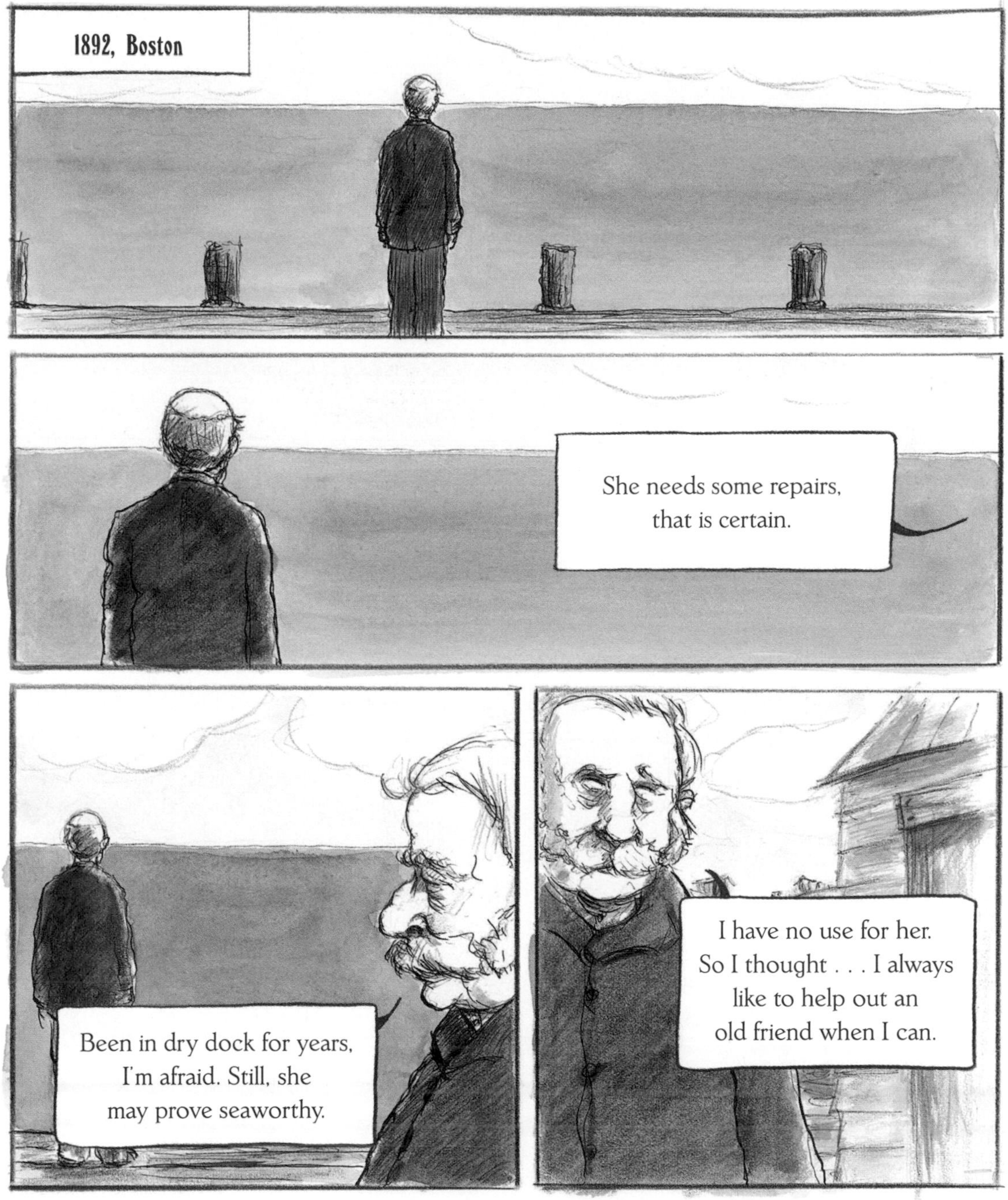
1892, Boston
She needs some repairs, that is certain.
Been in dry dock for years, I'm afraid. Still, she may prove seaworthy.
I have no use for her. So I thought . . . I always like to help out an old friend when I can.

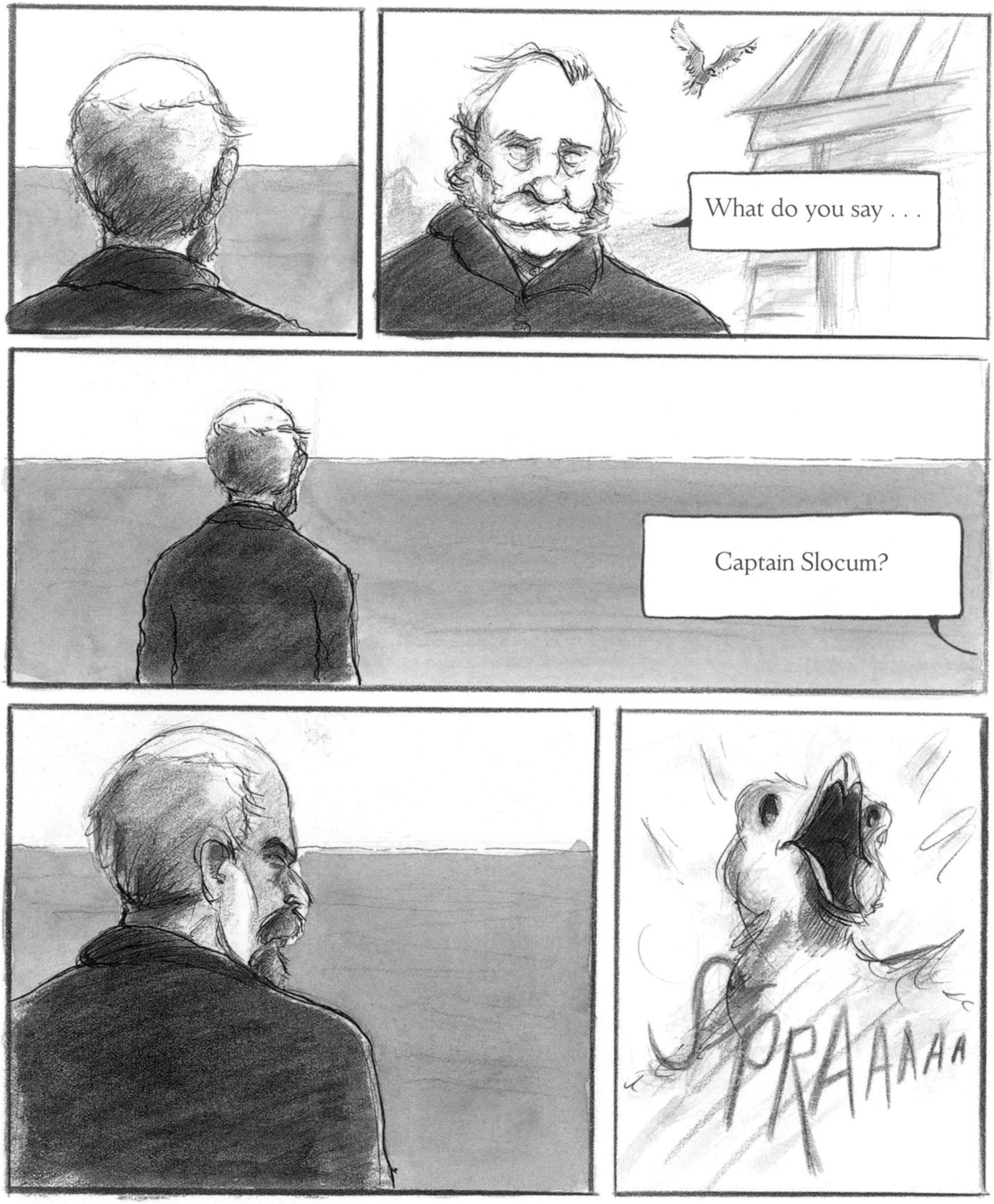
What do you say . . .
Captain Slocum?
SPRAAAA

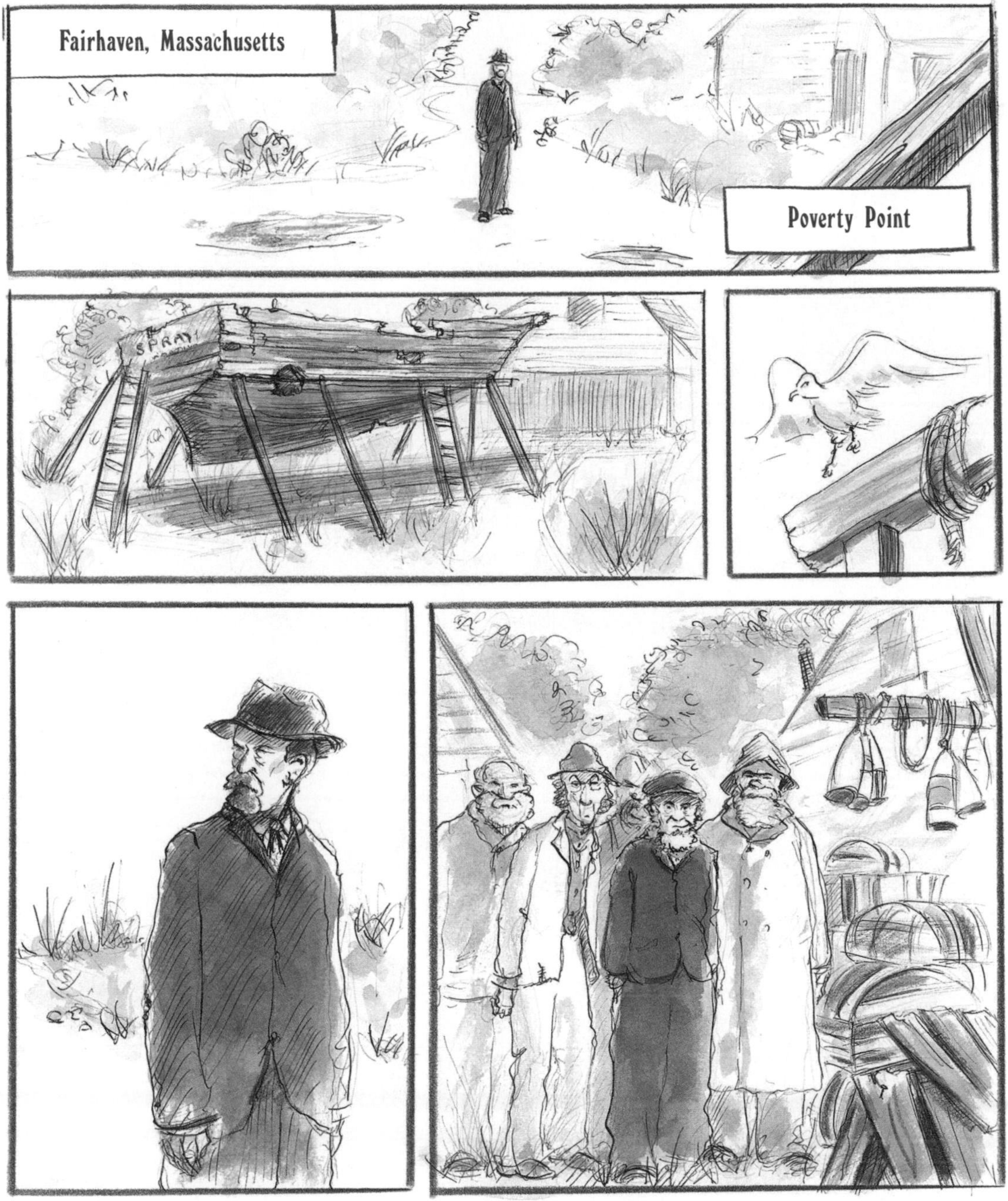
Fairhaven, Massachusetts
Poverty Point
SPRAY

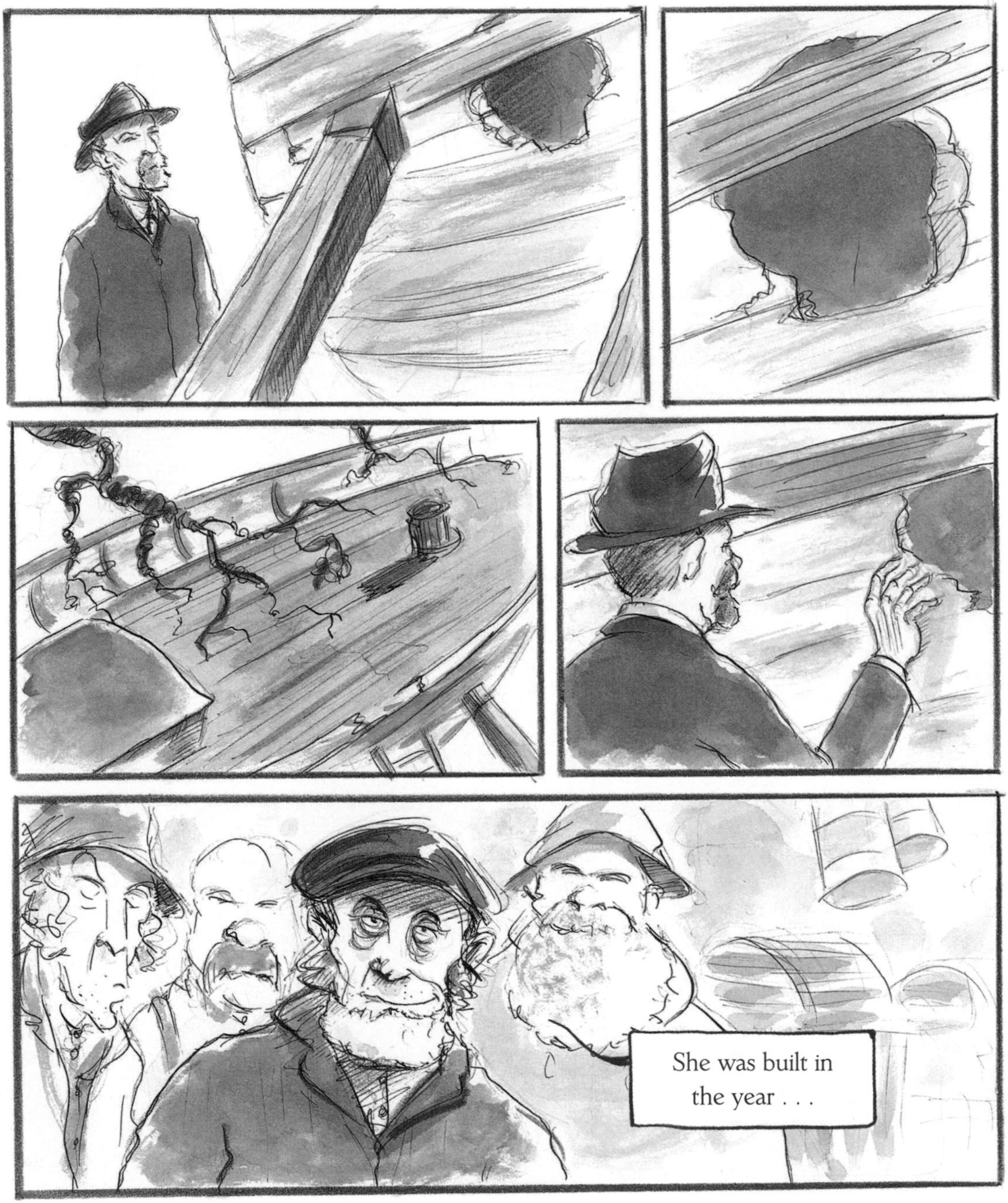
She was built in the year . . .

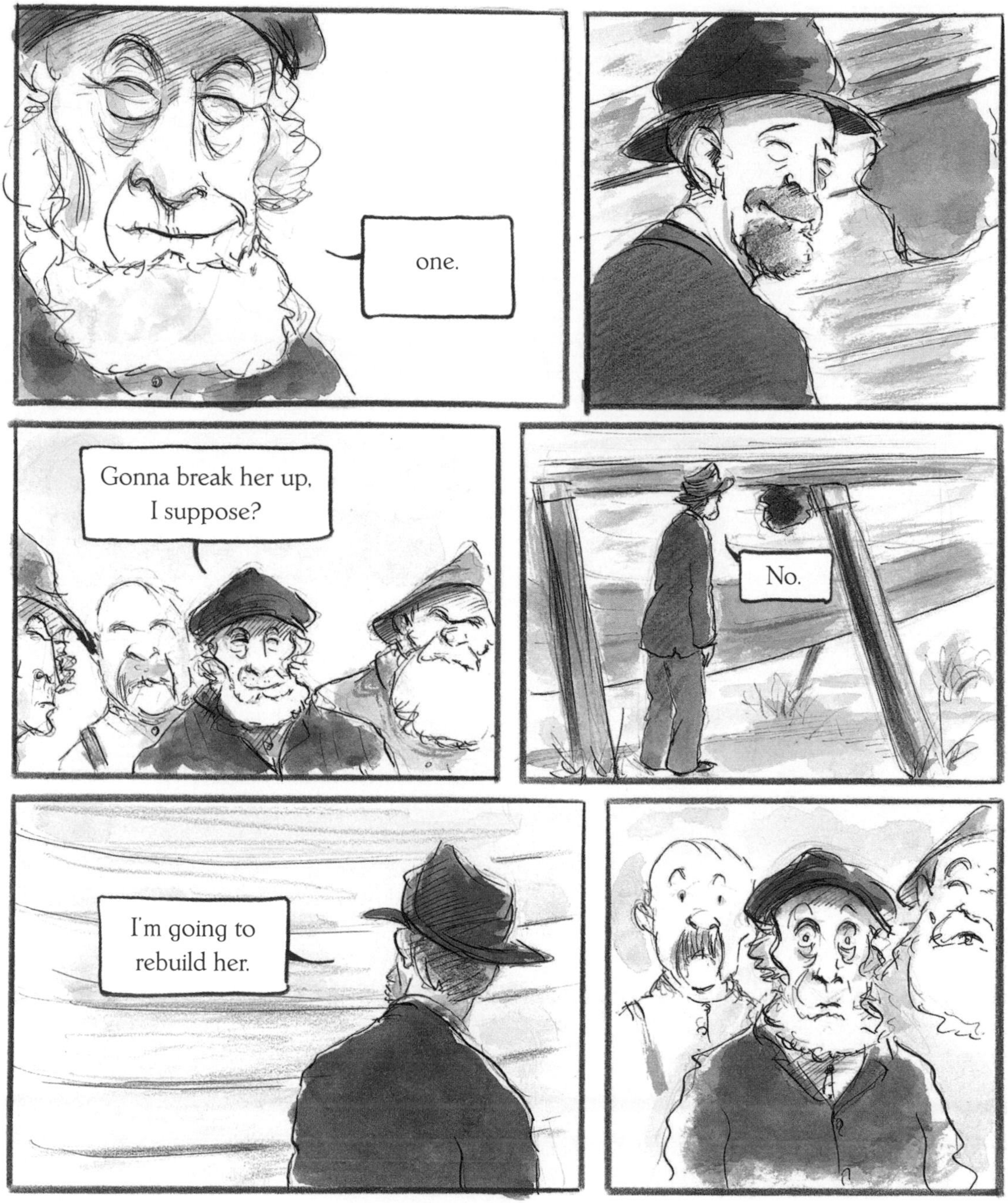
one.
Gonna break her up, I suppose?
No.
I'm going to rebuild her.

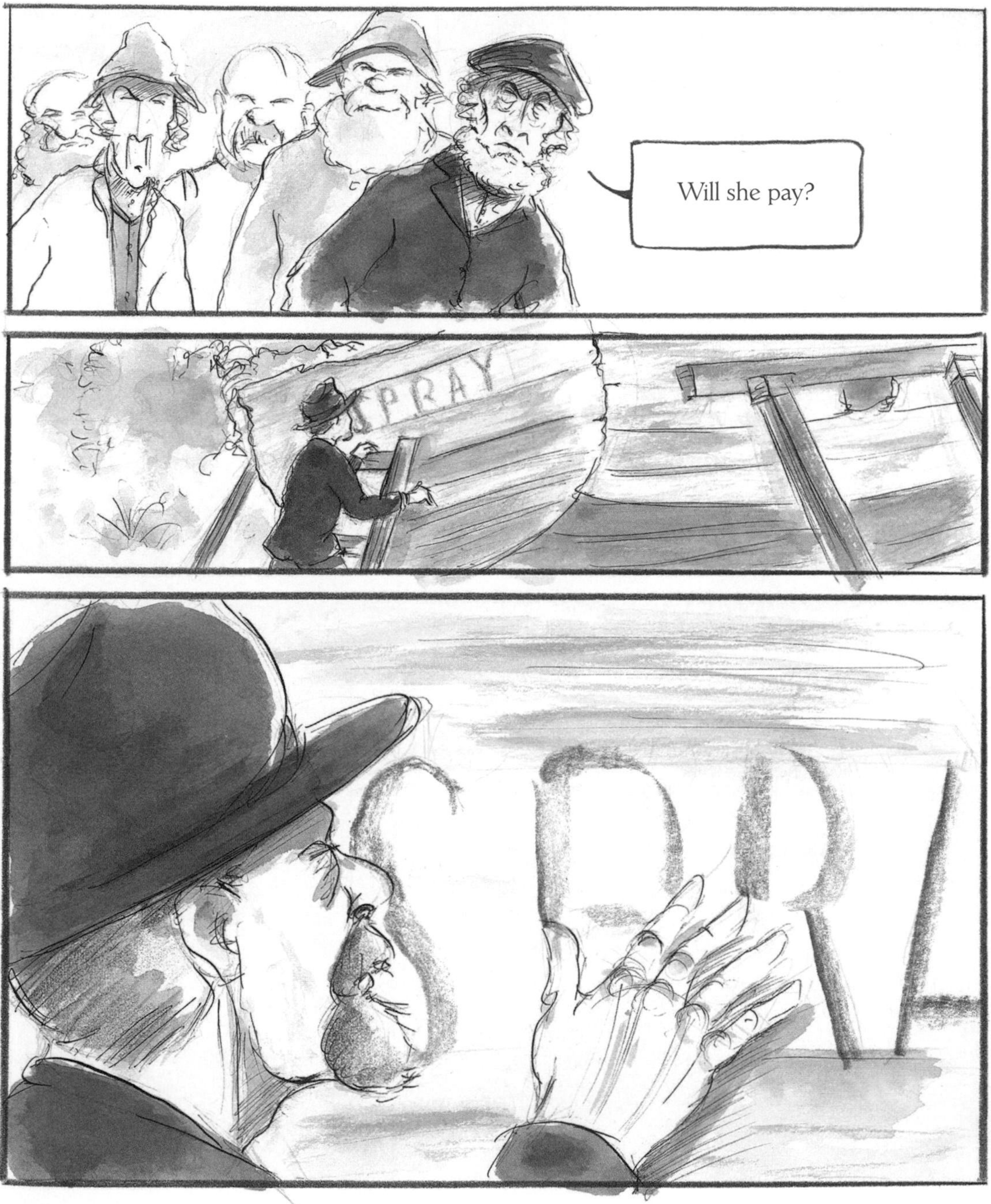
Will she pay?
SPRAY

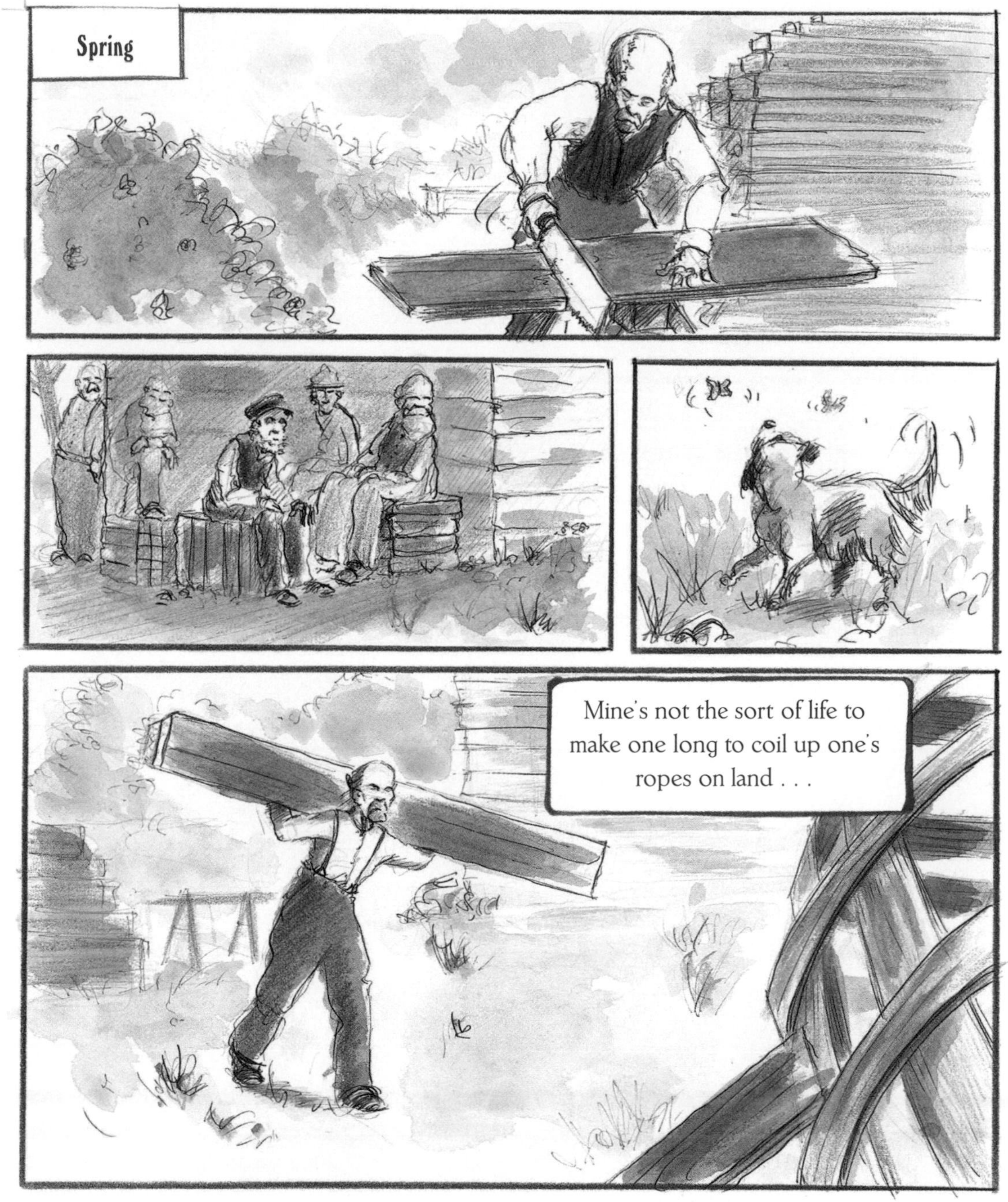
Spring
Mine's not the sort of life to make one long to coil up one's ropes on land . . .

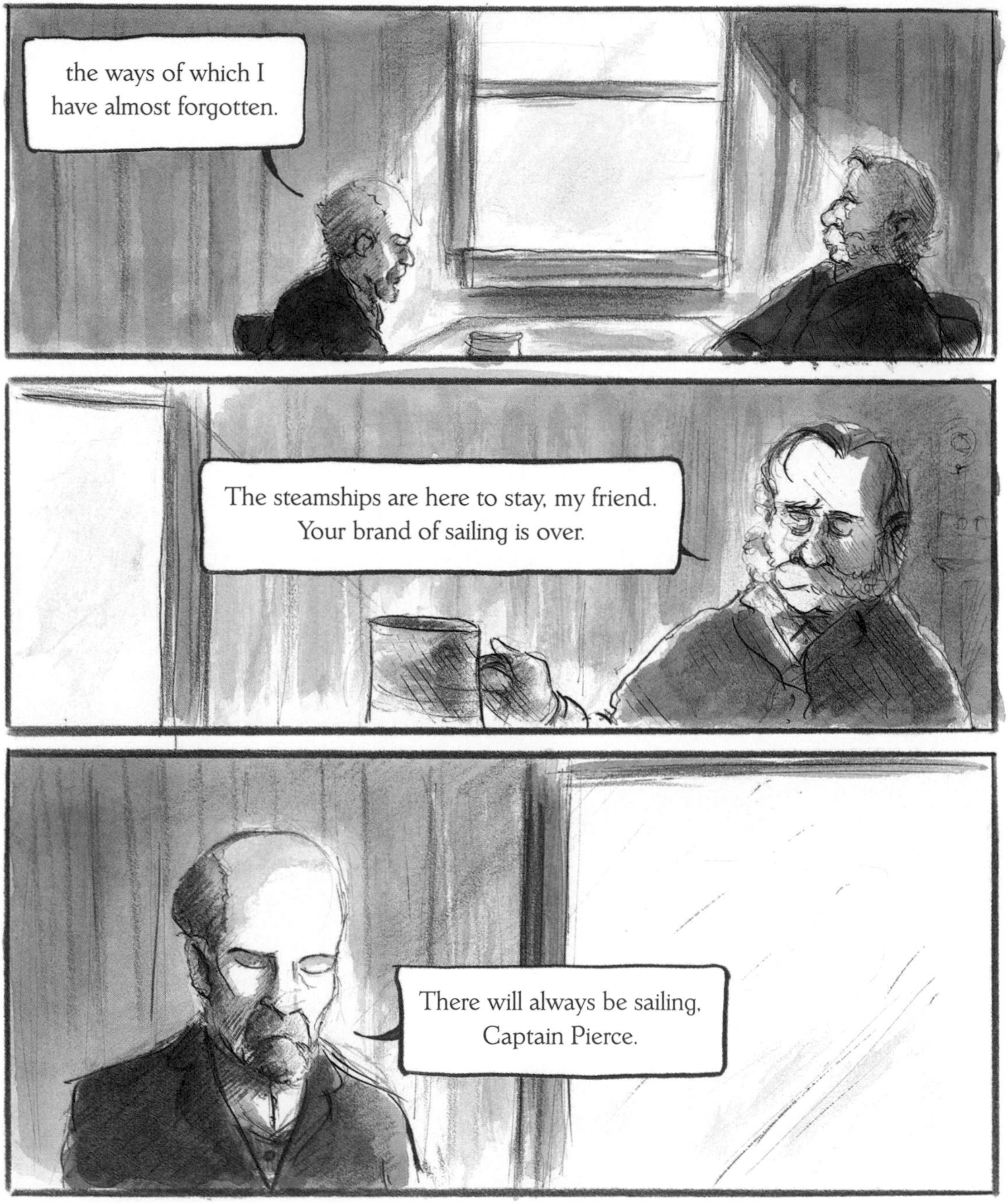
the ways of which I have almost forgotten.
The steamships are here to stay, my friend. Your brand of sailing is over.
There will always be sailing, Captain Pierce.

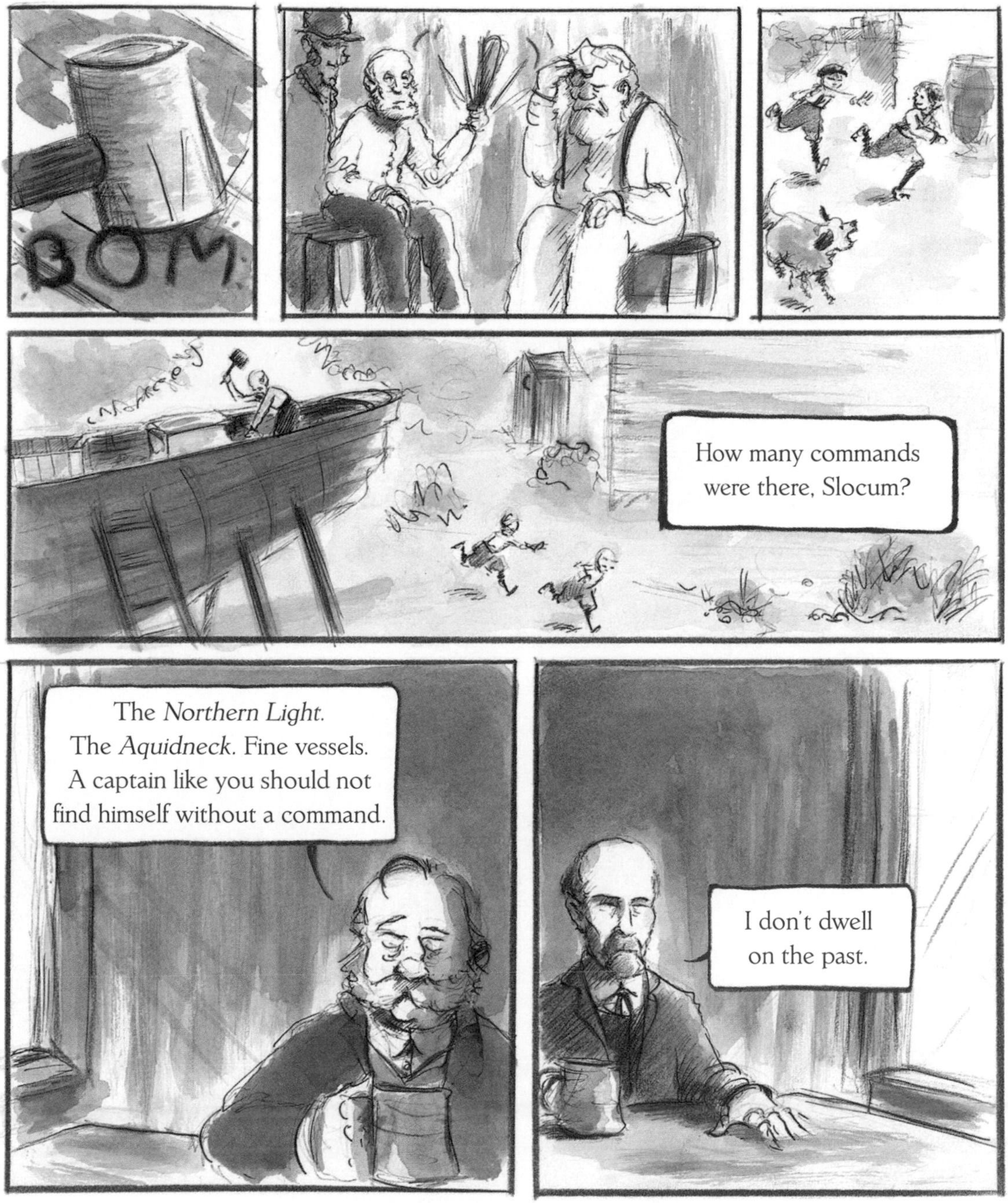
BOM
How many commands were there, Slocum?
The *Northern Light*. The *Aquidneck*. Fine vessels. A captain like you should not find himself without a command.
I don't dwell on the past.

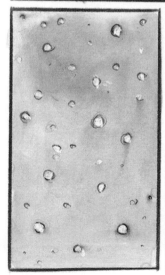

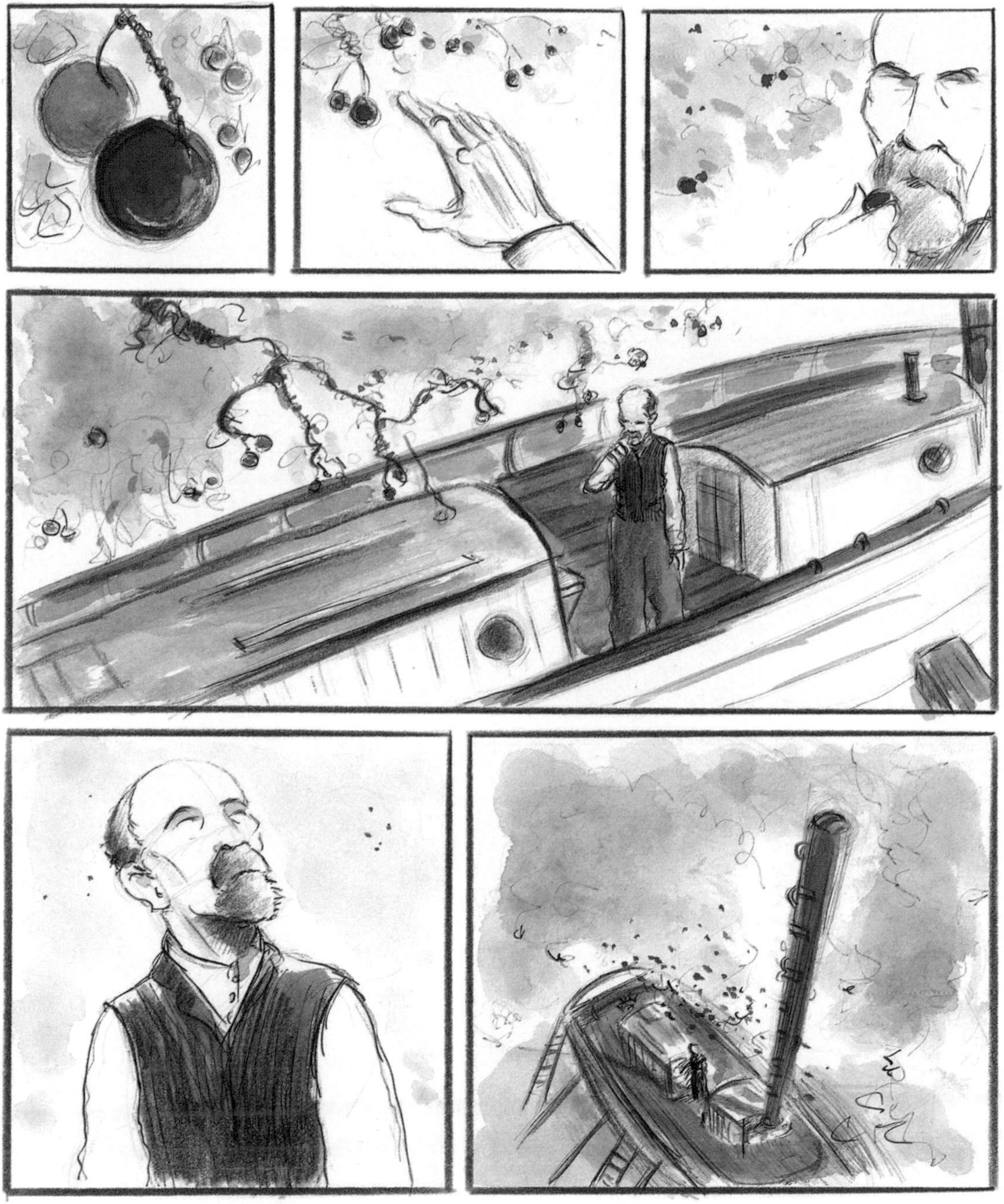

I suppose she might make it to Gloucester.

I was thinking of sailing her around the world.

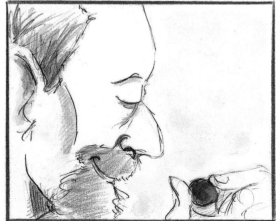

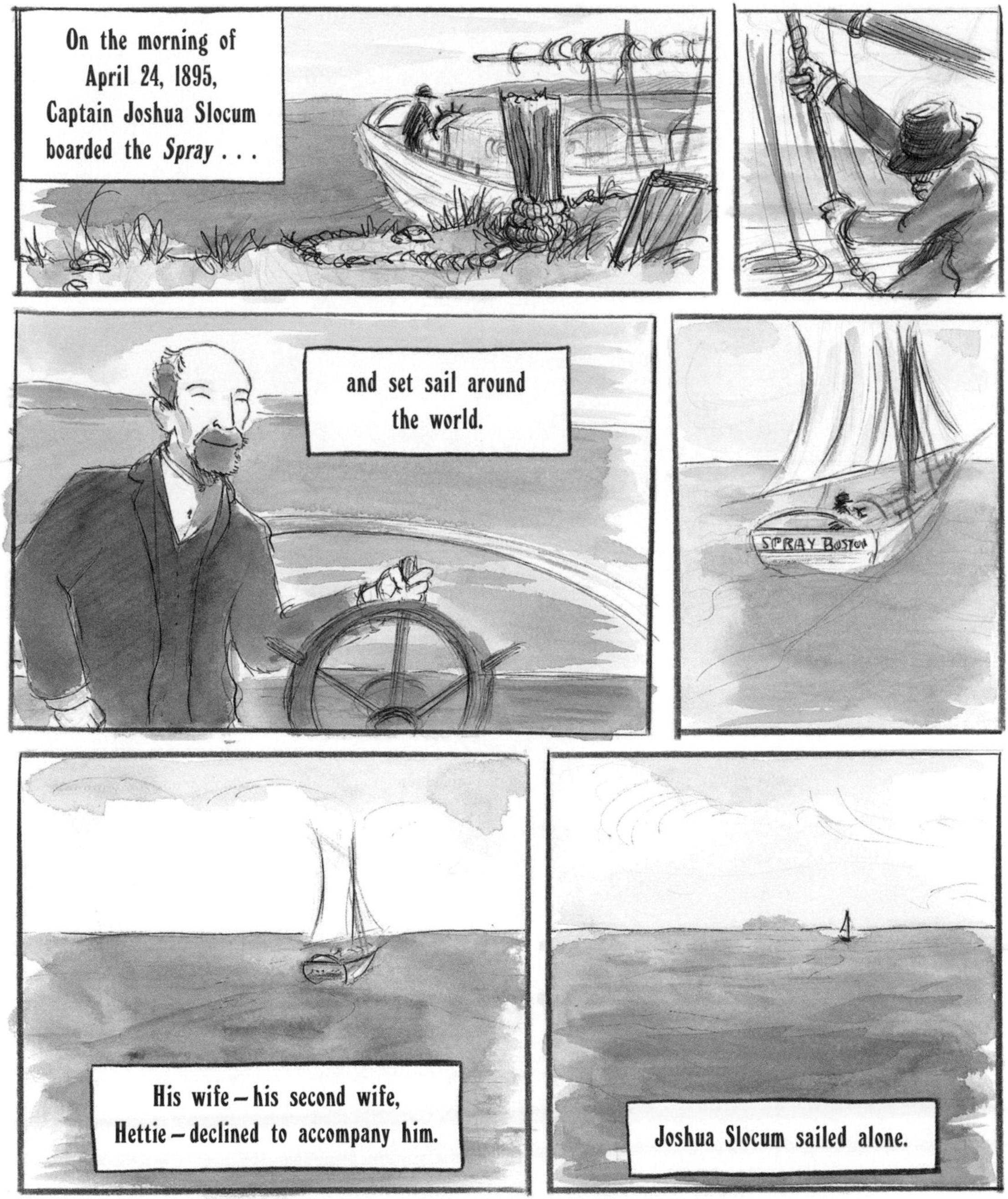
On the morning of April 24, 1895, Captain Joshua Slocum boarded the *Spray* . . .
and set sail around the world.
SPRAY BOSTON
His wife – his second wife, Hettie – declined to accompany him.
Joshua Slocum sailed alone.

The *Spray* measured thirty-six feet nine inches in length.
It was fourteen feet two inches wide and four feet deep in the hold.
The cabins rose above deck, allowing for ample headroom when below.

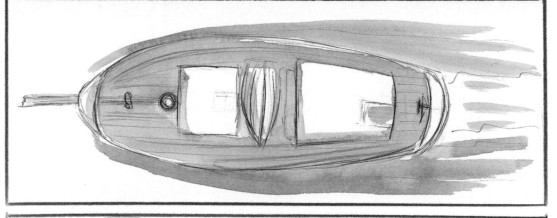

The captain's quarters were snug (ten feet by twelve feet) and comfortable.

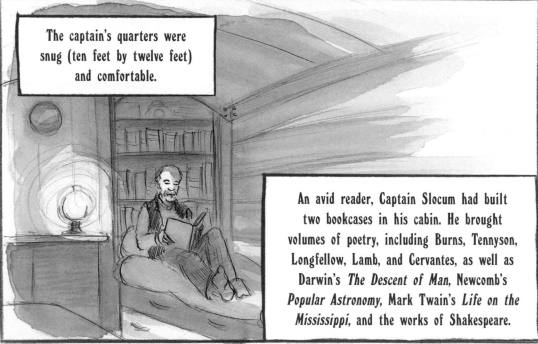

An avid reader, Captain Slocum had built two bookcases in his cabin. He brought volumes of poetry, including Burns, Tennyson, Longfellow, Lamb, and Cervantes, as well as Darwin's *The Descent of Man*, Newcomb's *Popular Astronomy*, Mark Twain's *Life on the Mississippi*, and the works of Shakespeare.

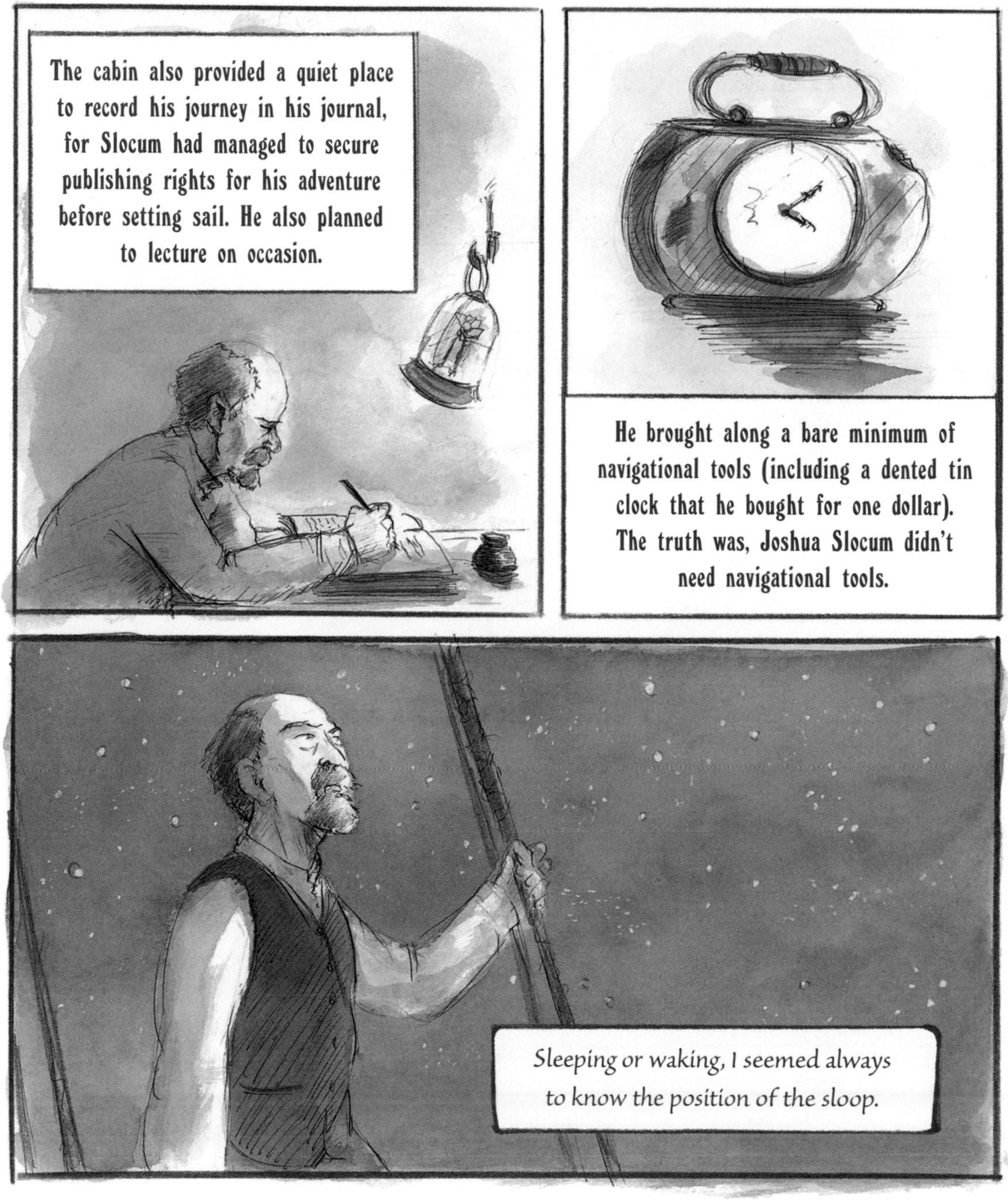
The cabin also provided a quiet place to record his journey in his journal, for Slocum had managed to secure publishing rights for his adventure before setting sail. He also planned to lecture on occasion.
He brought along a bare minimum of navigational tools (including a dented tin clock that he bought for one dollar). The truth was, Joshua Slocum didn't need navigational tools.
Sleeping or waking, I seemed always to know the position of the sloop.

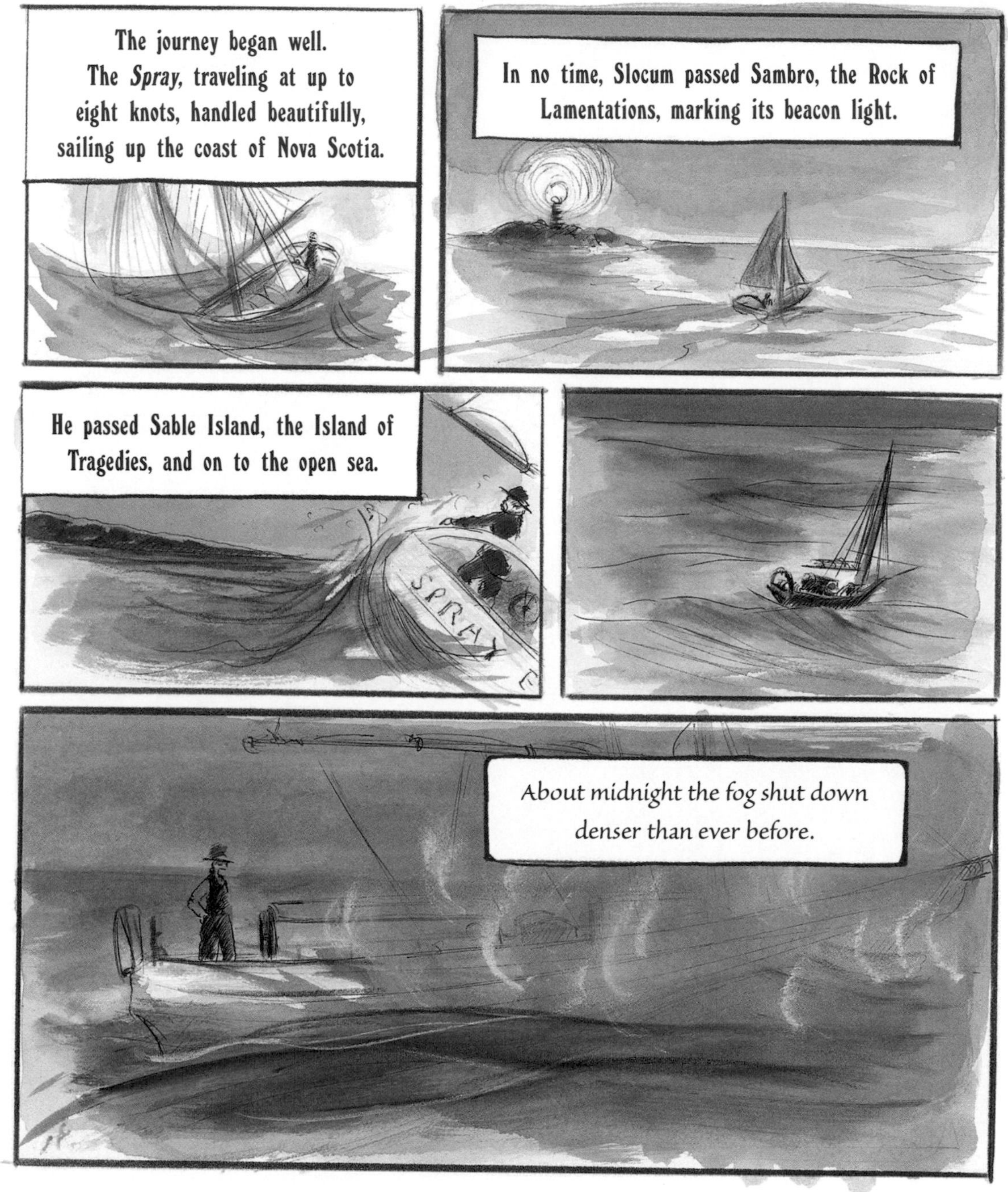
The journey began well. The *Spray,* traveling at up to eight knots, handled beautifully, sailing up the coast of Nova Scotia.
In no time, Slocum passed Sambro, the Rock of Lamentations, marking its beacon light.
He passed Sable Island, the Island of Tragedies, and on to the open sea.
About midnight the fog shut down denser than ever before.

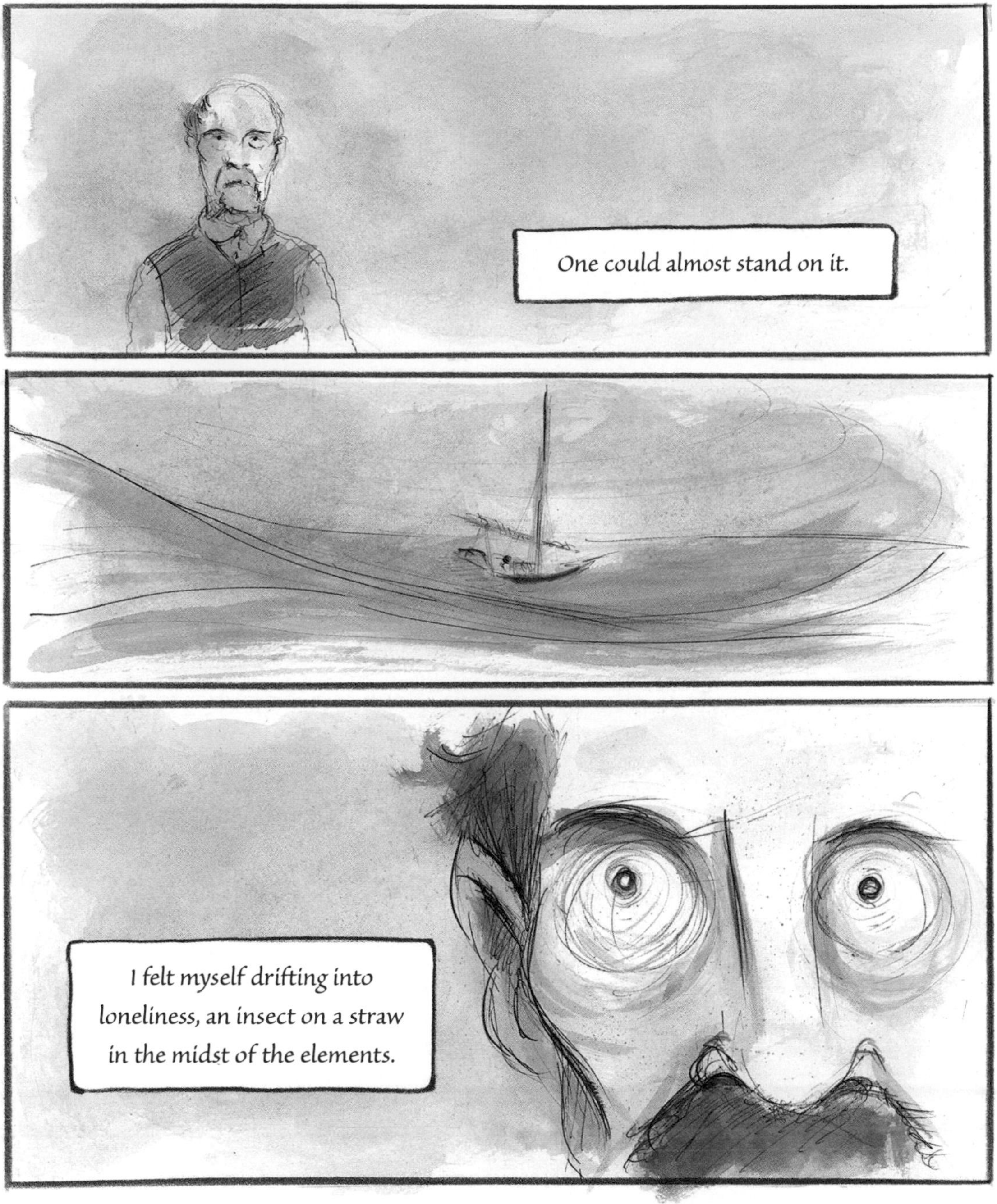
One could almost stand on it.
I felt myself drifting into loneliness, an insect on a straw in the midst of the elements.

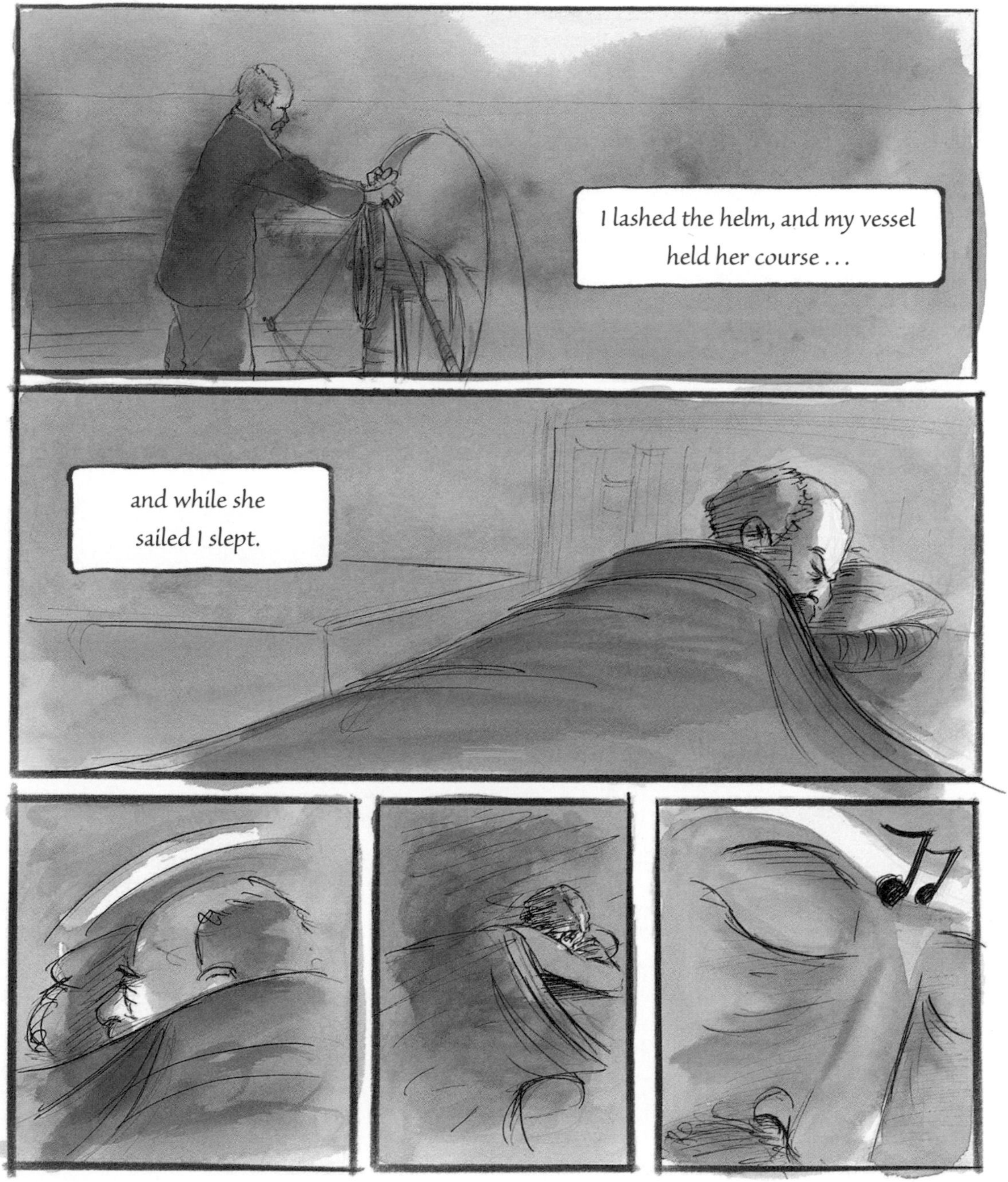
I lashed the helm, and my vessel held her course . . .
and while she sailed I slept.

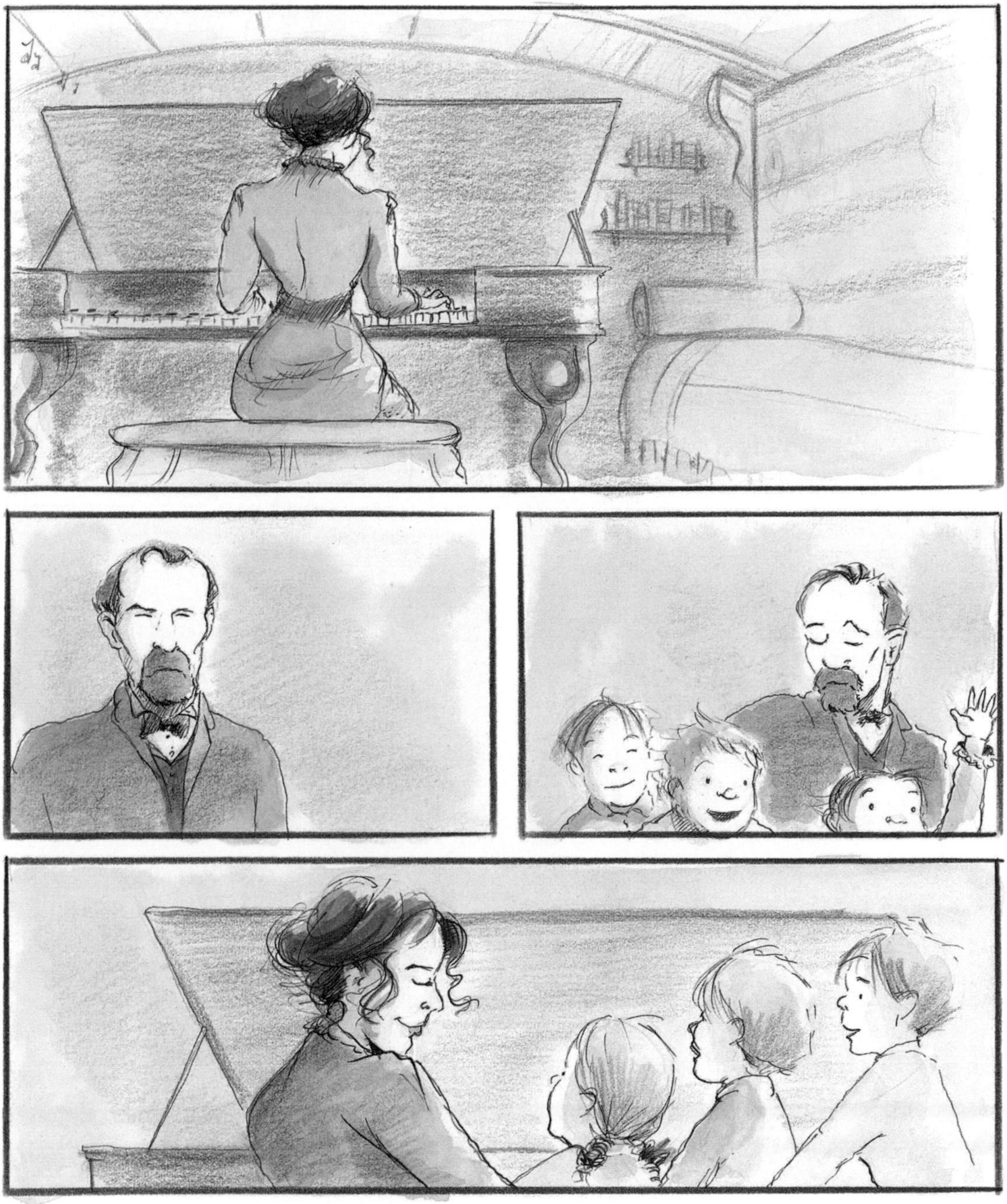

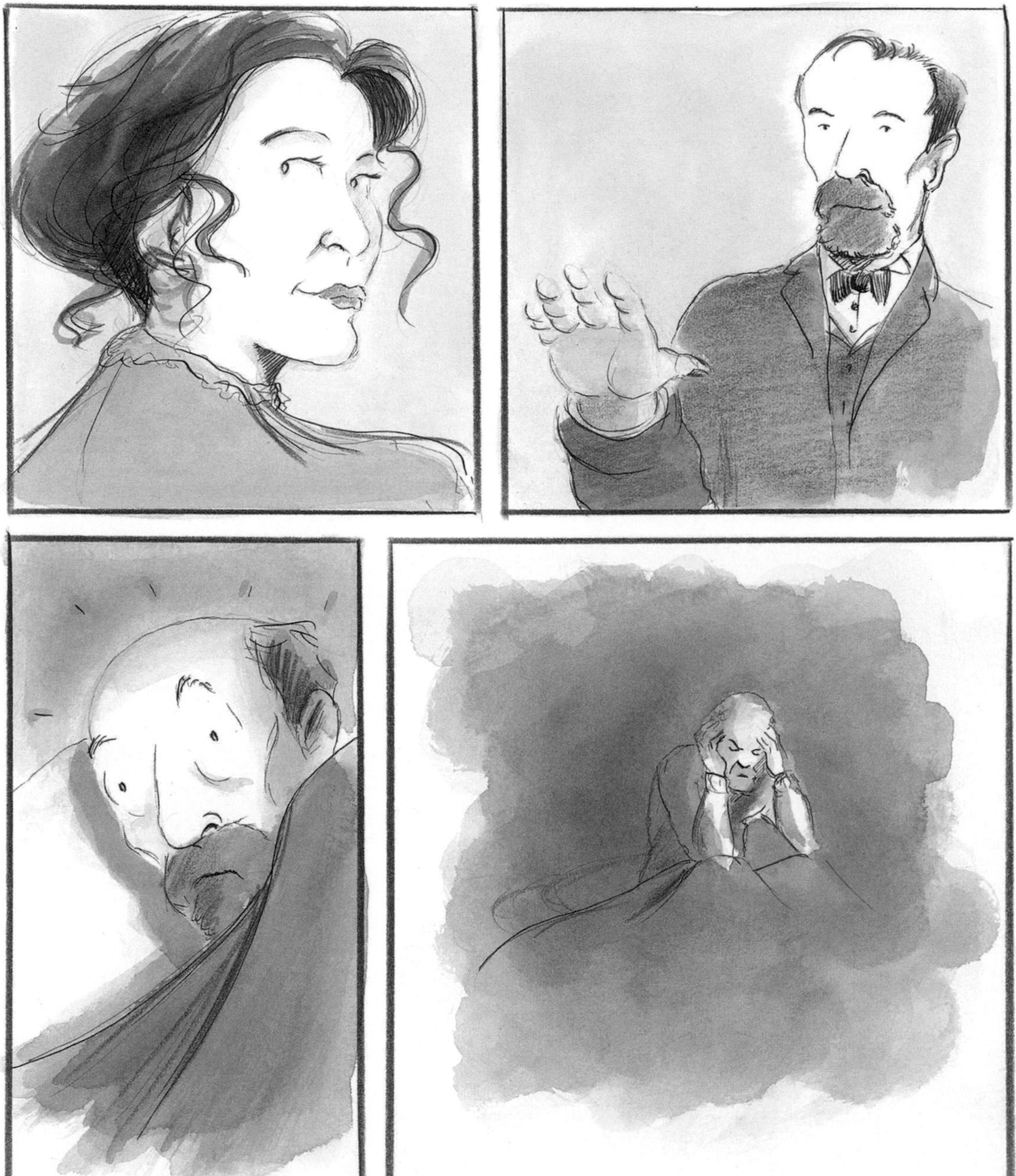

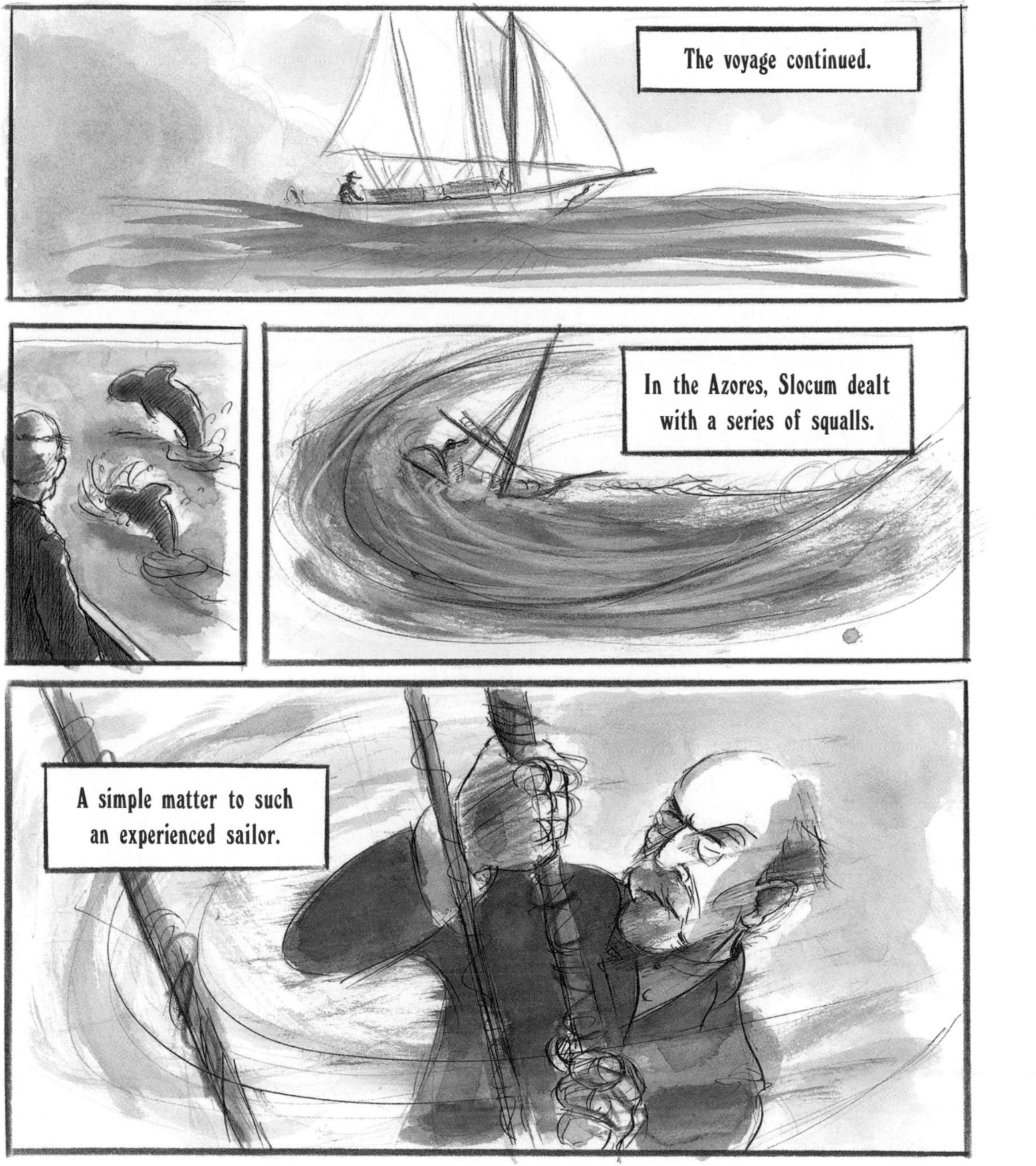
The voyage continued.
In the Azores, Slocum dealt with a series of squalls.
A simple matter to such an experienced sailor.

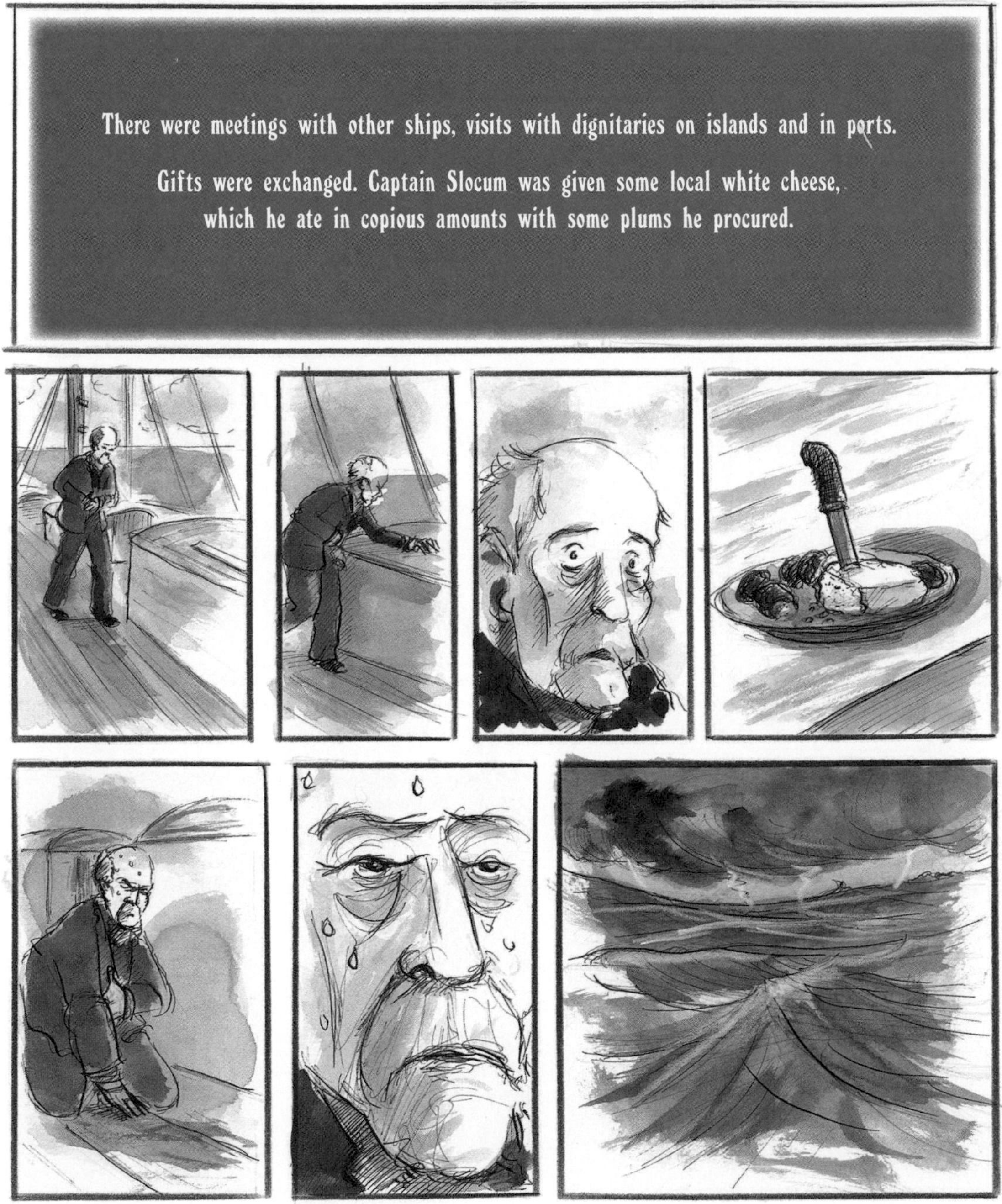
There were meetings with other ships, visits with dignitaries on islands and in ports.
Gifts were exchanged. Captain Slocum was given some local white cheese, which he ate in copious amounts with some plums he procured.

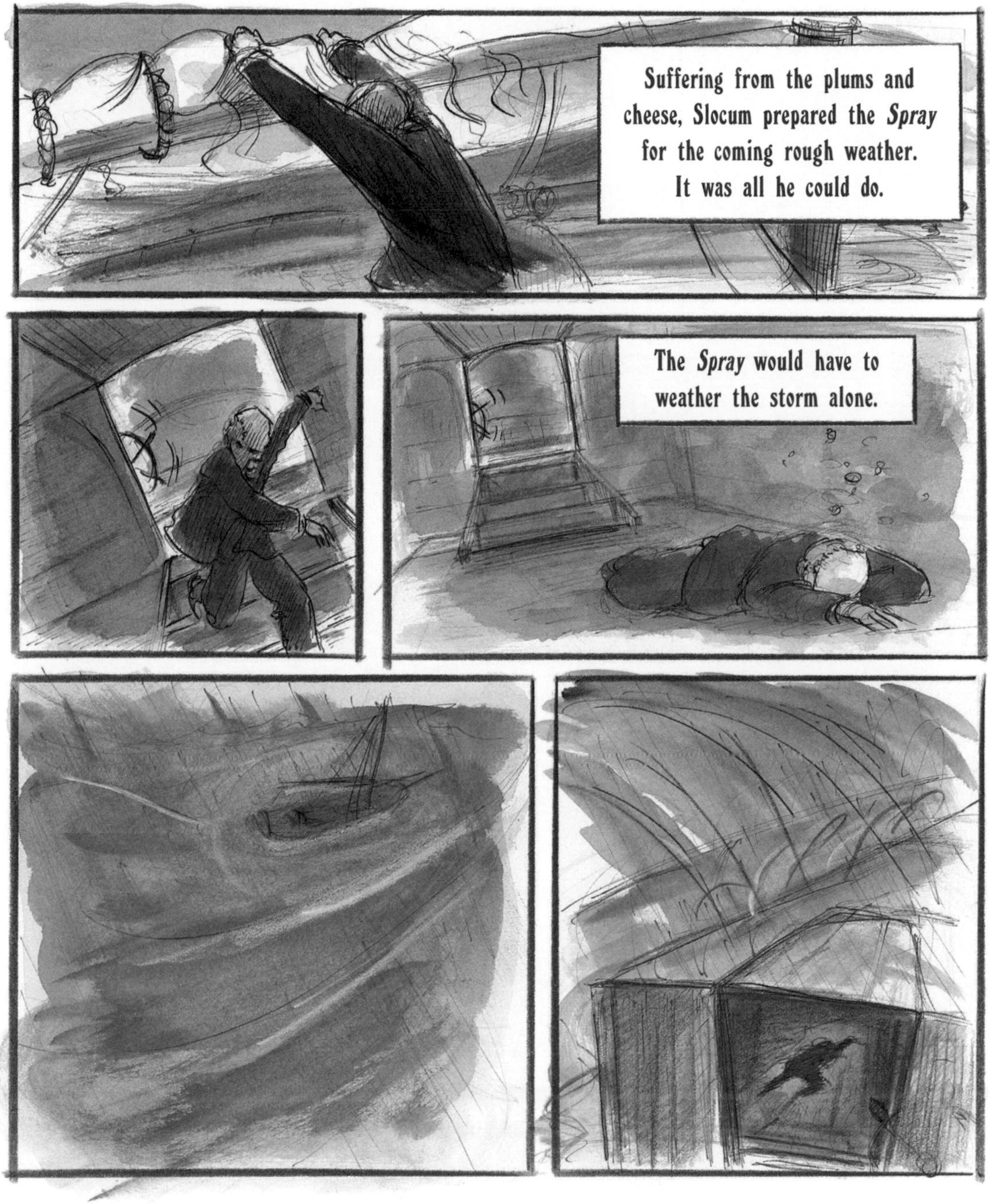
Suffering from the plums and cheese, Slocum prepared the *Spray* for the coming rough weather. It was all he could do.
The *Spray* would have to weather the storm alone.

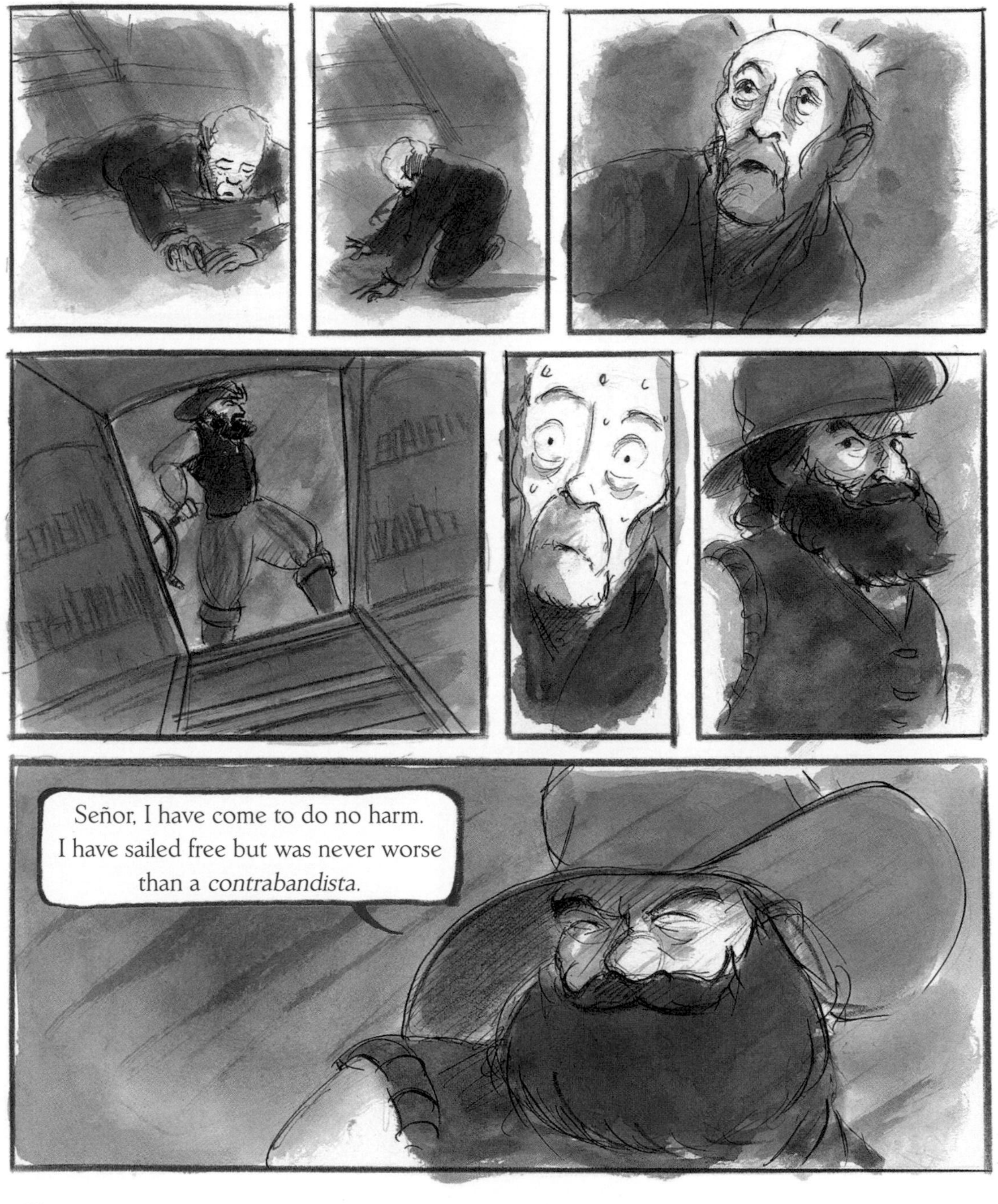
Señor, I have come to do no harm. I have sailed free but was never worse than a *contrabandista*.

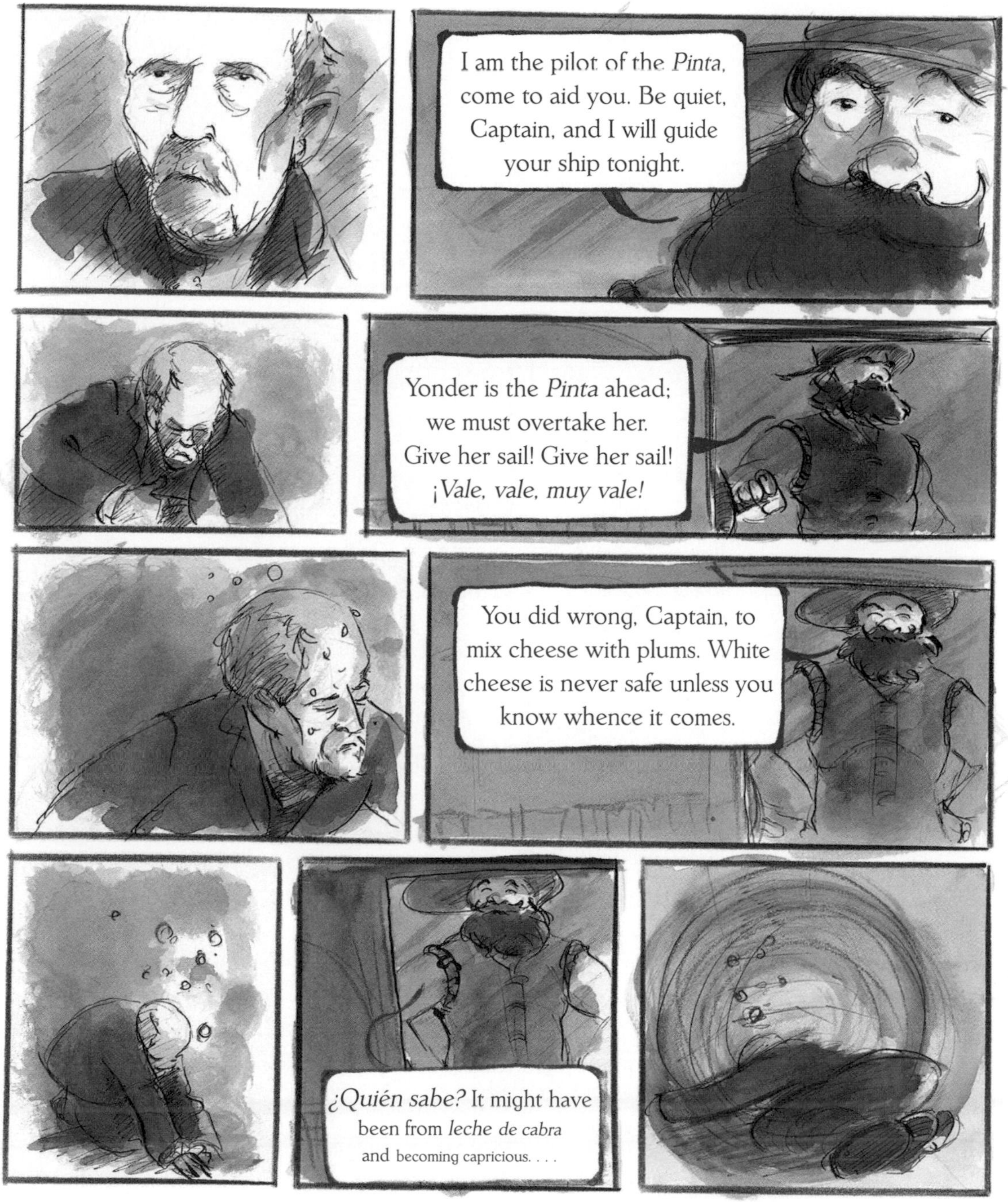
I am the pilot of the *Pinta*, come to aid you. Be quiet, Captain, and I will guide your ship tonight.
Yonder is the *Pinta* ahead; we must overtake her. Give her sail! Give her sail! ¡*Vale, vale, muy vale!*
You did wrong, Captain, to mix cheese with plums. White cheese is never safe unless you know whence it comes.
*¿Quién sabe?* It might have been from *leche de cabra* and becoming capricious. . . .

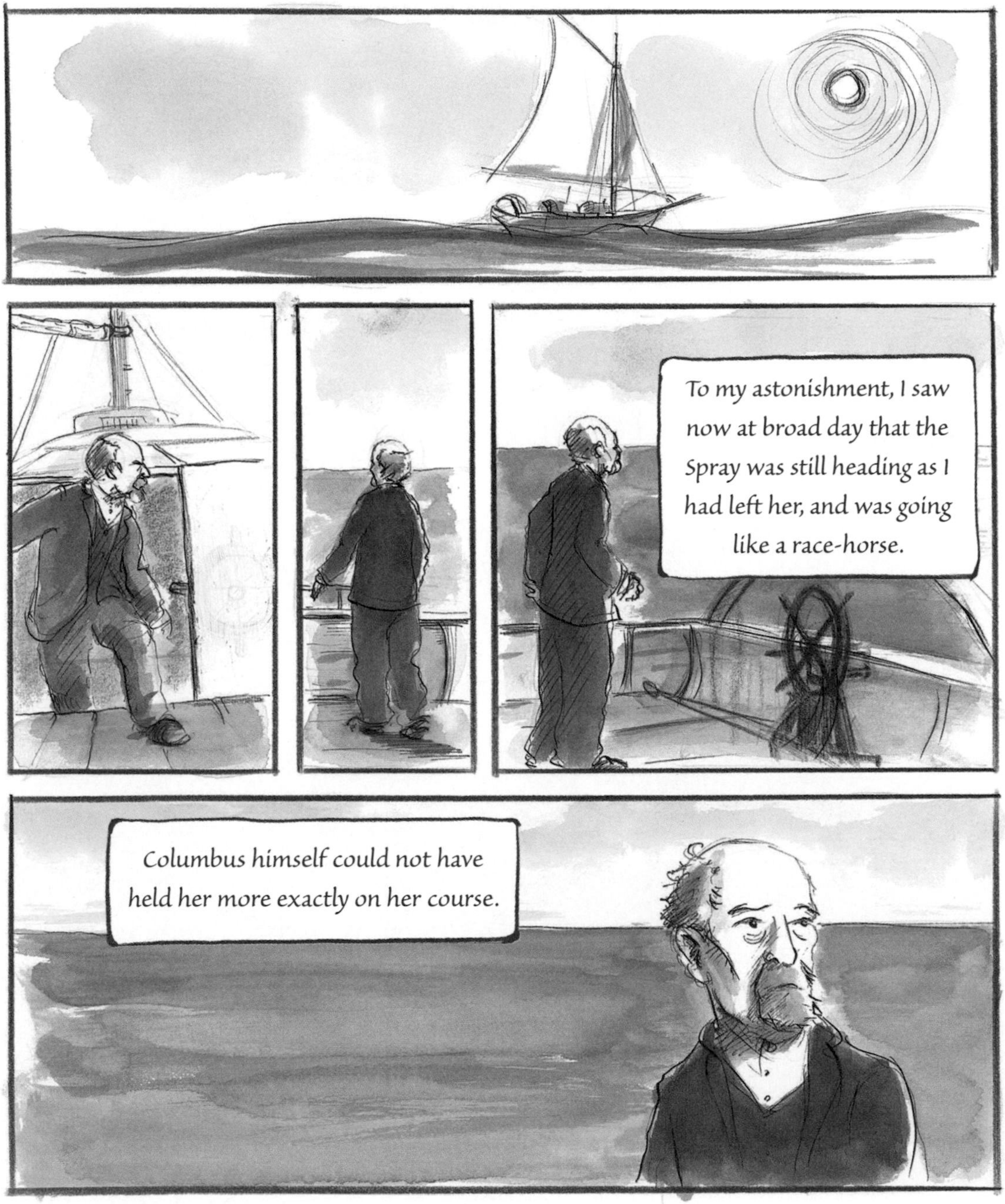
To my astonishment, I saw now at broad day that the Spray was still heading as I had left her, and was going like a race-horse.
Columbus himself could not have held her more exactly on her course.

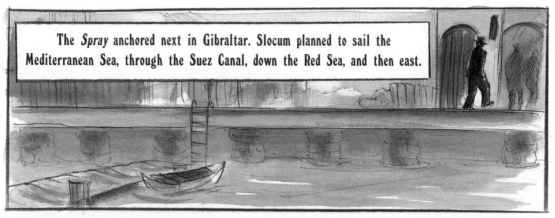

The *Spray* anchored next in Gibraltar. Slocum planned to sail the Mediterranean Sea, through the Suez Canal, down the Red Sea, and then east.

However, he was informed that the Mediterranean was a haven for pirates.

Slocum decided to recross the Atlantic to South America and then round Cape Horn.

Even so, the *Spray* was chased by pirates, but Captain Slocum skillfully outmaneuvered them.

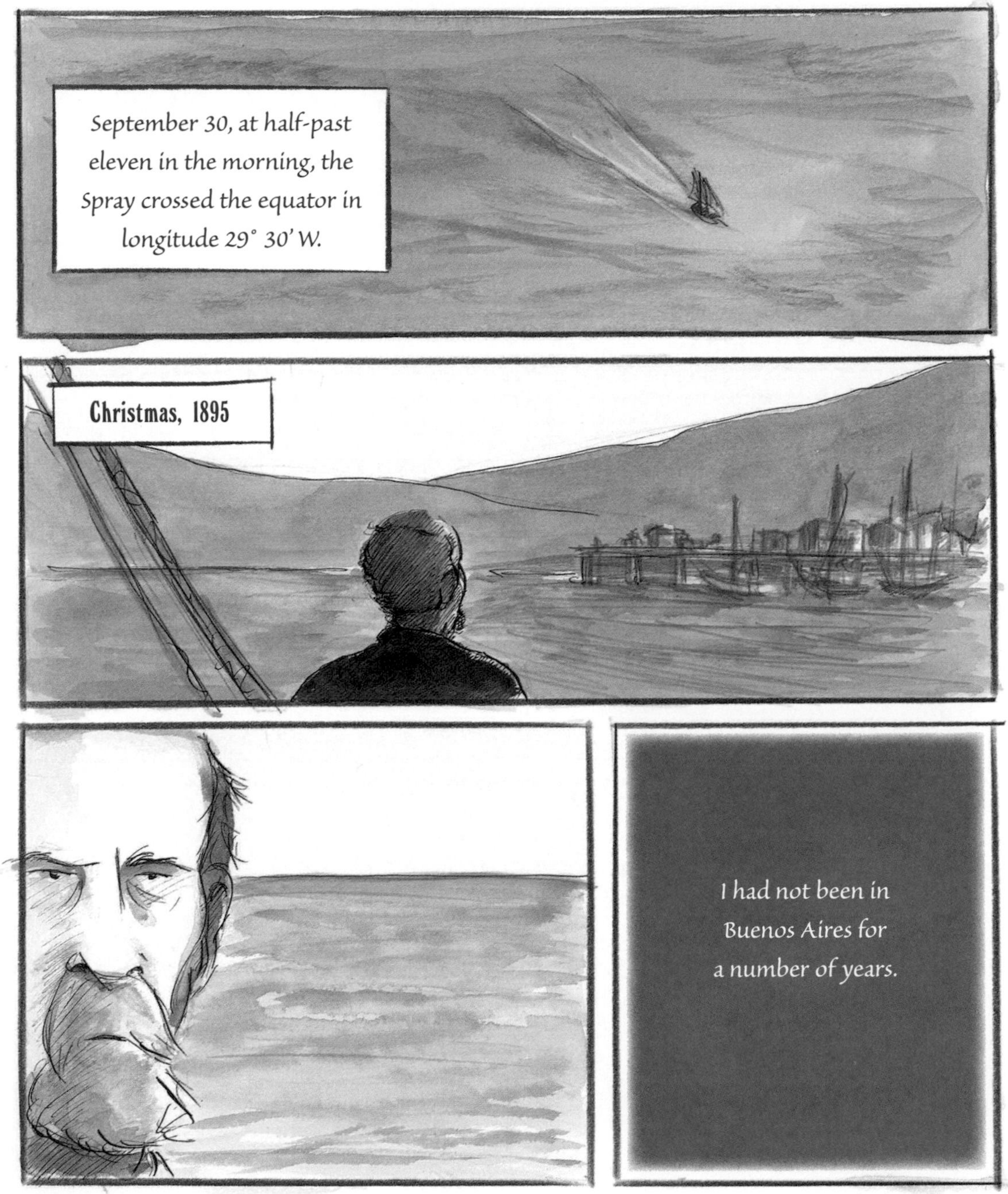
September 30, at half-past eleven in the morning, the Spray crossed the equator in longitude 29° 30' W.
Christmas, 1895
I had not been in Buenos Aires for a number of years.

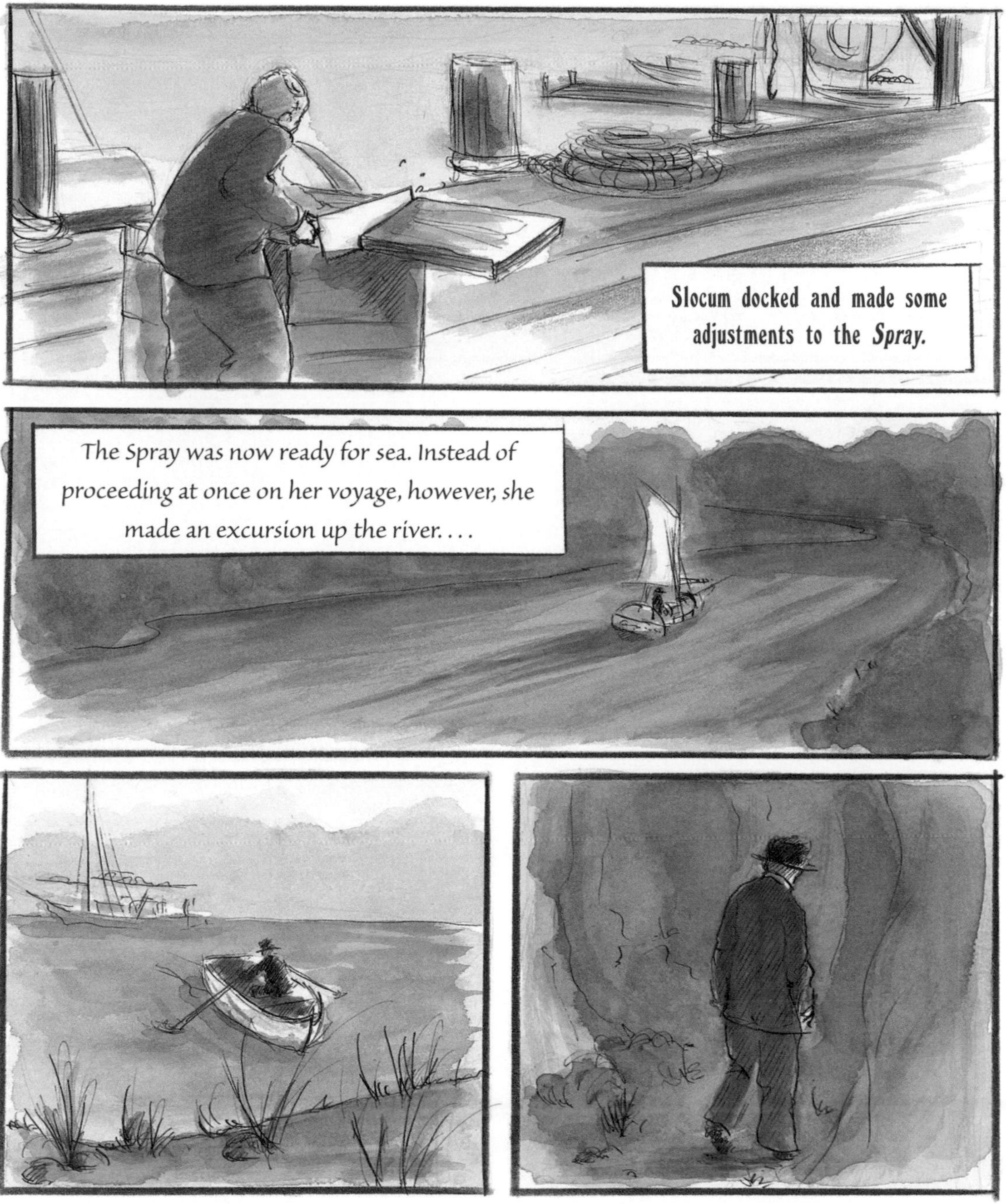
Slocum docked and made some adjustments to the Spray.
The Spray was now ready for sea. Instead of proceeding at once on her voyage, however, she made an excursion up the river. . . .

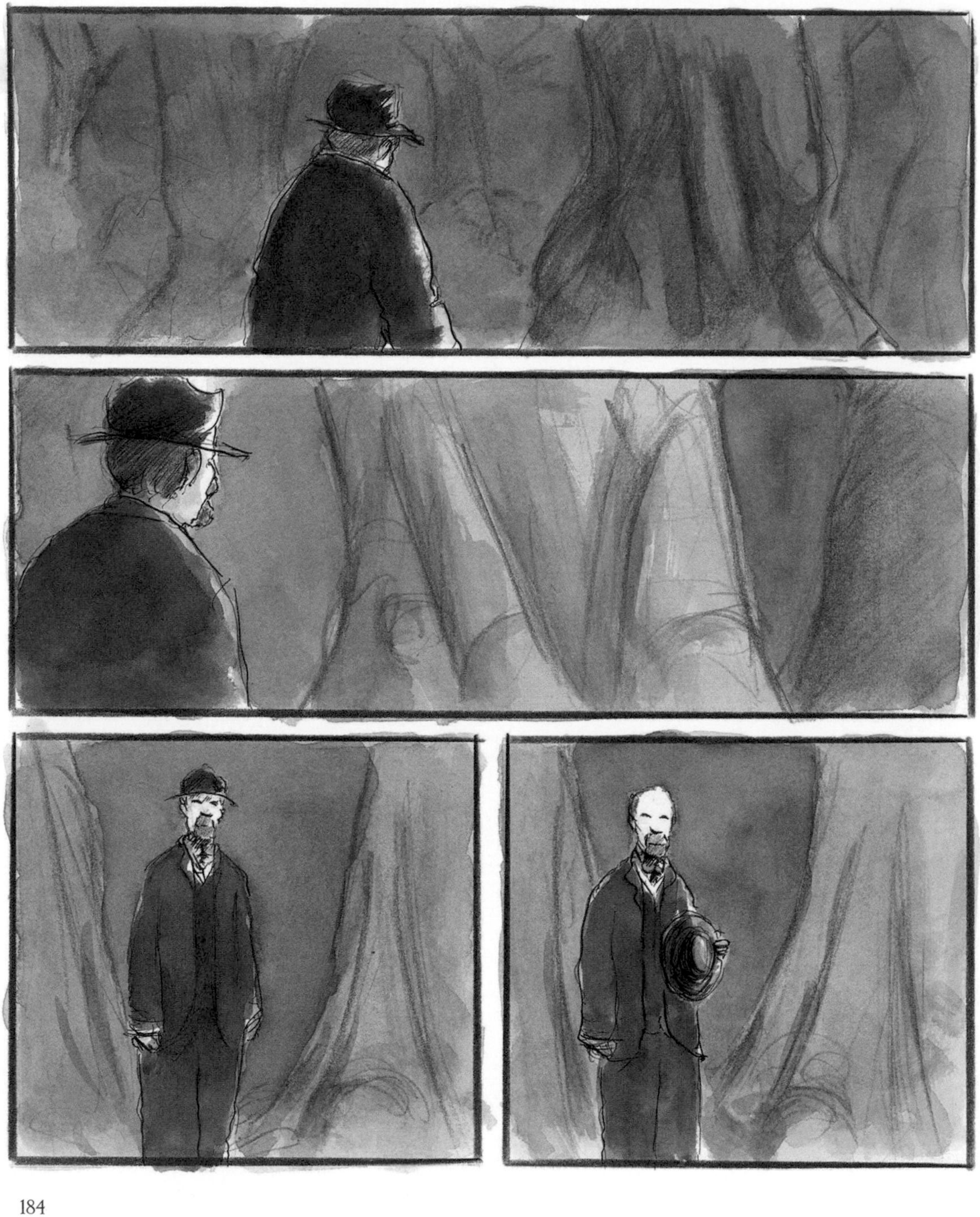

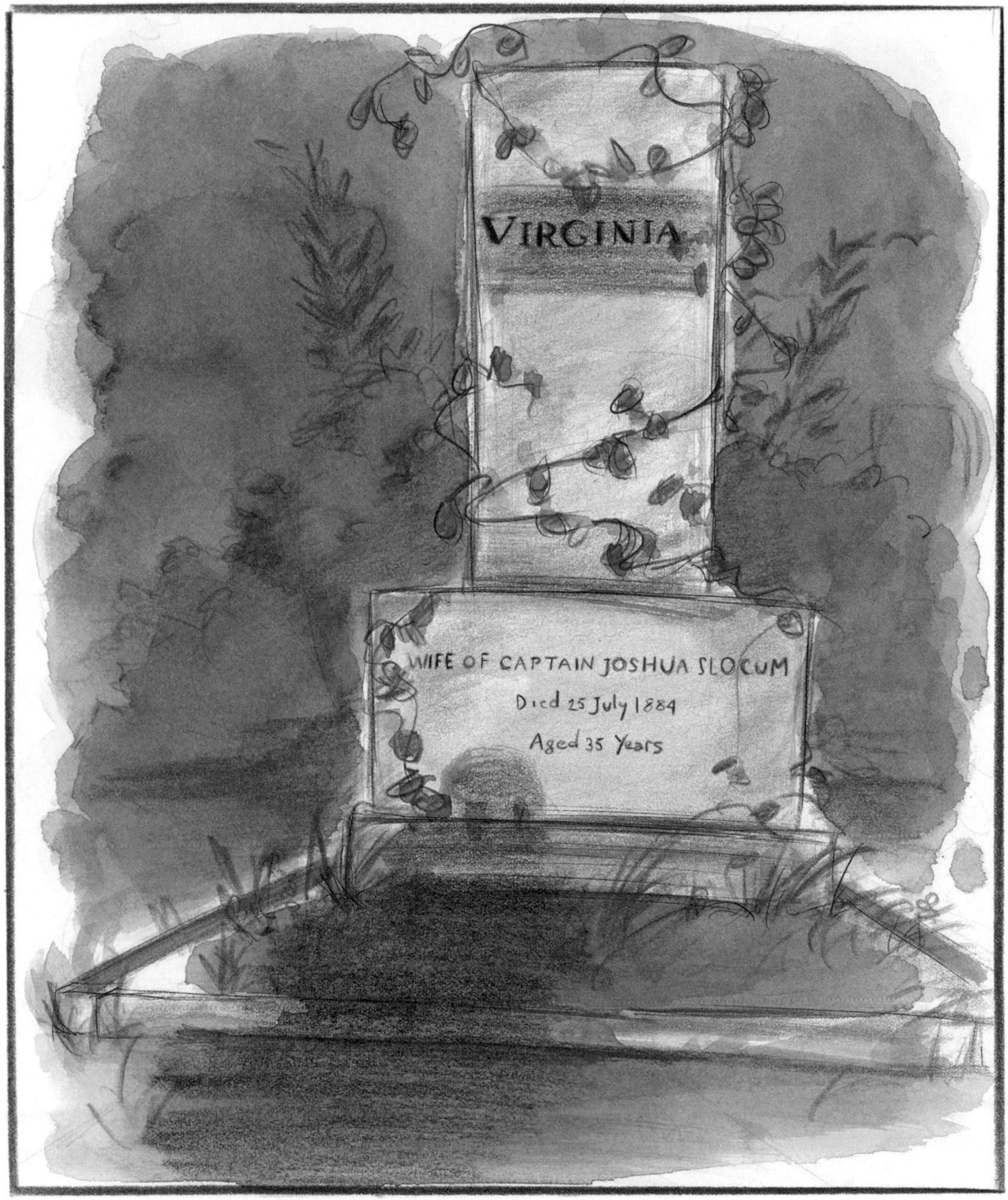
VIRGINIA
WIFE OF CAPTAIN JOSHUA SLOCUM
Died 25 July 1884
Aged 35 Years

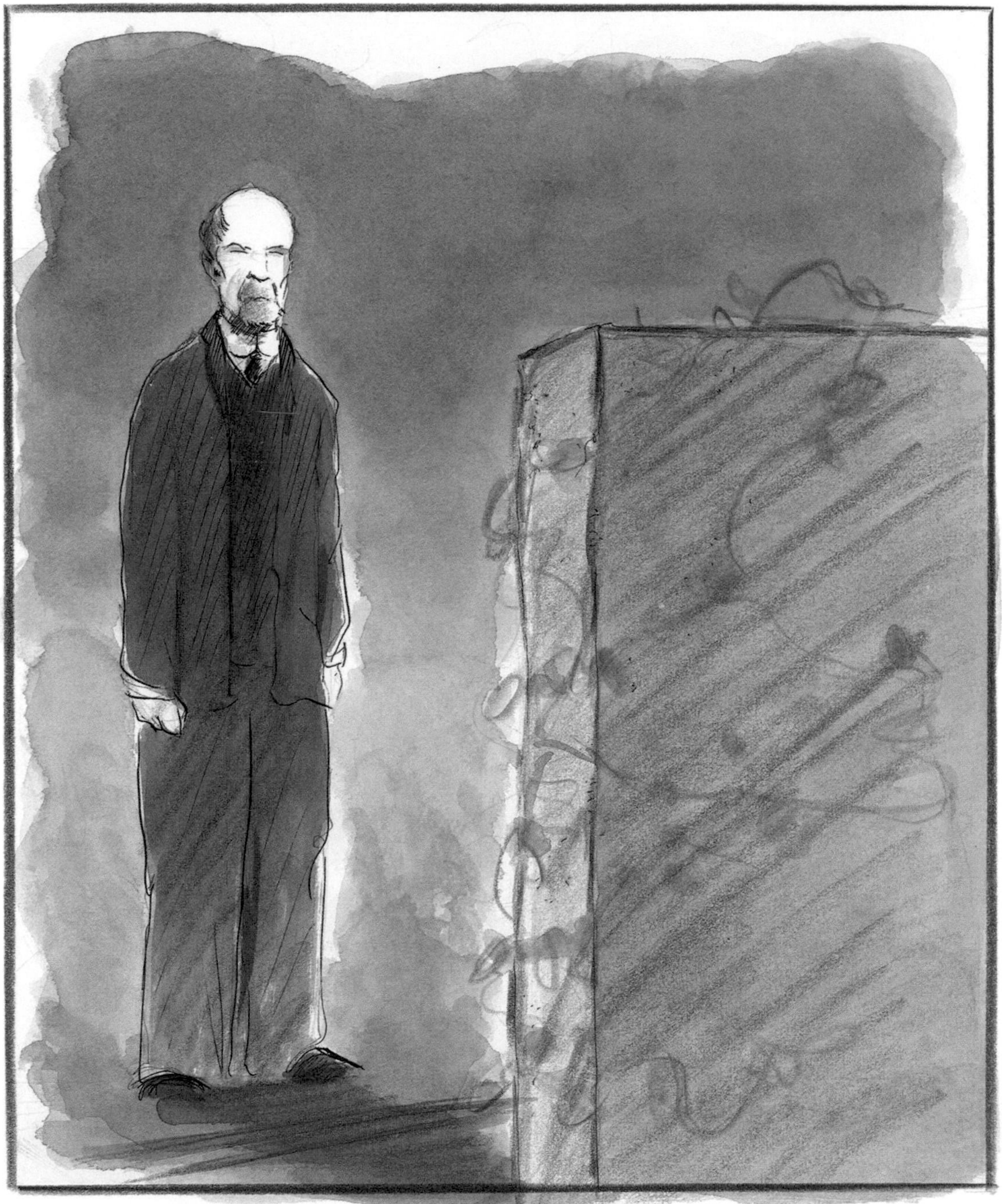

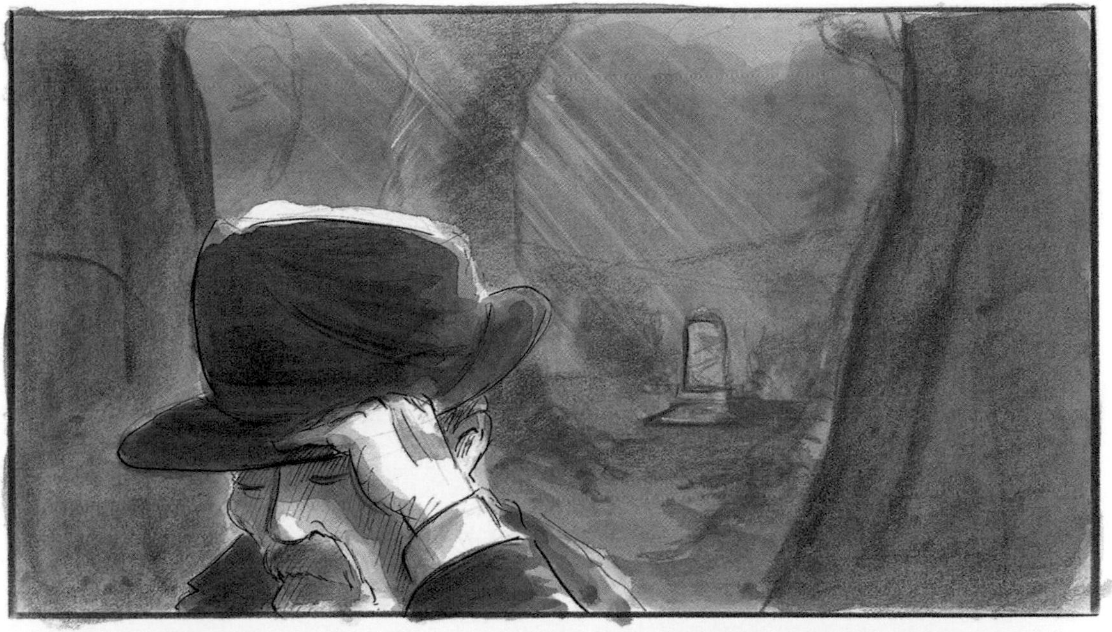

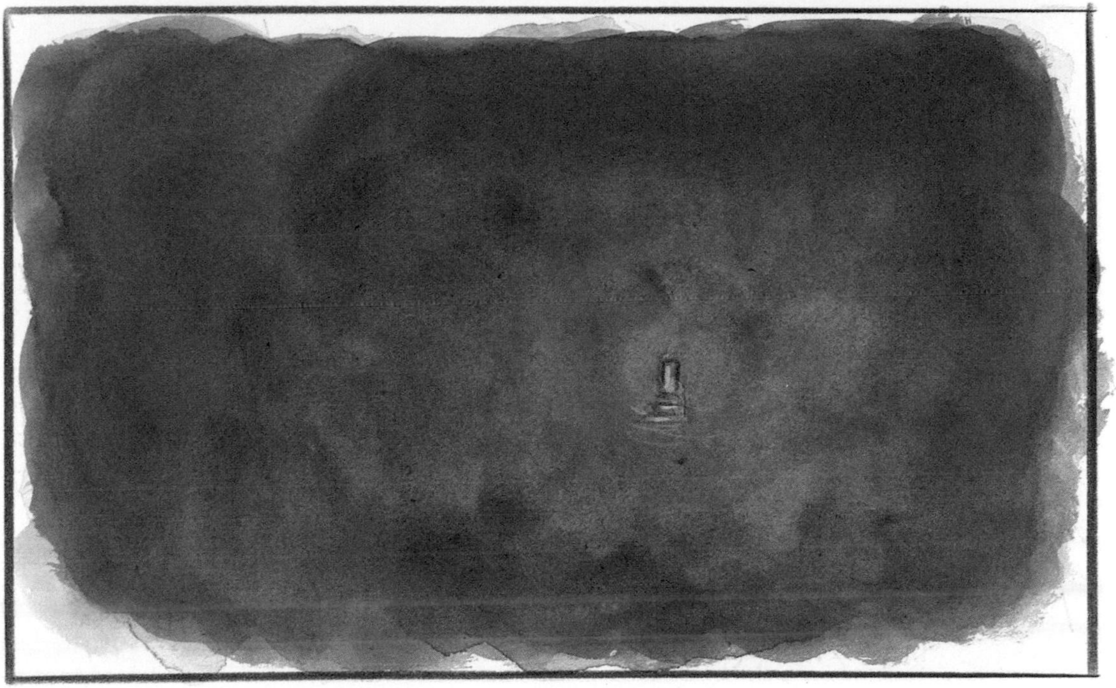

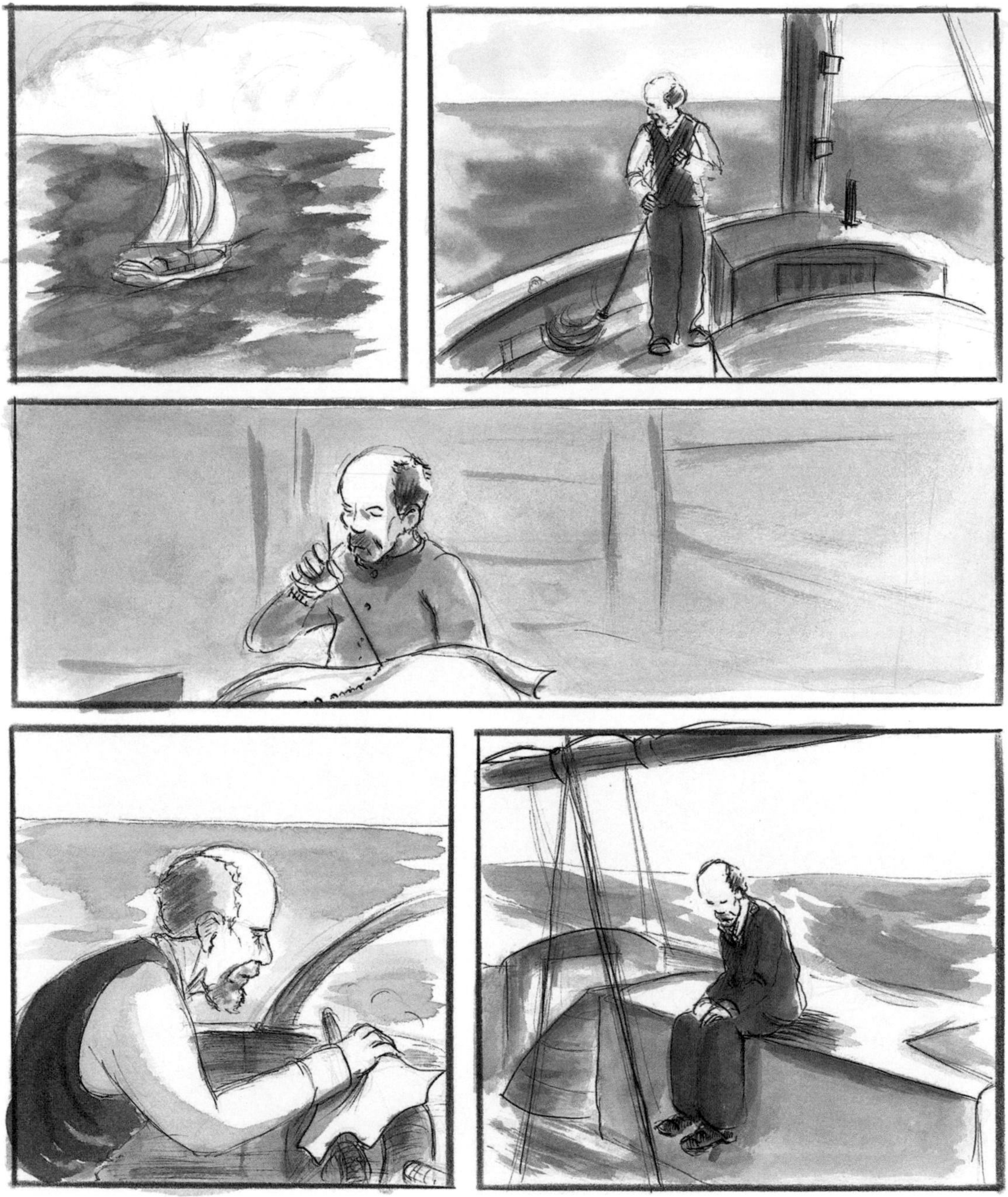

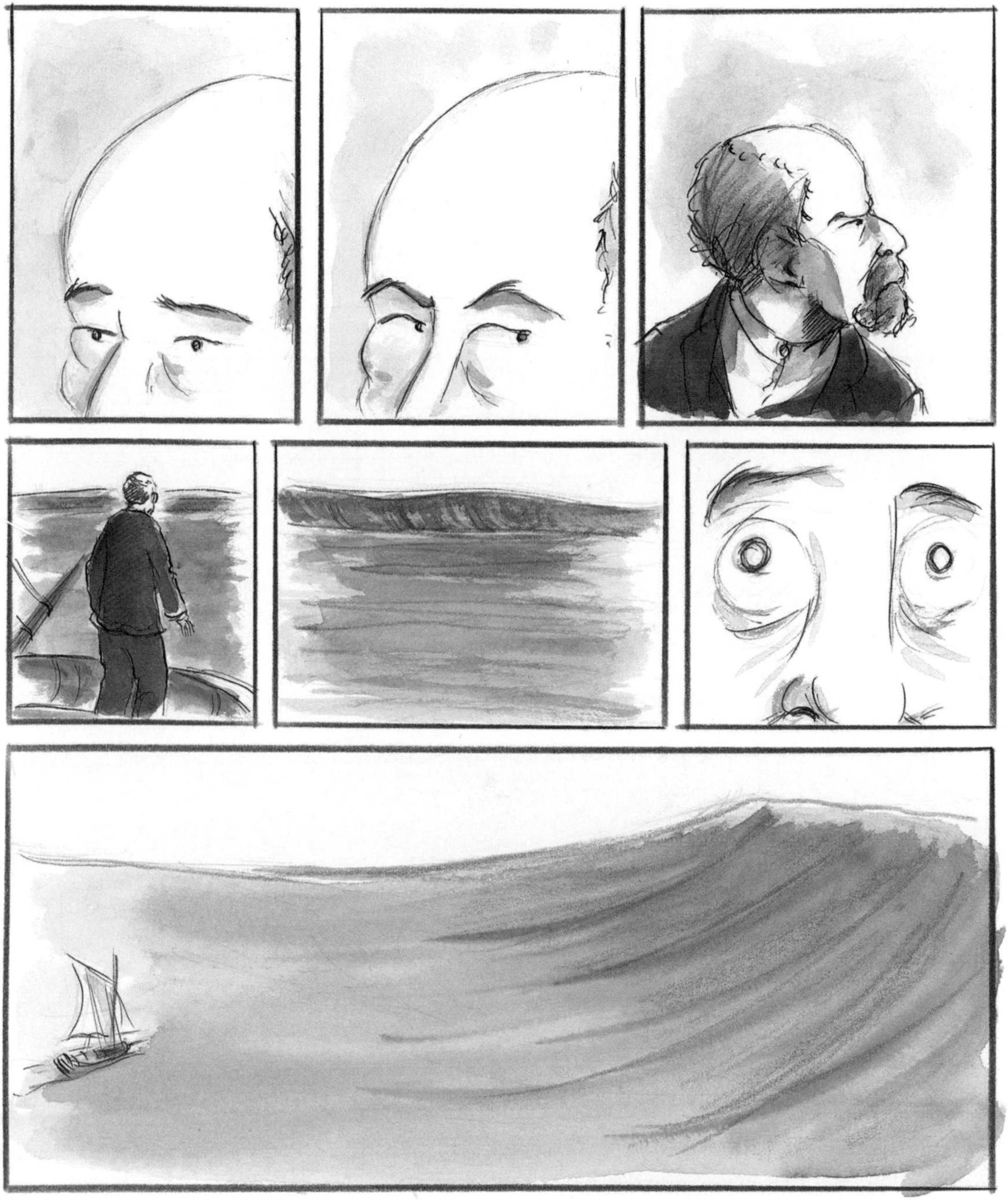

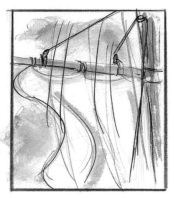

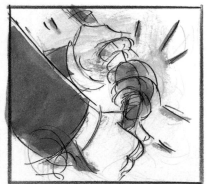

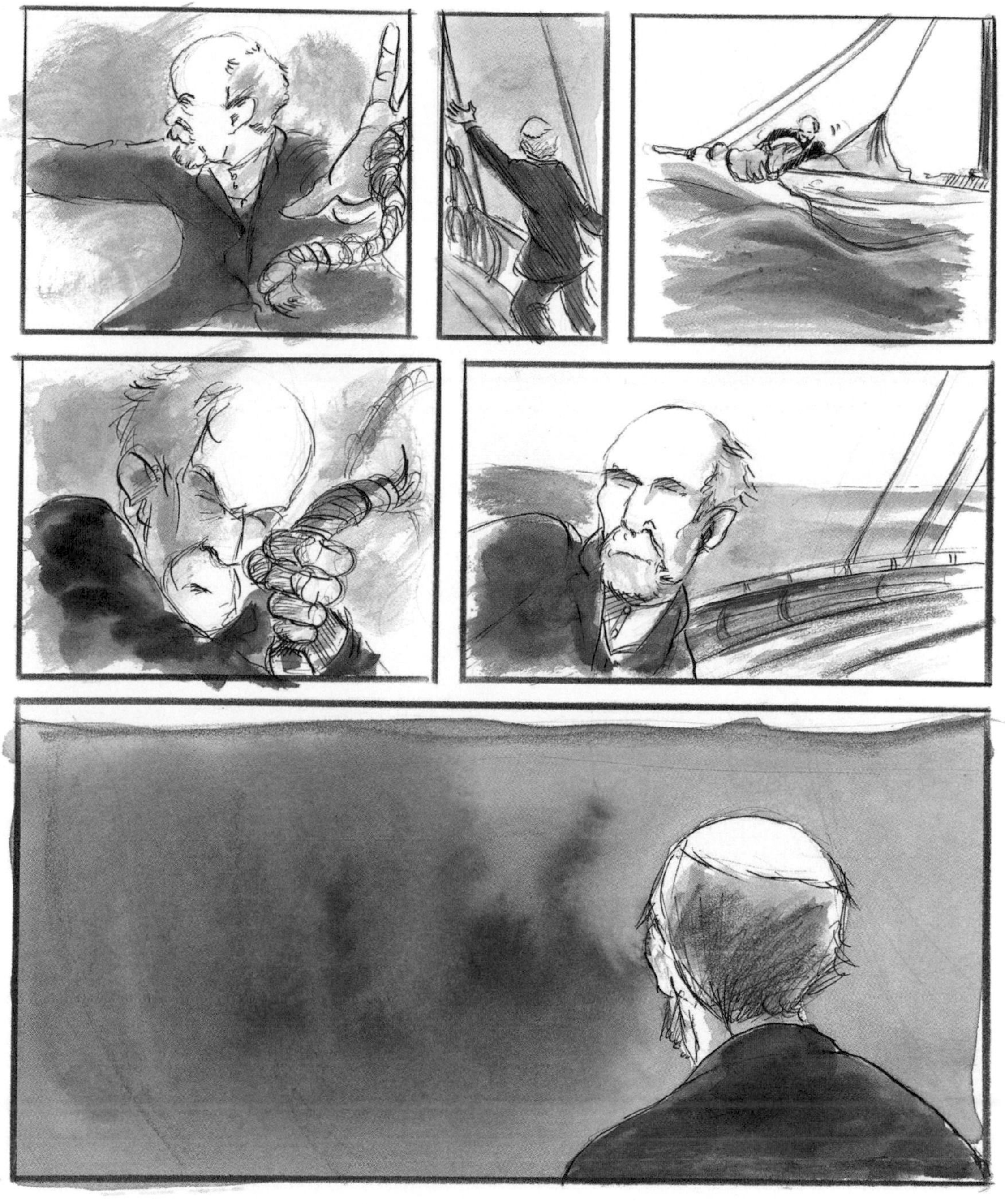

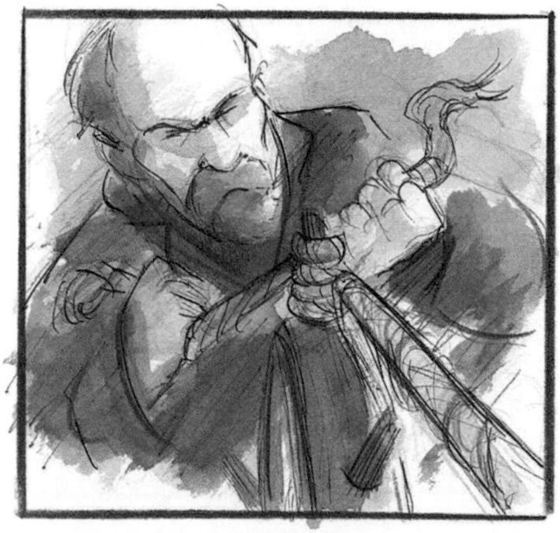

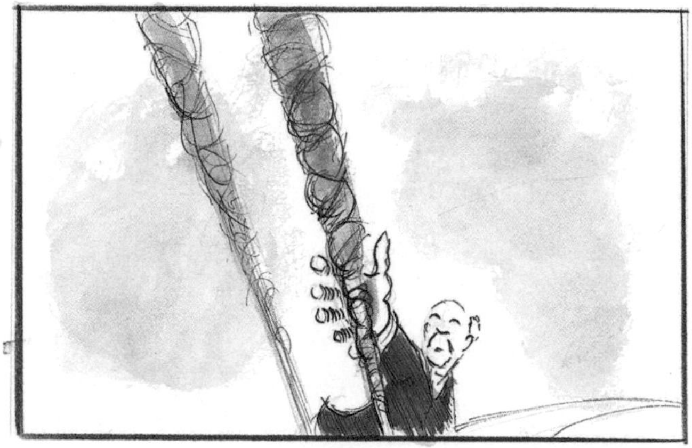

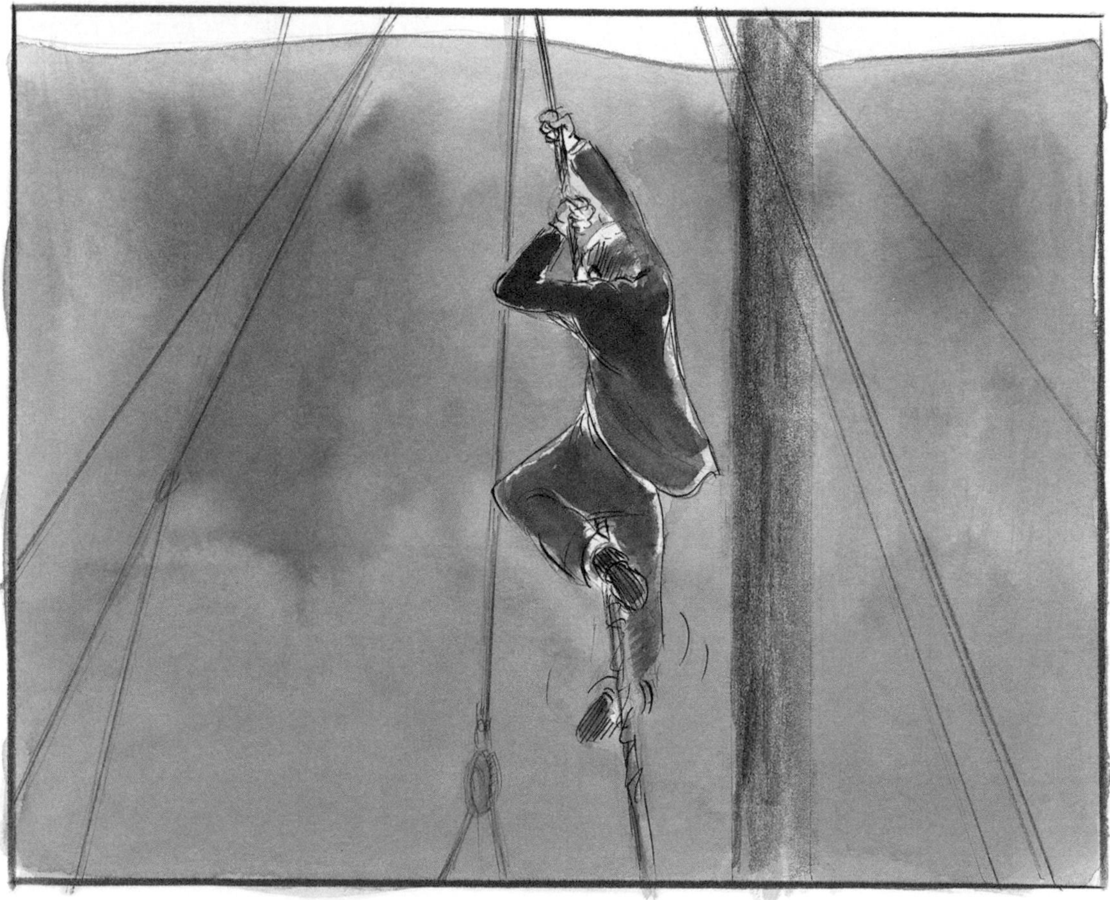

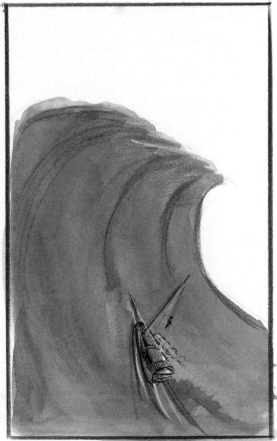

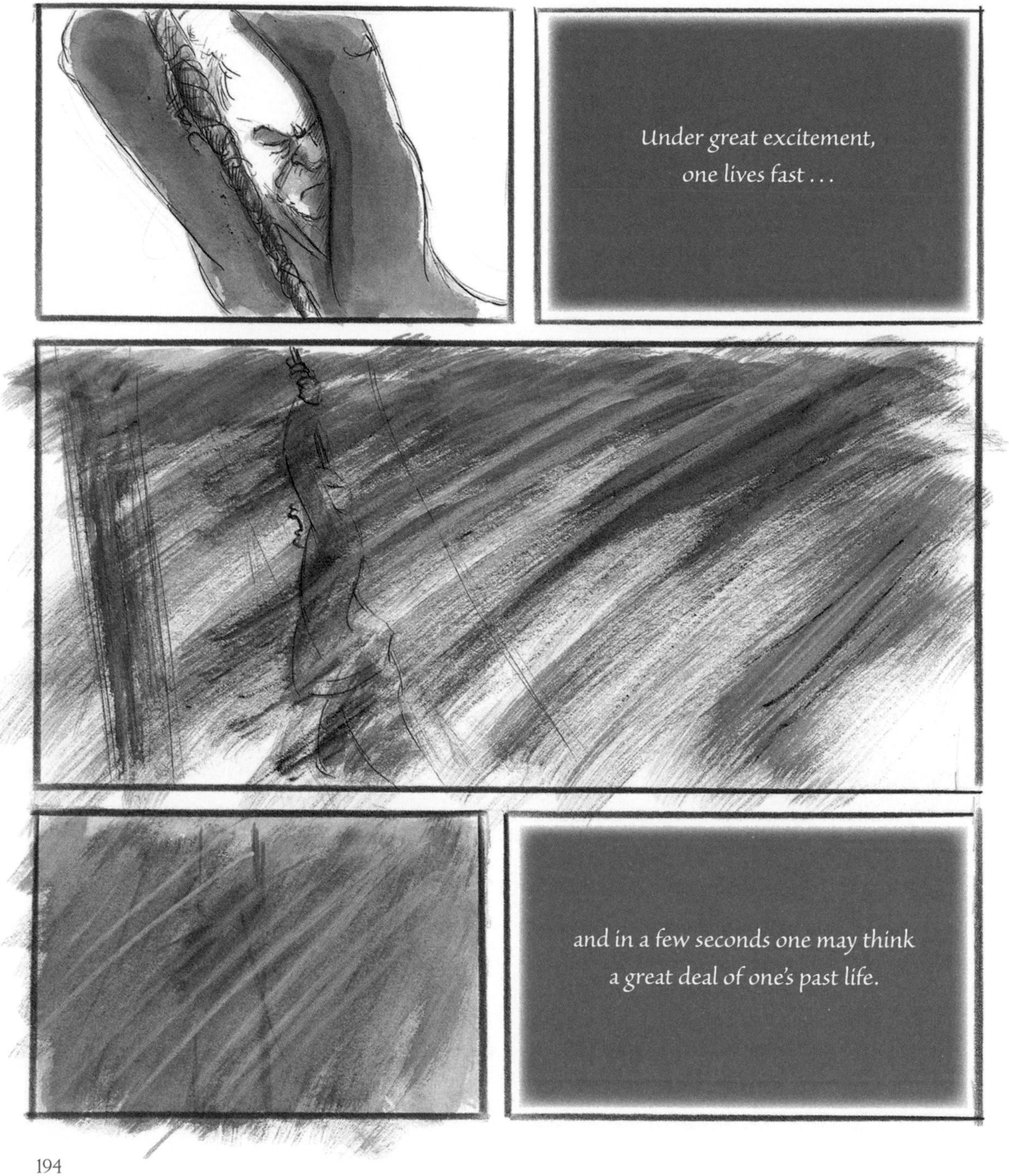
Under great excitement, one lives fast . . .
and in a few seconds one may think a great deal of one's past life.

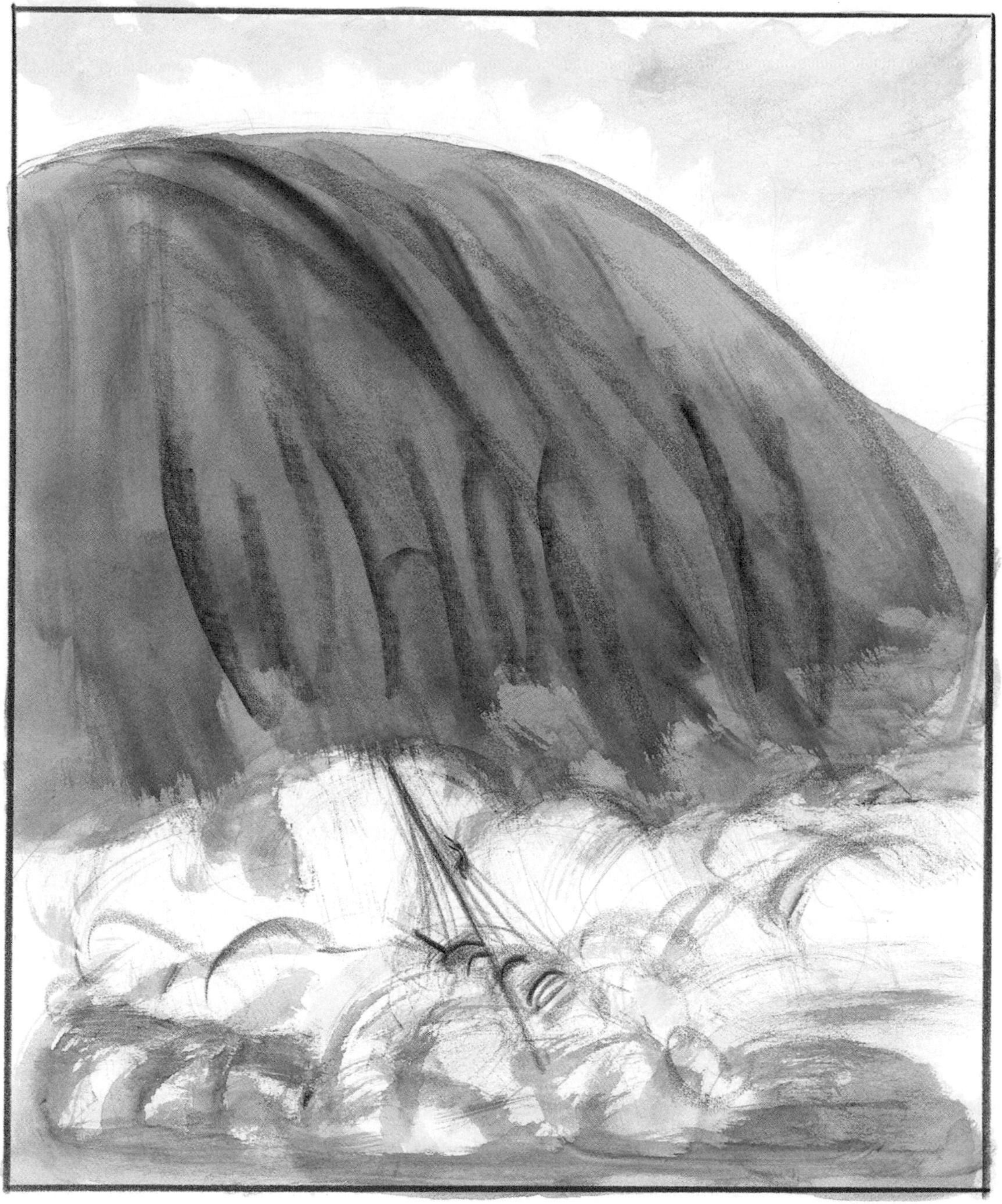

Joshua?

Why did you ever marry me?

For adventure.

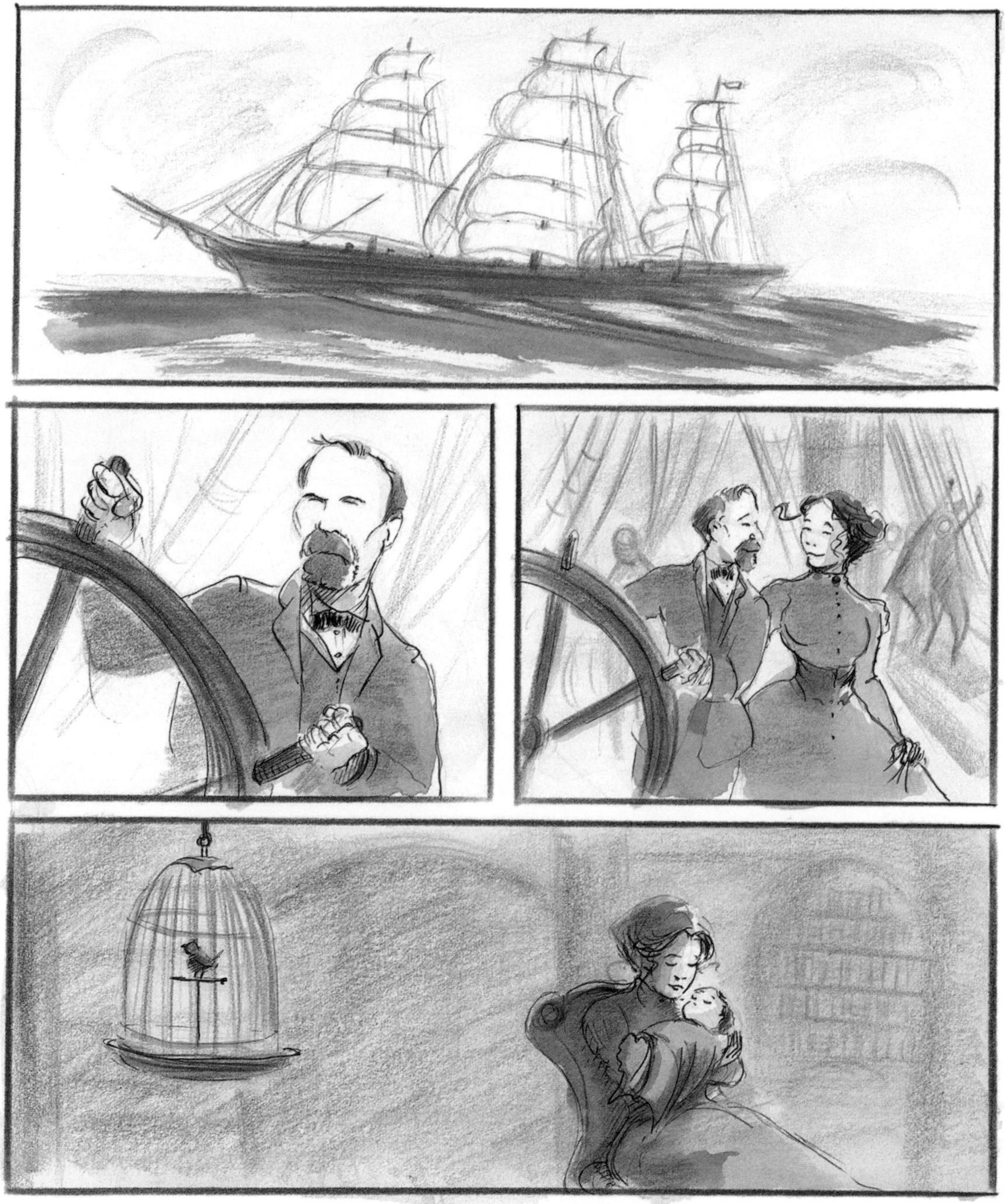

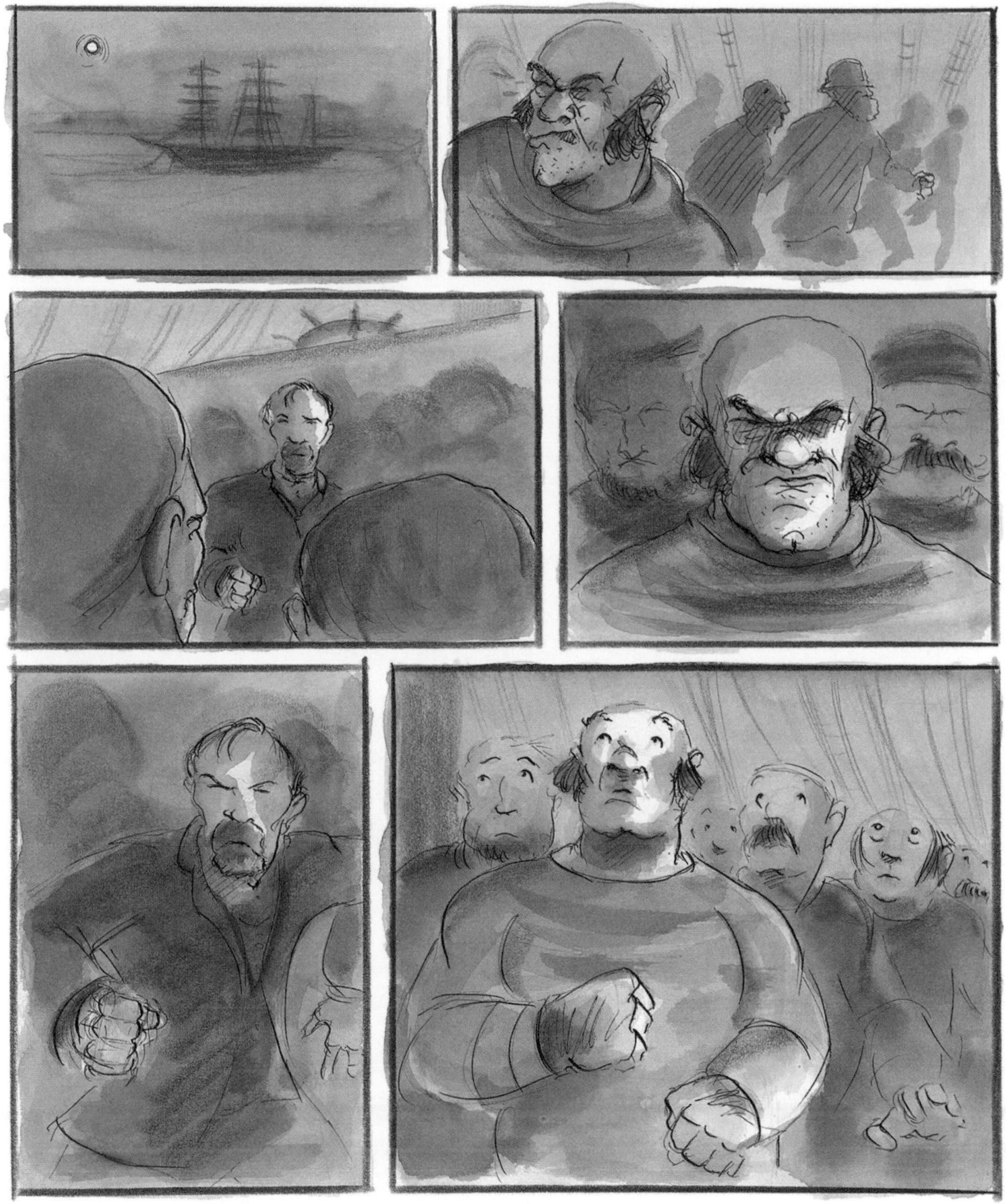

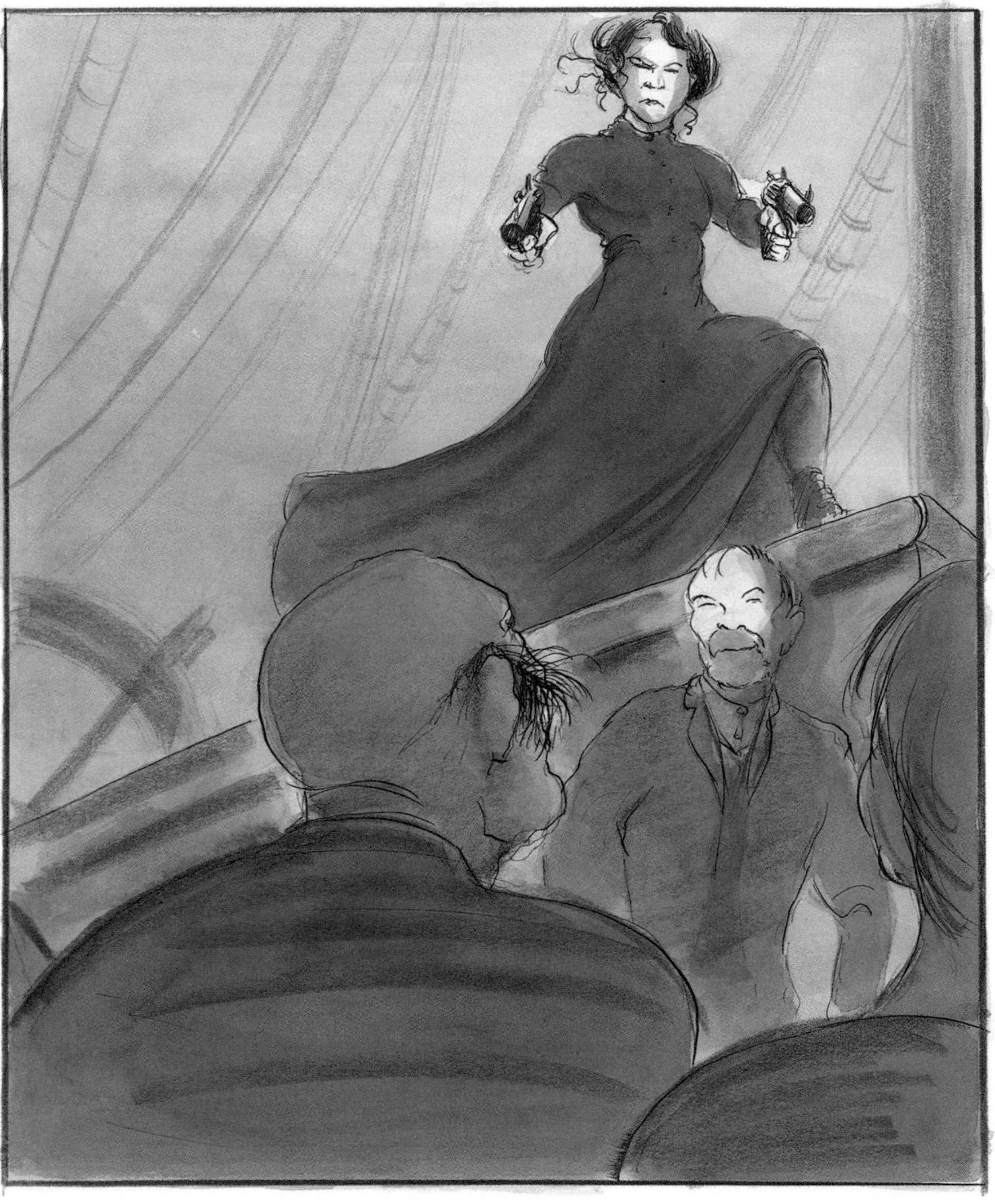

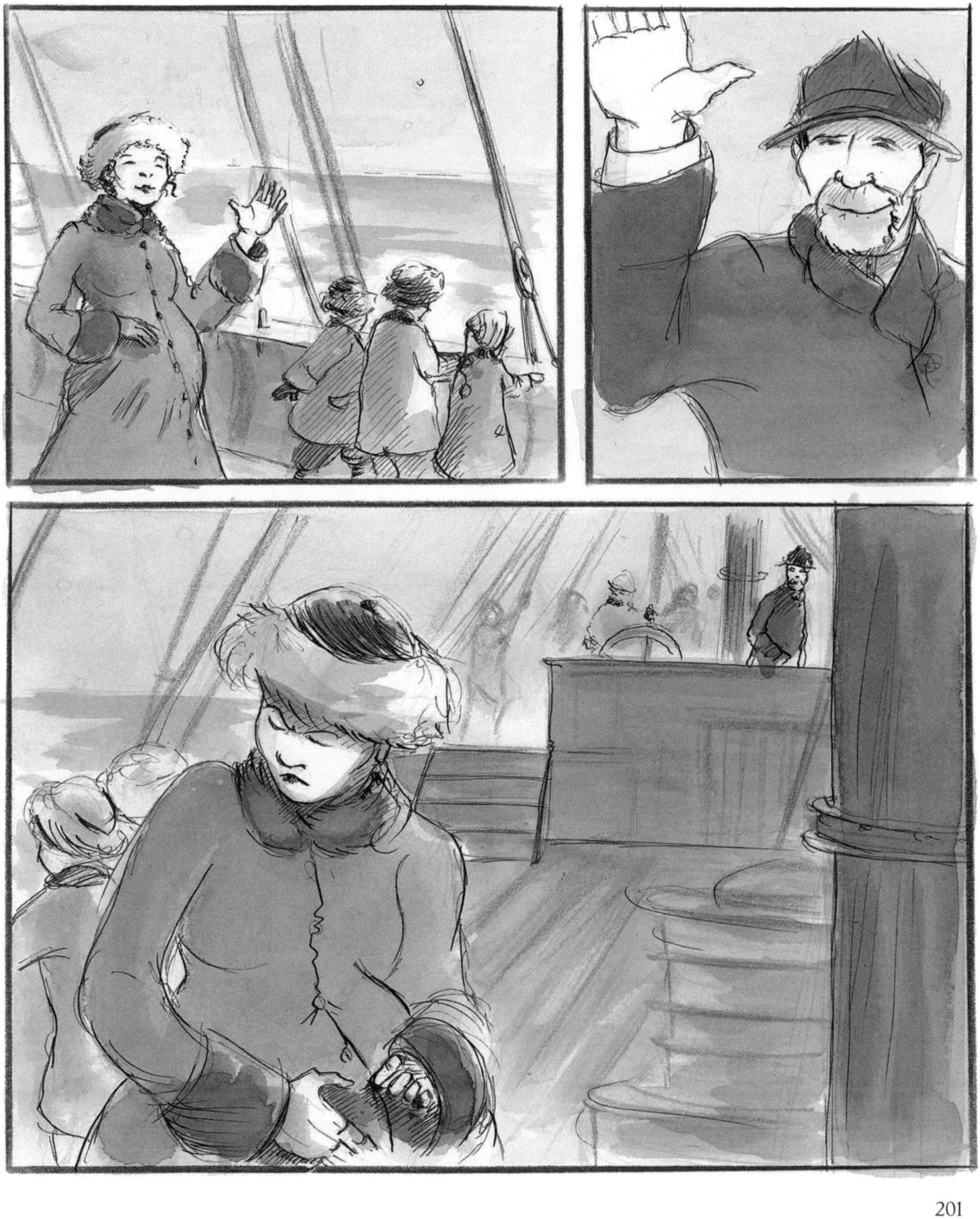

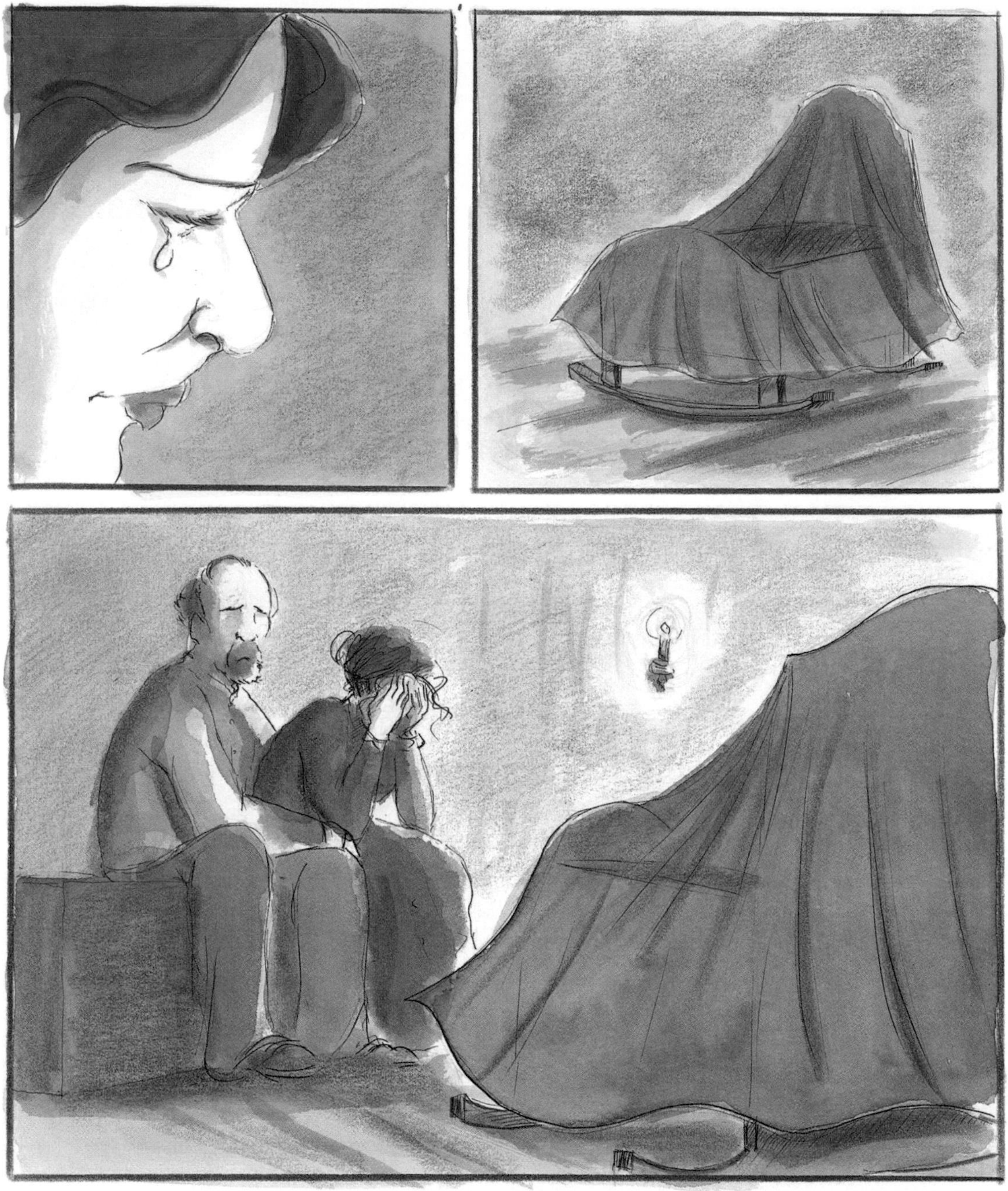

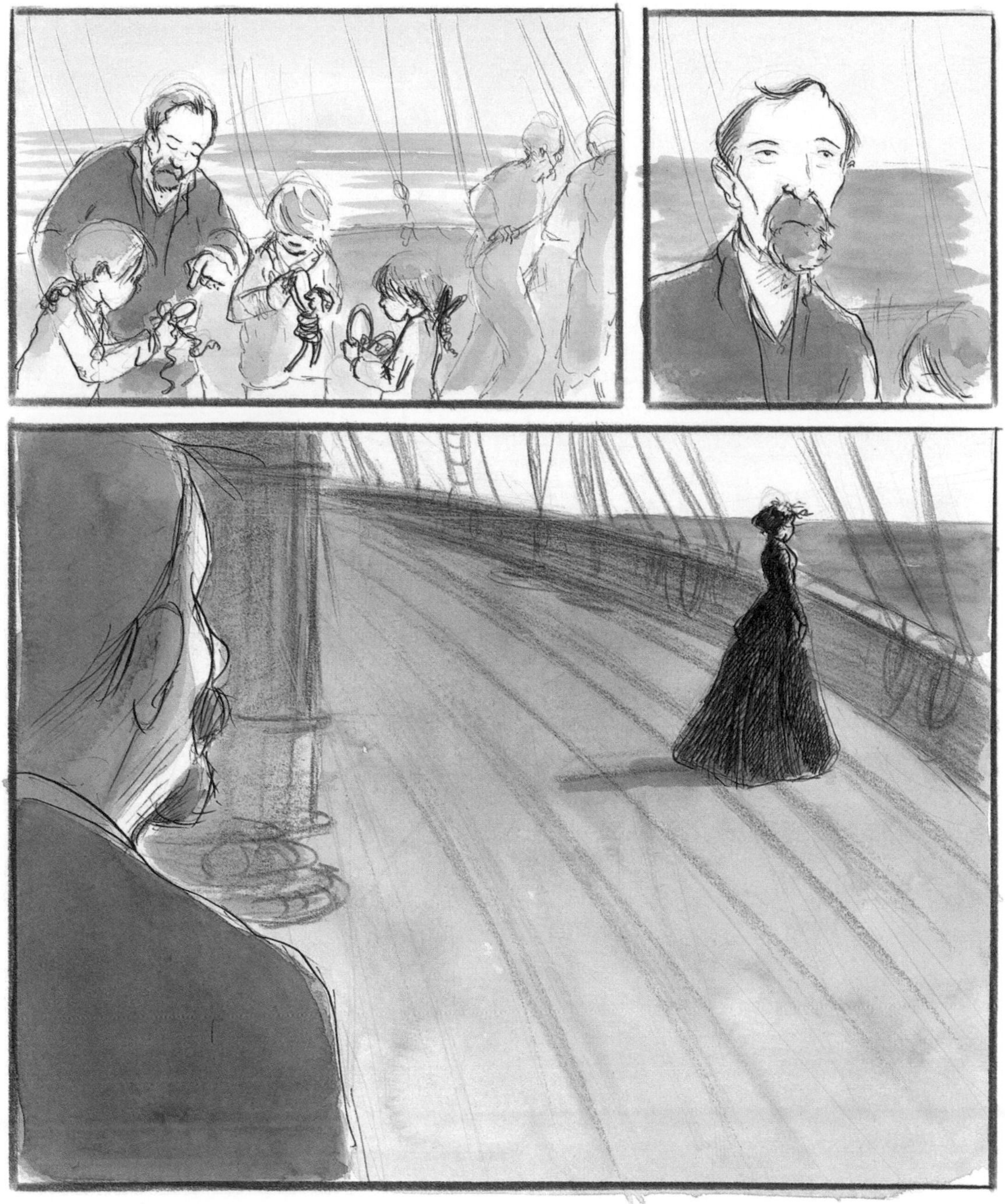

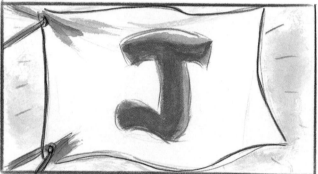

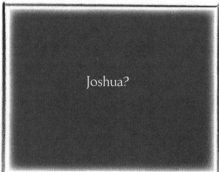

Joshua?

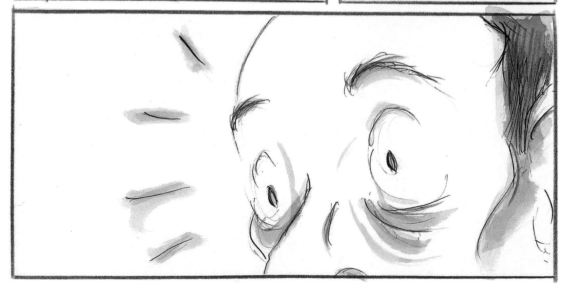

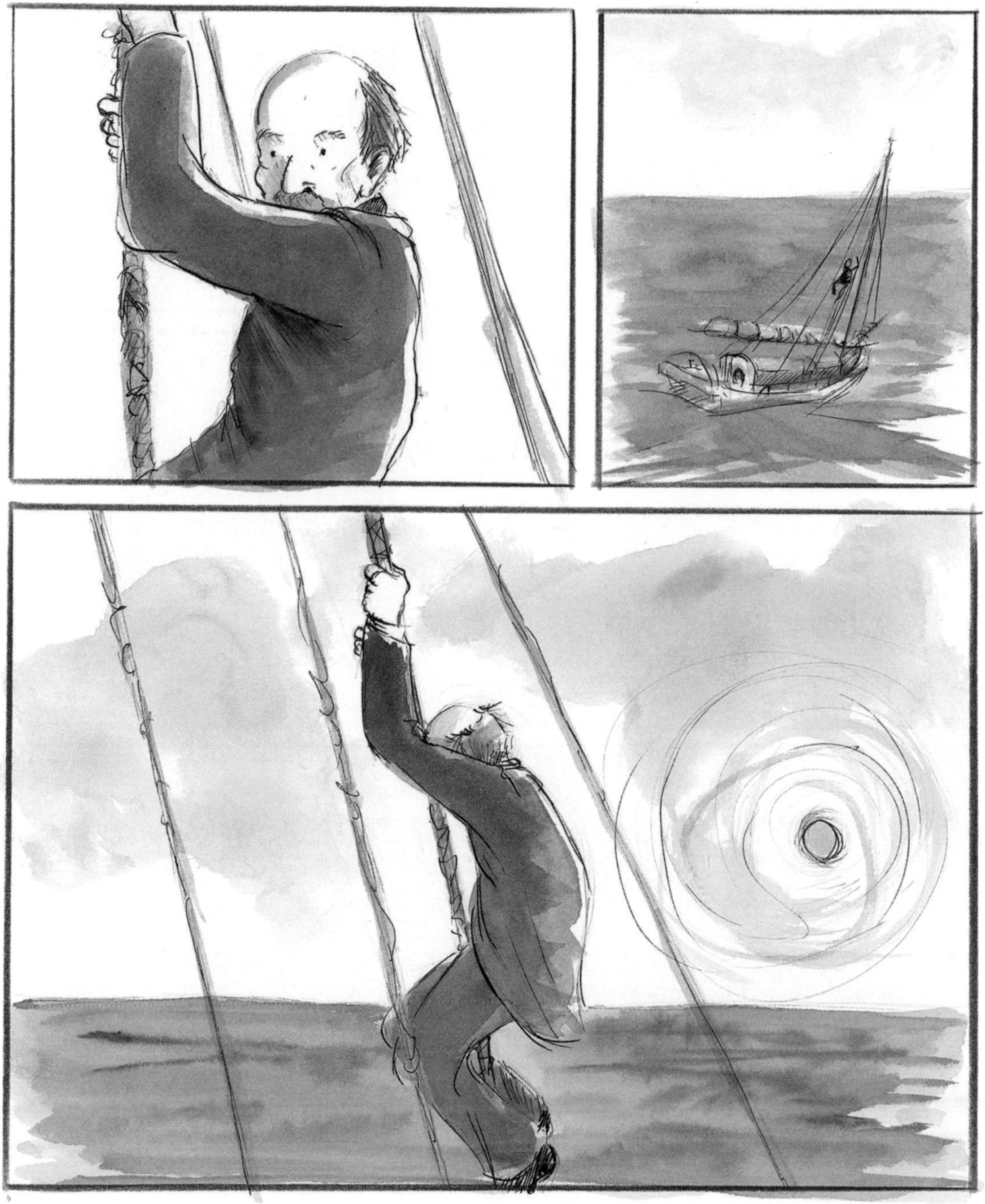

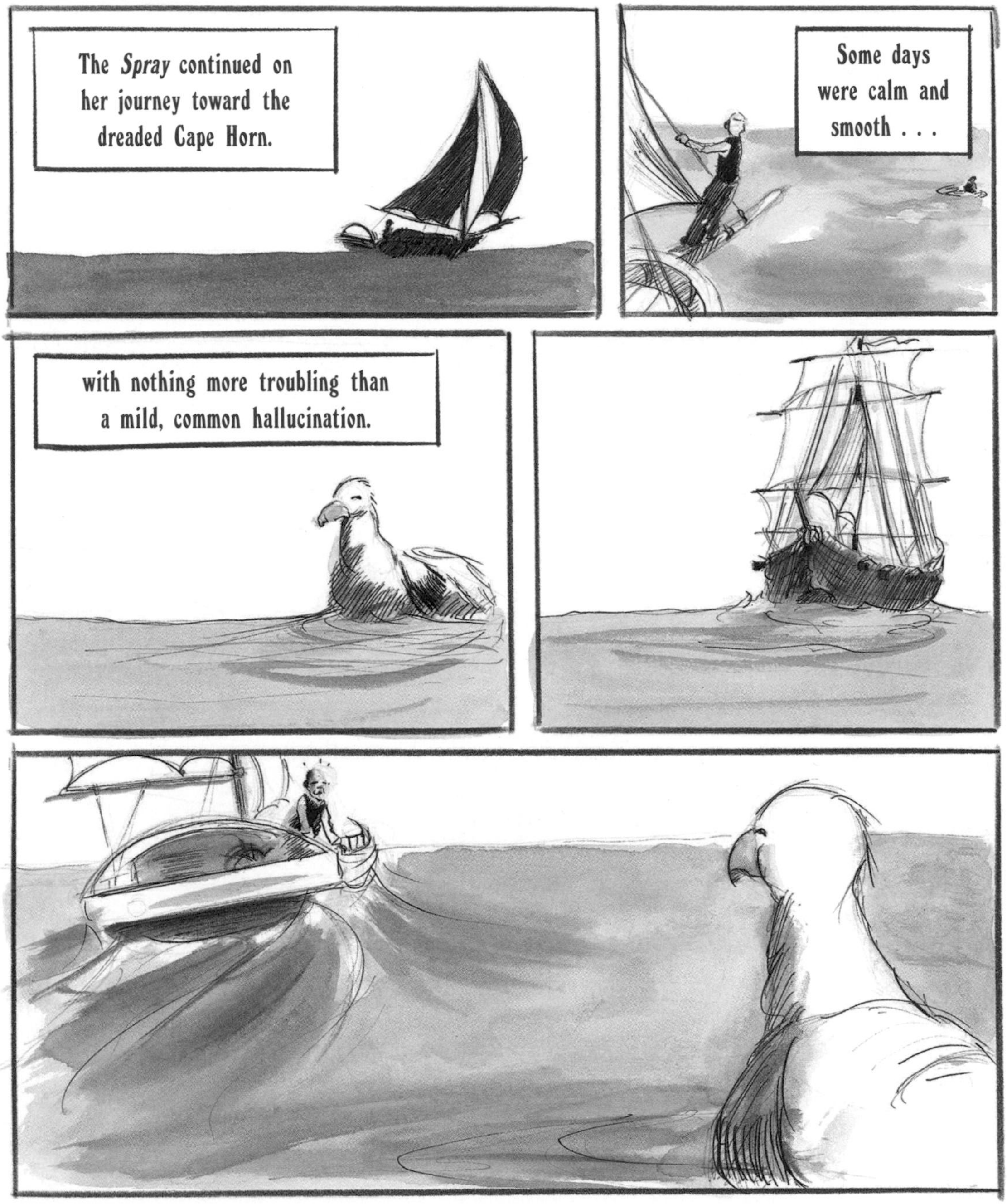
The *Spray* continued on her journey toward the dreaded Cape Horn.
Some days were calm and smooth . . .
with nothing more troubling than a mild, common hallucination.

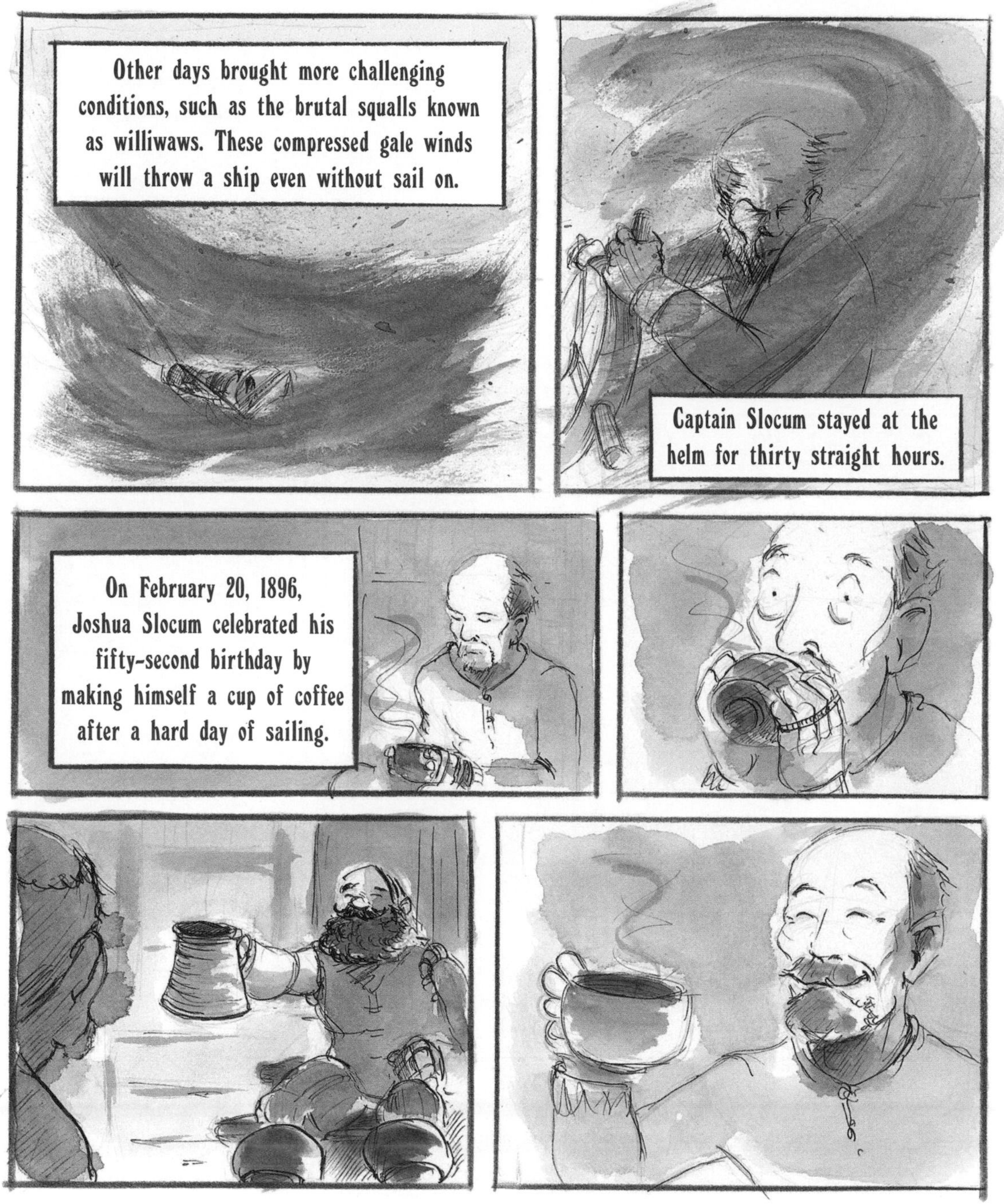
Other days brought more challenging conditions, such as the brutal squalls known as williwaws. These compressed gale winds will throw a ship even without sail on.
Captain Slocum stayed at the helm for thirty straight hours.
On February 20, 1896, Joshua Slocum celebrated his fifty-second birthday by making himself a cup of coffee after a hard day of sailing.

The *Spray* sailed for Cape Horn in a vicious storm, passing Cape Pillar, the "grim sentinel" of the Horn.

In no part of the world could a rougher sea be found than at this particular point.

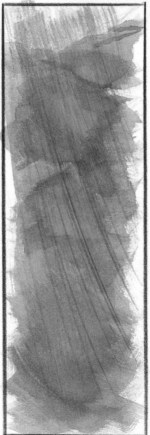

GRAN

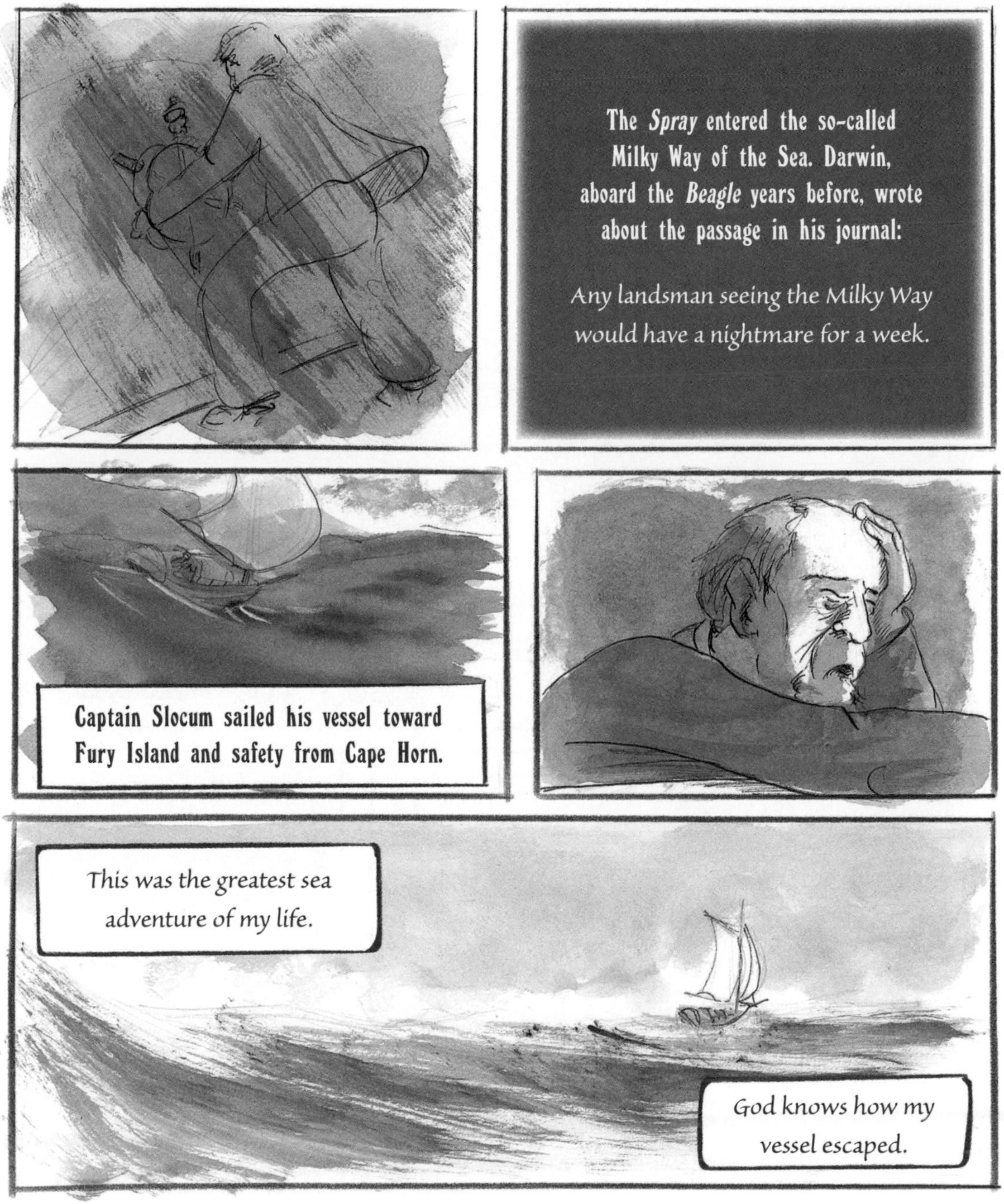
The *Spray* entered the so-called Milky Way of the Sea. Darwin, aboard the *Beagle* years before, wrote about the passage in his journal:
*Any landsman seeing the Milky Way would have a nightmare for a week.*
Captain Slocum sailed his vessel toward Fury Island and safety from Cape Horn.
*This was the greatest sea adventure of my life.*
*God knows how my vessel escaped.*

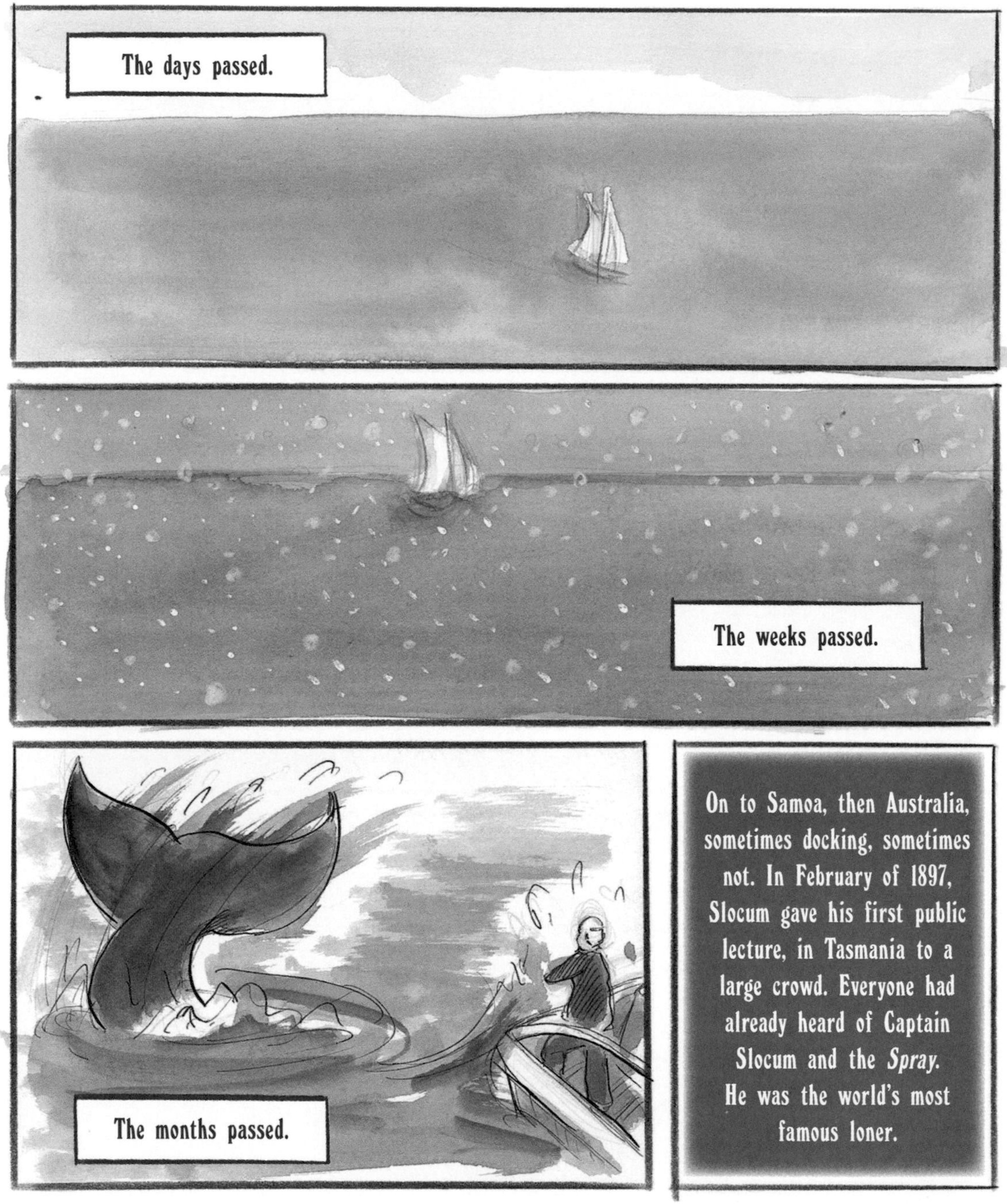
The days passed.
The weeks passed.
The months passed.
On to Samoa, then Australia, sometimes docking, sometimes not. In February of 1897, Slocum gave his first public lecture, in Tasmania to a large crowd. Everyone had already heard of Captain Slocum and the *Spray*. He was the world's most famous loner.

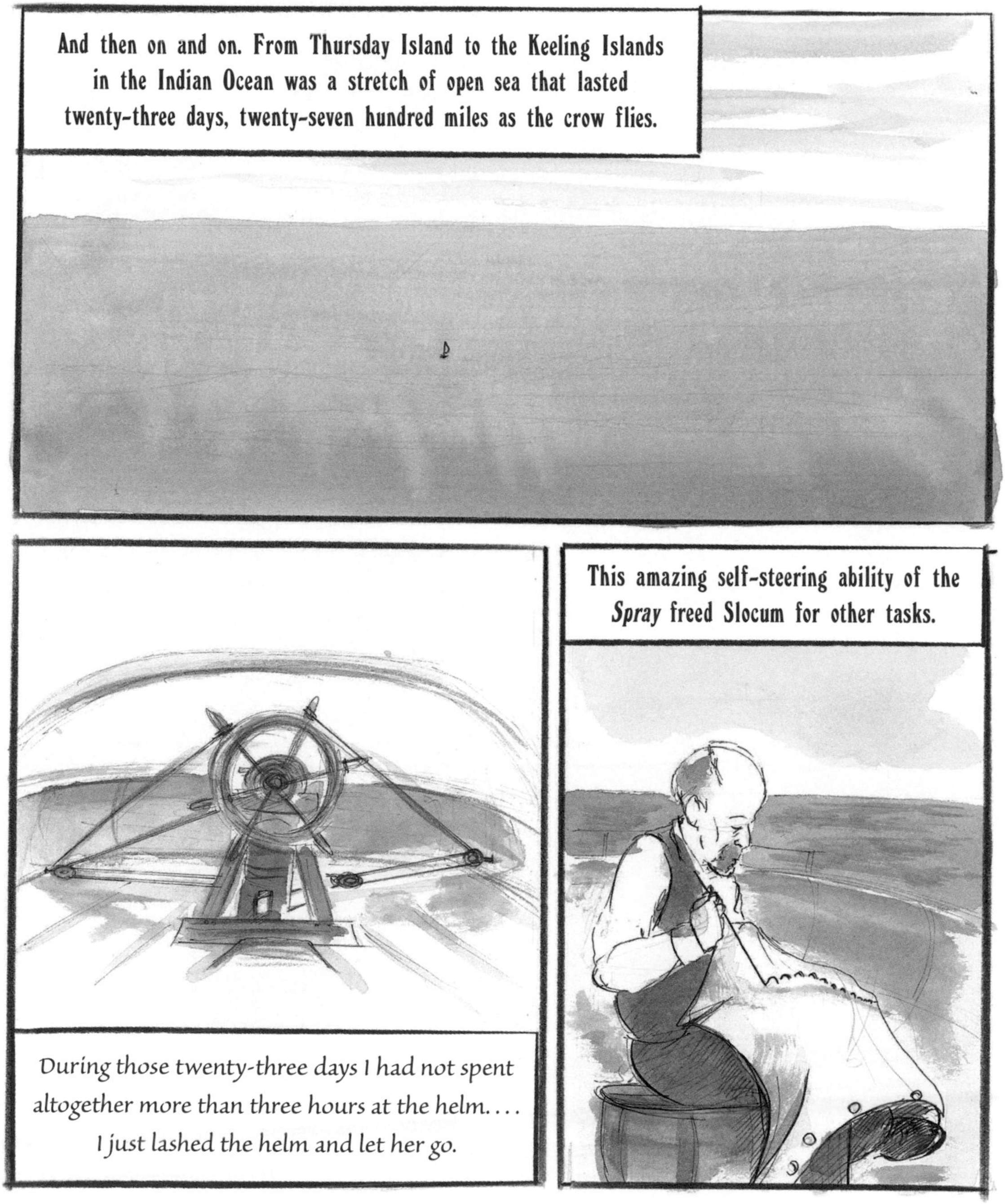
And then on and on. From Thursday Island to the Keeling Islands in the Indian Ocean was a stretch of open sea that lasted twenty-three days, twenty-seven hundred miles as the crow flies.
During those twenty-three days I had not spent altogether more than three hours at the helm. . . . I just lashed the helm and let her go.
This amazing self-steering ability of the *Spray* freed Slocum for other tasks.

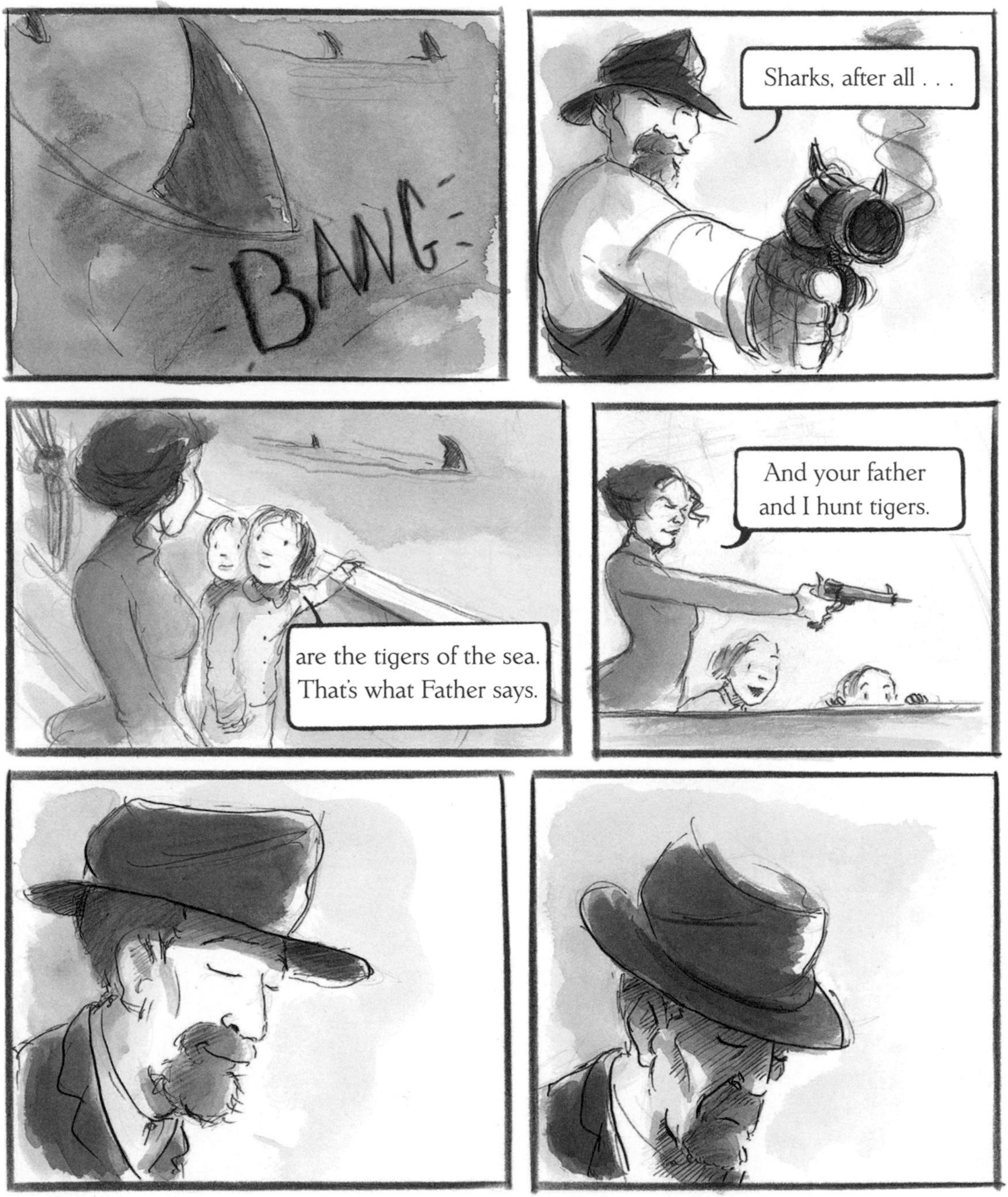
BANG
Sharks, after all . . .
are the tigers of the sea. That's what Father says.
And your father and I hunt tigers.

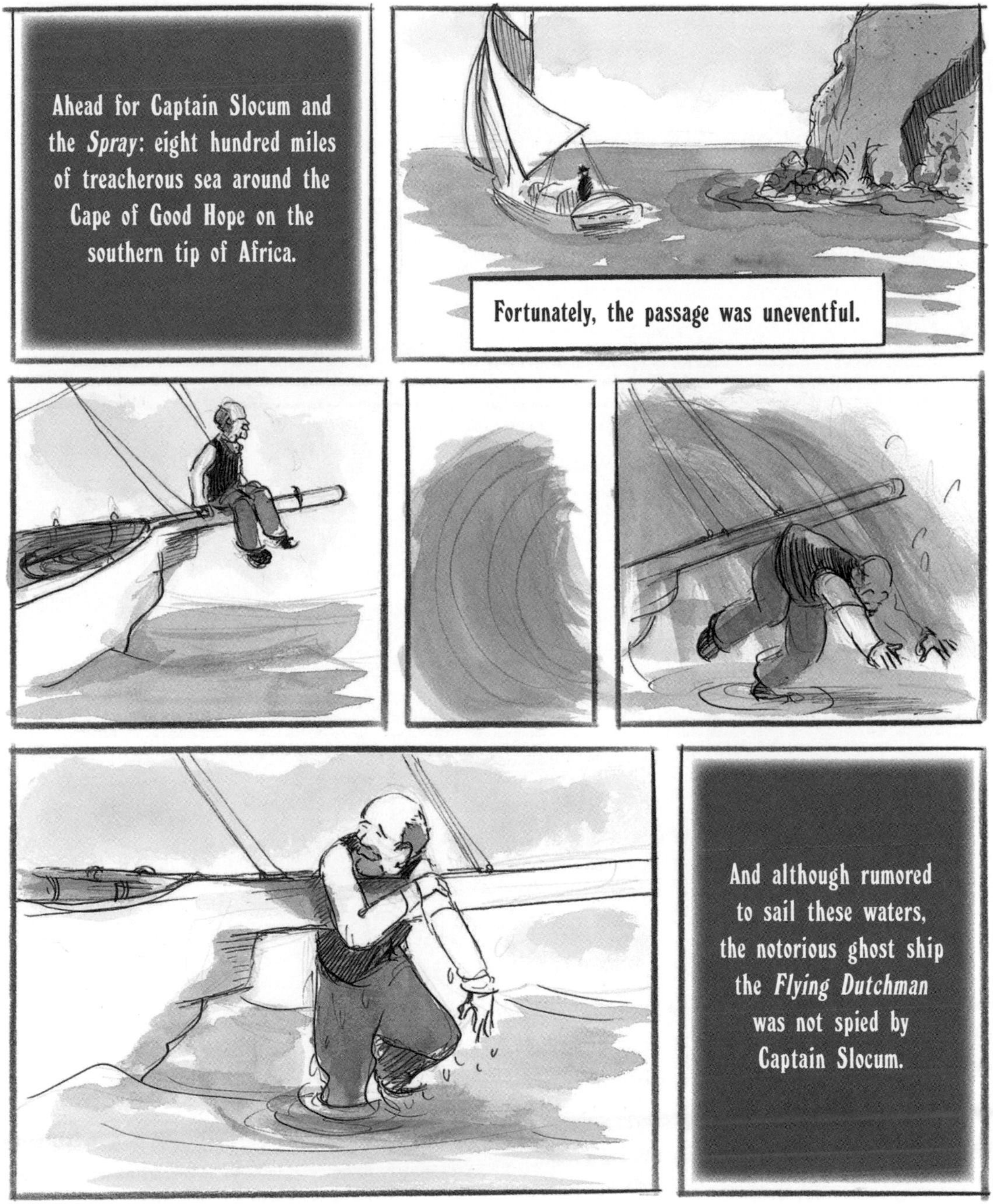
Ahead for Captain Slocum and the *Spray*: eight hundred miles of treacherous sea around the Cape of Good Hope on the southern tip of Africa.
Fortunately, the passage was uneventful.
And although rumored to sail these waters, the notorious ghost ship the *Flying Dutchman* was not spied by Captain Slocum.

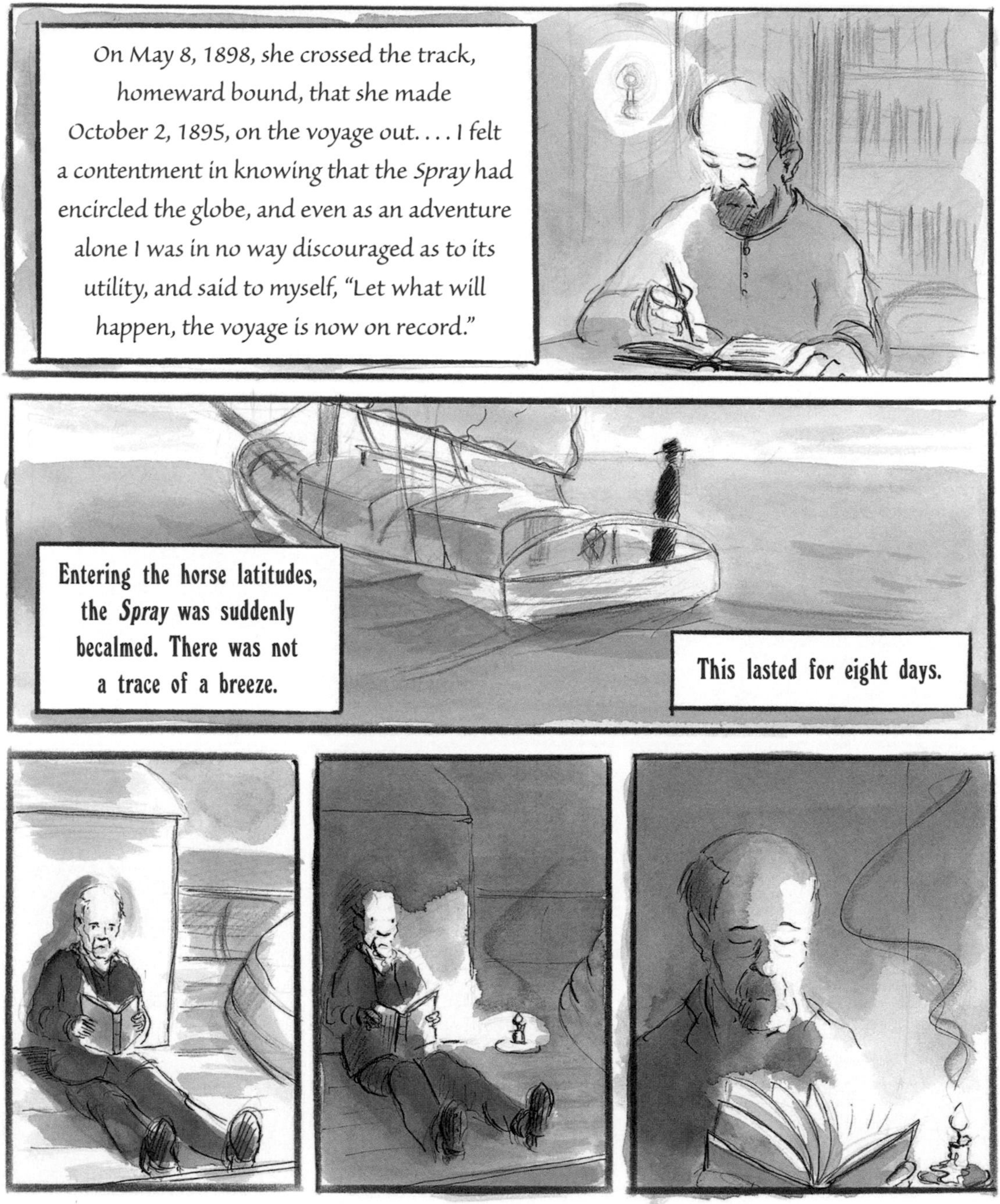
On May 8, 1898, she crossed the track, homeward bound, that she made October 2, 1895, on the voyage out. . . . I felt a contentment in knowing that the *Spray* had encircled the globe, and even as an adventure alone I was in no way discouraged as to its utility, and said to myself, "Let what will happen, the voyage is now on record."
Entering the horse latitudes, the *Spray* was suddenly becalmed. There was not a trace of a breeze.
This lasted for eight days.

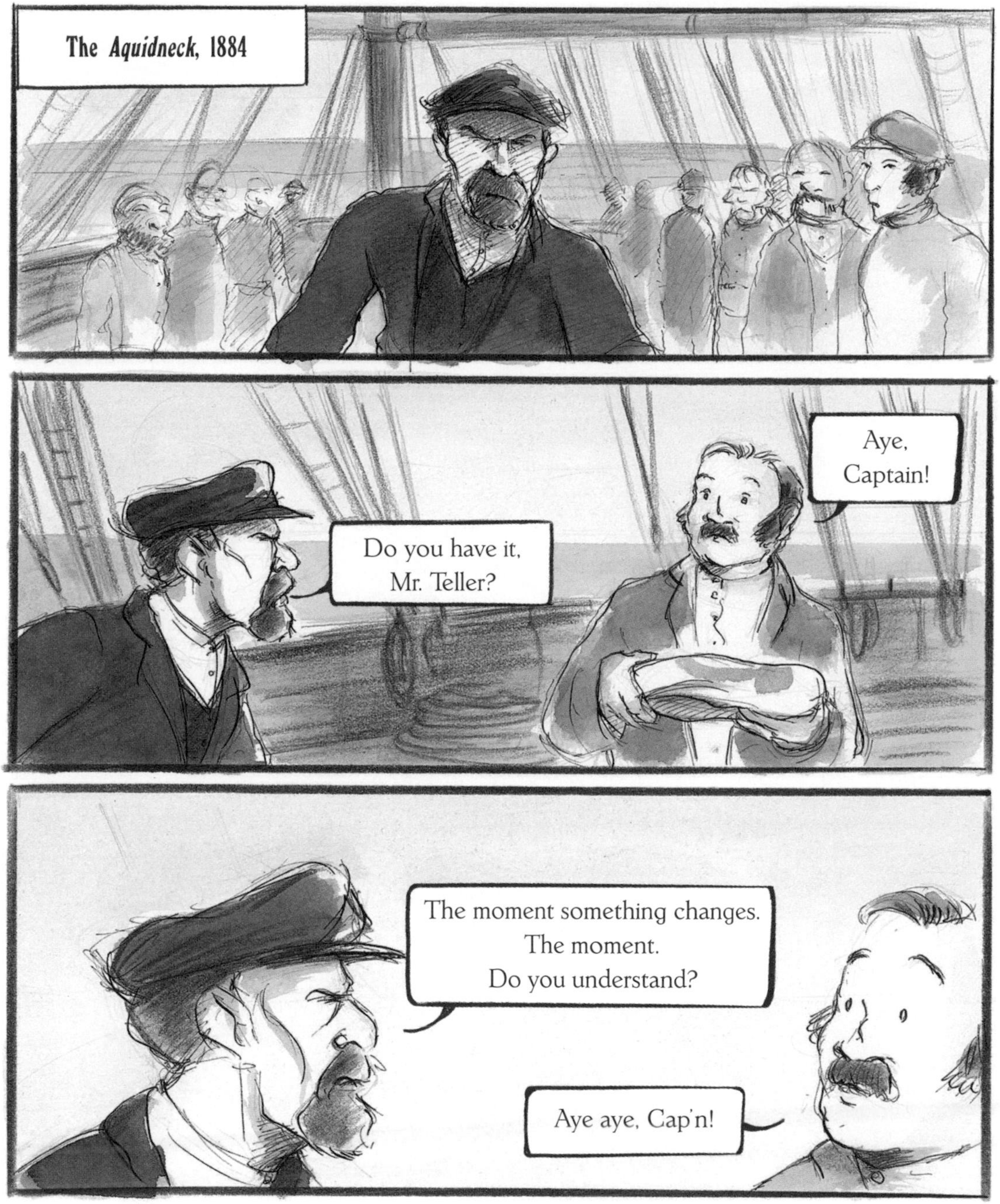
The Aquidneck, 1884
Do you have it, Mr. Teller?
Aye, Captain!
The moment something changes. The moment. Do you understand?
Aye aye, Cap'n!

Virginia, dearest. We've reached Buenos Aires. I need to go ashore to see about the cargo. Once it's loaded, we sail for Australia.

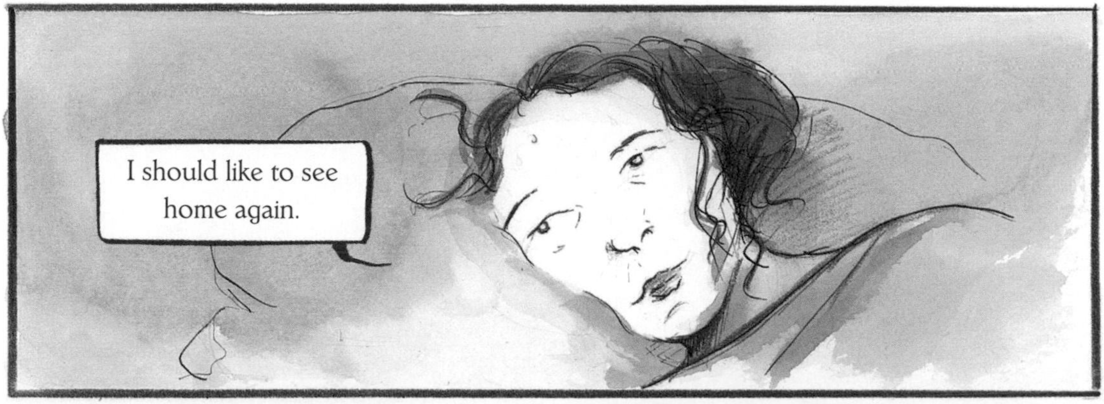
I should like to see home again.

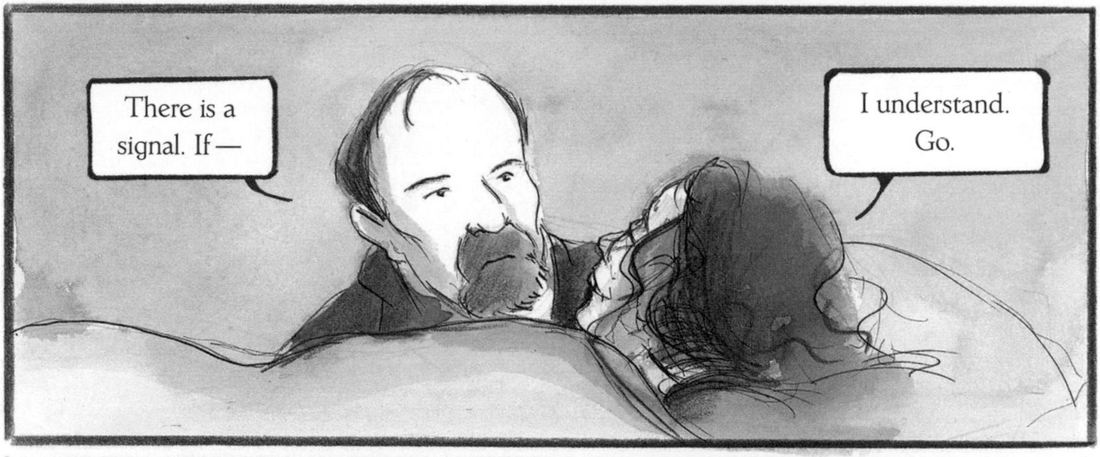
There is a signal. If—
I understand. Go.

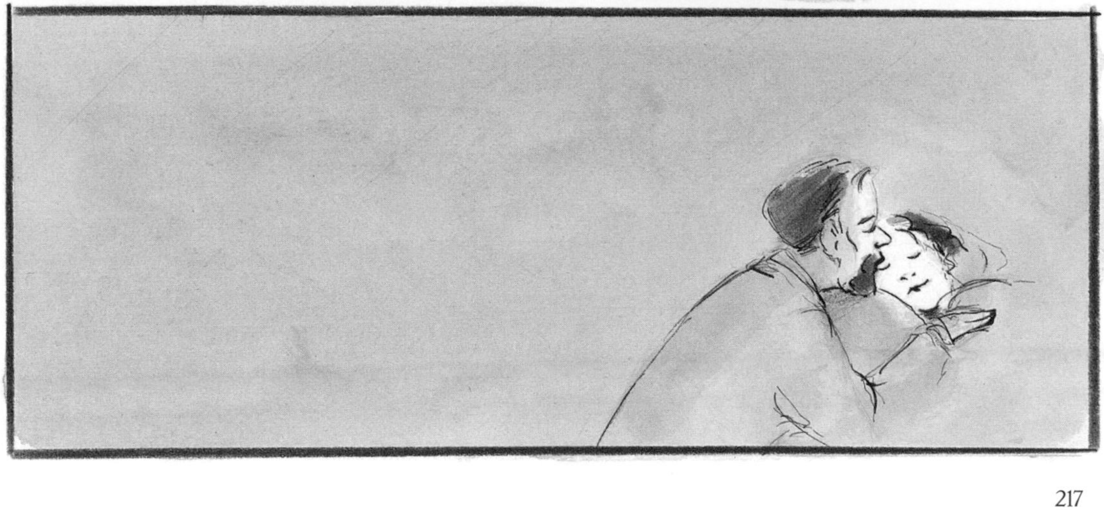

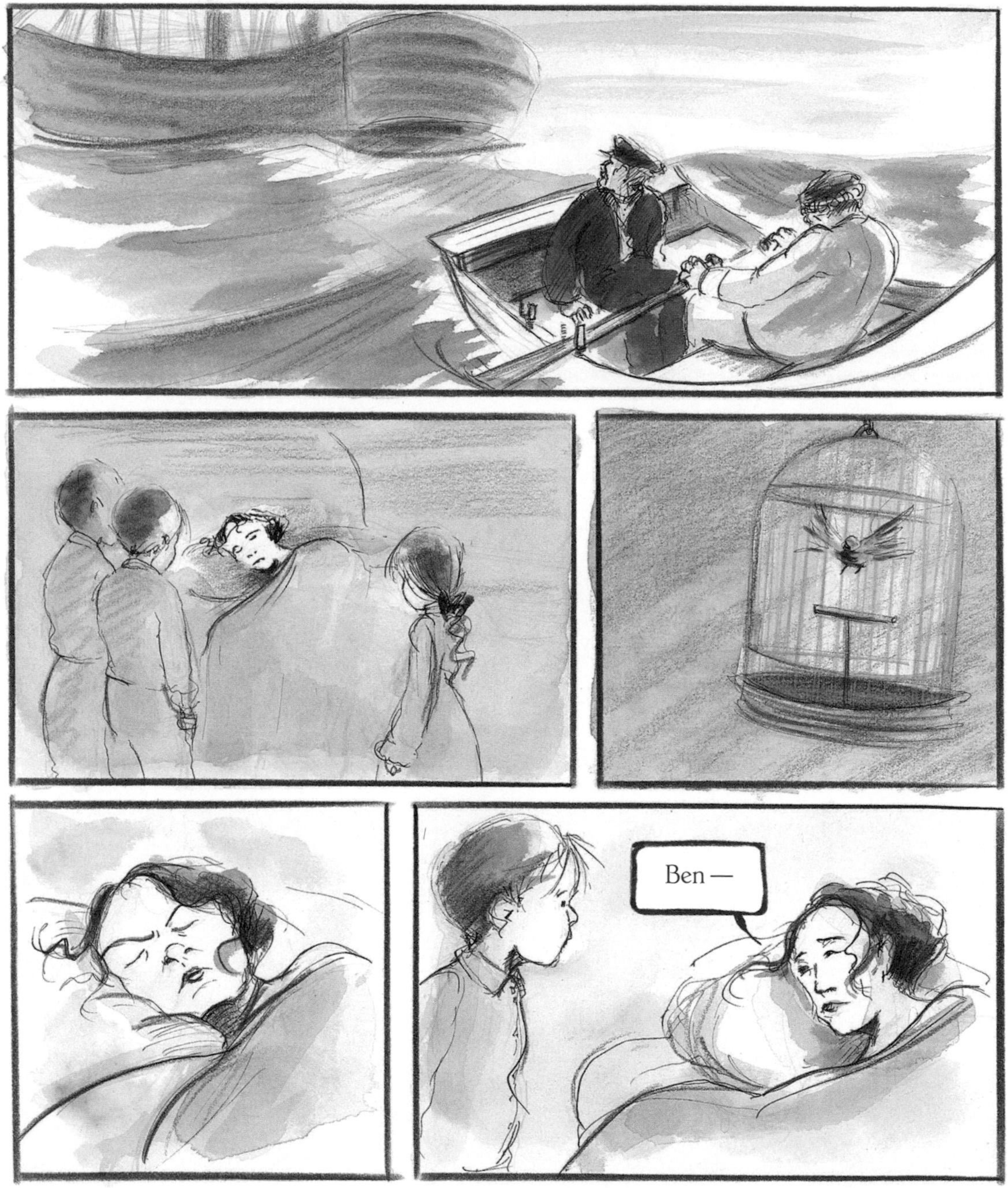
Ben —

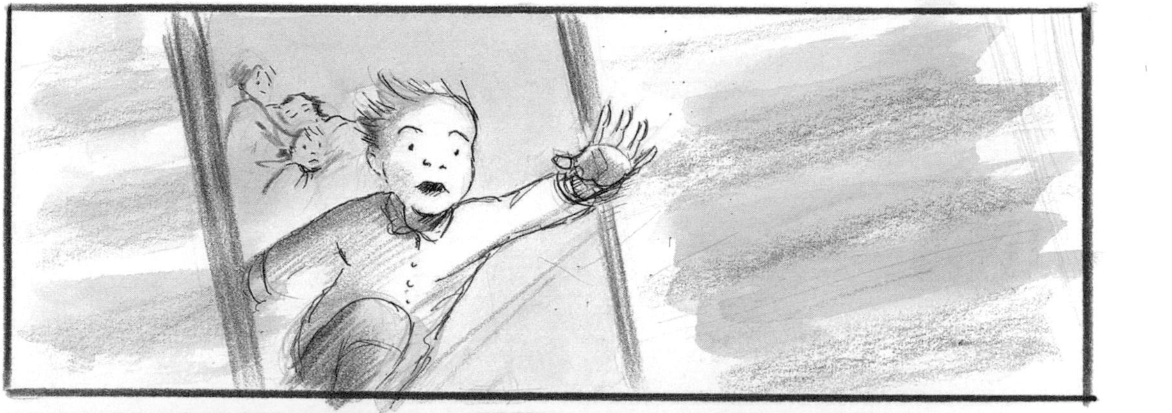

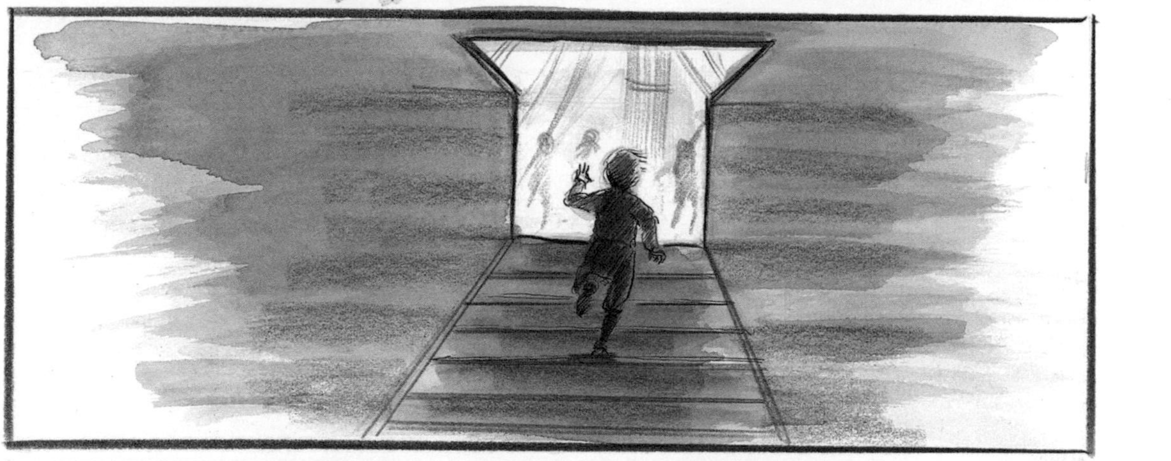

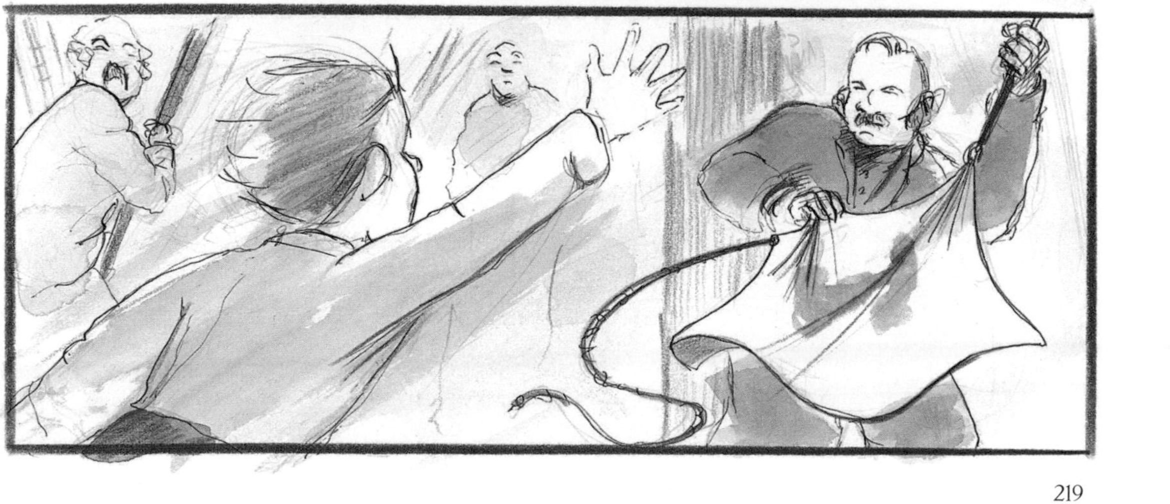

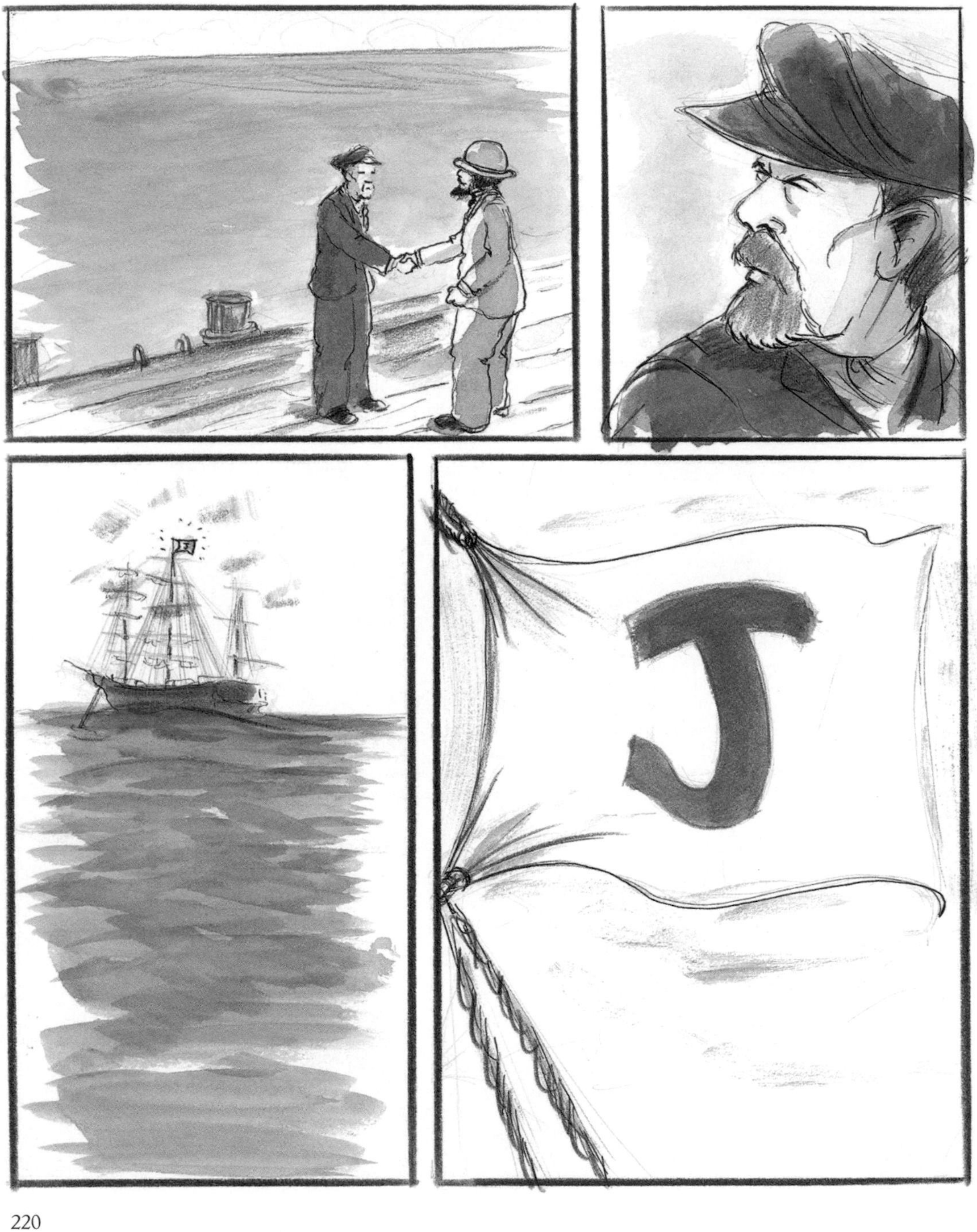
J

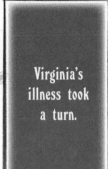

Virginia's illness took a turn.

There was nothing to be done.

Eight hours later, Virginia Albertina Walker Slocum died.

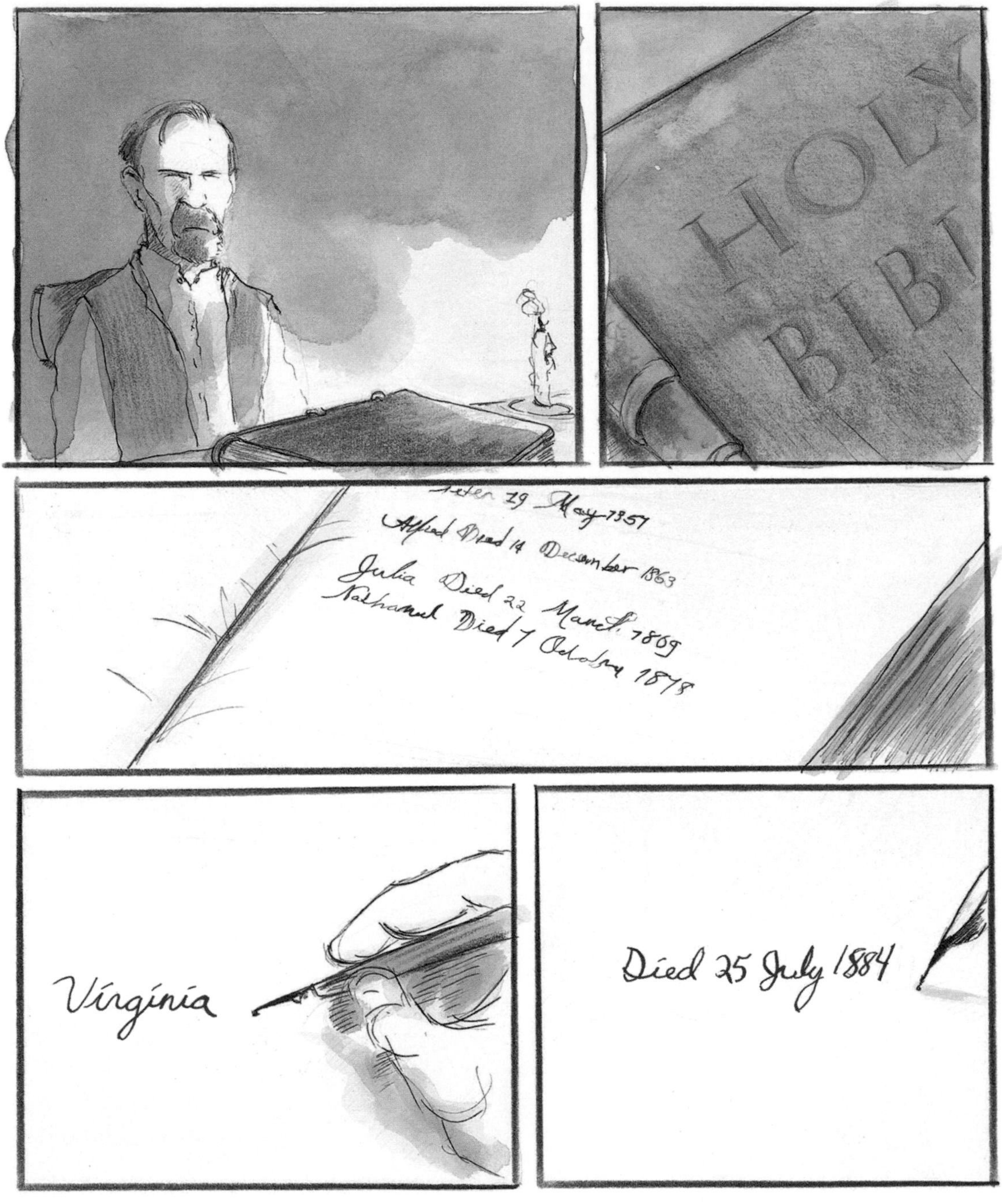

HOL
BIB
19 May 1857
Alfred Died 14 December 1863
Julia Died 22 March 1869
Nathaniel Died 7 October 1878
Virginia
Died 25 July 1884

Thy Will
be done

...l
...one not ours!

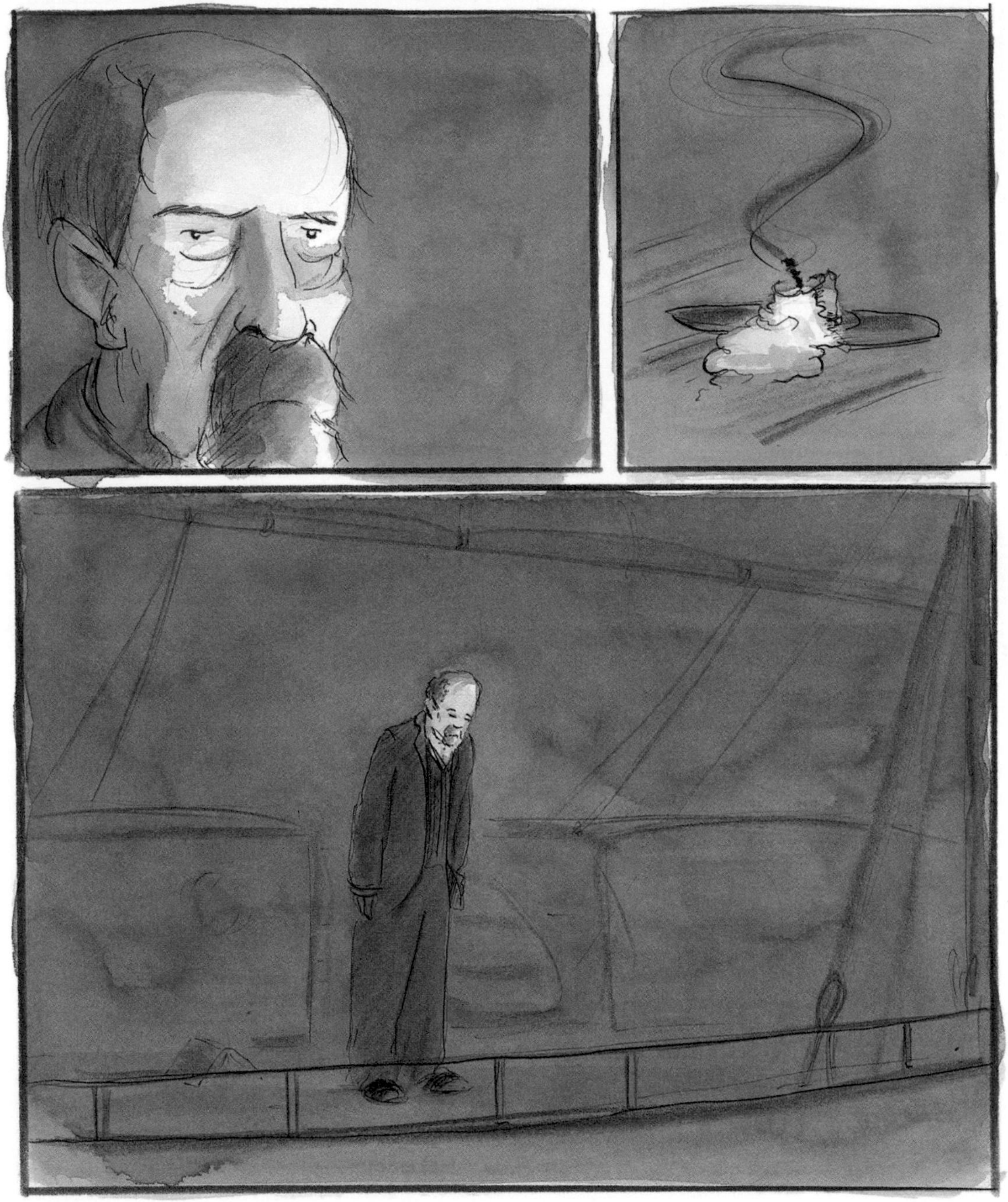

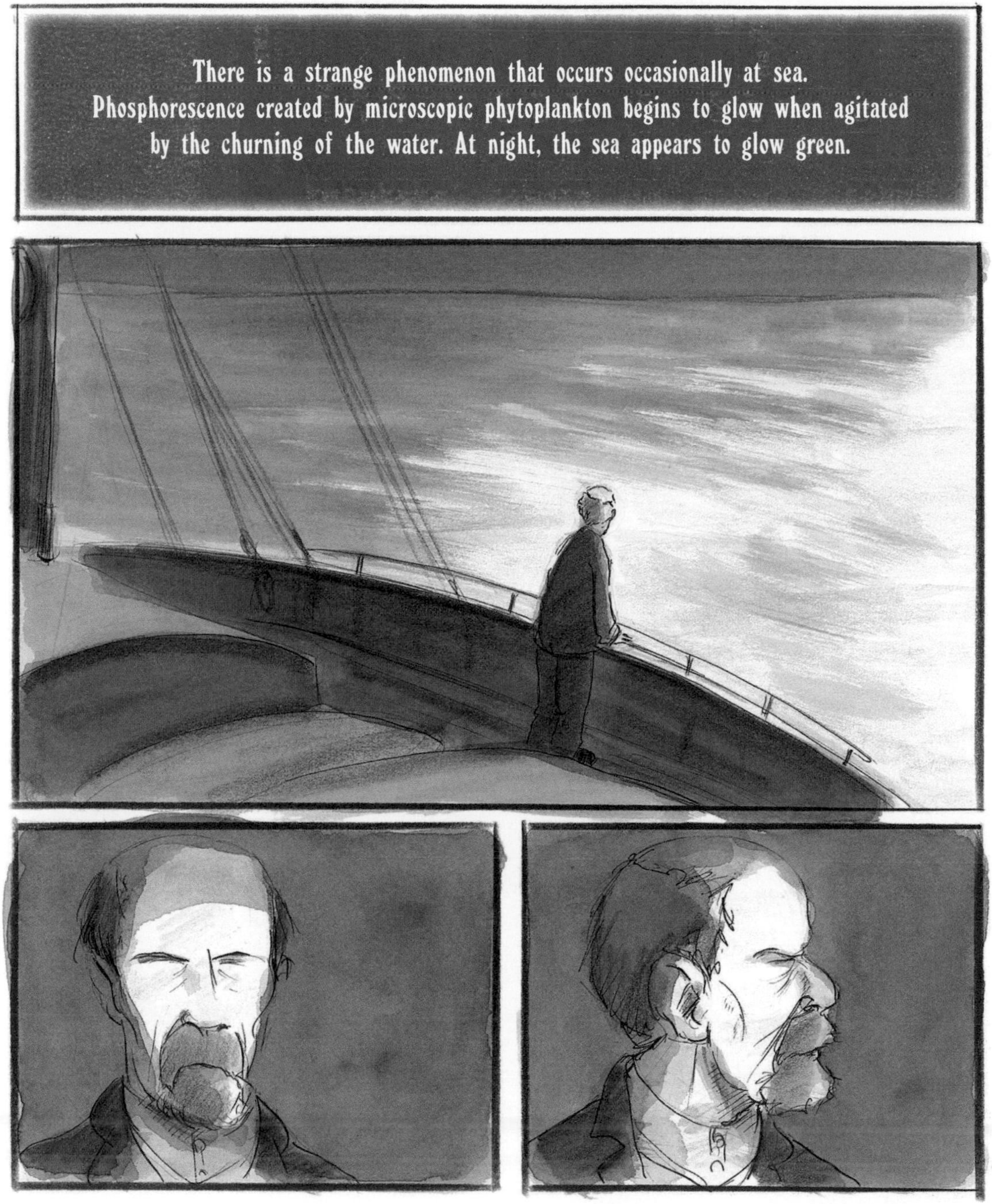
There is a strange phenomenon that occurs occasionally at sea. Phosphorescence created by microscopic phytoplankton begins to glow when agitated by the churning of the water. At night, the sea appears to glow green.

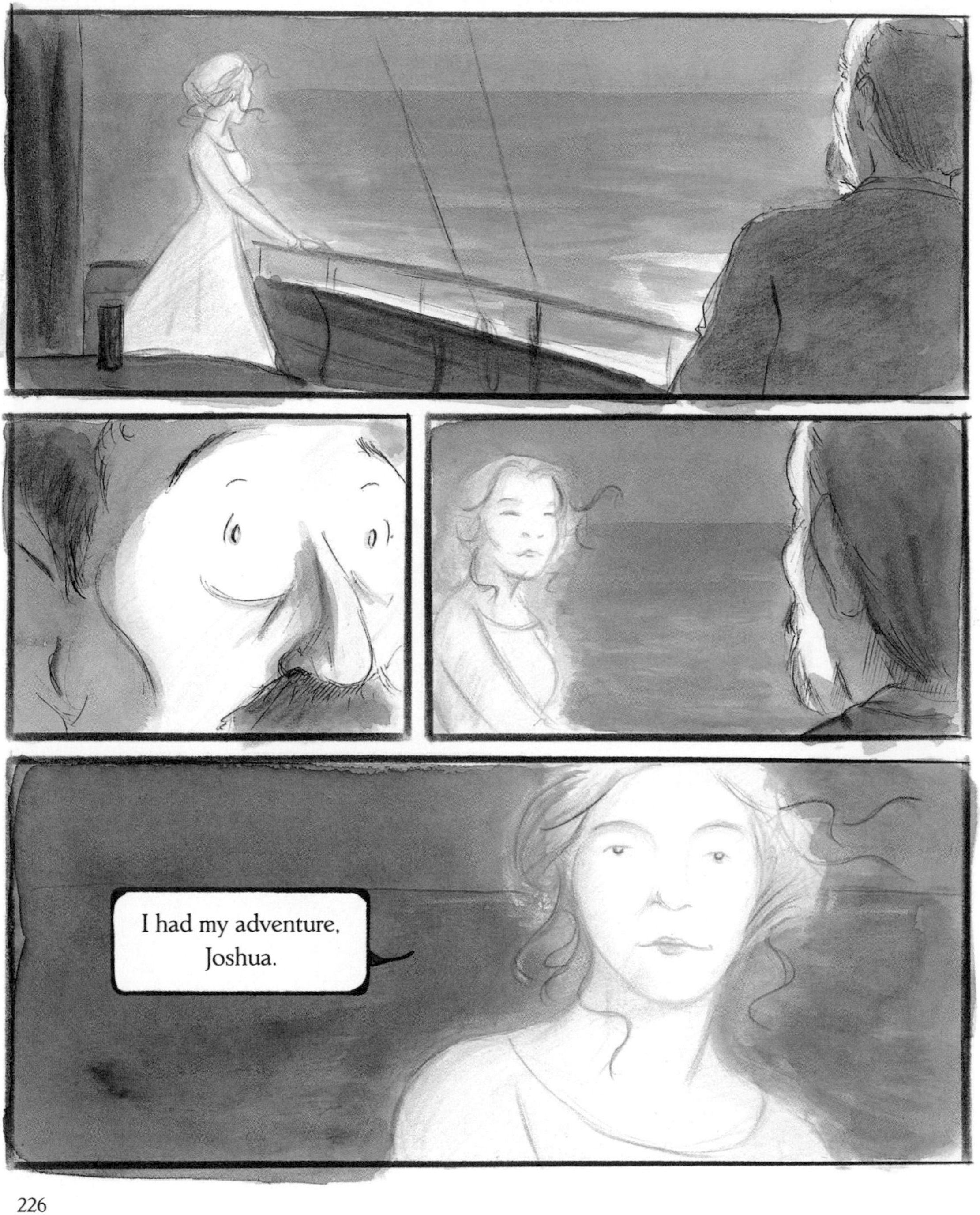
I had my adventure, Joshua.

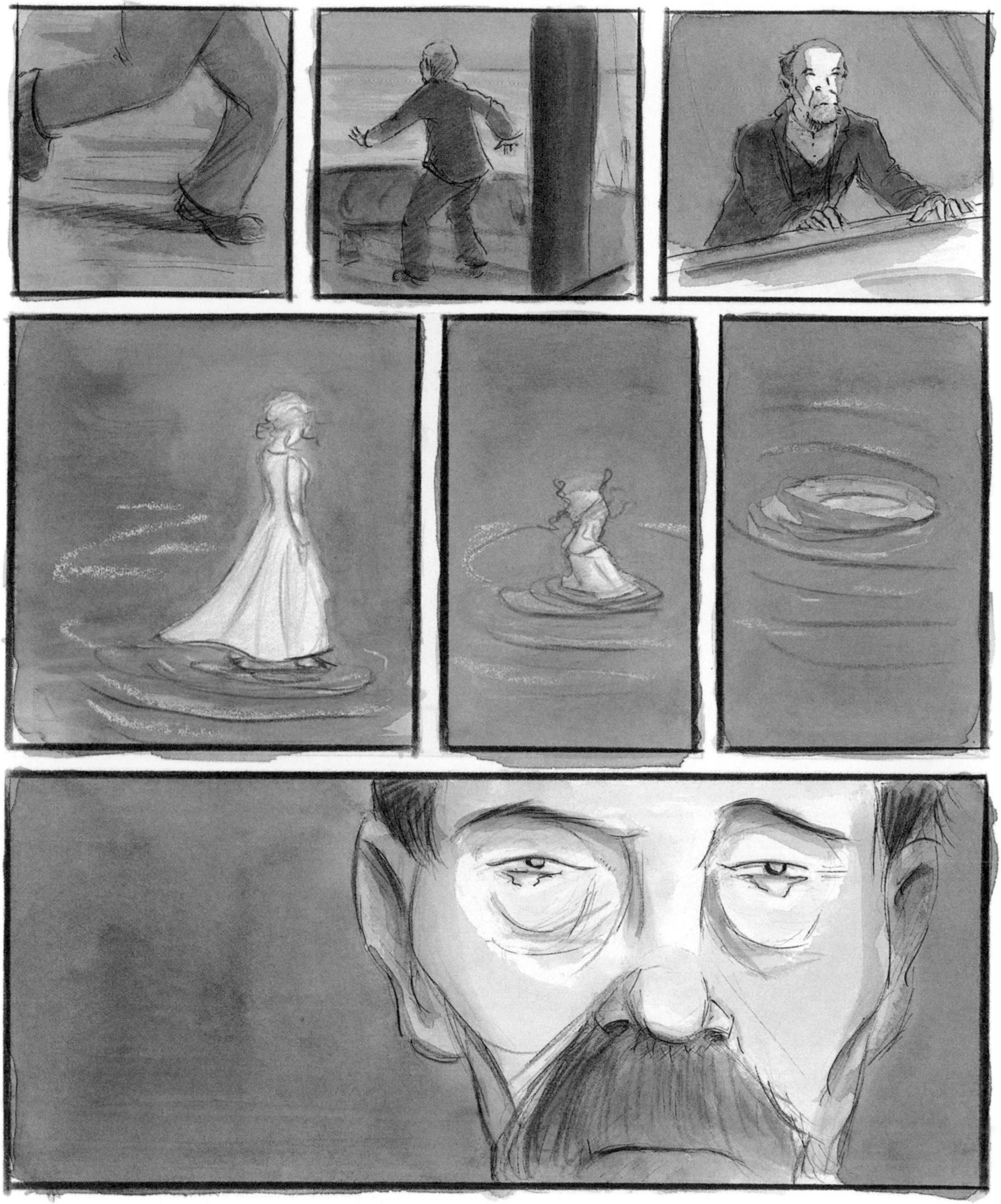

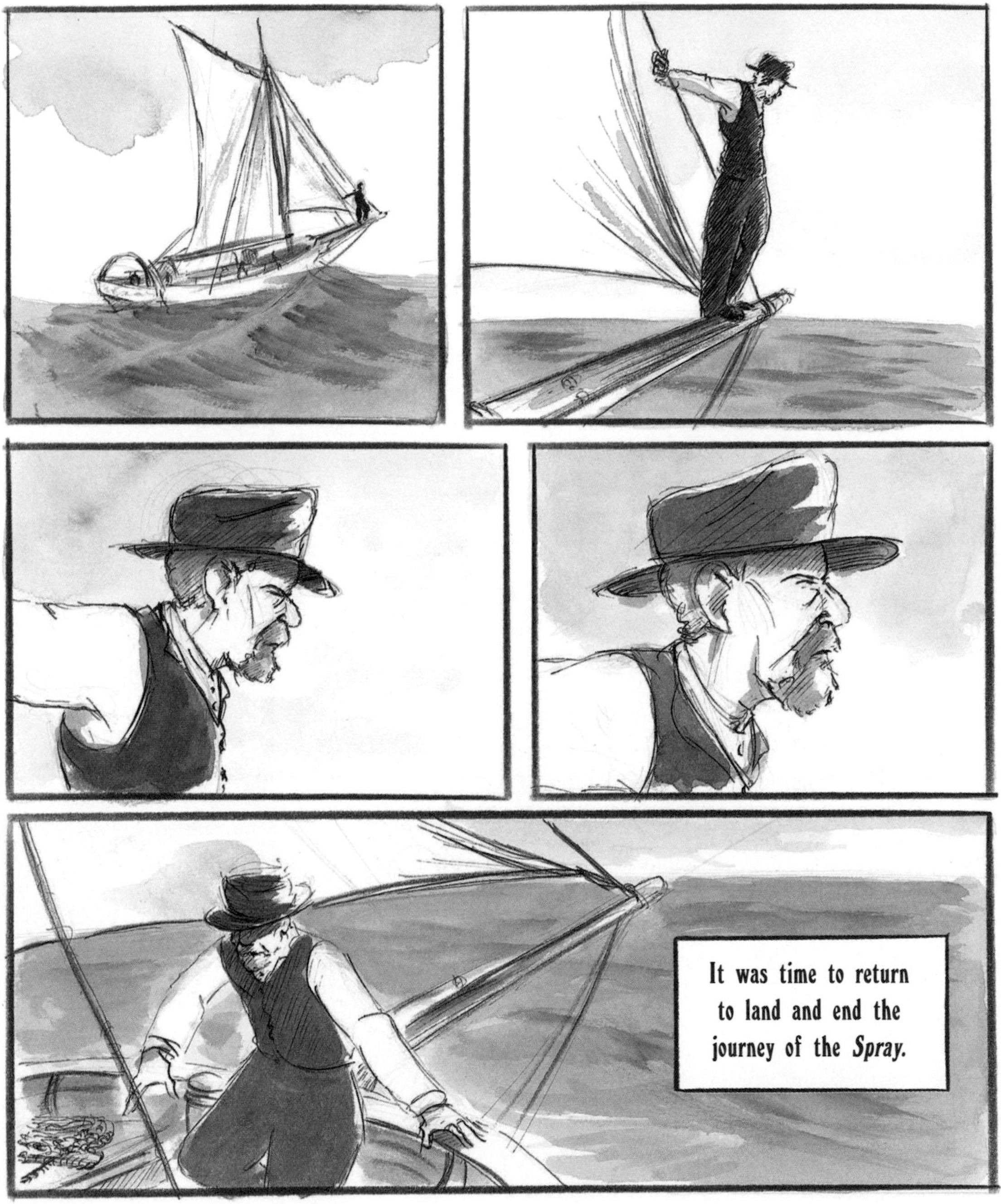
It was time to return to land and end the journey of the *Spray*.

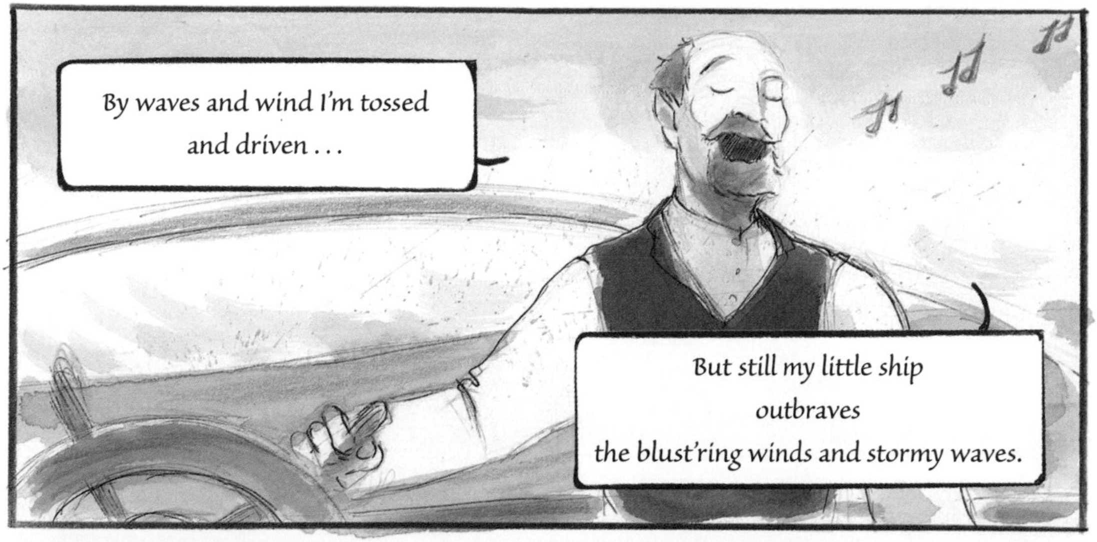
By waves and wind I'm tossed and driven . . .
But still my little ship outbraves the blust'ring winds and stormy waves.

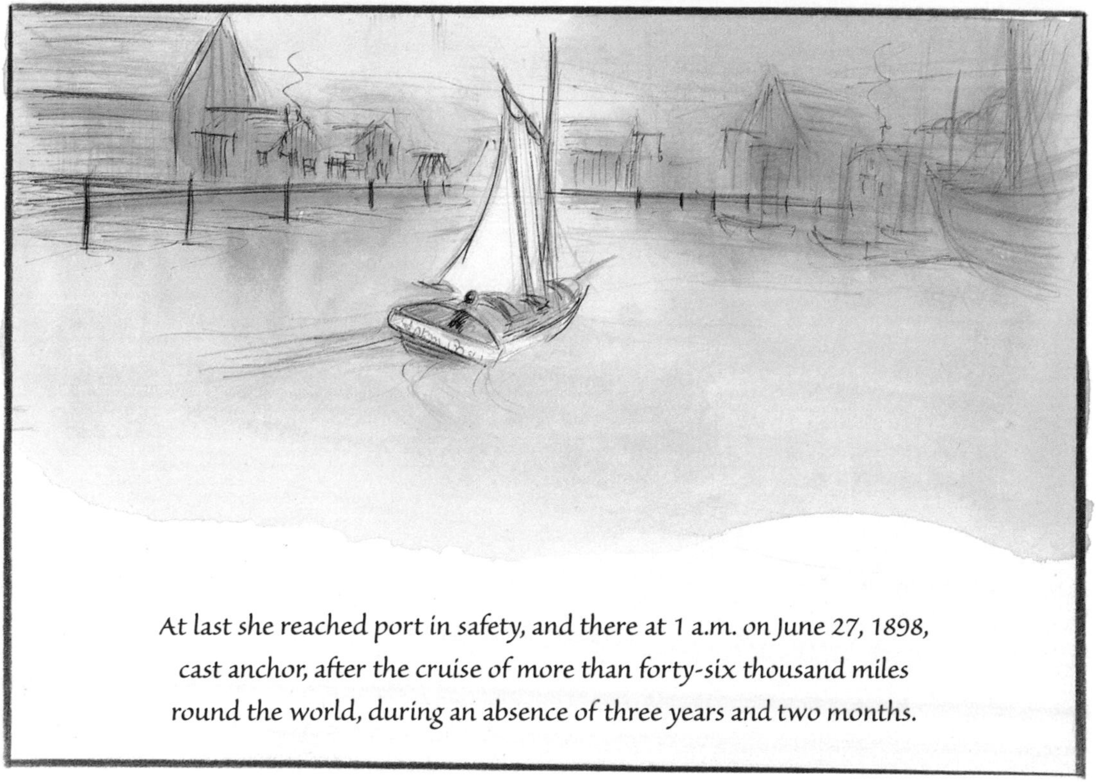
At last she reached port in safety, and there at 1 a.m. on June 27, 1898, cast anchor, after the cruise of more than forty-six thousand miles round the world, during an absence of three years and two months.

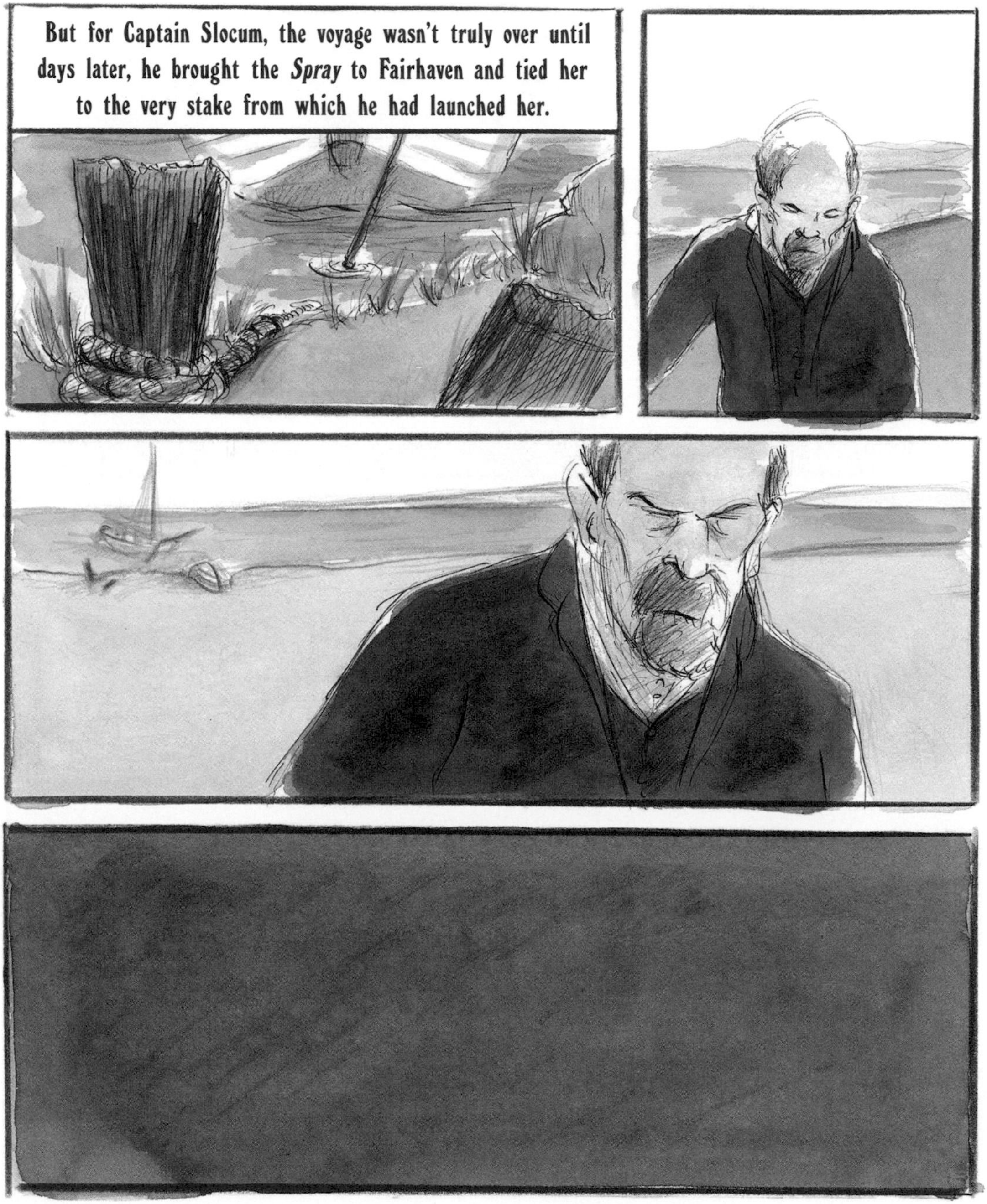
But for Captain Slocum, the voyage wasn't truly over until days later, he brought the *Spray* to Fairhaven and tied her to the very stake from which he had launched her.

EPILOGUE

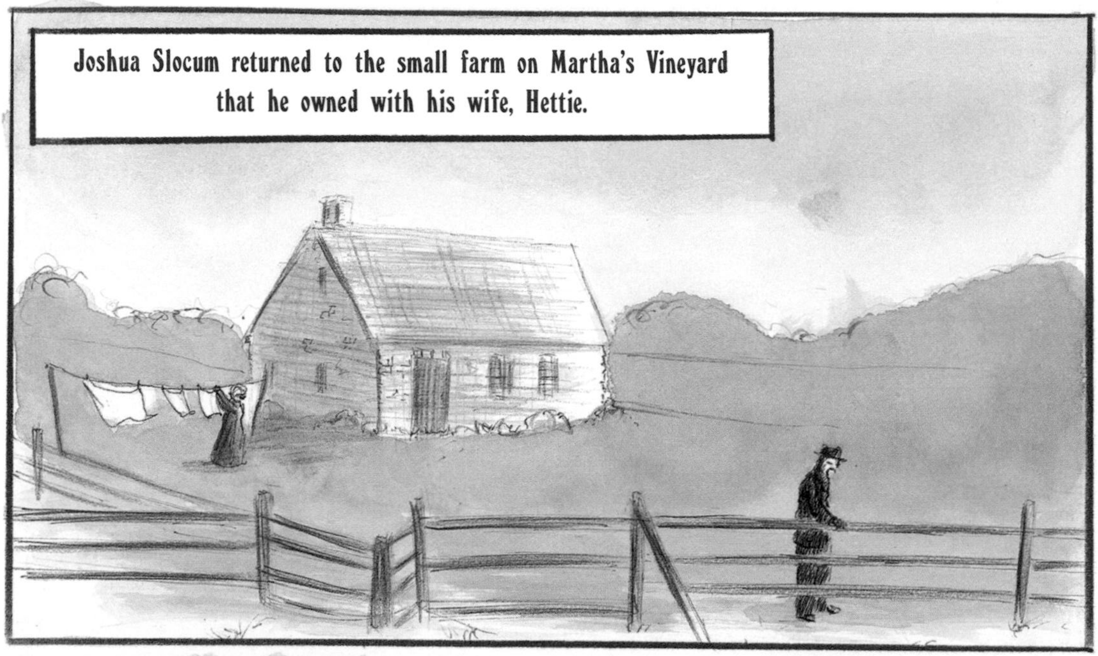
Joshua Slocum returned to the small farm on Martha's Vineyard that he owned with his wife, Hettie.

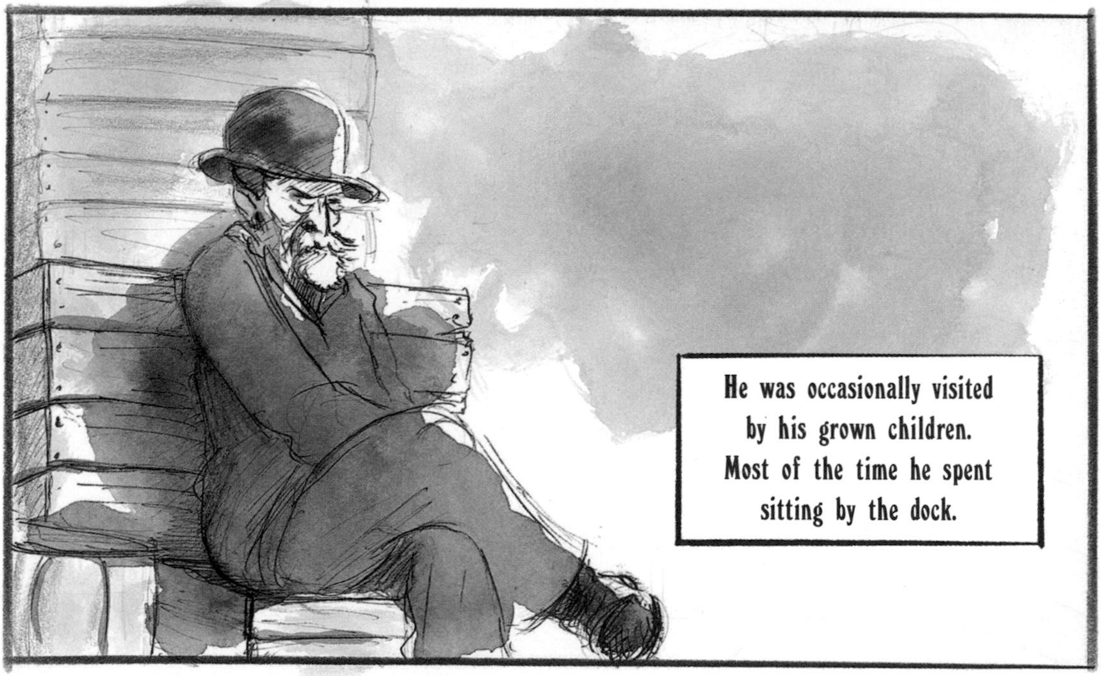
He was occasionally visited by his grown children. Most of the time he spent sitting by the dock.

People began to talk of his eccentricity.

Some talked of madness.

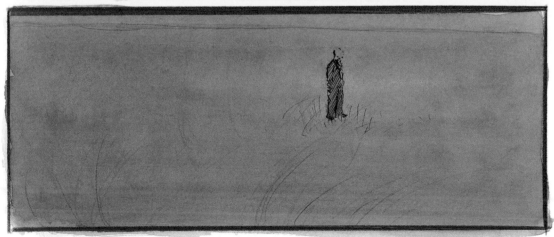

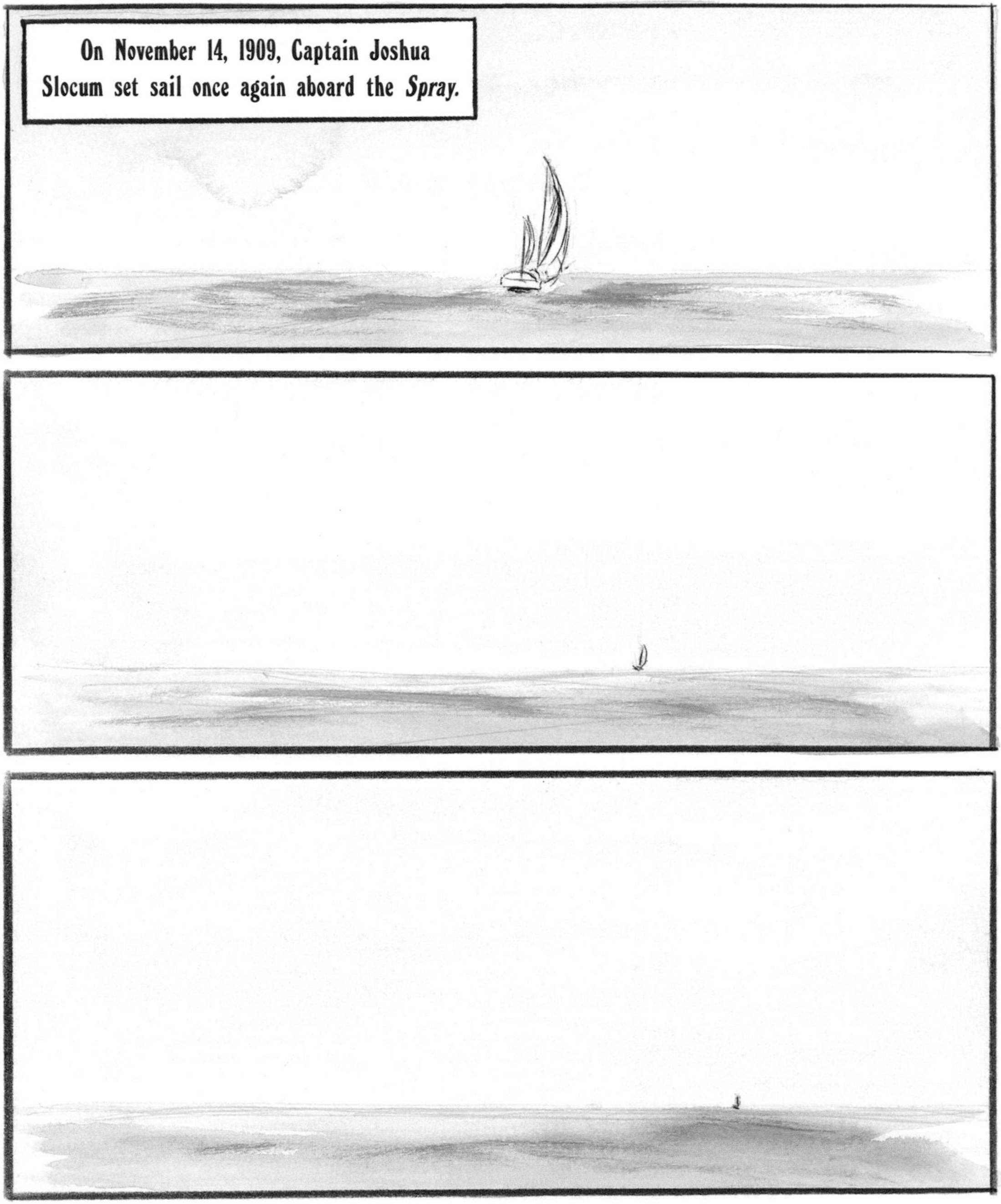
On November 14, 1909, Captain Joshua Slocum set sail once again aboard the *Spray.*

He was never seen again.

# AUTHOR'S NOTE

Pinned to my bulletin board is an index card with the words "the public journey & the private journey" scribbled on it. I wrote them down early in the process of working on this book, at which point I planned to simply dramatize the events in each of my subject's first-person narratives. The journeys were all extraordinary and fascinating on their own. My job would be primarily one of editing and pacing.

Or so I thought.

But as I researched the lives of Stevens, Bly, and Slocum, I noticed places where biography and narrative did not quite match up for me. My focus changed from *what* these real-life characters did to *why* they did it. Who were they outside the public spotlight? What were their motivations? What prior experiences might be traveling along with them? The public journeys (a straightforward presentation of events) began to shift to the private journeys (my interpretation of these events). My journey for *Around the World* started down one path but reached a different and surprising destination.

Isn't that how all good journeys should end?

I found the following books inspiring, invaluable, and engrossing:

Bly, Nellie. *Nellie Bly's Book: Around the World in 72 Days.* Edited by Ira Peck. Brookfield, CT: Twenty-First Century Books, 1998.

Herlihy, David V. *Bicycle: The History.* New Haven, CT: Yale University Press, 2004.

Kroeger, Brooke. *Nellie Bly: Daredevil, Reporter, Feminist.* New York: Times Books, 1994.

Slocum, Captain Joshua. *Sailing Alone Around the World.* Illustrated by Thomas Fogarty and George Varian. New York: Dover Publications, 1956.

Slocum, Victor. *Capt. Joshua Slocum: The Adventures of America's Best Known Sailor.* Dobbs Ferry, NY: Sheridan House, 1950 (reprinted in 2001).

Spencer, Ann. *Alone at Sea: The Adventures of Joshua Slocum.* Buffalo, NY: Firefly Books, 1999.

Stevens, Thomas. *Around the World on a Bicycle.* With an introduction by Thomas Pauly. Mechanicsburg, PA: Stackpole Books, 2001.

Teller, Walter. *Joshua Slocum.* New Brunswick, NJ: Rutgers University Press, 1971.

Verne, Jules. *Around the World in Eighty Days.* New York: Lancer Books, 1968